A DEAL WITH THE DEVIL . . .

Keane's smile widened. "You won't regret this, sweets. You've made a wise decision."

"Not like I had a great deal of choice," Esmeralda grumbled.

Ignoring her sulky tone, Keane stood beside her. "I believe now that we are in agreement, all that's left is for us to seal our bargain."

Esmeralda looked up warily. "Is that a regular procedure? I mean, don't we wait for the legal documents?"

"Certainly, but gentlemen always shake hands as a show of good faith after concluding an agreement."

His sultry expression caused Esmeralda to catch her breath. "But I am not a gentleman."

"Then we'll just have to improvise," Keane murmured, as he dipped his head down and captured her lips. . . .

Books by
Olga Bicos

By My Heart Betrayed
White Tiger
Santana Rose
More Than Magic
Sweeter Than Dreams
Wrapped in Wishes
Risky Games
Perfect Timing
Heat of the Moment

By My Heart Betrayed

OLGA BICOS

SPEAKING VOLUMES, LLC
NAPLES, FLORIDA
2016

By My Heart Betrayed

ISBN 978-1-62815-395-8

For my husband, Andrew, who encouraged me
to stay home and "make happiness."

Prologue

Northumberland, near Amberose Castle, 1840

Long-fingered shadows stretched across the moonlit ground, reaching out, grabbing at her. Panting for breath, Esmeralda MacClure fought the cutting branches and biting wind that sliced through her night rail. The hem of her lawn gown trailed and snagged in the bramble. Ignoring the needle-sharp thorns, she clawed her way into the protective darkness of forest shrubbery, trying to escape the moon's too-bright light. In her tension-whitened hand she clutched a strand of pearls.

What can they want? Help me, Allen. Help me!

Esmeralda pressed deeper into the thicket. The precious strand she carried caught on a branch. It snapped. Two pearls tumbled free, rolling beyond her reach. The necklace had been a comforting reminder of a mother not long dead. She'd slept with it at night; during the day she'd kept it safely strung around her favorite doll's neck. Now it lay broken in her hand. Two gossamer balls rested on the cold ground, reflecting moonlight like tiny beacons.

Her small body shaking, she wrapped her arms around herself. She dared not move to retrieve the pearls but remained hidden in the shadows, listening for the inevitable sound of pursuit.

It came. Much closer than before.

Her silent prayers became a chant as the rumble of approaching horses shook the ground beneath her. *Let them pass, please God, let them pass. I'll be good. I promise, I'll be good. But let them pass. Allen, where are you?*

The thundering noise grew louder, closer, and then trampling hooves raced by. Esmeralda stayed where she was, unable to distinguish between her heartbeat and the pounding of the horses' hooves. Before long she again heard someone approaching. This time her pursuer's movements were not marked by haste. The slow, plodding pace was somehow more ominous.

She heard a man dismount and whisper gently to his horse. Whoever stalked her now made no effort to dissemble. Through a gap in the branches she caught a brief glimpse of an elegantly dressed man, his fawn-colored breeches almost white in the moonlight. His back to her, he knelt down to examine an object on the ground inches from her hiding place. She stifled a gasp—the pearls!

"Esmeralda?" A comforting and familiar voice questioned the darkness. "Esmeralda, it's Allen. Come—"

Before the phrase finished, she squirmed out from beneath the bushes and launched her ten-year-old body into the welcoming arms of her cousin.

"Allen! Help me. Make them leave me alone."

"Shush, child." Allen's relief at finding his cousin was clear. "Dear Lord, Esmeralda, where have you been? I've searched for nearly an hour." Gently, lovingly, he stroked the waist-length, tangled curls of copper.

"Men—horrible, horrible men," she hiccuped, her

voice choked with tears. "They're chasing me. I couldn't find you. I called and called. But you didn't answer me! I had to hide, so I came here to the forest."

Esmeralda pressed her face into her cousin's hard, muscular chest, her head not quite reaching his chin. Seeking solace only he could give, she inhaled the familiar scent of tobacco and pine trees she loved so much. It calmed her like a balm. Looking up, she locked gazes with a face so like her own it could be a reflection in a mirror.

"They didn't find me," she said. "They just passed me by." Slowly she echoed Allen's smile, the secure sensation of his arms allowing her to feel her first real sense of relief.

"It was just a dream," Allen crooned, his hand still stroking the auburn tresses.

"No, Allen." Esmeralda pulled away, her childish voice pitched high with frustration. "They crept into my room. They thought I was asleep, but I just pretended. I ran out before they could catch me!"

Alert eyes stared down at the weeping child, and for a brief moment they reflected his irritation. He unclasped the arms that still hugged his waist and took her shoulders firmly in both hands. Esmeralda's stiffened features melted visibly under his now tender gaze.

"I have something for you, darling."

Esmeralda started. She furrowed her brow. "Shouldn't we get back to the house? Those men, they'll come back and hurt us if we don't hurry and get help."

Allen frowned. "Do you doubt I'll keep you safe? Don't you trust me?"

Looking into her cousin's intense eyes, Esmeralda nodded. He rewarded her with another melting smile.

"Good. Now, wait right here for just a moment."

Esmeralda knuckled her tired eyes and wiped her face clear of her tears while Allen walked to his powerful bay stallion. She watched him retrieve a bottle from a small leather satchel tied to the saddle. Fascinated by his actions, she stared as he took out a stark white handkerchief from inside his frock coat and dabbed it to the mouth of the bottle. When he looked over and saw her watching him, he smiled reassuringly.

Almost casually, he strolled toward her. "Come here, darling." He gestured with the hand carrying the soaked piece of linen.

Esmeralda remained where she was. Something in his eyes frightened her.

For the first time, Allen's feature's clouded. "I said, come here." This time his voice was not so light or friendly.

Taking in his glazed expression, Esmeralda shook her head and backed away. Something was terribly wrong; Allen never sounded angry or looked at her with hatred. When he continued toward her, she turned and fled.

An arm like an iron band across her stomach stopped her abruptly, then pushed her to the ground, knocking the breath from her. As Allen rolled her on her back and straddled her, her nightgown tangled on a branch and tore.

"You really should obey me. Believe me, I know what's best."

Esmeralda squinted, trying to focus. Two images of Allen floated over her until they meshed together into one figure. His eyes flashed poison green as he played with the pungent-smelling cloth in his hand.

"You know how much I care about you, darling. I love you, really I do."

"I love you, too," she replied automatically.

"Do you, darling? Do you really? Say it again, then. I want to hear it again."

Her senses finally clearing, Esmeralda felt a cold lump form in her stomach. She tried desperately to dislodge Allen from on top of her.

"Say it, dammit!" He grabbed her hands and held them down on either side of her face. "I want to hear it again!"

"Stop it, Allen. Please, you're hurting me."

Suddenly his features softened. Releasing her arms, he sat up, still straddling her. "I'm sorry. I don't want to hurt you. I love you, Esmeralda." Then looking at the cloth in his hand, he continued, "But it's all yours." He gazed about the forest with a blank expression. "Everything. You'll take it all from me."

"No, Allen, you're wrong."

"Oh, you won't want to." He touched his hand gently to her forehead, tenderly sweeping aside a copper curl. "But your husband will. And then it will be all for nothing. Everything I ever worked for will be gone. He really shouldn't have done that. He took everything that belonged to me, and gave it to you." His eyes were glassy and clouded with his memories, and she wondered if he was speaking of her father. "I'm sorry, my darling. Truly I am."

Before she knew his intentions, Allen slapped his sodden handkerchief over her mouth and nose. The acrid odor choking her, she struggled with all the force of her tired ten-year-old body. No longer able to keep her eyes focused on his twisted expression, she closed them and concentrated on trying to tear Allen's hand from her face.

I can't breathe. I can't breathe! I . . . can't . . .

Chapter One

Cincinnati, Ohio, April 1849

"His name is Henry."

Molly Egan looked up from the rocker where she sat sewing jet beads on the bodice of a sapphire gown. Her blue eyes wide and questioning, she stared at the tall, slender redhead poised before her. From the top of her tightly coiffed bun to the tips of her laced leather boots, Esmeralda MacClure beamed like sunshine reflecting off the clear waters of the Ohio.

"Henry?" A low fire flickered in the hearth of their one-room cottage, lighting Molly's Black-Irish features.

"Yes. Henry." Esmeralda paused to take aim before she tossed her straw bonnet at one of the pegs on a board that hung on the whitewashed wall. The hat brim caught, and it gently swayed into its place as she crossed the bare plank floor and added her cloak to the row of hanging garments. When she turned back to the stone hearth, the firelight sculpted shadows under her high cheekbones. Beneath fine, arched brows, emerald eyes challenged the dark-haired woman who sat by the fire. Esmeralda's full lips barely suppressed a smile. "Henry is very young and very handsome. And . . ." She let the word trail off like a baited lure.

"And?" Molly prompted, sitting on the edge of the arrow-back rocker.

"He comes from a well-to-do family who will pay a heavy purse to keep a lowly seamstress like me from marrying him!"

"Ye did it!" Molly shouted as she jumped out of her chair, throwing the satin gown and beads to the floor. *"Arrah,* I knew ye could do it!" She hugged the taller Esmeralda, who led the way in a fast polka around the near-empty room until Molly broke away and began a jig. As she copied Molly's dancing leaps, Esmeralda's curls escaped the few pins holding her hair in place and the copper strands swirled around her slim waist, while Molly's ebony curls bobbed about her shoulders.

"And Molly, his family owns Car—"

"Don't be botherin' me with details. He's rich! There's nothin' more I need to know about the cully." She launched into an especially energetic step.

In the corner, Molly's ten-month-old son, Peter, rose on wobbly legs and took several shaky steps toward them, laughing at the sight of his mother and Esmeralda dancing around the horsehair settee. Seeing Peter, Molly skipped to her bouncing son and picked him up in her arms.

"She did it, tyke!" Molly lifted Peter high above her head and his squeals of laughter grew louder. *"Musha!* 'Tis rich beyond the dreams of avarice we'll be!"

"Now, Molly," Esmeralda said, laughing. "We don't have the money yet."

"It doesna matter. Ye'll get it." Molly set Peter back on

his crocheted blanket and turned to Esmeralda. "Are ye not one of, if not the *most,* beautiful and charming—that is when ye choose to be—woman in Cincinnati?"

"Why, of course!" Esmeralda replied, immediately smoothing the folds of her·brown muslin gown and assuming a demure pose against the table's apron. She fluttered her long auburn lashes at Molly with mock modesty and molded her full lips into a perfect pout. But the humor reflected in her moss-green eyes spoiled her attempts to emulate the pampered young ladies who visited their dress shop on Pearl Street.

"And which of those whiny, pasty-faced colleens could ever compete with ye?"

"Not a one." Esmeralda snapped her fingers, cheerfully dismissing the imagined competition.

"Well, then, I ask ye—is it not just a matter of time before we git our hands on enough money to go back to England an' claim yer estate? Faith, ye got the dupe hooked! The money's as good as ours!"

Esmeralda's shoulders straightened in preparation for her exultant reply, but before the words left her lips, she slumped back against the table flap. "There are two problems."

Molly raised an eyebrow.

"Big problems." Esmeralda pushed away from the table. As she paced before the banked fire, the dimming light of early evening streamed through the room's curtainless window. Combined with the mute fireglow, the light formed multiple bobbing shadows across the hearth and floor. "My first problem is guilt."

"Guilt?" Molly visibly started.

"Why, yes, Molly. I feel guilty!" Esmeralda stopped and leaned over the gateleg table, her two hands braced against its scarred surface as she met the smaller woman's astonished gaze. "We are, after all, trying to manipulate a gently bred young man into falling in love with and proposing to me—a woman who has no intention of marrying the poor fellow."

"Bless us an' save us! That dribble again! If ye'd agreed to follow me plan earlier, 'tis halfway back to England we'd be." Molly marched back to the rocker and picked up the forgotten beads and gown and returned them to a cedar chest by the window. "But nay. She says 'One more month, Molly,' " she mimicked in a high, whiny voice. " 'Just one more month. I just know business will pick up, and then we can *earn* the money honestly.' " Molly looked back at Esmeralda's mutinous face. "If there were more opportunities fer women than seamstressin' and earnin' coins on their backs, we wouldna be in the pickle we're in now." Molly fetched the lamp from the split-log mantel and, using a spill made from a twisted strip of cornhusk, lit the lamp's rag wick. "So we're bein' a wee bit more inventive than most, and keepin' the wolves from our door by the effort . . . Is that a bloody crime?"

"I don't know if it's illegal, but it's wretchedly cruel."

"Musha!" Molly scoffed, placing the oil lamp on the table. Then crossing her arms, she challenged, "All right, me girl, if ye be feelin' so guilty, just marry this Henry. T'was yer decision not to. If he's so handsome and charmin', why not marry? Remember, yer an heiress in yer own right."

Instantly, Esmeralda pressed her lips together and creased her high brow. After her cousin Allen's betrayal, the thought of committing herself to marriage and trusting any man was completely abhorrent. "No. We'll stick to the original plan. We don't need anyone besides ourselves. If we succeed, I'll have the money to take care of you and Peter."

Molly strode to the corner where her son lay playing with his rag doll and wood blocks. Picking him up, she stroked his inky curls fondly as he rubbed eyes the color of the jet beads recently strewn across the floor. The muscles in her chest tightened when her sleepy son looked up and smiled, exhibiting a set of much-loved dimples. Sighing, she brought Peter back to the table and sat down, placing him on her lap.

"Look, Esme. If yer doin' this only fer me and the wee bairn, ye know we're not yer responsibility."

Esmeralda stared at Molly. Her mouth parted slightly in surprise at her friend's casual shrugging off of their past bond. The older by five years, Molly had been a mother and a friend to her for nearly a decade, helping her make the difficult adjustment from a spoiled girl unable to do a thing for herself to a young woman capable of surviving on her own.

She circled around her seated companion. "Tell me this, Molly Egan. Who helped me escape in London and smuggled me aboard the *Susanna?*"

"I suppose I helped ye out a bit."

"A bit? You've taught me everything I know about survival! Without you, I wouldn't know how to sew a straight seam, much less how to make a living doing it. You're responsible for the only income I've had since my parents died."

" 'Appens to be me only income, too, *mavourneen!*"

"Molly." She softened her tone. "You and Peter are the only family I have left."

By the dim light of the fire, Esmeralda knelt down at the foot of the chair and wrapped her arms around mother and son, resting her head against the small boy's dark locks. When Esmeralda had awakened on that rowboat nine years ago, nauseated and disoriented, she'd felt so frightened, so alone. She tried to remember how she'd gotten on board the boat, but her mind wouldn't cooperate. The evening's occurrences were a black void, and trying to recall them only caused a blinding pain at the back of her head. Then she heard the voices of the two men seated beside her recount what they planned to do with the money Lord Kielder, her cousin, had paid them to get rid of her. Without thinking, she plunged into the icy water and swam for shore, not even sure where shore was. It was Molly who had fished her out from the Thames and helped her to hide among some barrels while her abductors searched the London wharf for their escaped captive, all the while lamenting how much money a white girl with red hair would have brought on the slave block. It was Molly who had held her while Esmeralda cried out her grief for her cousin's betrayal. Molly had been taking care of Esmeralda ever since.

Molly felt a slight tightness in her throat as she stroked the younger woman's soft hair. Then, quickly dismissing the emotional moment, she barked through her constricted throat, *"Musha,* Esme. Stop yer caterwaulin'. When ye make it rich, ye can take care of me and the tyke like bloody royalty."

Placing her hand under the kneeling woman's chin, Molly turned Esmeralda's face up to hers and grinned broadly, exhibiting a slight but not unattractive gap between her even, white teeth. She stood and pulled Esmeralda to her feet. Seating Esmeralda down in the ladder-back chair, Molly plopped Peter on Esmeralda's lap before marching to the corner shelves where she removed an apron and wrapped it around her blue checkered dress like protective armor. Returning to the hearth, where a black pot hung on a crane laden with a dozen hooks of differing lengths, she used the edge of her apron to cover her hand as she lifted the kettle to a higher hook in order to reduce the heat. After stirring the pot's contents, she searched for and found two chipped wooden bowls and spoons in the small knotty-pine cupboard.

Esmeralda watched Molly ladle a watery stew into each bowl. She continued to bounce Peter on her knee as Molly set the dishes down with a piece of bread on the table.

"Eat up!" Molly announced, retrieving her son and placing him on the floor beside her chair.

Esmeralda stared at the bits of carrots and onions swimming with a few herbs in a pale liquid. Her stomach growled noisily as she broke off half of the day-old brown bread and dropped it by the side of her bowl. She threw a small piece of the bread into the soupy mixture and began to eat. As she sipped the hot but tasteless liquid, she stared at the exposed beams of the low ceiling, then shifted her gaze to the straw tick and bedding that served as their bed at night and now lay rolled up against the hearth.

It all came back to money, she thought. How to get enough of it to return to England and fight her cousin for Amberose, her family's estate in Northumberland.

When they'd left Charleston over a year ago—after Mrs. Gilbert, scandalized by Molly's pregnancy, had dismissed them from her dress shop—Esmeralda dreamed of making their fortune as owners of their own shop. On Molly's assurances, they gathered up every coin they'd saved over the past seven years and moved to Cincinnati. How lucky they felt when they first came here! And in some ways they *had* been fortunate. The owner of their dress shop, desperate to leave for the California goldfields, had leased it to them at an incredibly low rent, and they'd been able to find this cottage as well. Because it was far from town, it also leased at an affordable rent. That, however, had proved to be their only stroke of good fortune. Business had been bad. They owed back rent and they had used up their entire savings. Esmeralda had been quite desperate when she had finally agreed to Molly's scheme.

"What was the second problem?"

Molly's voice jolted Esmeralda out of her thoughts. "Pardon?"

"Ye said there were two problems. What's the second?"

"Oh." Esmeralda stirred the soup thoughtfully. "It's Henry. I'm not quite sure he's as gullible as he first seemed. He may not be fooled by any of this."

"Faith! So much for 'manipulating a gently bred young man,'" Molly grumbled. "He'll probably ask ye to be his mistress and think he's doin' ye a bloody favor." Molly took a spoonful of stew and fed it to Peter. "What makes ye think he's the right one, anyway?"

"Because he's known to have a certain susceptibility to feminine wiles, and, more importantly"—Esmeralda's cat-like eyes glittered in the lamplight—"he has an older brother who makes it his business to pay off Henry's soiled doves."

"The bloody blighter! He's perfect!"

Esmeralda smiled and her spirits lifted. "I met Henry about a month ago. He came into the shop with a beauti-ful woman—an actress, I believe—and ordered that mauve morning gown you finished two weeks ago. Then, just last week at the shop, I overheard those gossips, Mrs. Greenfeld and Mrs. Percy, talking about how Henry's lat-est light-o'-love disappeared without even bidding him good-bye. By coincidence, his older brother was seen leav-ing her rooms at the Spencer House the day before her mysterious disappearance." Meeting Molly's rapt gaze, she continued, "And they said it's not the first time this sort of thing has happened. According to Mrs. Greenfeld, Henry's already been involved in two unsuitable relation-ships before the actress, all of which the older brother had a hand in terminating."

At the expression of triumph in Molly's cobalt blue eyes, Esmeralda's smile widened. "The fact that he's fallen in and out of love three times this year alone makes this all a bit easier to do."

"Aye, that it does," Molly added happily. "What a dupe—an easy cull!"

"I could hardly break his heart if he falls in and out of love so easily."

"There ye go, me girl. A clean conscience to boot."

"In any event," Esmeralda continued, ignoring her friend's teasing tone, "Henry appears to be the only one who doesn't know of his brother's involvement."

"*Musha!* But will the brother be findin' a seamstress as undesirable as an actress? Will he be willin' to pay ye off?"

"That's the whole point. I'll have to captivate Henry but somehow let it be known that I'm some kind of vicious harpy out to marry for money. That should clinch the older brother's part. He won't want such riffraff in the family."

"Catching Henry's eye shouldna be a strain," Molly answered dryly as she examined her friend's exotic green eyes, and long, slender curves.

"Oh, Molly," Esmeralda admonished. "If I listened to you, I'd not step out the door without expecting some man to swoon at my feet. But it wasn't I who enticed some well-sought-after swain in Charleston."

"Stole him right out from under that hussy Lucille Decarte's nose, I did. Sometimes I wonder if Madame threw us out to avoid a scandal or because Miss Decarte refused to pay for the ball gown she ordered to get even with me."

Esmeralda watched Molly smile behind her wooden spoon. Her fine aristocratic features, translucent white skin, and large sapphire blue eyes belied her friend's rough manner—a manner that Esmeralda knew Molly took a gleeful delight in exaggerating for effect. Molly even exaggerated her accent. Esmeralda had taught her years ago how to speak without a brogue, but Molly quickly lapsed into her old habits and forgot Esmeralda's teachings. Yet despite her lack of polish, Molly was always spotlessly clean. And while she paid little attention to her looks, wearing her ebony curls short and loose around her oval face and her clothes heavily mended, her meager attire did little to hide the fine figure within.

From lowered lids, Esmeralda watched Molly soak a piece of bread in her stew and give it to Peter to eat. Despite her hunger, Esmeralda silently slipped back her own half of the bread to the center of the table.

Her throat tightened. If she ever found out who Peter's father was, the scoundrel who had romanced Molly while Esmeralda had been away on a shopping trip for Madame and discarded Molly like used-up goods, she'd make him pay! Damn that man! Sighing, she watched Molly toy with Peter's black curls. The name of Peter's father was a secret Molly guarded jealously. Esmeralda sensed there were other things—things about her friend's past—that she would never know. She tried not to be hurt by Molly's secretive nature.

In the silent and darkened room, Molly continued to feed Peter her share of the stew. When she saw the piece of bread still lying on the center of the table, she looked up and the two women's eyes met.

"Esme, are ye sure? We're not so poor we canna feed ourselves—not yet, anyway."

Esmeralda pushed the piece of brown bread toward Molly. "I'm not hungry, really."

Molly took the bread and crumbled it into the remains of her stew. "Tell me more about Henry. Is he interested enough in ye to draw his brother's attention?"

"I think so. He's been at the shop twice this week . . . alone. He hasn't bought anything, and I'm sure he's not involved with anyone else, or at least I haven't heard any gossip to the contrary. And today he asked me to the Rough and Ready to see the Bateman sisters in *Dumb Girl of Genoa.* He's calling for me tomorrow at the shop."

"Bless us an' save us, ye got him. Hook, line, and sinker!" Molly announced.

"You think so?"

"Arrah! Once ye set yer sights on someone, Esme, me dear, there is not a thing the poor cull can do to stop from falling for ye!"

Esmeralda looked doubtful. "Well, for my part, I plan to do my very best to enrapture him." She looked about the barren, dimly lit room.

Henry Carter could be their only hope!

Chapter Two

". . . And they alternate between the Stetsons' residence and the Carters'. Semi-Colon Club, indeed! Why, they're just a gaggle of bluestockings getting together to discuss silly radical ideas."

The loud, carrying whispers drew Esmeralda's attention away from her work. Annoyed, she looked up from the counter where she sat poised over a simple embroidery pattern and glanced at the corner of the narrow dress shop. There stood Mrs. Greenfeld, sharing the latest gossip with her cohort, Mrs. Percy.

"And that Samantha Carter—influencing nice girls like Harriet Beecher Stowe and the Cary sisters. It's a crime, I tell you. Next thing you know, she'll have them believing they should publish those silly stories."

"It's a wonder Mr. Carter permits her to get involved in such goings-on."

"It's not just that so-called literary club. You know she

went to Seneca Falls last summer with that Stone woman."

"No!"

"She most certainly did! Imagine, with that beautiful mansion of hers and those lovely boys, Jason and Henry. Why, the only emancipation I need is a home in the hills. And she already has that, and much, much more."

Picturing in her mind what Mrs. Greenfeld would look like covered in fine, white powder, Esmeralda fought the urge to pick up her pounce bag and throw it at the overblown matron. If she'd had the chance, she would have gone right along with Samantha Carter and Lucille Stone to last summer's conference on women's rights. It was just as Molly said: Women needed more opportunities in this life. Ladies like Samantha Carter and Lucille Stone were doing their best to secure those opportunities.

Sighing, she returned her attention to the embroidery pattern, continuing to prick holes in the parchment's design with a small stiletto. Ever since she'd been seen in public with Henry Carter the month before, these two rumormongers had become regular fixtures at the Pearl Street dress shop. At first, excited by the prospect of new customers, she'd attended them eagerly. But she soon discovered the women were not there to make a purchase. Instead, they waited like vultures hovering over a weakened victim, ready to gather whatever information they could about Cincinnati's latest *on-dit.*

"You know she would be cut dead if it weren't for her connections with royalty."

"Oh my, with the viscount back in town, I've been so anxious. Why, I just know if he met my Priscilla, they'd make the match of the season."

Esmeralda suppressed her urge to laugh when she pictured Mrs. Percy's rodent-faced daughter catching the eye of the popular Viscount Eldridge. Although she'd never met the man, and Henry never mentioned the British peer, everyone in Cincinnati knew he was an old friend of the Carters. He was also one of Carter Shipping's chief investors. The viscount's trips to Cincinnati were followed closely by its citizens, who, aside from the visit of the Marquis de Lafayette twenty years earlier, had little contact with nobility.

"Mark my words, viscount or not, some day that woman will go too far."

Esmeralda watched Mrs. Greenfeld finger the new bolts of patterned muslin displayed next to two fashion dolls, while the stick-thin Mrs. Percy hung on her every word. Vicious old biddies! Never had a decent thing to say about anyone. She found Mrs. Greenfeld particularly offensive. With a critical eye, Esmeralda examined the rotund woman. She wore an unflattering gown bedecked with layers of ruffles. The childish theme of her dress repeated itself in the multiple bobbing curls surrounding her plump face. Aside from her incredibly bad taste in fashion, the woman's only other memorable characteristic was her big mouth.

Trying to ignore the two harridans, Esmeralda finished piercing her embroidery pattern and pulled out her copy of *The Dressmaker's Handbook* from a shelf under the counter. She opened the book and began to read the instructions on piping and braiding, but Mrs. Greenfeld's grating tenor defeated her attempts to concentrate.

". . . You'd never believe Samantha Carter could be the mother of such fine gentlemen as Jason and Henry Carter."

"Well, I don't know," Mrs. Percy whined. "Henry Carter certainly exhibits a streak of indiscretion."

The room became silent as the two women turned to stare at Esmeralda. Seeing their interested faces from the corner of her eye, she shut her book and forced her most congenial smile.

"Mrs. Greenfeld, if those muslins are not to your liking, I would be happy to order any material you might want. Delivery would take only a few weeks by steamboat."

"No, thank you, Miss MacClure. I haven't quite decided what I'm looking for as of yet." Mrs. Greenfeld sniffed rudely, glaring down her prominent, bulbous nose.

"May I suggest Mrs. Mulliner's shop on Fifth? She has much more of a selection." Esmeralda smiled sweetly. "I'm sure you'll find what you're looking for there."

Clearly offended by the suggestion that she take her business elsewhere, Mrs. Greenfeld snapped, "Perhaps I shall!" Turning to Mrs. Percy, she said loudly, "Don't worry about Henry Carter—young men do have their dalliances before they settle down."

A look of triumph plastered to her porcine features, Mrs. Greenfeld marched out of the store with her companion in tow.

"Oh, bother." Esmeralda pressed her lips together. She'd done it again! She'd let her temper get in the way of her good judgment. Even if Mrs. Greenfeld never bought so much as a piece of ribbon, Esmeralda couldn't afford to be rude. Business was bad enough without inspiring that puffed-up fishwife to spread disparaging remarks about the shop.

Looking about the now vacant store, she experienced a surge of anxiety. Empty. The shop was almost always empty. Aside from the pine counter and the large worktable, the room's only decorations were a display table, two cane chairs, and a wire dress form covered with canvas. While the shelves lining the walls should have been stocked with rich materials, most remained empty. To make up for their lack, Esmeralda kept a large book of cloth samples and copies of the latest issue of *Godey's Lady's Book* on the worktable for clients to peruse. The many drawers that covered the wall behind the counter did contain ribbons, buttons, braiding, and other trimmings, and the tools essential for seamstressing could be found in the back room, where she measured her clients and fitted the garments. But basically the shop was modestly equipped.

When Molly and Esmeralda arrived in Cincinnati, they'd decided to set up shop in town instead of soliciting door-to-door for their patrons. They'd hoped owning their own shop would attract a greater and more sophisticated clientele. With twenty-three dressmakers in town, the competition to sell fashionable clothes was stiff—especially since most people in Cincinnati made their own homespun clothing. But now, over a year after opening the doors, they had barely enough business to make ends meet. And they'd accomplished that feat only by great sacrifice on both their parts. It appeared that, like the large shopping Bazaar on Third Street that had bankrupted Frances Trollope, Esmeralda and Molly would have to sell their business at a loss.

In an attempt to dismiss her gloomy thoughts, Esmeralda took a silk sleeve she had cut earlier and laid it out lengthwise across the pine counter. Placing the embroidery pattern on the shiny material, she was about to rub her muslin pounce bag over the perforated design when the door opened and a man entered the shop.

One word came to mind when she first saw him—*smooth*. Hair the color of creamed coffee complemented a lightly tanned complexion. Tall and distinguished looking, he paused at the entrance as he surveyed the shop with an air of authority. His dark chocolate morning coat and striped pants contributed to his suave demeanor as he strode toward the counter, carrying his beaver hat and ebony cane in one hand.

"Good morning."

His deep, distinctively British voice was a sound from home, a warming reminder of her past. When she looked up, away from the large, powerful hand he'd placed casually on the counter, her gaze met an exceptional pair of eyes. A light amber fringed with thick dark lashes, they accentuated his appeal and contrasted strikingly with his light, caramel-hued hair. Equally dark brows lifted slightly in question as her gaze followed the straight line of his broad nose, ending at his wide mouth and squared chin. Suddenly aware of her disheveled appearance, Esmeralda pushed aside the burnished curls escaping her tight chignon and brushed her chalk-dusted hands against the skirt of her peach muslin gown—all the while examining the man's elegant, expensive attire self-consciously.

"When you're through looking, I'd like to buy a hat." A slight, crooked smile tugged at the right corner of his lips.

Despite her effort not to, she felt herself flush, embarrassed to be caught staring. "A hat?"

"Yes. One of those little things women often wear on their heads."

"I know what a hat is." She forced herself to meet the man's mocking smile. *Arrogant beast,* she thought. How she hated these privileged gentlemen for whom fate had chosen to grant every extravagant whim while she and Molly struggled for each coin they earned. She glared up at him. "But you've come to the wrong place to buy one. This is a dress shop. What you want is a millinery store. If you go up Pearl Street, you'll find quite a large establishment—"

"But your shop comes highly recommended."

Esmeralda perked up. The thought of business improving helped to ease her hostility considerably. "Truly?" she asked with a smile.

"You are Miss Esmeralda MacClure, aren't you?"

Her smile widened. "Indeed I am."

"Then I'm certain I've come to the right place."

Something in his tone caused her smile to falter. Quite suddenly his height, over a head taller than her own five feet six inches, seemed menacing, his casual stance before the counter almost looming. For a fleeting moment she thought she caught a glimpse of something strange in his expression, something . . . could it be dangerous? But when he smiled, his features became so relaxed and friendly that her misgivings seemed out of place.

Straightening her shoulders, Esmeralda renewed her enthusiasm for the potential sale. A customer was nothing to take lightly. "Well, Mr. . . . ?"

"Marshall, Keane Marshall."

"Well, Mr. Marshall, as you've heard about our fine merchandise and workmanship, which I assure you is of the best quality you can find in Cincinnati, could I perhaps interest you in a gown or some other article of dress? We happen to have some beautiful—"

"Only a hat." He cut her off in the clipped voice of a man accustomed to being obeyed. But the smile remained the same: warm and cordial.

"I'd certainly hate to turn down a prospective client," she said jokingly, trying to relieve some of the tension in the room. Seeing that he would not be swayed to purchase something else, she plunged ahead before he could change his mind and leave. "Perhaps we can accommodate you after all. What kind of a hat would you like?" Surely, with Molly's talent, she could come up with something. She tried to calculate in her head how much it would cost to purchase an inexpensive hat from the millinery shop up the street and fix it up by adding ribbons and bows.

"I'd like three hats, actually. One for each of my sisters. I always buy them presents when I travel."

"How very thoughtful of you." *Three!* she thought. This was turning out better than she'd hoped.

Eyes the color of brandy met Esmeralda's direct gaze. They really were extraordinary, she thought, so warm, almost intoxicating. As she stared into their inviting depths, wondering how his lashes and brows could be such an unusual dark color and his soft curls so contrastingly light, she felt curiously unsettled. She reminded herself sharply that a man with such handsome looks and easy manner was most probably an accomplished rake, accustomed to girls like herself trying to capture his attentions. . . .

". . . So if you could help choose—Miss MacClure?"

"Certainly." Esmeralda snapped to attention. That was the second time she'd made a fool of herself in front of this man. What was wrong with her! "You were saying?"

His lips turned upward in a smug line, as if he knew exactly how distracted she was by his presence. "The hats? If you could help me choose them?"

"My pleasure." She smiled broadly, trying to make up for her past clumsiness. "Perhaps if you told me a little about your sisters, I would know what might suit them best." She clasped her hands on the counter and leaned forward, determined to be especially attentive from now on. But instead of exhibiting the professionalism she strove for, she accidentally swiped the embroidery pattern with her elbow and sent the pounce bag sliding into Mr. Marshall's gloved hand. A spray of white chalk plumed out of the muslin sack, leaving a powdery residue on the brown kid leather.

Horrified, Esmeralda grabbed a remnant from beneath the counter and began to wipe at the chalk stain. "Oh, I'm so sorry!"

Keane Marshall merely shrugged his shoulders and smiled. "Don't worry. I don't think it's fatal."

"But I've ruined your glove." Clutching his hand, Esmeralda continued to scrub his glove with the piece of velvet.

"Miss MacClure, if you don't ease your grip, I'm afraid I'll lose more than my glove."

Startled, Esmeralda looked up. Following his sharp gaze, she glanced down to the counter where she literally had the poor man's hand pinned, her own knuckles turning white with the effort. She immediately released her grasp and gaped at him, completely at a loss for words.

His only reaction was to throw his head back and laugh. His unrestrained mirth made Esmeralda's lips twitch and soon she joined in his infectious laughter. It really was rather funny, she thought. For a moment she felt a certain camaraderie between them.

Smiling down at her, Mr. Marshall set his hat and cane on the counter, careful to avoid the white spot produced by the pounce bag. After removing his gloves, he dropped them into the pocket of his coat. The matter thus dealt with, he leaned casually against the counter, his arms crossed over his broad chest.

"Charlotte, the oldest, is *most* practical," he began, as if nothing unusual had occurred. "She's almost my height, but married to a man not nearly so tall." He lifted his dark brows comically, and Esmeralda laughed at the image of Charlotte looming over her poor husband. "I've always believed that was part of the attraction for her— she can be a bit dictatorial. What do you recommend?"

"A military cap perhaps?"

Mr. Marshall shook his head slowly and eyed her with mock disappointment. "So obvious, Miss MacClure?"

"It was just a thought." She grinned. Then, trying to appear serious, she stated, "I think the *very* practical Charlotte deserves a *very* sensible straw bonnet."

He nodded appreciatively. "Then there's Annabella. She's younger than I and spends most of her time reading romantic novels and poetry. Her head is forever in the clouds, so half the time I expect her to walk into a wall or a bush."

"Has she made her debut yet?"

"No, but I'm certain *that* auspicious event will occur soon enough."

"Then how about a party hat? One with lots of ribbons and flowers."

"That would do admirably." His smile made Esmeralda feel as if her suggestion were a stroke of genius.

Pausing as if for effect, he sighed dramatically and added in a sober voice, "Then there's Katherine Nicole."

"Katherine Nicole?" The name didn't sound particularly ominous.

Keane nodded solemnly. "We'll have to be particularly careful with Nicky."

"Indeed?"

Keane leaned over the counter and whispered, "I'm afraid Nicky would be quite offended by such a feminine gift as a hat, so we must be very clever in choosing it."

Esmeralda looked at his laughing eyes suspiciously. Was he teasing her? "How old is Nicky?"

"Ten. But she considers herself much older. She's always giving me advice about my riding. Says I don't sit back far enough on my hunter when I take the fence. She predicts someday I'll lose my seat—but I'm afraid she didn't phrase it quite so delicately."

"Ahh!" Esmeralda barely suppressed her own smile, enjoying his teasing depiction of his sisters. "And I gather Nicky would prefer something not so dull as a hat. Perhaps a riding crop?"

"More like a Wesson rifle," he said dryly, causing Esmeralda to break into uncontrolled giggles. "I admit she's a talented shot. We call her Nicky because she's such a scamp. She's the baby of the family and terribly spoiled. I fear that's my fault," he added with a smile.

"How shall we ever find a hat that Nicky won't throw back into your face for the insult?"

Keane held his hands out in a mock plea. "I'm at your mercy."

Esmeralda tapped her forefinger against her lips in thought. Then, her eyes sparkling, she said, "Definitely a hunting cap for Nicky."

"Perfect!" Keane stepped back and bowed deeply in an exaggerated fashion. "I am forever in your debt, Miss MacClure." Returning to the counter, he picked up her hand and kissed it softly. The touch of his strong fingers and the feel of his warm lips against her bare skin startled her. Distracted by the unsettling sensation that spread through her, she watched helplessly as he lingered over her hand, his darkened eyes holding her emerald ones in an intense stare.

"You see, you really do have a knack for hats," he said

in a rough whisper. "Maybe you should consider expanding business?"

Despite her confused emotions, Esmeralda beamed from his praise. "Thank you, Mr. Marshall. But wait until you see the hats." Setting aside the odd sensations he'd caused, she gathered her confidence from his charming compliments. "I'm sure you'll not be disappointed."

Keane reached into his coat pocket and removed a gold coin and a card. As he placed them carefully on the counter before Esmeralda, she noticed for the first time a gold signet ring he wore on his left hand. She couldn't quite make out the insignia engraved on the ring's surface.

"I'm staying at the Burnet, should you need to contact me. You can deliver the hats there." Flashing the same crooked smile that had made her stomach flip-flop, he stated in a voice warm with appreciation, "Thank you very much Miss MacClure. It's been a real pleasure." Picking up his hat and cane from the counter, he granted her one last melting smile and then strode out the door.

Esmeralda stared at the closed entrance, fighting her sense of disappointment at his leaving. She'd enjoyed their banter. It wasn't often she had the chance to meet an interesting man, and she'd certainly never known one so charming or good-looking. She shook her head at her own foolishness, thinking again that the man was probably a rogue, well aware of his effect on women. She'd not fall for one such as he. Look what had happened to Molly when she had left her senses and became enamored of Peter's father!

Turning her thoughts away from the seductive image of Mr. Marshall, she transferred her attention to the gold coin on the counter. She picked it up and rubbed its cool surface with her fingers. It was a large sum to pay for three hats, especially ones designed by a professed novice. With this one coin, she and Molly could pay off the rent they owed on the cottage *and* the shop, and still have money to spare! She sent a silent thanks to the mysterious Mr. Marshall for his generosity.

Her train of thought returning to her benefactor, she set aside the gold coin and picked up the thick cream-colored calling card he'd left. As she read the bold letters embossed in gold, her eyes widened, and she whispered under her breath, "Oh, my."

Chapter Three

Keane Marshall, Viscount Eldridge, heir presumptive to the Marquess of Amesbury, glanced across the card table into the jet-black eyes of his opponent. The stocky, dark-haired gentleman raised a bushy brow and met Keane's penetrating gaze with a brooding stare. *No help there,* Keane thought; his friend, Jason Carter, always looked brooding.

Shifting his eyes to his left, Keane examined an older, more distinguished-looking version of Jason. It wasn't often that Derek Carter, Jason's father, joined in their card games. But tonight, after a splendid dinner prepared by the Carters' talented chef, the retired businessman had met with them in the parlor for a game. He seemed to be thoroughly enjoying himself, despite what Keane guessed was a less than pleasing draw.

"Derek, I believe it's your turn to bet." Keane watched the handsome, lined face carefully.

Tossing his cards amiably on the felt surface of the table, Derek Carter folded. "Well, I'm done for. This appears to be a game for the young."

"If it suits the young in heart, then you've given in prematurely."

"That's what I like about you, Keane." Derek chuckled. "Always the diplomat." Reaching for the cedar box on the mahogany tripod table beside him, he offered Keane a smoke. When his guest refused the hand-rolled cigar, Derek removed one for himself, bit off the end, and lit up.

Keane watched as the older man sat back in his chair and rolled the cigar between his teeth, ready to enjoy the game as a spectator. Now that Derek was no longer responsible for the financial well-being of Carter Shipping, a burden he'd shifted to the younger, stronger shoulders of his elder son, Jason, he could relax enough to lose gracefully.

One opponent taken care of, Keane turned his attention to the player on his right. His discerning glance took in a very different picture from that of the other two, powerful Carters. Chewing on his lower lip, tall and slender Henry Carter stared at his cards as if he wished he could magically transform them. Keane watched him pull distractedly at a lock of pale hair and mentally counted how long it would take the younger man to fold.

He'll turn his cards in right about . . . now.

Henry threw his cards down. "Drat. I always have the damndest ill luck when I play against you, Keane!"

Keane's expression remained impassive as he turned to the only remaining competitor. "That leaves you and me again, Jason."

"That's right." Tossing enough money into the center of the card table to match Keane's last bet and raise the stakes, Jason smiled like a man intent on winning.

In the tension-filled room, all eyes focused on Keane.

He evaluated his options in a fraction of a second. Jason, a conservative attorney not prone to reckless betting, must have a good hand. But there was more than one way to win at poker. Without looking down at the meager pair of threes he held, Keane immediately slid across the green felt surface a small pile of coins—enough to match and double Jason's bet.

He met Jason's brooding expression with a smug smile and an arrogant lift of his brow.

Hesitant after his opponent's bravado, Jason's coal-dark eyes narrowed on Keane's unwavering gaze. "God help me, if you're bluffing. . . ."

"Your bet, Jason," Keane stated in an even voice.

Jason's lips tightened while Keane's remained fixed in a complacent grin.

"You win again!" Jason gathered his cards together and slapped them facedown on the table, forfeiting the game to his opponent. "Mark my words, Keane, someday the tables will turn."

Keane scooped up his winnings and stacked them neatly along the cross-banded edging on the lip of the table. He tilted his head thoughtfully, as if trying to recall something important. "Why does that threat sound so familiar? Ah . . . yes." Keane leaned back in his chair and played with one of the many substantial stacks of coins before him. "An oft repeated prediction that has yet to come true." He clicked his tongue in disappointment. "Your talents as a soothsayer are questionable, Jason. Best stick to lawyering. I understand you're much more successful at it than cards."

"If you weren't so closefisted," Henry teased his brother, "you could have fronted the money just to see if he was bluffing."

"Were you?" Jason stared intently as Keane picked up the cards and shuffled them with ease.

"Now, Jason," the commanding voice of his father intervened. "If you wanted the answer to that, you should have called Keane's bet."

"It's not the money that stops me," Jason grumbled.

"It's the thought of having to put up with that smug look when he fans out the winning hand, one blasted card at a time." Directing his comment to Keane, Jason added, "I absolutely *hate* when you do that."

"If you find me so offensive, why do you play against me?" Keane cut the cards with one hand several times while watching Jason with an amused expression. He then placed the deck in the center of the table for Derek Carter to shuffle and cut.

"Because"—Jason smiled, displaying a set of seldom seen dimples—"I keep thinking it will be *me* waving the winning hand under *your* nose." Jason reached for a cigar and clamped down on the end. "Besides. I like to see anything well done—even if it's an obnoxious friend beating me at cards."

"Why, Jason . . . was that a compliment?" Keane parried.

"Deal the cards!" Jason barked while Derek and Henry laughed.

"By the way," Jason asked when the laughter died down, "did the boys at White's ever set up a game between you and that Lord . . . Now what was his name? The one that was so all-fired hot for a match between you?"

"Lord Kielder."

"That's the one."

"Not a chance." Keane flipped a round of cards to each player across the felt. "I didn't even bother to send my card around to Kielder's town house for an introduction. Not only is the man a rumored cheat, there was some unsavory business surrounding his ward. Not to mention his possible insolvency."

Jason looked up surprised. "You don't say?"

"He's left unpaid vowels at all the clubs." Keane continued dealing the cards with an easy rhythm.

Derek Carter lifted a corner of one card and sneaked a

peak. "You're right to avoid the fellow, Keane. Best to stay away from his type."

"My thoughts exactly," Keane replied.

Just then, the doors to the parlor burst open. A tall, willowy woman dressed in a light fawn gown of figured barege paused dramatically before winding her way past one of two empire settees. Stepping toward the card table, she adjusted the white curls around her slender, unlined face with a sweep of one hand. Then, pulling the gros point covered stool away from the tapestry screen, she set it beside her husband's chair. Before any of the four men could stand, she lifted her hand in a commanding gesture, indicating that they should remain in their chairs. Once seated, she adjusted the heavy skirt of her gown and granted each man a dazzling smile before taking her husband's cigar.

"Gentlemen, deal me in." She took a delicate puff.

"Mother!" Jason grabbed for the offending cigar while his father merely chuckled and sat back, ready to watch the antics of mother and son.

Blasting Jason with a basilisk stare, Samantha Carter held the cigar out of his reach. "Did that snobocrat call *me* 'Mother'?"

Jason threw his hands up in the air and expelled an exasperated sigh while Henry snickered.

"Impossible!" Samantha examined each man with a look of astonishment. Replacing the smoking cigar on the edge of the card table, she added, "No son of mine could be so narrow-minded as to deny a woman equal access to the entertainments afforded men."

"Botheration." Henry stood and straightened his waistcoat. "Mother, if you're going to make this a forum of debate between you and Jason, I'm leaving for my club. Maybe I'll have better luck there."

Leaning over toward Samantha, his face beaming with admiration, Henry kissed her powdered cheek. At that moment, the extraordinary resemblance between mother and son was evident. While Jason's stocky figure was a copy of his father, Henry's doelike eyes and tall, slender physique favored Samantha Carter.

"Don't stay out too late, dear." Her features softened as she gently patted Henry's face.

Henry donned his jacket and smiled. "Only as long as it takes to recoup my losses."

"That should be all night," Jason scoffed.

"Jason." Henry swatted at an imaginary piece of lint on his sleeve. "Do try not to be a total boor. Good night, all." With a slight wave and a flash of white teeth, Henry turned and left the parlor.

Jason stared out the double doors of the room. "Young pup. Shows me no respect."

Samantha squeezed her elder son's hand. "You simply must learn to relax, Jason. I worry about you and your exaggerated sense of propriety." Then, smiling at Keane, "Do pass the cards, dear. I feel lucky tonight."

Jason turned with a pleading look to Derek Carter while Keane gathered up the cards and shuffled with exaggerated concentration, trying to suppress his laughter.

"Perhaps we should excuse ourselves, Sam. I'm sure Jason and Keane have more important things to do than play cards with us." He smiled indulgently at his wife.

"Don't patronize me, Derek."

"Sam, really. I risk my own reputation gambling. If any member of the council should get wind of this, much less your joining in . . ."

"Oh, bosh! They're all so above themselves these days. But such snobbery does not go unnoticed. Why, just yesterday I walked by that purse-proud Mary Dicker's house, and someone had strung a pair of old shoes on the doorknob! About time people reminded that woman her father was a cobbler before he made a cent in land."

"You didn't have anything to do with that incident, did you, Mother?"

Samantha examined Jason closely. "You're starting to get worry lines, darling."

"Mother?"

Ignoring Jason, she turned to her husband. "He's too young for wrinkles, Derek. You're overworking him."

"Will you please answer me, Mother?"

"Jason, if you're so concerned about my . . . ah . . . activities, why not try distracting me." Leaning close to her son and smiling, she suggested, "Now, if for example you should marry and have a son . . ."

This time, Keane couldn't hold back his laughter. The horrified expression on Jason's face was just too funny.

"Oh, for goodness' sake, Keane, he's three and thirty and never cared about anything more than making money and more money. It's no wonder I search for ways to spend my time. But if I had a grandchild . . ."

Jason rubbed his face with his hand, and Keane continued to chuckle.

"You wouldn't leave your mother without grandchildren, would you, Keane?"

Still laughing, Keane answered the distinguished-looking woman across from him. "Luckily, Charlotte has already taken care of matters. Her brood keeps Mother busy."

"But the title, Keane. Surely that's a consideration." Samantha looked at the handsome British peer with interest.

"Yes." Keane tried to keep a straight face as he explained, "But since I'm three years away from Jason's decrepit age, Mother hasn't been too concerned." Keane glanced at Jason from the corner of his eye. His friend's bushy eyebrows looked as if they were about to pop off his scarlet face. Keane added in a solemn voice, "It appears I still have time. But Jason . . ." He shook his head sadly.

Samantha lifted her shoulders and sighed. "Oh, dear, I do hope he gets on with it before I'm too old to enjoy the little ones."

Before Jason could think of a retort, Derek stood, pulling his wife to her feet. "Well, gentlemen, if you'll excuse us. I believe Samantha has had her fun for the evening."

She smiled congenially at her husband. "Do you think he'll ever forgive me?" She glanced anxiously at Jason.

"He always forgives you, darling."

As Jason and Keane began to stand, Samantha held her hand up, requesting that they remain seated. Leaning over Jason, she kissed him on the top of his dark, curly head. "Good night, darling." Smiling at Keane, she bid him a good night and added, "Please, leave him a few pennies."

Keane grinned as he watched the distinguished couple walk out, hand in hand. Shaking his head, he laughed. He really liked the Carters.

"I hope you enjoyed yourself!" Jason grumbled.

"Most thoroughly."

Jason strode to the satinwood table covered with crystal decanters of various sizes and shapes. He splashed cognac into two glasses and offered one to Keane. His dark eyes sharp and assessing, he asked in a low, gruff voice, "Did you see the MacClure woman?"

Keane stood and leaned against the marble mantel. He took a slow drink and then examined the cognac's amber color with rapt interest. Lifting his gaze to meet Jason's intent stare, he answered, "Yes."

"And?"

"Henry's a lucky man."

Jason waited, impatiently tapping his fingers against his bell-shaped glass, but Keane remained silent.

"Is that all you have to say? Come now, Keane, I didn't send you to the shop to report sentimental slop. I want to know if she's after his money!"

Keane thought about his visit that morning to Miss MacClure's store. When he entered the shop, he saw a sparsely furnished establishment, and, acting on a hunch, he asked for something he knew a dressmaker would not normally provide. It was a test to see just how desperate she was for business. He was not surprised when she finally accepted his offer and agreed to make the hats.

"She needs the money," he stated softly.

"I knew it!"

"But I don't think she's the fortune huntress you suspect."

"And why is that?"

Keane furrowed his brow. Why indeed? He pictured the copper-haired girl he'd sought out under Jason's instructions. She'd eagerly waited on him, trying almost desperately to please him despite his arrogant demand. Her face had hidden nothing: not her need for the sale nor her interest in him. She'd been so solicitous, so . . .

"Naïve. She's just too naïve to fleece Henry."

Jason looked doubtfully at his companion. "Are you sure you're not taken with the girl yourself? I've seen her. She's not your ordinary bit of fluff. Can you be sure your judgment is not clouded by a nice figure and a pretty face?"

Keane turned sharply toward Jason. His hand tightened around the brandy snifter and his eyes narrowed as he shook his head slowly. "I can recognize a scheming woman."

Catching Keane's steady gaze, Jason's eyes clouded momentarily. "That you can, my friend."

In the silence, Keane reflected on the glowing embers warming the salon. A gambler with excellent instincts, he seldom lost. He played to win. But he hadn't always been able to see through a good bluff. Slowly the mesmerizing flicker drew him into memories that after twelve years he still couldn't escape.

It was Jason's habit to look after his own. During the years their fathers had spent developing a solid business relationship, Keane and Jason had formed a deep and lasting friendship. They treated each other like brothers. In the same way Jason monitored Henry's actions here at home, he'd counseled Keane during his wild years at Oxford. Not unlike young Henry, Keane had ignored Jason's sage advice about Alysha.

Alysha Cranborne was ten years older and widowed—hardly a good match for an eighteen-year-old boy. But Keane would not be warned off. He loved her with the energy and desperation of untried youth. In the end, untutored in the bed games of the upper class, he pleaded for her to marry him. Her resulting refusal was responsible for the tight lines around his full lips and the parallel marks between his wide-spaced eyes.

Alysha had laughed at him, of course. He was only the second son of a viscount—hardly adequate compensation for the ambitious woman, who had set her sights on an aging earl. It was only later, when the death of his older brother and father in a sailing accident further hardened his handsome face into its present chiseled planes, that Alysha's attentions returned to the new Viscount Eldridge, now the potential heir to a marquess. Having left his studies and taken over management of the family estates and vineyards, Keane's many responsibilities overshadowed any thoughts of a renewed romance with the conniving Alysha. His tremendous sense of guilt over the death of his father and brother drove him to double and then triple the family fortune. Many said he had the Midas touch, and it was true that his seemingly daring investments almost always paid off. Eventually Alysha had lost interest in her pursuit and had landed her earl. Yes, he knew about calculating women.

Slowly Alysha's dark image dissolved into burnished curls and haunting green eyes. Jason was right. Esmeralda MacClure was beautiful enough to be distracting. While normally immune to pretty packaging, Keane had been drawn by her ready smile and exotic eyes. He'd found himself trying to attract her, playing off her obvious admiration of him, despite the fact she was Henry's choice. Perhaps his vision *had* been less than clear. Could he be sure she was not just a younger, less experienced version of Alysha? And what would it cost Henry if he were wrong?

Taking a steadying sip of the brandy, Keane asked, "What makes you think she is after his money?"

Jason rose, depositing his glass on a silver salver left for that purpose. "Henry has no sense when it comes to women. Three times now I've had to get rid of the parasites. The last time it cost me a bloody fortune." Jason leaned against the curled arm of the inlaid rosewood settee. "No sooner did Rose Murard disappear than Henry became entangled with Miss MacClure. This time I'm afraid things are more serious. He's speaking of marriage." Jason raked his hair back off his brow. "Considering Henry's past record, I have to be very careful."

Keane remembered his own painful experience with love. If he could spare Henry that sort of humiliation, he would. "I can hardly tell you the woman's intent after one visit. What do you need me to do?"

Faint dimples accented Jason's smile. "I want you to get to know her, talk to her, find out if it's Henry she wants or his money. She would be less guarded around you."

"Of course." Keane smiled over the rim of his brandy glass. "Getting rid of Henry's past light-o'-loves has hardly made you a candidate for confidences."

"Don't joke about it, Keane. When I said Henry is a bad judge of women, I was being generous. So far my brother has lost his heart—and his wallet—to an actress, an operetta singer, and another man's mistress!" Jason returned to the settee and sat down, leaning back against the tapestry cushions like a man tired of shouldering a heavy burden. "And if any one of these women had truly loved Henry for anything other than what his inheritance could buy her, I'd have granted her my blessing without a second thought. But not surprisingly, each and every one has been more than happy to accept my money and leave. The last even had the bad manners to bargain for a better price! I'm not a snob; it's not their status in life that I find objectionable. Why, I myself . . ." A pained expression crossed his face and Jason turned away. "I want only Henry's happiness. You and I both know, women can be a treacherous lot."

Jason's words reminded Keane of his friend's own bitter experience at thwarted love. "There's a certain danger in applying our own experiences to Henry's life," he warned softly.

"Balderdash! That young pup doesn't know if he's on his head or his heels around women. And I'll not have him or this family strapped to a money-hungry harpy out to ruin him. Now, are you with me?"

Keane sighed. "You may be right. Henry is your brother and my friend. I'll do anything in my power to protect him."

"Fine. For the moment, I would appreciate your keeping a close watch on Miss MacClure and finding out anything you can about her. I'm giving a ball to celebrate Henry's birthday. Miss MacClure will be present. Romance the chit if you have to—just find out what she really wants."

Chapter Four

Esmeralda sat stiffly, her back straight against the jarring carriage seat. She pulled the black silk cape around her and adjusted the fall of her heavy green satin skirt. The dress and wrap were on loan from the shop—articles purchased with the viscount's gold that would later be transformed by Molly's talented hands into unrecognizable creations and sold. Her hair lay in soft, flowing curls against her smooth shoulders, with gently floating wisps outlining her heart-shaped face.

Guilt weighed heavily on her conscience.

She'd been seeing Henry for over a month. During that time, she'd learned of his kindhearted and selfless nature, his youthful charm, and his droll wit. Any woman who didn't fall in love with him would have to be completely heartless. And, of course, she didn't love Henry. Her only interest in him was a cold desire for money.

I've turned into a conniving shrew!

She sighed. It did no good to berate herself. No matter

what the consequences, they needed the money. If she had to sacrifice Henry's pride to get it, so be it.

That's all it was: pride. He would get over her in much the same way he had forgotten the actress and the singer. Besides, what about Molly and Peter? She owed them this chance. Once she regained Amberose, she could take care of them.

Esmeralda shook her head, deep in thought. It was always the same: first guilt, then justification. A conscience was a tedious thing.

She held back the fringed velvet curtain covering the carriage window and stared at the busy, gaslit streets of Cincinnati. Even at this late hour, hundreds of carriages, light wagons, and trotting baskets crowded the streets and evidenced the city's thriving life-style. The "Queen City of the West" was booming with business. Unlike other towns, Cincinnati had weathered the financial tempest of '37 admirably, earning its reputation as a place where many could make money just by turning a hand over. But the city was best known for its efficient pork-packing industry. Hogs roamed the streets, doing their best to clean up the garbage left behind by the less than effective city scavenger carts and granting Cincinnati its other pseud-onym, "Porkopolis."

Despite its commercial progress, Cincinnati was essentially a country town. Maples, ailanthus, and sycamores lined the immense blocks of buildings made of brick. Well-kept gardens surrounded the red-and-white homes and attractive villas. Elegant carriages and horsemen on magnificent mounts from Kentucky ranged the wide, paved roadways. Coming into town each morning from Walnut Hills, Esmeralda would admire the majestic double curve of the Ohio River sweeping between the steeple-topped peaks of the Ohio hills and Kentucky. The primeval forest that was still visible in the hills provided a dramatic background for the city's many gilded spires, which glittered with captured sunlight.

Nibbling on a fingernail, Esmeralda watched out the window as the carriage passed the Western Museum where Count d'Orfeuille's dramatic depiction of Dante's *Inferno,* "The Infernal Regions," still lured curious sightseers. Henry had taken her to see the exhibit last week, and she'd been amazed by the caverns, molten lakes, and imaginative figures of imps with eyes that rolled and shot flames and dwarfs who grew into giants at a touch. And when she ventured too close to the exhibit fence, she received an electric shock that made the macabre show even more unforgettable. At the time, she hadn't seen the irony of her visit to the nether regions. Only later did she realize how fitting it seemed that Henry should give her a preview of Hell.

Oblivious to her tormented thoughts, the hired coachman directed the carriage down Fourth to Pike Street. Up ahead ran the canal, the bend of which citizens had dubbed the Rhine. A huddle of short, cramped streets and stout, red-brick buildings, the Rhine area was Cincinnati's German community. Esmeralda visited the ethnic quarter often, enjoying the smells from the *Backerei* that would make her mouth water as she listened to Bach chorales chimed from the clock towers of the stone churches. On warm days, women would knit on the whitewashed steps before the sidewalks where men could be found smoking long-stemmed clay pipes they called chibouks. It was always a pleasant detour, and she treated herself to it whenever she had the time.

But tonight the German quarter was not her destination. Bright lights and rows upon rows of carriages marked her goal. Esmeralda silently examined the majestic two-story structure as her carriage rolled up to the walled entrance of the Carter mansion. The lively cadence of a quadrille permeated the jasmine-scented air. From behind the imposing pillars that supported the portico, she could see that dancers already occupied the ballroom on the top floor.

Like an actress preparing for her debut, Esmeralda inhaled a steadying breath. *Tonight Henry will propose,* she predicted. Stepping down from the carriage with the help of a footman, she gathered her wide skirts and her courage before continuing toward the paved walkway leading to the house.

When Henry entered the ballroom with Miss MacClure on his arm, Keane quietly excused himself from Priscilla Percy's rapt and unsolicited attention. He'd been watching for the lovely seamstress all evening. Now, well into the second hour of the night's entertainment, she'd finally arrived.

Taking a proffered glass of champagne from a passing waiter, he leaned against a mahogany pillar and took a moment to observe her. The elegant young woman who walked gracefully beside Henry, her shoulders straight and head held high, presented quite a different picture from the likable, slightly flustered girl he'd joked with less than a week ago. The tight bun she wore at the shop had disguised the mass of copper-hued curls that now framed her face and cascaded over her bare shoulders. Despite her disheveled appearance at work, he'd known she was a beautiful woman. But tonight she appeared devastatingly attractive. The stylishly clinging bodice of her emerald gown, with its black lace flounces, exhibited a praiseworthy figure, while the daring cut of her décolletage displayed ample, pale breasts. Keane stared as she glided across the room like the goddess Hebe and, with Henry, joined the many couples swirling across the dance floor. The intensity of his desire for her was both surprising and instant.

"Your mouth's flapped open like a trapdoor. I suggest you shut it before you start salivating like a starved hound." Jason spoke from behind Keane. "You're being quite obvious. All the proud mamas here will swoon in despair."

Keane chuckled softly. "At least I'm not alone." He gestured with his glass to the many spectators Miss Mac-Clure's entrance had attracted.

"A real stunner, isn't she?" Jason asked, his own scrutiny of Miss MacClure as intent as Keane's.

"That is an understatement." Keane's gaze continued to follow Henry and his partner as they executed a *tour de deux mains* together. "She's breathtaking."

With a worried frown, Jason examined his companion's steadfast focus on the dancing couple. "I wonder, Keane, if you're up to the project we discussed."

"Jason, I have never been more 'up' for anything in my life. You'll excuse me?" Never taking his eyes off Esmeralda, Keane handed Jason his empty glass and advanced toward the dance floor.

Samantha Carter lifted her crystal goblet to her lips and sipped the bubbly champagne. Dressed in a gown that shockingly mimicked her husband's attire, complete with lapels and scarf tied *à l'Americaine,* her light brown eyes centered on her younger son and his dance partner.

"She's extraordinary." Derek Carter stood almost level with his wife, but his muscular, barrel-chested physique was no less manly for its lack of stature.

"Yes, Miss MacClure is quite pretty."

"First time he's brought a woman to meet us. What do you think, Sam? He says he wants to marry her. Maybe Henry will make up for all the time Jason's wasted."

Samantha compared the young woman's distracted gaze to her son's intense interest and frowned. "I think not. Somehow I don't believe Miss MacClure is that . . . involved. Such a shame, too. She's a seamstress. Just the kind of hardworking woman who could turn around our frivolous Henry."

"A seamstress, you say? I'm not sure Henry should—" He stopped at his wife's disapproving glare. "Well, just the same, how can you be so sure about her feelings?"

"I can't. But I know where I can find out more information."

"Jason?"

Samantha Carter's lips curled in a secretive smile. "He's not his mother's son for nothing."

Esmeralda's heart pounded as she watched the viscount stroll toward them. If possible, he looked even more handsome than the first time she'd seen him. Dressed in a black swallowtail coat and trousers, he made Henry's tight-waisted jacket with its flared skirt seem almost feminine. She closed her eyes and tried to steady her breathing—and stepped on Henry's foot.

"I believe this is my dance."

She swallowed her apology to Henry, nearly jumping out of her skin at the sound of the viscount's deep, mellow voice, and watched as Henry recovered from his irritation at having their dance interrupted. He stepped beside Esmeralda and touched her elbow in a proprietary gesture.

"Since I personally made certain that Miss MacClure's dance card was devoid of the names of any scoundrels like yourself, Keane, I can only assume you are impatient to meet this beauty." Henry proudly drew her forward. "Esmeralda, my dear, I wish to present—"

"The lady and I are already acquainted."

"Oh, really?" Deflated, Henry failed to disguise his disappointment.

"At the shop," Esmeralda quickly interjected, concerned that the viscount's tone had implied something more intimate than a business acquaintance. "The viscount purchased a few items for his sisters."

"Well, Keane, if you promise to behave"—Henry graciously stood back—"I believe you can steal this one dance."

As she stepped into his arms, Esmeralda immediately felt the difference between Henry's polite waltz stance and this man's embrace. Before she could catch her breath and object to the intimacy of his hold, he swept her into a tight turn that brought their bodies even closer. When she lifted her gaze to protest, she met his eyes and nearly gasped. It was a sin to put such beautiful eyes on a man—too great a weapon.

Their amber color reminded her of a brooch she'd once seen in Charleston, worn by one of Madame's rich customers. Locked within the precious amber jewelry had been some prehistoric insect. Staring now into the depths of Keane's eyes, she felt a little like that trapped bug.

"He's too young for you."

She felt her stomach drop at his words. Small laugh lines appeared at the corners of his eyes, but his humor was different from the easy camaraderie they'd shared at the shop. His intense gaze and solid grasp reminded her of the moment when he'd stood beside the counter and she'd wondered fleetingly if this man were somehow dangerous. Now his actions as well as his words elucidated the threat: He was a friend of the Carters' and a man not easily deceived. She would have to be careful around him. She couldn't let his charm and good looks lure her into giving her plans away.

Esmeralda wet her lips nervously. "I don't understand your meaning, Lord Eldridge, but it would appear not to be polite."

"Shall I change the subject, then?" His dark eyebrows rose to meet a lock of tawny hair. "How about this: Esmeralda—what a beautiful name." His dry tone and dandified expression imitated Henry perfectly. Despite her anxiety, she found herself choking back her laughter.

"It's an odd combination, Esmeralda MacClure." This time, he sounded genuinely interested.

"Not really. My father was Scottish. My mother, while a very proper British lady, was only half-English. I was named after my Spanish grandmother." She narrowed her eyes and watched him speculatively. "And you, my lord. Why did you withhold your true identity at the shop?"

He frowned. "Withhold my identity? I remember distinctly making a proper introduction."

"But you didn't mention your title."

"Ah, the title!" He grinned down at her, and Esmeralda felt a cold, pleasant tingling below her stomach. "I meant no deception. While here in Cincinnati, I prefer to use my given name. It's so much more . . . democratic."

"But once people know who you are, surely they address you properly?"

Leaning forward, he murmured in her ear, "My friends call me Keane." Then he lowered his eyes to where Esmeralda's breasts strained against the material of her bodice, but the look was so fleeting, she wondered immediately if she'd imagined it. She willed herself not to blush—and managed to tread on his instep.

"I'm so sorry."

"Apologizing again, Miss MacClure?" He lowered his hand to her waist and gave a slight squeeze. While Esmeralda believed his touch was meant to be reassuring, it felt surprisingly like a caress. "You needn't ever apologize to a man who is holding you in his arms. The privilege is well worth the risk of a small pain or two." Laugh lines again appeared as his eyes met her questioning gaze. His expression was accompanied by a smug smile.

She felt as if she were caught in a game of cat and mouse. Once again, she was acting like a complete nitwit. She wanted to appear controlled and sophisticated to this world-wise man, but instead she felt awkward and unsettled in his presence. She didn't know if she was expected to remonstrate with him for his intimate hold or thank him for dancing with her despite her clumsiness. And now, as she looked at his arrogant smile, she realized he must be laughing at her and her lack of sophistication. That made her angry.

Bracing her hand against his shoulder, Esmeralda pushed herself away from him. She could see Henry watching them from the corner of the room, his expression reflecting his disapproval of Keane's improper hold. It was imperative to gain control of the situation. "Really, Lord Eldridge, people are beginning to stare."

"A waltz should be danced close," Keane whispered in her ear, completely undoing Esmeralda's hard-fought-for composure. "It's a very romantic dance."

Despite her full skirts, she could feel Keane's thigh press against her leg with each turn. She took a deep breath and tried to ignore the responding warmth she felt where their bodies touched. But with the feel of his breath against her cheek, her resistance dissolved. Each whispered word tingled and trailed down her neck. Her body unconsciously leaned into his.

"How serious are you and Henry?"

Although spoken in a butterfly-soft voice, his blunt question brought Esmeralda out of her sensual haze. Her body straightened. "Very!"

"What would it take to change that?"

"Nothing you could offer."

"Give me a chance. I may surprise you."

His hand gently caressed the small of her back through the tight material of her bodice, but Esmeralda eased her elbow under his to force the offending hand away.

"You, sir, have the manners of an octopus!" She tried to step gracefully out of his arms and off the dance floor, but he somehow translated the move into a cordial escort toward the the balcony. Not wanting to cause a scene, Esmeralda walked with him through the French doors. He held her hand imprisoned on the crook of his arm, anchored there by his steady grasp. Only when he pulled her to a far corner, away from any prying eyes, did she twist her hand free and attempt to return to the ballroom. She didn't get far. Keane grabbed her wrist and guided her back into his arms.

"I find that I suit my actions to the circumstances." Wrapping his arms around her waist, he drew her body against his, ignoring her resistance.

When Esmeralda's gaze met his beautiful eyes, her desire to fight waned dangerously. Reality seemed to recede with the warm touch of his hands as they caressed her back. As if sensing her change in mood, Keane drew her closer.

"Spanish, Scottish, red hair—any of the three alone could make claim to a bad temper. All three together . . . an interesting combination." Slowly, he lowered his lips to hers.

Her heart hammered in her chest; she was having trouble catching her breath. Turning away from his kiss seemed absurd. Instead, she closed her eyes and lifted her face to his. At the touch of his lips, she plunged into a fantasy she'd been reliving in her dreams since the day they met.

His mouth felt warm and soft as he gently brushed it against hers. His firm grasp on her waist was a haven of comfort. He felt right, like a missing piece of puzzle. And when he fitted their mouths together, his hand entangled in her hair while he stroked her neck, she leaned into his touch, savoring the taste of champagne and tobacco. She lifted her arms and wrapped them around his neck, melting into the sensation of his body against hers. This kiss was everything Henry's genteel embraces were not: passionate, exciting, creating sensations she never wanted to stop. But then, she couldn't blame Henry for his shortcomings when compared to Keane. Henry *was* just a boy, while this man—

This man was a real threat to all she held dear.

Esmeralda twisted her head free. Pushing her hands against his chest, she tried to put some distance between their pressed bodies. What could she be thinking of? Henry was just beyond the French doors, and she was carrying on with his friend on the balcony! She continued to try and pull out of Keane's embrace, but his hold remained firm. Looking up briefly, she caught his amused expression. He looked as though he were indulging a child. She responded in kind.

"You spoke of my potential for ill humor, Lord Eldridge. Well, if you don't let go of me, I'm going to kick you in the shins. How is that for a bad temper?"

"Please, spare my shins."

He flashed a crooked grin, as if pleased by their banter. When he lowered his face to kiss her again, she could think of only one way to stop him. The crack of her hand against his cheek startled them both.

Keane immediately released her, his pleasant smile fading as he rubbed his face where she'd slapped him. "I believe I've misjudged the situation." He stared down at her, his expression unreadable. "I must be losing my touch. I'm not usually so clumsy." His lips curled upward. "Shall we join the others?" Tucking her hand in the crook of his arm, he escorted her back inside.

When they entered the ballroom, he stopped before the French doors. "It's been . . . enchanting. But I leave in fear of greater injury to my shins than that which you've just delivered to my pride." He neatly bowed over her hand. To anyone watching, he appeared to grant a cordial kiss; only Esmeralda felt the gentle nip of his teeth on the skin above her lace glove. "That's not a bad right you have," he whispered. "I'll remember that next time."

Esmeralda stared after his retreating figure, still stunned that she'd actually slapped him. She unwittingly stroked the back of her hand where his mouth had touched her skin. It was still moist.

"I hope Keane didn't offend you?"

Startled, Esmeralda spun around to meet Henry's concerned expression, whipping her hand behind her back as she did so.

"No. No, of course not."

"He can be very tiresome when he chooses. He really is an old friend. My brother and he get along famously. Anyone Jason likes so much . . . I mean . . . I never would have left you if I thought he meant anything insulting, really."

"It's all right, Henry."

"Well, fine, then. It's just that the way he danced . . . it was a bit in poor taste."

Taking pity on Henry and his floundering apology, Esmeralda linked her arm through his and directed them toward the banqueting rooms. "It was just an innocent flirtation. You mustn't be concerned." Esmeralda's laugh sounded brittle to her own ears. "Really, I can take care of myself. What I need now is a glass of punch."

Reassured, Henry patted her hand on his arm. "I just wanted to make certain you were all right." He smiled lovingly at her as they walked toward the hall.

"I'm fine, Henry. Just fine," Esmeralda answered absently, her eyes scanning the room for a tall, caramel-haired man in a black swallowtail coat.

"The finesse of an elephant in heat, Keane, that's what I would call it."

"So blunt, Jason?" Keane pitched his cheroot into a large stone urn. He leaned against the balcony rail, his arms and legs crossed. His sharp glance challenged Jason's disapproving glare.

"That's the sort of activity that happens at the end of the evening, after a large dinner and too much drink, not the moment a woman walks into a room."

"Oh, so it's my timing that has upset you."

Jason took in Keane's rebellious stance. "What exactly are you planning?"

"Understand this, Jason, I'm not your naïve younger brother. You can't orchestrate my actions."

"Where Henry's happiness is concerned, I damn well have a say in what you do." Jason's clipped tones cut Keane's defiance short. "I asked you to get to know the woman, not seduce her on the dance floor for all to see!"

"As I remember, your instructions were: 'Romance the chit if you have to.' "

"But it wasn't you who was doing the romancing! You looked like any other moony-eyed buck out there. I didn't ask you to help me just to have you become infatuated with the girl!"

Keane sighed, relaxing his aggressive pose. "All right. What do you want me to do?"

"I want you to find out if she's a fortune huntress. Now, did your display out there reap anything other than scandal?"

Keane thought about the impression she made when she first entered the ballroom. She looked so sophisticated, so controlled—not at all the young innocent he'd first assumed her to be. When he asked her to dance, he did so with the intention of matching wits with a worldly woman, something with which he had a great deal of experience. But after he began his assault, she appeared confused, ill at ease with the game. When she slapped him, he realized for the first time that her easy blushes might not be feigned coyness, that perhaps she really was a naïve, young girl out of her element. His thoughts turned to her responses to his touch, responses she did not seem to give to Henry. Could she be playing Jason's brother for a fool? He unconsciously rubbed his jaw where she'd slapped him. Though tardy, her rebuff had been real enough.

Keane knit his brow, concentrating, then shrugged his shoulders in defeat. "I don't know, Jason. I would guess she's not in love with Henry. But she doesn't strike me as calculating or deceptive. I feel it here." He pressed a clenched fist to his breastbone.

"Wrong, Keane. What you're feeling involves a part of your anatomy located a good deal lower. You want that woman." Jason raked his fingers through his hair. "You and half the men in that room. I don't see how you can make a valid assessment of her intentions."

"I want her, yes." Keane surprised himself by admitting it. "But that need not conflict with our plans."

Jason stopped and turned toward Keane. "You're joking."

"Can you think of a better way to discover Miss MacClure's true intentions than using live bait?" Keane stretched out his arms, dramatically presenting himself. "Here stands before you a thirty-year-old bachelor, wealthy, complete with title. I ask you, could any self-respecting fortune huntress resist me?"

Jason's dark eyes showed a slight wavering of his distrust. "What about Henry? I don't want him humiliated. He'll look like a fool if you seduce the woman he's planning to marry."

"First you're afraid he might marry some trollop after his money. Now you're concerned I might woo her away? You're not making sense, man."

"Don't ask me to make sense; we're talking about Henry's happiness."

Keane steered Jason to a more private corner of the balcony. "When do you want him to find out about Miss MacClure, before or after the wedding?"

After a considerable pause, Jason executed an almost imperceptible nod. Keane smiled like a man showing aces in a high-stakes poker game.

"You realize, of course, that this is just an excuse for you to do exactly what you damn well please?"

Not one to delude himself, Keane answered, "I know."

Esmeralda nervously glanced about the moonlit garden. Her eyes shifted from Henry's entreating expression to the scrolled woodwork of the rose arbor, then back to Henry as he droned on about her virtues. Her palms felt moist in his hands, her back rigid against the cool marble bench. The sweet perfume of damask rose was suffocating.

"I want you to know how much I care for you, Esmeralda."

"Henry, I think we should be getting back inside."

"In a minute, darling. There's something important I must ask you first."

My Lord! This is it. He's going to propose! This was the moment she had worked for. Here, at last, was her ticket to England.

"Esmeralda, I know we've only known each other for a short time. . . ."

Panic seized her. Her carefully made plans suddenly appeared makeshift and ridiculously transparent. Would Jason Carter truly pay her off? Was she ready to face Henry's business-astute brother? And what if she were wrong, and Henry deeply cared for her?

The image of mocking eyes and a crooked smile hovered before her: an enticing package wrapped in form-fitting trousers and a swallowtail coat that within a span of minutes had shown her just how clumsy and flustered she could be—and how ill equipped she was to go through with this farce.

"I must go now." Esmeralda jumped up off the bench, nearly unseating Henry. "Absolutely this very second, I must leave."

Henry stood, confused. "But it's only midnight."

"Midnight! My goodness, it's later than I thought. Now I must certainly leave." Esmeralda gathered her skirts and set out for the house. Henry strove to keep up with her.

"But I thought tonight we could discuss our plans for the future," Henry persisted.

"Why, of course. My calendar is completely free for the next week. Just send me a note in plenty of time to prepare. I'll leave all the details to you, dear Henry. You're so good at planning spectacular outings."

"I was thinking more in terms of the *distant* future."

"Nonsense. You know I'd simply die if I had to wait too long to see you." She came to an abrupt halt; Henry, who had dogged her steps, nearly collided with her. "How about next Friday?"

"Well, certainly. We can go to the new Hiram Powers exhibit."

"Wonderful! I knew you'd come up with something splendid. Friday it is, then. Now, Henry, I want you to go back in and enjoy your party. No sense in escorting me back and missing all the fun."

Still smiling, Esmeralda backed away toward the garden doors. She stumbled on the long train of her dress but managed to keep from falling. When Henry reached to help her, she held up her hands, as if warding him off.

"No, Henry . . . I . . . so sorry."

Esmeralda hitched up her skirt and fled.

Chapter Five

Darkness engulfed her as she struggled through the thickened air for breath. Flashes of light revealed monstrous reptiles intent on devouring her. She tried to run, but her legs felt leaden, nailed to the ground. A torchlike flame shot at her from the ebony eyes of an imp, and the creature grew into a colossal figure with emerald eyes. Eyes so like her own.

She was on the ground. Allen stared down at her, glassy-eyed. He slammed his handkerchief over her nose. She struggled but could not dislodge his hands.

I can't breathe. I can't breathe! I can't . . .

Esmeralda bolted upright in bed, gulping huge breaths of air. Cold sweat soaked her face and nightgown. *It's just a dream,* she reminded herself. *Just a dream.*

Outside the curtainless window, lightning split the night sky, filling the room with its brilliance. A crack of thunder immediately followed.

"Did the storm wake ye, Esme?"

Still breathing heavily, Esmeralda glanced at the woman beside her on the straw pallet. A second bolt of lightning illuminated her companion's concerned blue eyes. So she'd waked Molly again.

"No."

"Yer nightmare again?"

Snuggling under the coarse cotton sheet and itchy wool blanket, Esmeralda nodded. She stared at the window. The low glow from the embers still burning in the hearth reflected off the rain-splattered pane. She could hear raindrops as they drummed against the window and roof.

"Why can't I remember when I wake up? Why do I always forget what I dreamed about? If only I could remember."

Molly sat up, her cropped, black curls brushing against her shoulders. "Trust me, *mavourneen,* the mind knows what it's doin' when ye blanks out things."

"But the dream . . . it always frightens me so. Maybe if I remembered . . ." She shook her head, trying to break free of the spell. Drawing her legs up, Esmeralda wrapped her arms around them and rested her cheek on her bent knees. She shivered. "I just wish I'd stop having this nightmare."

"Were ye thinkin' of home today? That usually brings on the dream."

Esmeralda nodded. "Looking at the fields on my way into town this morning reminded me of the purple heather that covers the hills near Amberose during spring and fall."

Esmeralda's heart tightened at the thought of her childhood home. She recalled the sharp sting of the wind on winter nights and the old granite mansion, so cold and cavernous, and yet filled with warming familiarity. Amberose. How she longed to see her home again!

Another crack of thunder shook the room, Esmeralda watched Molly sweep back the covers and pad over to the corner of the room where Peter slept soundly in his large pine cradle. While Molly fussed with his blankets, Esmeralda thought about the child's future. Unless matters changed dramatically, prospects looked dim indeed.

Oh my stars! Henry! Esmeralda bit her nail as a blade of anxiety knifed through her.

"What ye thinkin' about?"

Esmeralda started guiltily. She searched her mind for something to say. "Nothing, really. I was just wondering how life could be so unfair."

"Musha!" Molly whispered, scampering back to the pallet and tucking the bedclothes under her arms. "That's what's wrong with ye, Esme, me girl, all that moralistic nonsense. How's that to be gettin' us Amberose? Now *my* plan—"

"Is probably going to get us into a lot of trouble!"

"Shhh!" Molly warned, looking meaningfully at the cradle.

"Sorry." Esmeralda lowered her voice. "Try and get some sleep. Good night, Molly."

Molly reached back and squeezed Esmeralda's hand reassuringly. "Good night, me girl."

Esmeralda stretched out her legs and leaned back against her pillow, squeezing her eyes shut. She hadn't had the nerve to tell Molly what she'd done. Best to wait until morning for that. Trying to banish her anxiety about her actions that night, she continued to gnaw worriedly on her nails. *I should have let Henry propose. I won't make that mistake again!* she vowed.

But what about the viscount? a small voice inside her asked gleefully.

"I'll have nothing to do with that womanizer," she challenged the darkness.

As soon as the words were out, she covered her mouth with both hands. Glancing over at Molly, whose back was to her, she watched her friend's shoulder rise and fall in slumber. "Wonderful, now I'm talking to myself," she whispered.

Womanizer, maybe, but certainly handsome, continued that small voice. No man had ever made her feel that way —like warm taffy melting. And the way he held her when he kissed her, as if he wanted to make her a part of him.

Esmeralda shook her head clear of the seductive image. What had all those wonderful emotions ever gotten Molly? Abandonment, that was what, and a child to raise alone. Men were all the same. Just when they had your love and trust . . .

Allen. He was all she'd had after her parents died. She'd loved him with all the trust of a young child. And he'd betrayed that trust.

Pressing her lips tightly against the flow of emotion, Esmeralda held back her tears. She wouldn't cry about him. Not this time.

Nor would she ever be fool enough to love again.

The next morning Esmeralda woke to the sounds of Molly's soft voice crooning an Irish lullaby. She opened her eyes slowly, then quickly shut them against the bright morning sun streaming through the room's window. Pulling the small pillow over her head, she proceeded to drift back into a deep sleep.

It seemed like seconds later when she was awakened by an annoying gurgling sound next to her ear. She turned her head toward the disturbing noise and met Peter's enthusiastic, slobbering smile.

"I thought that'd do the trick," a satisfied Molly stated as she gathered up her son. "About time ye got out of bed, I'm thinkin'."

"What time is it?" Esmeralda groaned.

"Time for ye to be gettin' up! If ye hurry, I'll even save ye a hasty pudding biscuit."

Esmeralda reluctantly tore herself away from the warm haven of the bed. After making use of the heated water Molly had set out and a bar of Messrs. Procter and Gamble's soap, she dressed in a blue checkered dress of soft muslin and pulled her long curls into a tight bun at the back of her head. The smell of freshly baked biscuits drew her to the hearth where the Dutch oven stood with embers glowing under its trivet stand and covering its thick iron lid.

"Sit," Molly commanded, motioning toward the table. "I'll get ye some tea."

Esmeralda reached for a biscuit, one of their few weekend luxuries, and split it open with her hands. Fragrant steam rose from the two halves. She inhaled the tempting aroma. Molly's hasty pudding biscuits were always light and fluffy. Whenever Esmeralda attempted the biscuits, made from cornmeal and flour flavored with molasses, they always tasted mushy in the center. Somehow she had never conquered the cast-iron baking pot that stood in the fireplace on tripod legs. Molly was, however, a master.

Esmeralda watched Molly scurry about their kitchen. Using the same poker with which she had stoked the fire, Molly maneuvered two eggs out of the ashes where she'd set them to roast for Peter's breakfast. Eggs, butter, and milk were part of the payment they received from the neighboring bachelors, for whom Molly did mending. After retrieving the eggs, Molly lowered the water kettle to the stone hearth and added steaming water to the teapot.

"What happened to ye last night?" inquired Molly, pouring tea into a chipped china cup.

Esmeralda's hand froze midway to her mouth. She returned the inviting morsel to her plate, thoughts of last night destroying her appetite. She stared blankly at the plank floor.

Molly pulled up a ladder-back chair and took up one of Esmeralda's hands. Each nail had been chewed to the quick.

"This must be serious. Do ye want to talk, *mavourneen?*"

Esmeralda withdrew her hand and placed it on her lap, the urge to jam her fingers into her mouth almost overpowering. She remained silent, staring down at her steaming tea.

Molly sighed. *"Ochone.* The telling isn't goin' to get easier, Esme, me girl."

Esmeralda shrugged helplessly. "Molly, I don't know where to begin. Last night was a disaster."

"He didn't propose?"

Esmeralda laughed dryly. "Oh, he tried, believe me."

Molly sat back into the chair and crossed her arms. "Why do I get the feelin' I'm not goin' to be likin' this story?"

"I couldn't do it, Molly. I couldn't go through with it."

"Esme, we've been through this already. 'Tis not like—"

"I know, Molly. It's not like I'm the first woman to spurn Henry for money. I know he's young and will quickly mend from the hurt. I *know* how badly we need the money," Esmeralda continued more forcefully, ticking each item off on her fingers. Plaintively, her gaze turned to Molly. "Somehow, all that didn't matter last night. When Henry tried to propose . . . I ran away."

At the sight of her friend's reddened eyes, clearly irritated by more than the cooking fire filling the room with smoke, Molly gave up arguing. If Esme was this upset about their scheme, it was not worth pursuing. She patted Esmeralda's shoulder, trying to comfort her.

"Well, ye tried, Esme." She rose and returned to the fire for the teakettle, smiling at Esmeralda reassuringly. "Don't ye be worrin', now. We'll think of some other way to get the money."

Molly poured water into a large basin and carried it to their ancient sideboard. Wiping her hands on her grease-stained apron, she turned to check on Peter, who lay on a faded hook rug examining his small, pudgy hands.

Esmeralda watched Molly, knowing she should help but feeling rooted to her chair. After a brief silence, she admitted, "There's something I forgot to mention."

"Oh?" Molly began to clean and cut the few early vegetables their small garden yielded, in preparation for a stew that would simmer throughout the day until dinner.

"I'm not sure if Henry is the reason I couldn't go through with our plans."

Molly stopped chopping.

"There was this man last night."

Placing the knife on the sideboard, Molly closed her gaping mouth and slowly turned to examine her friend.

"Of course, he's terribly handsome." Esmeralda trickled spoonful after spoonful of molasses into her tea.

Knowing Esmeralda seldom sweetened her tea, and certainly never so generously, Molly left the vegetables and returned to sit at the table, her attention focused on her friend.

"He's also arrogant, smug. A complete rogue. A scoundrel," she said, gathering steam. "Everything I hate in a man. Last night, he was all hands and no manners." Esmeralda lifted her teacup to her lips. "He made a spectacle of us on the dance floor." After taking a small sip of tea, she returned the cup to its saucer and stared at the contents as if they were dregs from the Ohio River.

Molly pulled the cup toward her and poured Esmeralda a fresh one. "Ye think he's the reason ye stopped Henry from proposing?"

"Of course not!" Esmeralda argued. Then, eyes wide with confusion, she added, "I don't know, Molly."

Esmeralda felt miserable. She'd spent sleepless hours justifying last night's disaster. Just when she'd managed to convince herself that Keane Marshall had nothing to do with her rejecting Henry, she'd picture the viscount's laughing eyes and fawn-colored curls, feel his soft mouth devouring her lips. Thoughts of Keane buzzed over her with irritating regularity. And no matter how often she swatted it away, a short time later, his memory returned.

"How'd ye meet him?" Elbows planted on the table,

Molly rested her chin in her hand, eyes alight with interest.

"He's a friend of Henry's brother."

"Is he rich?"

"Oh, yes." Esmeralda remembered the gold coin he'd used to pay for the hats. "And a viscount to boot."

"Well, then, what's all the hullabaloo? Drop Henry and marry the viscount. Then we all live happily ever after."

"Are you paying any attention to what I'm saying, Molly?" Esmeralda leaned over her teacup and glared into her companion's guileless blue eyes. "Have the words 'scoundrel' and 'rogue' no meaning for you?"

"Look, *mavourneen,* the word 'rich' has plenty of meaning."

Esmeralda threw her arms up in despair. "Fine, then you marry him! I'm going to the shop." Esmeralda stood and marched to the pegboard to gather her cloak.

"Glad to hear it." Molly smiled. "About time, too." Taking up Esmeralda's rejected cup, she sipped the cooled liquid and grimaced. "Too bloody sweet."

"Besides, after what happened last night, I came up with an idea on how to speed the plan forward." Esmeralda swept through the room scooping pieces of cloth and ribbons into her travel sack. "I don't want this to take any longer than is absolutely necessary."

"Let's hear it." Molly shot her friend a doubtful look. "Though lately I'm doubtin' ye can come up with a decent thought about money."

"I've decided to confront his brother directly."

Molly raised her eyebrows.

"Why should I wait around for Henry's brother to approach me?" Esmeralda questioned. "If I go to him and tell him that I intend to marry Henry, he'll pay me off that much quicker."

"Maybe. Then again, he might throw ye out."

Esmeralda snapped shut her travel bag. "I don't think so. Remember, this brother is *very* familiar with the procedure of paying off women." She wrapped her cloak around her and smiled smugly.

"Ye may be right." Molly improvised a change in plans. "And ye should do it soon, before Henry starts thinkin' about yer actions last night and questions yer feelings."

Esmeralda's smile wavered. "I thought I should wait until Henry is out of town."

"Oh, no. That may be too late. No, it's best that ye be meetin' the brother soon, today even."

"I suppose you're right."

"Of course, I'm right. Aren't I always?" Molly picked up the two, mismatched tea cups and carried them toward the sideboard.

"All right then. I'll go to Carter Shipping and confront—"

At the sound of crashing dishes, Esmeralda whipped around to face the sideboard. A few feet short of her goal, Molly stood, her face ashen, pieces of broken porcelain at her feet.

"Molly, are you all right?" Esmeralda rushed to her friend's side.

Molly bent down and picked up the broken pieces. "Why Carter Shipping?"

"That's where Henry's brother works. Jason Carter is the president of Carter Shipping. It's the family business."

Molly's hand tightened around a fragment of china until a trickle of blood seeped through the gaps between her fingers.

"Molly!" Esmeralda wrenched open Molly's hand to remove the broken pottery. She snatched a handkerchief out of her carpetbag and wrapped Molly's hand with it.

"J-Jason Carter is Henry's brother?"

Esmeralda stared at Molly's suddenly pallid features. "What's the matter?" she whispered.

"Nothing!" Molly jerked her hand away. "Why did ye not tell me Henry was a Carter!"

"I tried! But you said not to bother you with details.

You said you didn't need to know anything about him other than he had the money."

"But a *Carter.*" Molly collected the broken cups. "They're such an important family. Imagine, us takin' on the bloody Carters." Then, looking at Esmeralda accusingly, she snapped, "Bless us and save us. When I told ye to find someone rich, I didn't mean the most important family in Cincinnati!"

Esmeralda followed Molly to the sideboard. "Molly, something *is* wrong."

"There's nothin' wrong. I just dropped the cups and I'm bloody mad, they're bein' our best an' all." Molly fumbled with the handkerchief around her hand, before Esmeralda stopped her botched attempts and tied it for her.

"They were our only cups."

"Musha, must ye be always correctin' me!"

"Molly?"

Peter's distressed wail claimed Molly's attention. Turning away, she picked up her son and rocked him in her arms. Then looking back, she continued, "Esme, why don't ye pick up some cups today at the Wade Street market-house? We're not exactly destitute, you know." Her voice was now cool and controlled.

"Of course," Esmeralda answered mechanically, completely confused by this strange behavior.

"And maybe ye should hold off meeting Henry's brother," Molly added as an apparent afterthought.

"But didn't you just say I should see the brother today?"

"Arrah, ye know how impulsive I am, Esme. Always wantin' it to be done yesterday. But this operation deserves a more delicate approach."

Esmeralda's confusion dissolved into suspicion. She'd lived with Molly for nine years, ever since she left England. She knew when Molly was lying or hiding something. And judging from her frightened reaction to his name, Jason Carter was definitely involved.

"Oh, I see." Esmeralda crossed her arms and waited. Give her enough rope, and Molly would trip herself up. "What would you suggest I do, then?"

Molly continued to sway back and forth with Peter in her arms. "I'm thinkin' that the handsome viscount—"

"Molly . . ." Esmeralda warned.

"All right, just a thought." Seeing her son rubbing his eyes, Molly took him to his cradle. Once he was nestled inside, she returned to continue preparing the vegetables for their evening stew.

"I've been thinkin', Esme, and ye were right all along. It's despicable, our takin' advantage of that poor boy."

"Henry?"

"That's right. The poor mite don't deserve to be hurtin' just cause we need money and all."

Esmeralda couldn't believe her ears. An attack of conscience? Molly? The woman who at fifteen, when they first arrived in America after stowing away aboard a merchant ship, had used her skills as a pickpocket and called it enforced charity? Something about how it was easier for a camel to get through the eye of a needle than for a rich man to get into heaven. Only Molly could make stealing sound like a Christian obligation.

"You think we should forget the whole thing?"

"Aye." Molly sighed with relief. "It's just not proper. I don't know how I ever let ye talk me into it."

"It was your idea, Molly."

"What?" Molly looked up, momentarily flustered. *"Musha,* Esme, of course, it was me plan. But you shouldna have let me talk ye into it!"

"So I shouldn't go see Henry's brother?"

"Henry would be *really* hurt if he ever discovered ye only wanted his money." Molly chopped vigorously, reducing the vegetables to an inedible mush. "Leave the man some dignity. Just let him know that ye find him attractive, but no sale. Marriage just isn't in the cards."

Esmeralda thoughtfully watched her friend destroy their dinner. Why didn't Molly want her to go to Carter Shipping? Did she truly think the Carters were too much for them? Or was there something particularly threatening about Henry's brother? Molly was so protective, she probably wouldn't tell Esmeralda if there was. Well, there was one way to find out for certain.

Esmeralda gathered her bag and headed to the door. "I'll see you later tonight, Molly."

"Don't ye forget to bring me Mrs. Dilger's gown. We promised it would be done this time next week."

"I'll remember."

"And, Esme"—Molly gave what Esmeralda knew was her most sympathetic smile—"try to be gentle with the poor cull."

Esmeralda paused slightly before answering. "Don't worry, Molly. I'll take care of it."

After the door shut behind her friend, Molly placed the knife on the sideboard and wiped her hands on her apron. She walked to the cradle and watched Peter's sleep-sealed eyes and flushed cheeks. Gently, so as not to wake him, she reached down to touch his jet curls. With a sigh she whispered, "Bless us and save us. Jason! Of all the luck."

Chapter Six

Polished double doors barred the entrance of the four-story brick building before Esmeralda. A shiny brass plate embedded in the brick announced, CARTER SHIPPING, CINCINNATI HEADQUARTERS.

She inhaled a deep breath and stepped onto the columned portico. The brass knob felt cool as her hand's determined twist and push propelled the door open, and she entered the building's darkened interior.

Once her eyes adjusted to the change in light, she walked toward an efficient-looking young man behind a large oak desk at the end of the entrance hall. A thick wool runner of rich burgundy cushioned her steps down the corridor so that the walls, decorated with brightly hued Greek mosaics, had no sound to echo.

"May I help you?" The young man's thin hand pushed his small round glasses back onto the bridge of his hawkish nose. His lips met in an almost invisible line under an unfashionably bushy mustache. Esmeralda took a mo-

ment to compare the abundance of hair above his mouth
to his thinning hair line.

"Miss?"

"My name is Esmeralda MacClure." She attempted a
confident tone. "I'm here to see Mr. Jason Carter."

Glancing down at the large, red-leather volume opened
before him, the man furrowed his brow. He looked up at
her, his expression doubtful. "Do you have an appointment?" Drawing a long, thin finger down page after page,
he leafed through the appointment book before executing
a smug smile. "I don't see your name anywhere. Mr.
Carter is a very busy man. Now if you return a week from
next . . . ah . . . Wednesday at two o'clock, you may
see—"

"But that's almost two weeks away! I need to speak to
him much sooner than that."

The secretary looked astounded by her interruption,
causing Esmeralda to reconsider her tactics. She smiled
pleasantly, but did not manage to make a chink in his
stubborn expression. Feeling as if she had been examined,
judged, and found lacking by this keeper of the gate, she
nonetheless tried to wheedle a concession.

"I'm sure if you look again, you'll find one short moment Mr. Carter can spare to speak with me."

"I'm sorry, miss. As I said, Mr. Carter is a very busy
man. One can't expect to just appear at his door and see
him."

"Perhaps I may be of some assistance to the lady?"

That voice! Crisp as an English morning and just as
seductive as memories of home. Slowly, Esmeralda turned
to meet Keane Marshall's imposing figure. From the
white linen shirt with its rolled collar to the requisite Wel-
lington boots, he made an impressive picture. A tight-
fitting coat molded his broad shoulders and his trousers
displayed each turn of his muscular thighs. A matching
fawn-colored hat dangled from his hand. Esmeralda

found herself responding to him with suffocating intensity.

"Viscount Eldridge," the voice behind her replied with previously withheld warmth. "Mr. Carter is expecting you."

"Thank you, Mitchell. But, please, give Jason my apologies. Tell him I'll be entertaining Miss MacClure. He'll understand."

Esmeralda watched, fascinated, as Keane held out his hand.

"Shall we?" His wide mouth turned slightly upward on one side and the corner of his eyes crinkled pleasantly.

Esmeralda pressed against the receptionist's desk. Remembering their last encounter, she ignored his outstretched hand. "Lord Eldridge," she began rather sharply, overcompensating for the attraction she felt.

"Keane, please."

"Lord Eldridge, I came to see Jason Carter."

"So I heard. He seems to be detained. I thought I might do as well."

"I'm afraid not. My business with Mr. Carter is personal." Her voice sounded steady to her own ears despite the hammer pounding at her temples. It made her feel better, more in control. She stepped forward confidently but managed to knock a pile of loose papers off the desk behind her with her carpetbag. The white sheets floated in circles to the floor like dried leaves. Esmeralda dived to pick them up.

"Oh, I'm so—"

"Sorry?"

"I'm not normally this—"

"Clumsy?"

Keane's dry tone made her stop her frantic gathering. She looked up from the floor where she was kneeling and found Mitchell hovering behind the desk, a stricken expression plastered on his disapproving features, while Keane stood above her, his lips pressed together tightly, it appeared, to keep from laughing. She was not so disinclined, however, and her laughter echoed down the empty corridor.

Keane's smile was wide with approval. He extended a hand, which she gladly took to help herself up from the floor. The papers she left for the obnoxious Mitchell to retrieve.

"I suppose I needn't apologize," she sighed, this time smiling with her eyes as well as her lips.

"Never." Though he answered with a sober expression, Esmeralda detected an amused glint in his eyes.

"You know, it would greatly help my self-esteem if you should chance to trip once in a while. Do you think you might manage?"

"For you, anything."

"I shall look forward to it." Turning her attention back to the secretary, she continued without missing a beat. "I'm certain if you tell Mr. Carter that I'm here, he will see me."

"As I said before—"

"She's right, Mitchell," Keane broke in before the secretary could put her off again. "Certainly Jason can make time for Miss MacClure. Perhaps dinner?" Keane executed a barely perceptible nod toward the secretary over Esmeralda's head.

Knowing from past experience never to gainsay the viscount, Mitchell answered without gazing at the appointment book. "I'll schedule it now. The Gibson House at seven?" He looked to Keane for approval, completely ignoring the lady at his side.

"No, the Burnet." Turning his attention back to Esmeralda, Keane smiled. "You see. Anything is possible if you know the right people, even a meeting with the impervious Jason Carter."

Esmeralda felt relieved for his help. Now that she had her meeting with Jason Carter, she could find out what Molly feared and maybe even resolve the situation with

Henry. Perhaps she'd misjudged Keane. Unlike last night, today he was pleasant, not pushy, and very thoughtful. And the Burnet House was a fine establishment, the newest and most expensive in Cincinnati. Much nicer than the Gibson, which the rude Mr. Mitchell had suggested.

"Thank you, Lord Eldridge. That was very helpful."

"Fine. To where shall Jason send the carriage?"

"That won't be necessary. My shop is close by. I'll meet Mr. Carter in the lobby of the Burnet after I close."

"I'm sure Jason would be happy to escort you there."

"Please, there really is no need. If you'll excuse me?"

"Of course."

As she skirted around him, her arm lightly brushed against his. Even that small contact ignited a response within her, belying all the calm rhetoric she'd just used to determine that matters were now clear between them. She dismissed her reaction impatiently, angry at her instant attraction to this rogue. Better to ignore this giddy lightness in her heart. *Forget about last night and his wonderful kiss and focus on the evening ahead.*

Stepping up to the double doors, she called over her shoulder to Mitchell, "Seven o'clock?" At his confirming nod, she disappeared across the threshold.

After Esmeralda's departure, Mitchell turned to Keane, clearly confused. "My lord, Mr. Carter always schedules his business dinners at the Gibson. He has a table reserved especially for that purpose."

Keane stared distractedly at the doors through which the delectable Miss MacClure had exited. A secret smile of pleasure pulled at the right corner of his mouth.

"You're absolutely correct."

Outside, Esmeralda skipped down the steps of the Carter building, kicking up her skirts so they swirled about her ankles before she quickly glanced around to ascertain if anyone had witnessed her loss of decorum.

The street was devoid of traffic, except for a few industrious hogs searching the hard-packed earth for garbage.

Walking down the brightly tiled footpath, she merged into the busier traffic on Sycamore Street toward the National Theater. On her left, she could hear the bells in St. Peter's giant stone steeple ring out the hour. On her right, the Cincinnati Observatory lay nestled on its hill at Mount Adams, a suburb named after the president who laid the cornerstone for the United States' first small observatory.

Excitement bubbled inside her as she walked through the lower street market toward Pearl Street, ignoring the shopkeepers peddling their goods in high, booming voices and stepping around the wagonloads of vegetables crowding the street. The Burnet House! So many times she had walked past that hotel dreaming of the day she could go inside. She'd always admired the superb stone building. It towered an incredible five stories high, with two wings that stretched forward like the paws of the Sphinx and flanked its domed center unit. The front portico had Ionic pillars reached by sandstone steps and the entire facade was covered by a beehive of windows. Why, the building was so large, it encompassed a good part of Vine and Third! She always went out of her way to pass the fashionable establishment while walking to work from the omnibus station. And tonight she would be dining at one of its fine tables.

She knew Molly wouldn't worry if she came home late. She often stayed at the shop after hours to organize for the next workday or to do some last-minute touch-ups. Molly seldom came into town, preferring to stay at the cottage where she could work and watch Peter undisturbed, leaving Esmeralda to tend the customers at the store. Whenever they came close to missing a deadline, Esmeralda would stay late in town, completing the last-minute flounces and bows, or even complicated beadwork, by candlelight. Though they faced no such deadline today, she could always tell Molly she'd been working on Mrs. Dilger's gown. No need to mention she'd met with Jason Carter.

As Esmeralda turned onto Pearl Street and headed toward the shop's entrance, she thought of the lovely gown Molly had requested she bring home. Mrs. Dilger was normally conservative in her taste in clothes, but this time Molly had convinced the society dame to order a gown quite different from the normal fare. Unlike the current fashion of multiple-layered skirts, it was simple and cut close to the figure. Only its many sparkling beads defied its elementary design. When Mrs. Dilger had tried the gown on at her initial fitting, she'd been impressed by the arrangement, but rejected the dress, nonetheless, explaining that she was no fashion setter. Molly had promised to change the skirt to a full one and replace the off-the-shoulder design with more demure bishop sleeves.

It was a beautiful gown, one of Molly's best, and Esmeralda couldn't help thinking it was a shame to destroy its symmetry with a wide skirt and flounces. And the lovely drop sleeves were perfection, enhancing the complicated beadwork of the bodice.

Retrieving her key from her carpetbag, Esmeralda opened the shop door and entered. She removed her cloak and, as she always did, turned the sign on the door to indicate that the shop was open for business. Not that the hordes of customers Molly had promised had ever materialized.

Sighing, Esmeralda glanced about the dress shop for the gown. She found it folded on the worktable, ready to be disassembled. Picking up her small tailor scissors, she pulled out a chair and prepared to snip Molly's minute stitches.

"What a shame, my pretty," she explained sadly to the shimmering satin covered with white seed pearls. "Now you'll be just like the rest of them."

Lovingly, she stroked the thin beaded sleeves, then paused. She bit her lip. Did she dare?

She thought of the sophisticated ladies who would dine at the Burnet and their elegant gowns. A gradual smile spread across her face. Slowly, purposefully, she set aside the scissors and dress and stepped toward the shop door. Not letting herself dwell on the consequences, she locked the entrance and turned the sign over to proclaim the shop was CLOSED.

Jason stared at the columns of figures on the report before him, but the black scratches blurred insignificantly before his tired eyes, defying his attempts to concentrate. His mind was elsewhere—in Charleston, almost two years ago, with a woman whose sapphire eyes and loving ways still haunted him. *What could I have done to make you stay, Molly?*

It was a question he'd asked himself repeatedly.

What could he have done, indeed. Jason dropped his quill, oblivious to the splats of ink its moistened tip trailed across the report. As if his actions had ever had any power over that Irish whirlwind. He managed a smile when he thought of his nickname for her. She'd been such a bundle of energy, always thinking up new ways to please him, to make him laugh. The two weeks they'd spent together at the cabin had been heaven.

His whirlwind had been filled with surprises, not the least of which had been her virginity. He incorrectly assumed from her facile acceptance of their relationship that she was familiar with the physical aspects of romance, and her aggressive responses to his embrace only served to confirm it. Yet the first time they made love, he found the evidence of her innocence on the blood-flecked sheets beneath them. It had been quite a shock to find he'd deflowered a virgin, something he had always avoided. Afterward he'd determined not to let her out of his life.

Then she'd left. Without a word of explanation.

Slowly, hesitantly, Jason opened the top drawer of his desk and removed a long satin-covered case. He opened the clasp and stared down at the string of brilliant sapphires on a bed of white velvet. A deep, rich, cobalt blue, they were the exact color of Molly Egan's eyes.

He'd given her the necklace their last night together. He recalled her curious, knowing smile when she opened his present and carefully lifted the sapphires from their velvet setting. Her eyes had been glassy with tears, and he remembered how moved he felt by her show of emotion. Molly never cried. "Ye want me to be yer mistress, do ye not, Jason?" she asked. And he laughingly replied that she'd always be the mistress of his heart. She accepted the necklace thoughtfully and told him—for the first and last time—that she loved him deeply. Their lovemaking that night had been especially tender and satisfying.

He should have declared himself then. Maybe if he'd asked her to marry? But he hesitated because, for all her beauty and lively personality, she was an Irish immigrant working as a seamstress, and he wasn't sure their different backgrounds could be reconciled in marriage. So he waited, believing they had all the time in the world to test the strength of their love. He came to regret that decision.

Come morning, he turned in his sleep and reached for her small, satin-skinned body to warm him. His fingers instead found the cold, empty sheets of the bed. Molly was gone. Only the cool necklace of sapphires lay on the pillow next to him.

He wasted valuable time searching the grounds about the cabin. It never occurred to him she would leave . . . taking the only means of transportation with her. But he'd misjudged his Irish whirlwind. A costly mistake—he missed her more and more each day.

Jason snapped shut the jewel case. It wasn't like him to dwell on his errors in judgment, but he couldn't seem to help himself where Molly was concerned. Lately he'd take out the necklace and, like a penitent, purposefully dredge up this quagmire of emotions. Damn her! Why had she left? He could have given her anything. He would have given her everything.

When his office door opened and Keane entered unannounced, Jason slipped the case back into his desk guiltily. His actions were too late. Keane's smile faltered and he stood frozen by the door.

"I'm sorry, Jason. I thought you were expecting me."

"Blast you, come in."

"I can come back later."

"Get in here."

Keane shut the door behind him but remained at the threshold. "I told you to sell the necklace." His voice was quiet but firm. "I don't know why you insist on keeping it."

Jason smiled bitterly. "Because it pleases me to remember."

"Jason, not all women—"

"Shut up and sit down. It makes me nervous when you start giving romantic advice." And when Keane still hesitated, he added, "For God's sake, man, sit down. We have a lot of ground to cover this morning."

With a sigh, Keane dropped his hat and coat at the rack by the door and stepped to one of two leather chairs before Jason's large desk. Sitting down, he made a steeple with his hands and watched Jason riffle through the many papers littered across the desk top.

"I found some vineyards that look promising. Nicholas Longworth is also considering them, so we'll have to move fast if you're interested. Now, here's their asking price"—Jason handed Keane a set of papers—"but I'm sure we can do better than that."

Keane absently glanced down the paper. "Why didn't you ever try and find her?" He turned to the second page of the proposal, looking up at Jason briefly before returning his attention to the papers in his hands.

Jason caught his breath. "You're like a hungry mongrel

with a bone, Keane. You never let go until you have all your answers, do you?" Jason leaned back against his chair.

Both men stared at each other in silence.

"All right." Jason furrowed his dark brows. "Pride? I give the woman a necklace worth a small fortune and tell her I want to spend the rest of my days with her—and her response? She sneaks out of my bed in the dead of night." Jason crossed his arms and stared at the ceiling of his office, trying to control the surge of anger and pain that flooded through him. The soft ticking of an ormolu clock on the mantel dominated the silent room.

His throat felt thick when he finally answered. "Her message was clear enough. She wanted to be left alone; I've only complied with her wishes. If she should ever need me, she knows where to find me."

"You'd take her back?"

Jason's obsidian stare met Keane's challenge. "I don't know. She was like a dream—we were so happy. For so short a time, she made me forget dreams don't come true."

As soon as he'd said the naïve words, Jason's anger returned. Standing up brusquely, he sent his chair sliding back a good two feet and turned away from Keane's penetrating gaze. Jason stared out the large window behind his desk. "Blast it, man. Leave off," he warned in a rough voice.

Keane sighed and tossed the report back on the desk. He realized he'd pushed Jason too far and now regretted his prodding. Well, if he couldn't solve Jason's problems, he could at least distract him from them. "Miss MacClure came to see you this morning."

Jason spun around. "The deuce you say. I knew the chit was after his money. Is she outside?"

"Not anymore. Mitchell sent her on her way."

"That bumbling fool." Jason started toward the door.

"At my suggestion." As Jason stared at him, incredulous, Keane examined his finger nails with a bored expression. "I thought we'd decided that I was to take care of Miss MacClure."

"You're joking. That was before. No doubt the woman was here for money."

Keane looked up. "Jason, has it ever occurred to you that there is something unsound about paying off the women Henry courts?"

Jason bristled, his olive skin turned a brilliant shade of pink. "And what else am I supposed to do? Let them ruin his life?"

"No. But getting rid of unsuitable women need not involve money. That only encourages others to follow a very profitable example. Now, if Miss MacClure were found in a compromising position, by, say, the brother of her intended victim, wouldn't a threat do as well?"

Jason expression turned speculative. "Maybe."

"Mitchell just scheduled a meeting for Miss MacClure to have dinner with you. At the Burnet. Suppose you don't show up. Suppose, I have dinner with her . . . alone . . . in my suite. And suppose you arrive later, much later, and find her in the arms of another man?"

"Rather disgusting methods."

"Disgusting, yes, but effective. I doubt any other woman would target Henry for money if it's known that his brother is not so forthcoming with a payoff."

"Do you think it will work?"

"One way or another we'll have our answer. We've already discussed my substantial appeal to a woman out for money, not to mention my innate charm." Keane smiled wolfishly. "Either she succumbs to the temptation I present, or I receive a sound upbraiding for my ungentlemanly advances and we know Henry's girl is the sweet, unspoiled gem she appears to be. Now, what do you think?"

Jason picked up the discarded report and shuffled through its pages thoughtfully. "What time should I get there?"

Chapter Seven

For the third time in fifteen minutes, Keane glanced at the gold numerals of the clock above the lobby entrance. Seven thirty—she was late.

Arms crossed, he stood next to one of the many fluted columns that graced the enormous lobby of the Burnet House. He gathered from the admiring feminine glances he received that the care he'd taken in preparing for this meeting had not gone unappreciated.

The bait was set. The question was, would she take it?

Finding Miss MacClure at Carter Shipping had been fortuitous. Never one to pass up Lady Luck, he'd taken full advantage of the situation, intending to know her true feelings for Henry before the evening's end. His lips curled in a satisfied smile as he recalled her childlike delight when he suggested the Burnet House rather than the Gibson. The Burnet was the most fashionable hotel in the city, its popularity secured last winter when national and international newspapers alike raved about 800 tons of ice ordered from Dayton and Sandusky for the coming season. Its clientele were people of means and social standing, and many who hoped to better their social status attended the grandiose balls held there weekly in order to associate with the beau monde. It was also astonishingly expensive. Despite her own strained circumstances, Miss MacClure apparently preferred the very best.

Moving away from the pillar, Keane placed his hands in his pockets. Quarter to eight—the possibility that she might not come appeared more likely.

Damn, if he didn't need a smoke! He glanced about the black-and-white checkered floor and gazed at the many brass receptacles placed for tobacco chewing. He could never understand why smoking was considered improper in the presence of ladies without first obtaining their acceptance, when no permission was needed for tobacco chewing and spitting. Personally, he thought the latter habit was far more offensive, especially since many of the strategically placed spittoons went ignored.

With growing annoyance, he searched the crowded room for the absent Miss MacClure. Despite his desire to smoke, he hesitated to go to the gentlemen's parlor for a cheroot and risk missing her arrival. Just as his patience came to an end, he looked up and recognized the subject of his thoughts as she entered the lobby.

The gown floated and shimmered around her. She wore no gloves, and the combination of bare arms and shoulders added to her seductive sensuality. Her hair fell down her back in artless curls with a spray of small white roses framing her face. Apparently she had taken equal care in preparing for the coming battle. He smiled in anticipation of discovering who would seduce whom.

When Esmeralda entered the Burnet, she felt hot, harried, and harassed. She had no gloves or evening cape for Molly's magnificent gown, and she was wearing the same shoes she'd worn for work. With only one old petticoat, the gown clung indecently to her shape—not to mention that two hours of alterations had done little to make it more comfortable. The dress had been made for a tall but slighter woman, and even after she let out the generous seams Molly always kept until the final fitting, it was still snug around her breasts.

At the shop, she'd had a devil of a time fixing her hair with the few pins she used this morning to secure her chignon. In the end, she opted for a simple style. Loose down the back and pulled off her face, it was enhanced, she hoped, by a few somewhat wilted roses she'd purchased for the shop earlier that week. Although she felt like one of those stuffed sausages Cincinnati was so famous for, and had to breathe in short, shallow breaths lest the gown's low neckline lose its precarious hold on her burgeoning bosom, she was satisfied about one thing—she was here. She was finally in the Burnet House. And she was not disappointed.

She took in the enormous size and splendor of the lobby. The marble floors, forest of Corinthian columns, and four grand staircases were awesome; the Grecian paneling decorating the ceilings and the chandeliers, brilliant. Elegantly dressed ladies and gentlemen leisurely strolled in and out, exiting through the many corridors. In the *Cincinnati Commercial,* she'd read that there were 340 rooms, all with sophisticated furnishings and all connected to the front desk by J. P. Jackson's Annunciator or hotel telegraph. She could even hear the jangling bells clamoring for service. No other hotel surpassed the Burnet's magnificent ballroom, seventy-eight feet square, where one could dine and dance to the music of Joseph Tosso's orchestra. The Burnet House was the talk of Cincinnati. Being here was like stepping into a fantasy.

Reality intruded when her wandering gaze connected with Viscount Eldridge's intense stare.

He wore a black evening jacket and trousers, set off smartly by a silver brocade waistcoat and a dove white shirt and scarf. When their eyes met, Esmeralda felt her stomach plummet to her toes.

Before this moment, she hadn't been concerned about a lack of chaperon, assuming that, while marginally correct, meeting Henry's older brother for dinner at this distinguished establishment would not be too frowned upon. In any event, she hadn't had much choice; she couldn't very well ask Molly to come along. Nor could she trust anyone else to overhear what she planned to discuss with Jason. But now, seeing the viscount strolling toward her, she felt a chaperon would have been a marvelous addition.

Esmeralda didn't know if her light-headedness was due to the handsome man approaching her or to the snug fit of her dress. She'd removed the light corset she'd donned this morning—totally ineffective for tight lacing—in order to give herself more breathing room in the heavily padded and many-stayed gown. It had taken Betsa, the woman she and Molly occasionally hired to help around the shop, fifteen hot, sweaty minutes to fasten her in. Yet when Keane took her hand and kissed it, she knew better than to blame her breathlessness entirely on the gown.

"I was beginning to worry you wouldn't come." His lips curved into the crooked smile she found so appealing.

"Funny, I was under the impression *you* wouldn't."

"Jason was detained. He asked me to entertain you until he arrives. Then I shall magically disappear and leave you to your private matters." He hooked her arm on his and escorted her to one of the four stairwells. "I took the liberty of ordering dinner sent up to my suite. All the private dining rooms are engaged."

Esmeralda almost tripped. They were headed to his suite! And Jason Carter was nowhere in sight. She stopped abruptly.

"Shouldn't we wait for Mr. Carter in the lobby?"

Seeing her vivid green eyes widen with apprehension, Keane almost took pity on her and agreed to her request . . . almost. "I'm afraid he won't be joining us until dessert. He had some urgent business. But if you would rather wait for some other time to speak with him, I'm sure he'll understand. I do believe I overheard Mitchell say he would be available a week from Wednesday?" Keane kept his expression bland.

Esmeralda jammed her pinky in her mouth, biting her nail nervously. Heavens above, all this for nothing? She'd just spent the last four hours practicing her clever speeches to Jason Carter. And to be put off almost two weeks. It was too much. She wanted—no, *needed*—the answers to her questions now.

Keane grinned as he watched Esmeralda's face go through a series of mercurial changes. The poor woman hadn't a clue that she was so obvious. His smile widened —she was delightfully transparent, and yet adorably unaware of it. Clearly she hadn't been prepared for his dining plans, yet she lacked the sophistication to extricate herself from the situation. He suspected that although she hesitated to come to his suite, she warred with her reluctance because of her great desire to speak with Jason. It was that latter need that he wanted to explore.

"You're certain Mr. Carter will come?" she asked.

"Absolutely. He's looking forward to it."

"Well then, Viscount Eldridge, let's not wait for him on the stairwell."

Taking her by the arm once again, Keane covered her hand with his and said amiably, "Keane, please."

When they arrived at his suite, Keane's valet had everything ready. In the salon there was a small dining table, covered by a starched white table cloth, placed strategically before the fireplace. A charming fire, set not for warmth but for atmosphere, burned therein. The different courses were safely covered and set aside for serving. The wine, already decanted and allowed to breathe, had been poured into goblets.

"Would you care for some wine?" Keane asked.

"Please."

Keane handed a goblet to Esmeralda and toasted, "To a successful evening."

"Success." She barely managed the single-word response as she lifted her glass to Keane's.

For Esmeralda, the clink of the Baccarat crystal had an ominous ring. The scene before her was made for seduction. Lilies and roses arced out from large porcelain vases and perfumed the air. Gaslight sconces cast soft shadows on the pastel blue walls. A candle-lit table was set before the hearth, with many silver-covered dishes crowding the sideboard beside it. Only the short, elderly man with a paunch and a balding pate who stood guard beside the serving dishes granted her some peace of mind.

"Thank you, Higgins. That will be all for now. We will be serving ourselves."

Her peace of mind thus dismissed, Esmeralda took a long, fortifying drink of her wine.

"I hope you're hungry."

"Famished." It amazed Esmeralda how her mind could be screaming *run* at the same time that her audible voice calmly said the word "famished."

Keane pulled out her chair before the dining table and waited. Judging from her expression, it was time to execute some of that charm he'd boasted about to Jason. Her face mirrored the pale color of her dress, and he didn't think it was from rice powder. Her hands were steady enough, but he suspected that was due to the solid grip she had on the wineglass.

As always, Keane's assessment was quick: The woman was no experienced seductress. She presently resembled a terrified girl, not the *femme fatale* Jason feared. Whatever she wished to discuss with Henry's brother was most likely innocent and did not require the heavy-handed tactics Keane had planned to use. It was a good bet that the evening would be an uneventful affair—they'd sit and chat, waiting endlessly for Jason to make his grand entrance.

As she took the seat he offered, Keane happened to glance down at the neckline of her magnificent gown. There, two perfect white globes threatened to escape their tether—effectively destroying the little-girl image. Sitting down opposite Miss MacClure, he leaned against the cushioned back of his chair, revising his hasty opinion. The evening could prove to be trying indeed. He wasn't good at playing nursemaid when confronted by the face of an angel. His gaze dropped a fraction. And a pair of beautiful breasts.

"So, tell me. What brought you to Cincinnati?" He hoped she could at least carry on a distracting conversation until Jason arrived.

By now Esmeralda had taken several fortifying sips of the mellow red wine, as well as a couple of deep breaths. The combination was effective. "Cincinnati was recommended by a friend." Now there, a complete sentence—that was a step forward.

"And is business here successful for you?"

"Not very, I'm afraid." Esmeralda managed what she hoped was a charming smile.

"That's a shame. Maybe things will change with the coming season."

"We do seem to do better in the warmer months." Warmer, yes, the room was definitely warm. Hot even. She looked accusingly at the small fire burning in the grate as she gulped another mouthful of wine. "Isn't it rather stuffy in here?" She fanned her hand back and forth quickly over her breasts.

Dear, God—Keane watched the tempting pale flesh above her décolletage sway gently with the rhythm of her hand—*I'm not made of stone.* He might have given up his plans for seduction, but in her own innocent way, the chit across from him was doing an admirable job of seducing him.

"I'll have it taken care of." Keane lifted the small silver bell beside his plate, and the paunchy man reappeared instantly. "Higgins, the room is too warm. Please, see to it."

"Yes, your lordship."

Esmeralda watched the small, round man extinguish the fire before leaving the room. She felt better. She was still warm, but as she looked into Keane's amber eyes and compared the color of his ebony lashes to that of his sandy brown hair, it just didn't seem to matter as much.

"And you, what brings you to Cincinnati?" she asked. "Are you here to check on Carter Shipping? I understand you're a substantial investor in the company." She lifted her glass to take another drink of wine but found it empty. She stared at the crystal stupidly, as if she couldn't understand where the contents had gone.

"Allow me." Keane refilled her glass. "Actually, I'm investing in vineyards. Some very fine wines have just started to come out of Cincinnati. You're drinking one now. What do you think?"

Esmeralda stared at the ruby liquid before setting it aside. "It's lovely." And quite strong. She already felt a bit befuddled, but the evening stretched long before her and there was something to be said for Dutch courage. Facing Jason Carter, not to mention the unexpected evening with the viscount, had shaken her more than she'd anticipated. She picked up her glass and gulped down several more swallows.

"Try the boiled buffalo tongue; it's quite good. Or would you prefer the paté?" Keane held up one of the many silver dishes.

Esmeralda selected a piece of toast covered with goose-liver spread. Remembering that it was the first thing she'd eaten today, she realized she was very hungry. She stared speculatively at the man across from her as she nibbled on the bread. The candlelight reflected deeply in his eyes, warming their amber shade to a deep sienna. His soft tawny hair curled attractively around his square face, and playful shadows danced across his chiseled features with the wavering light.

"Viscount Eldridge—"

Reaching across the table, Keane placed a warning finger gently on her mouth. "Keane, I insist."

His soft touch burned against her lips. It was an intimate gesture that made her feel strange and desirable . . . special. "Keane," she amended with a smile of her own. "I've always wondered how one judges a good wine."

"Ah. It's quite an art. I was taught by a master, my father. For a red wine, like this"—he picked up his glass —"one judges several things. First the bouquet." He swirled the wine with a smooth rhythm while inhaling, then lifted his dark brows, his expression suggesting something pleasant. "Nice. Very nice." He tipped the glass until the scarlet liquid barely touched the crystal edge. "Then we look for body." He held his glass to the candlelight for her to see. "The stringy formations on the side of the glass are called legs. The longer the legs remain visible, the greater the body."

Esmeralda watched, fascinated, as the streams of carmine faded into translucent pink, then eventually disappeared. She looked back to Keane for confirmation.

"Excellent." His smile of pleasure took in both her and the wine. "But most important is the taste." Bringing the glass to his lips, he paused, locking gazes with her as if he could somehow make her taste the rich flavor through his own senses. He tipped his glass back and slowly, oh, so slowly, swirled the liquid in his mouth before swallowing. Esmeralda sat on the edge of her chair. His lips still glistened with the moist red wine when he answered, "Truly outstanding."

Esmeralda's breath quickened; she could feel her heart hammering in her chest. Grabbing for her water glass, she hit the wine goblet with the back of her hand, but managed to steady the crystal before it tumbled over onto the white linen cloth. Shaken by the close call, she ignored the water and lifted the wine goblet to her lips.

"Outstanding," she echoed Keane's assessment, then emptied the glass.

Watching Esmeralda's reaction to his narrative, Keane almost lost sight of the evening's objective. Seeing her soft pink tongue capture a drop of wine from the corner of her mouth, he felt his blood thicken. What at first had started as a simple lesson on wine tasting had turned into an extremely sensual experience. He watched, riveted, while she set down her glass and leaned forward on the table to reach for another slice of paté-laden bread. The movement caused her breasts to press together against the material of her gown.

"Mmmm. This is delicious." She ate as if the paté were ambrosia. Her face reflected such sensual pleasure, he felt himself grow excited just watching her eat the damn toast. *There's only so much of this a man can take.*

"Oysters?" He reached behind him to the sideboard and extended a dish toward her.

"No, thank you. The paté is fine."

As she took another bite of the toast, Esmeralda searched in her mind for a piece of conversation. Something casual to distract herself from Keane's compelling eyes.

"Tell me about yourself, Keane." Didn't all men love to talk about themselves?

She was leaning forward, resting her elbows on the table. As Keane stared at the creamy expanse of skin exposed by her pose, he lost the slim hold he had on his control. Jason and their plans for the evening faded, and Keane's tension-racked body settled into the calm of a man who knew his hunger would be sated. "I'd much rather talk about you." His voice was low and consciously seductive.

Esmeralda smiled wanly and shook her finger at him. "Now, now, I asked first."

"In that case." He reached across the table, took the piece of bread from her fingers, and returned it to the serving tray. He picked up her hand and pulled it toward his lips. One finger bore a small trace of paté. "I like goose-liver pâté." Taking her index finger into his mouth, he sucked the spread off. Soft, wet kisses followed, as his mouth caressed each knuckle. "I ordered this one special." Guiding her hand toward his wine glass, he dipped her index finger into the cool liquid. "And I like good red wine." With languorous swirls of his tongue, he proceeded to lick the dripping liquor from her finger.

Esmeralda felt an icy, tingling sensation begin at her stomach and creep up her spine. She could feel the wine singing in her veins. With each successive touch of his lips, her goals for the evening melted. Unable to stop herself from doing so, she obediently followed when he stood, pulling her toward him.

"But I especially like fine, satin dresses and the ladies who wear them." He stood only inches away. She could smell tobacco and a fresh lemon scent, as he continued to brush her fingertips against his soft full lips while his other hand stroked her satin-bound waist. Then, releasing her wrist, Keane enclosed her waist within his two large hands, his thumbs gently massaging her rib cage under her breasts.

For Esmeralda, nothing existed outside this cocoon of physical sensation. She leaned toward Keane and pressed her hands on his chest as his hands traveled to her breasts. Looking at her with the same expression he'd worn when tasting the wine, he grazed the side of one breast with his knuckles. Instinctively, she responded by closing her eyes and tipping her head back, giving him access to her lips. Keane's mouth immediately descended on hers.

Tender lips explored her mouth, caressing the corners and trailing kisses along her cheek to her ear. His tongue outlined her earlobe and then the recesses within, his tickling, moist breath causing a sharp contraction within her. She reached around his neck with her arms and pulled his mouth back to hers.

Keane licked her lower lip, then bit it gently, seeking entrance. She obligingly opened her mouth and his tongue's feathery touch elicited her low moan of pleasure. He tasted as mellow as the wine.

Yet despite her total concentration on Keane and the feelings he was creating, something nagged at the back of her mind. "Keane." She barely managed the word. "Keane, please."

In apparent reply to her passion-thickened voice and its plea, he pulled his mouth away and examined her beneath hooded eyes.

"Keane"—her breath came in short, soft pants— "when will Jason be here?"

Keane's only reaction was to smile. Then, his lips descended to continue their kiss.

"Forget Jason."

Chapter Eight

Who could think about schemes and plots with this beautiful woman in his arms? Her lips were so ripe, so full of
promise. One moment Keane wanted to bite them, hard,
and the next he wanted to brush them softly against his.
Her breasts felt warm and lush against his chest. Still
exploring her mouth with his tongue, he cupped one
breast in his hand and stroked the satin-encased tip with
his thumb. The nipple stiffened in response and he longed
to rub his lips against the hardened nub.

No matter how methodical his actions originally, they
were no longer calculated or controlled. Putting a halt to
his wondrous exploration of her mouth, he searched Esmeralda's eyes for a response. He found those green jewels
full of emotion, holding nothing back. Her wealth of passion fed his own, and he clasped her to him, kissing her.
When she returned his embrace in full measure, he noted
with no little surprise that what he experienced now felt
different from ordinary lust. He felt possessive, primitively

so. The irony of his feelings was almost amusing—he'd become the victim of his own planned seduction.

Keane chuckled deep in his throat as his mouth opened and his tongue traced the contours of her neck down to the heated valley he'd watched all evening. He could hear as well as feel her sharp intake of breath when his lips reached the crevasse captured by the gown's square neckline. Soft and warm, the tops of her breasts pressed against his mouth and he gently nibbled the tender skin where it met the cool satin.

Imagining the exquisite feel of her naked body against his, he reached around her back to unhook the fasteners of her gown. He found the top hook and pinched the material together in order to release it.

Nothing happened.

He tried again. The gown remained closed.

Some of the sensual fog surrounding his mind began to clear. Concentrating on what his hand was doing, he tried once more to manipulate the first hook open. Still the material didn't budge.

More than a bit frustrated, he grabbed Esmeralda's shoulders and pulled her lips from his. "What the hell do you have on? A full-length chastity belt?"

Musical laughter floated around him. Her emerald eyes teased. "Is something wrong, my Lothario?" She emitted an undignified hiccup, then collapsed against him as if seeking the strength to stem any similar lapses.

Keane felt as if someone had just dunked him in ice water. "You're drunk."

Still smiling seductively, Esmeralda bobbed her head up and down. She slipped away from his slackened hold and stood before him, swaying slightly. Face flushed and with a few tendrils of hair curling around her heart-shaped face, she appeared more exciting and desirable than ever.

The image of wanton beauty evaporated with another loud hiccup. This time, she broke into uncontrolled giggles.

"Damn it! No one gets foxed on two glasses of wine." Keane grabbed her and pulled her to him, examining her face closely.

"It was very good wine." Her tiny pink tongue began to trace his lips.

Keane jerked away, raking his fingers through his hair. She was drunk as Bacchus on two glasses of wine. "My God, don't you ever drink?"

Ignoring his question, she wrapped her arms around his neck and commanded breathily, "Kiss me, Keane, with your tongue. That feels ever so nice."

With startling clarity, Keane remembered his earlier assessment of her character: She was no experienced seductress, out to fleece Henry. But with that thought came the realization that her breasts were firmly pressed against his chest. *For God's sake, I'm not a saint.* He looked down at her parted lips. Her eyes remained closed as she waited for his touch. *Sorry, Henry, old boy, but fortune huntress or not—she's not the girl for you.*

Keane's lips met her provocative challenge. He wrapped his hands around her slender figure, reaching for the fasteners at her waist. Using both hands he managed to undo three hooks. Once these barriers were breached, it was a simple task to undo the rest.

Esmeralda felt Keane's large warm hands part the material of her dress and slide the beaded sleeves down her arms. His lips followed the path of his hands, causing her to suck in her breath with pleasure. When he'd unfastened her bodice, she lost any sense of release to the sexual tension building inside her.

As Keane watched, her gown slipped down her pale breasts to her waist like a curtain unveiling a work of art. He followed the luscious curves caressed by the thin cotton of her chemise as the gown pooled at her feet. By lamplight, her nipples appeared as mere whispers of shadow. His mouth went suddenly dry and he realized everything he'd felt beneath the satin was real—no artificial molding involved. He reached for the tapes of her petticoat and pulled. The material joined the gown on the floor. A current of desire swept away the last threads of his control as he stared at her nipped-in waist and gently flared hips.

"My God, you're not wearing a corset." He breathed the words against her lips.

"I couldn't fit into the dress with it. It was too—" She stopped abruptly when he opened his mouth across hers. As he sucked on her tongue, a sharp frisson of sexual excitement crescendoed through her with each pull of his lips.

She wanted this, needed him to touch her and never stop. Now she knew why Molly had run away with Peter's father. To feel this—like something incredible opening, blossoming deep within her. She felt drunk, drugged, languid. Yet every exposed surface of her skin sparked with sensations. Where he touched her, there was heat; when he kissed her—a bit of heaven.

Keane swept her into his arms and carried her to the bedchamber adjoining the salon. He kicked the door shut and set her on the cream-colored counterpane of the large canopied bed, then stripped off his clothes until only his trousers remained.

Esmeralda lay on the bed's coverlet, waiting, wanting.

He unlaced and removed her shoes, then reached up and playfully snapped a garter above her knee before he unrolled one stocking, and then the next. When he untied the ribbons of her plain cotton chemise, he saw that the skin of her lovely breasts was marred by angry red indentations where the stays of her gown had bitten into her. He removed her chemise and traced one pinkened line with his tongue, trying to wipe away the mark with a caress. When his wandering mouth found her nipple, he groaned and covered the swollen tip with his lips, sucking gently.

That's when he first heard it: the soft, insistent tapping at the door to his bed chamber.

"Your lordship?" Higgins's tenor also breached Keane's awareness. "It's Mr. Carter. He insists upon speaking with you."

Jason! He'd actually forgotten about him. And their plan.

Keane quickly moved off the bed and headed to the armoire for a robe. Then, thinking better of it, he searched the room for his discarded clothes and began to dress.

Esmeralda was not so quick in her reaction. Still wrapped in a sensual haze, she watched, confused, as Keane pulled on his boots. "Keane? What's wrong?"

Keane groaned at the sight of the woman on his bed. Dressed in only her drawers, her auburn tresses wrapped seductively around her luscious body, she made him ache to return to her side. He took a deep breath. "It's Jason. It appears he couldn't wait for dessert." Keane began to re-tie his cravat, then launched it in disgust to the opposite side of the room.

Esmeralda felt as if she'd been punched in the stomach. Grabbing her chemise, she quickly drew it over her head and searched desperately around the room. "My dress, where is my dress?"

Keane stopped his own frantic actions. His features set into a sympathetic expression. "In the salon."

"Oh, my lord. What have I done!"

Taking pity on her, Keane stepped to the bed and tried to wrap her in his arms. She slapped them away. Still trying to console her, he advised, "I'll get rid of him. He needn't know you're even here." As he said the comforting words, Keane realized he was speaking the truth—he would lie to Jason if necessary. He no longer believed Esmeralda was after Henry's money. And he was responsible for her current predicament. He felt a pang of guilt at his conscious seduction of a woman none too sober. Yes, he must protect her as best he could.

"But my dress is in the *salon!* Where is Mr. Carter waiting?"

Keane sighed. "The salon, I imagine."

"Heavens above!" Esmeralda dived into the pillows.

He couldn't help grinning. "Maybe he won't notice?"

Esmeralda pounded her frustration on the hapless pillows, while Keane stroked her back, trying to give her some solace. "I'm sure I can talk to Jason; ask him to be discreet—"

"You don't understand!" Esmeralda sat up. She flung the words at him, completely out of control. "You've ruined everything! Everything! Now, I'll never get the money!"

Esmeralda clamped her mouth shut and sat back, frozen in place. Keane's features turned deadly serious. "What money?"

She shook her head and began inching away, up the mountain of pillows until the headboard blocked her progress.

"What"—Keane grabbed her shoulders, roughly—"money?"

To his surprise, she turned a ghastly shade of green that mocked the lovely color of her eyes. She clapped her hand over her mouth and lurched forward. Knowing immediately the cause of her distress, Keane guided her to the washbasin across the room.

"Higgins!" he shouted over his shoulder.

Holding her lovely auburn hair off her face as her body shuddered and spasmed, Keane's lips settled in a tight line. So the little minx couldn't hold her liquor. Nor had she experience enough to know its effects.

She moaned, collapsing on the floor next to the highboy that held the wash basin. "I feel awful."

Keane sat down beside her. He pressed her head to his shoulder, stroking her hair in a steady, soothing rhythm. "When was the last time you ate?"

Esmeralda thought about the biscuit left uneaten that morning and shuddered. "Yesterday sometime."

Keane shook his head in disgust. "Don't you even know enough not to drink on an empty stomach?"

"Ohhh," she groaned again, leaning helplessly against him.

At that moment, Higgins appeared. The proper valet showed no surprise at the sight of Keane holding the scantily clad lady in his arms.

"Your assistance is needed, Higgins."

"Perhaps a wet towel, your lordship?" His features remained completely bland.

"That should do admirably for starters."

"Very good, sir." Higgins turned toward the door, then, his shiny brow knitted in concern, he added, "About Mr. Carter, sir. He is most insistent. He mentioned something about being part of the plan?"

"Tell him to cool his heels. I'll be there shortly."

Esmeralda felt absolutely wretched, both physically and mentally. She hadn't a clue how she was going to escape from this mess. She had tried to come up with some believable excuse to explain her outburst, but she couldn't think. If only the room would stop spinning.

Keane continued to stroke the soft curls draped about her bare shoulders methodically. A cold, hard knot formed in his stomach. "I need to go speak with Jason. But don't think for one minute this conversation is over. I expect some answers when I return."

"You can't keep me here!"

Keane smiled a not-so-nice smile. "You're welcome to go into the salon and retrieve your dress."

She was trapped. Esmeralda felt the bile rise again, backing up in her throat. The room continued to spin faster and faster. "Please, I don't feel well."

"So I gathered."

"No. You don't understand." She looked up at him, hating the pleading tone of her voice. "I'm sick. I . . ."

The room's gyrations prevented her from finishing. When he started to pick her up, she waved him away. But he ignored her, hauling her to her feet despite her protests.

"You'll feel better once you're lying down."

"Please, just . . . leave . . . me . . ."

As she crumpled against him, Keane scooped her up in his arms and carried her to the bed. Her arms anchored themselves around his neck. Once he'd set her on the bed, Keane pulled back the counterpane and settled her under the covers. Tucking her in, he stroked back the curls from her heated face.

"Rest. It's the best thing for you right now."

Esmeralda didn't respond. She merely shut her eyes tightly, as if fighting off pain.

Higgins appeared with a wet towel and a steaming cup in hand. "I thought a remedy might be in order, your lordship."

Keane smiled at his valet's efficiency. "Splendid, I'll leave you to your patient, Higgins. Make her as comfortable as possible. But by no means is she to leave. Understand."

"Certainly, your lordship."

Without a backward glance, Keane left the ailing Esmeralda to Higgins's efficient care. He didn't envy her. One of his valet's remedies could be punishment enough for any crime.

Keane entered the salon dressed in the same clothes he'd worn that evening for dinner—minus one elegantly tied cravat. He examined the neat room with a sense of relief. Higgins had removed all evidence of dinner and the discarded dress.

Still in his work clothes, Jason stood by the fireplace. He held a snifter in his hand and his face was drawn in a familiar brooding expression. At Keane's approach, Jason turned. "Where's Miss MacClure? I rushed here straight from the office and that valet of yours barely let my foot past the door. What the deuce is going on?"

Keane poured himself a brandy, focusing on the task as if it were a delicate process requiring his complete concentration. "There's been a change in plans."

Jason frowned. "I don't understand."

Keane took a long drink of brandy; the warming sensation it created was a satisfying distraction from his cold thoughts. He felt like a fool. Convinced of her innocence, he had badgered himself for seducing the chit. And all the while he'd been the one duped. His pride bristled. He, the accomplished gambler, taken in by a girl hardly out of the schoolroom.

"I want an explanation, Keane."

He turned his attention back to Jason. "I wish I had one," he answered softly. At Jason's confused expression, he added, "Don't worry; our plan is still intact. Miss Mac-Clure had to postpone our little meeting. But it's only a matter of time before we catch the girl out."

Jason noted the change in his friend's attitude. "You're keeping something from me."

"Do you trust me, Jason?"

Jason lifted his dark brows, surprised by the unexpected challenge. "You know I do."

Keane stared at the cold grate of the fireplace. "Then leave Esmeralda MacClure to me."

Chapter Nine

Esmeralda hopped off the milk wagon, clutching the man's gray coat protectively around her. She waved her thanks to Mr. Cooper, happy for the ride up the incline to Walnut Hills. She wondered if the delivery man believed her story about working late at the shop. Probably not, she thought glumly, as she plodded down the dirt path to the cottage, engulfed in Keane's greatcoat. Although quite likely, the story certainly didn't explain her strange attire.

Traveling down the path, Esmeralda squinted against the early morning rays streaming through the latticework of branches. She could feel the sun's warmth fall on her slumped shoulders. She walked as if she carried a great load—but her only burden was a mental one: how to recoup from last night's blunder?

Even now she couldn't say how it happened. How did she end up in Keane's bed, naked, begging for his kisses—blithely forfeiting everything she and Molly had worked for? It was as if she lost her will when he touched her.

Could a man's embrace lead to such insanity? Apparently so, or neither she nor Molly would be in this mess.

She should have been on guard after the ball. She'd known then, after she had returned his passionate embrace while Henry waited in the next room, that he had this wretched power over her. Yet at the time she thought it a fluke, a slight miscalculation that she'd not repeat. And after his kindness at Carter Shipping, she believed herself safe. How naïve she was. The man was as safe as a python.

Silently padding across the porch, she sighed. Regrets were useless now. Better to concentrate on how to recover from last night's disaster. She paused at the door, her thoughts returning to the end of the evening. After his meeting with Jason, Keane had come back, seeking to speak with her. But she feigned sleep, unable to face the viscount, whose seductive embrace had elicited her wanton behavior and extracted a partial confession. She waited for what seemed hours to avoid his cross-examination. When he finally left her bedside, she cautiously sneaked out of the hotel, ignoring the astonished glances of the late-night hotel staff. But somehow she sensed Keane's interest would not be so easily eluded.

As she unlocked the door, she prayed she'd find Molly asleep on their pallet near the hearth. Aside from the incriminating hour, she didn't look forward to explaining Keane's greatcoat—borrowed to conceal her partially unhooked dress—and the silk sash from his robe, the only thing she could find to hold her gown together at the waist. Easing the door open, she felt like a recalcitrant child trying to avoid a scolding. But when she stuck her head in the door after sliding it open without even a squeak, she saw she would not be so lucky. Like one of the Queen's ever-alert sentinels, Molly sat in the rocking chair, facing the door.

Molly started at the sound of the key turning in the lock. Her heart thundered with relief when she saw Esme's dear face peek around the door. She'd been terrified, ready to bundle Peter up and head into town to look for her friend. But when she saw Esme was in fine health, her relief passed and anger seeped in, taking over her emotions. How dare Esme stay out all night without even sending a note?

Then she noticed Esme's clothes.

"That's a very fine coat, Esme. Though it's a wee bit big fer ye. It goes nicely with Mrs. Dilger's dress. That is her dress I see peekin' out, is it not?" Molly didn't wait for an answer. "I guess, I dinna need to ask ye where ye been while I sat here all night worrying meself gray, wonderin' how, with the tyke in tow, I was to find ye."

Realizing the depth of Molly's anger, Esmeralda avoided removing Keane's coat and sat in one of the kitchen chairs, facing her irate friend. If Molly saw the disgraceful state of Mrs. Dilger's gown, she'd know for certain what Esmeralda had been up to last night.

"Molly," she said, shoulders sagging with guilt, "I can explain."

"This better be good, *mavourneen,* 'cause I'll not be believin' what me eyes are seein'."

"Please don't be angry."

"Angry?" Molly stood abruptly, sending the rocker into wild movements that almost toppled it to the floor. Arms akimbo and wide gray skirts swinging with each slow, purposeful step, she walked to Esmeralda.

Esmeralda flinched. Molly's red-rimmed eyes burned like the blue-hot center of a flame.

"Oh Esme, me darlin' girl, I'm not angry," Molly whispered, leaning over her guilt-ridden companion. "Furious as a banshee is what I am!" She quickly swung away as if trying to gain control. "I could chew ye up and spit ye out, I'm so mad! I sat here worrin' about ye. Thinkin' of all the horrible things that could happen to ye without me there for protection. Then ye show up, sneakin' in like . . . like ye just come home from a night of dancin'!" She whipped around to face Esmeralda. "What in ballyhack are ye doin' in Mrs. Dilger's dress? And yer hair? What did ye do to yer hair? It's all a mess, like ye just got out of bed."

Esmeralda felt her face heat up like a newly struck lucifer, while Molly's eyes grew saucer-big with understanding.

"Esme?"

Esmeralda dipped her head downward, trying to hide her shame.

"Were ye out dancin'? Is that why yer hair is all a mess?" Molly said in a low voice. When Esmeralda shook her head, Molly's heart plummeted. For a few agonizing minutes, she watched Esme's slumped figure. Only the tick of their iron clock on the mantel broke through the silence.

"Molly . . . ?"

"Arrah, Esme. What have ye done?"

Molly rushed to Esmeralda. Before she could react, Molly grabbed open the coat and stared at the sagging sleeves of Esmeralda's gown and the man's sash at her waist. Esmeralda's gaze met turbulent blue eyes before Molly propelled her up and around, yanking the coat down. What Molly saw made her gasp.

"Bless us an' save us!"

Molly's words reeked disapproval, adding to Esmeralda's own sense of misery. "Molly, let me explain—"

Molly grabbed Esmeralda's shoulders. "Who did this to ye, Esme? Henry? Did ye let'm do this?" She accented each question with a shake.

"Please, Molly—"

"Did ye let'm do this or did the cull force ye?"

Esmeralda swallowed hard. Her head pounded harder with each teeth-rattling shake.

"Who did this to ye?"

Something inside Esmeralda snapped. Tired and frightened by last night's happenings, she was much more in need of Molly's understanding than of her disapproval. "Don't you mean who bedded me?" she lashed out. Molly drew in a breath at the scandalous phrase, granting Esmeralda a perverse sense of satisfaction. "Funny how I didn't ask you that same question when you disappeared with Peter's father."

Molly's hand cracked against her cheek, but Esmeralda hardly felt its sting. Egged on by her own hurt and pent-up anger, she added, "I never made you feel cheap or dirty when you walked in after a two-week absence, leaving only a short note explaining you'd be gone. And months later, when you found out you were with child, you made it clear you had no intention of telling me the father's name. I was hurt, Molly, deeply hurt that you didn't confide in me. But I tried to understand. I tried not to condemn. And in the past year, I have never once held you in the contempt you're so generously heaping on me now. I never once *demanded* you tell me who Peter's father was."

"Well ye should have, Esme," Molly screamed. "Maybe if ye'd known Jason Carter is Peter's father ye'd not be in this bleedin' mess!"

Esmeralda stared, incredulous, as Molly collapsed to the floor and burst into tears. Without a word, Esmeralda knelt down and wrapped her arms around her, shocked into silence by Molly's confession.

"This is all me fault," Molly cried. *"Musha,* if I'd only told ye, but I didna want ye to go half-cocked after Jason." She gazed up at Esmeralda, her face marred by tears. *"Arrah!* All the lies, not just Jason . . . but ye were such a fine lady, Esme, with fine manners and learnin'. So much better than I deserved for a friend." Molly looked down into her lap, choking on her words. "I didna want ye to be ashamed of me and leave."

"Oh, Molly." Esmeralda heard her own unsteady voice. "Did you really think I'd ever be anything but proud to call you my friend?"

"There's things about me I've never told ye. About me past—me mother." Molly was quiet for a moment, the pain she felt written on the tight lines around her eyes and mouth. "A fine example I've been to an innocent like ye. Going off with some man I had just met. Peter and me living with you, taintin' ye—a young lady. And because of me pride, sure as I acted as if what I did wasna wrong."

Esmeralda felt her heart constrict at Molly's words. "Going off with *some* man? You loved Peter's father! You always told me nothing was more special than the love between—"

"Aye. But when I said those things, I wanted ye never to be scared of the marriage bed, like those milk-toast ninnies who call themselves 'ladies.' I never meant for ye to do it before you got married."

"But you and Peter's father . . . ?"

"That's just dandy." Her angry tone was directed at herself. "I tried to pretend I was just as good as ye—and now ye've taken after me! Ye could have had so much more!"

"More?"

"Yer a lady, Esme. I am a bastard." Molly pushed away her friend's hands. She lifted her chin slightly, defiantly. "I have the blood of Irish kings, thanks to me father, the earl. Though it matters for little; I'm a bastard nonetheless. Me mother and father weren't married." Her voice was flat, without emotion. "There. Now ye know. She was only a paid mistress in Ireland. And God rest her soul and that of me poor brother, she wasna worth the cost of savin' her or her family from starvin'. One fine day, the earl closed up his country estate, packed up the legitimate family, and left without even a by-your-leave. I buried them both, me mother and Donald, before I left. I only managed to save meself because I'd learned a trick or two from some rough sorts in town. I'm no lady, Esme. Until I met ye, I didna even know how to read." A tear slipped down Molly's cheek, belying her stoic expression. She wiped her eyes impatiently.

Esmeralda grabbed Molly by the shoulders. Tears burned behind her own eyes for Molly's pain. "And now you know how to read and write and keep our books . . . Molly." Esmeralda pronounced each word distinctly and with the strength she wanted to infuse into her friend. "You are worth ten times more than any of those blue bloods. If it weren't for you and your good common sense, and a couple of your 'tricks,' I would never, *never* have survived." When Molly turned away, Esmeralda shook her, trying to force her friend to understand how much she meant to her. *"Survived,* Molly. I owe you my life. A friend can't give more than that."

The two women sat on the floor, facing each other. Slowly, understanding and forgiveness dawned in their eyes. Molly hugged Esmeralda forcefully, as if trying to convey the extent of her love by the pressure of her arms. The relief was such that both started to laugh while a few tears escaped down their faces.

"And *you* had nothing to do with what happened to me last night."

"If I'd told ye about Jason, maybe we wouldna be spendin' the next fortnight wonderin' if yer to have Peter's bleedin' cousin."

Esmeralda felt a cold knot of anxiety tighten in her stomach. "There's no chance of that. I wasn't with Henry."

A small ray of hope crossed Molly's face. "The viscount?"

Esmeralda nodded solemnly.

"Well, then." Molly wiped her eyes, gathering her resolve as quickly and efficiently as she gathered her seams. She stood, pulling Esmeralda with her. "I'll be seein' that he marries ye. Tell me a little about him, so I can plan how best to hook him. I could pretend to be yer sister, lookin' out for your welfare."

"I'm not marrying anybody."

"Of course ye are—leave it to me. I'll tell him about your background, that way he'll know yer in his class. That's important to these gents."

"No, Molly, you don't understand. I don't *want* to marry Keane Marshall."

Molly placed her hands on her hips, her face set in a mulish expression. "Want to or not, me girl, that's out of yer hands now. Ye have no choice; yer ruined for anybody else. An' marry him ye will." Her expression softened for a moment. "Don't ye be gettin' scared. Ye must have felt something for him if ye was willing to do what Eve and Adam did. Love will come, believe me." She moved away to collect her hat and coat. Midway to the peg board, Molly stopped abruptly and turned back to Esmeralda, her hands at her chest. "He's not married already, is he?"

Esmeralda caught Molly by her elbow and steered her to the worn horsehair settee, seating Molly next to her. "No, but it makes absolutely no difference to me whether Keane is married and has twelve children or is eagerly looking for a wife," she explained as if speaking to a child. "Stop talking about Keane! We need to discuss Peter."

"Peter? Are ye touched in the head? We have to strike while the iron's hot. I'm going to drag that no-good lecher of a viscount out of bed, if I have to. He's got to know right off he's responsible for ye."

"And what of Jason Carter's responsibility to you and Peter?"

Molly shook her head with disbelief. "Don't ye be tryin' to distract me. Where's the snake staying?"

"If you never planned on confronting Jason with your pregnancy," Esmeralda continued mercilessly, "why did you *insist* on moving to Cincinnati?"

Molly slumped back into the settee. She knew that look. Once Esme had her head fixed on some notion, deflecting her questions was like trying to unravel a knotted skein of fine thread. "I meant to." Molly sighed, giving in to Esmeralda's greater resolve. "In fact, I came here to cut off his nutmegs and make *sure* he'd not catch another girl short-skirted." Molly smiled sheepishly. "But then I remembered it really wasna his fault I got aproned up. Even though I'd never been with another man, I was no naïve colleen; I knew what I was doin' when I went away with him. So after I got over me anger, and stopped losing me breakfast every morning, I decided to tell him nice-like, after the bairn was born. I used to practice what I'd say to him. 'Here ye are Jason, is he not cute? An' all yers, too!' " She shrugged her shoulders. "But then I had the tyke an' I didna want to give him away. I would make up these silly excuses—'I'll tell him after I wean Peter,' or 'A bairn needs its mother; later when he's a boy, I'll send him on to his father.' Now, I look at Peter, and he's so perfect and lovable, the image of Jason. He would be so proud of his son." Molly's eyes clouded up with fear. "But what if Jason wants to take him away from me? He's so bloody rich, so powerful; he could do it. I just canna lose me bairn—not even to Jason."

Esmeralda held Molly's hand sympathetically, but inside she seethed. So Jason Carter was the man who had run off with Molly, gotten her pregnant, and discarded her. What did it matter if he knew about Peter's birth or not? She'd met him; the arrogant and conceited lout was like all men. He would have abandoned Molly just the same. He might have even offered to pay her off as he did all of Henry's light-o'-loves! And to think she had felt sorry for Henry. Jason Carter deserved to be punished. One way or another, she was going to make sure he paid for what he'd done to Molly.

"Molly." She turned eagerly toward her friend. "We can still get the money from the Carters."

"Oh, no, Esme."

"Peter deserves a share in Carter Shipping!"

Molly didn't like the way the conversation was going, not one bit. She had to make Esmeralda understand that the right solution *was* marriage to the viscount—*not* an attack on the Carters! Therein lay only disaster. She vaulted to her feet, standing nose to nose with Esmeralda. "Yer going to marry the viscount if I have to drag the both of you to the priest! That man's ruined ye—"

"I am not ruined!" Esmeralda shouted, pointing her index finger in Molly's face.

Molly swatted Esmeralda's hand away. "Wake up, Esme. This is real life, and no man of any standing, much less of yer class, is goin' to be marryin' a woman with a muddied reputation."

"That's fine, Molly, just fine. Did it ever occur to you that I have absolutely, positively—without even a smidgen of a doubt—no plans to marry?"

"Yer talkin' like a babe. What yer cousin did to ye is cloudin' yer thinkin'. When ye get back yer estate, what are ye plannin' to be doin' with it? Ye goin' to take care of it all by yerself? Esme," she said in a softened tone. "I know Allen made ye bitter—him tryin' to git rid of ye an' all—but someday yer goin' to want a home and bairns to inherit Amberose. An' yer goin' to have to live with a man to do it."

"I don't want to hear this." Esmeralda turned away and headed to the rack where her dresses hung.

Molly followed and helped Esmeralda dress in a faded brown gown of cotton. "They're not all bad, *mavourneen*. Why, I bet this viscount is a fine man. Just tell me where I can find the blighter and I'll make sure he lives up to his duty."

Esmeralda pushed Molly's hands away from the hooks of her gown. "Would you stop—"

Three sharp knocks interrupted their argument. Both women froze in place. Esmeralda and Molly had no friends in the area. The shop clientele never visited the outskirts of town where they lived. And no one ever paid a call on a Sunday.

But now someone's fist was banging down the door.

Molly hurried forward, but Esmeralda grabbed her arm and pointed to the hooks of her gown. Quickly fastening her up, Molly again started toward the door, only to be swung aside. Esmeralda indicated that Molly should stand behind the door while she opened it. Her face set in a stubborn expression, Molly obeyed.

The pounding on the door continued. Esmeralda dried her palms on the skirt of her dress and swung it open. Just as she'd feared, Keane stood before her, his cognac-hued eyes fuming and his square chin set.

Chapter Ten

"I came for my coat."

Esmeralda met his cold gaze with an equally cool expression. "By all means," she responded. "How did you know I'd taken it? Do you take inventory every time a woman spends the night?"

Keane stepped forward, up to the threshold. Tipping her chin up with the crook of his finger, he leaned toward her until she could feel his breath against her lips. "That's why I have Higgins." The right corner of Keane's lips turned up just a bit. "He keeps track of my things . . . and the persons who abscond with them. He's also astute enough to have them followed."

With his soft breath caressing her mouth, thoughts of last night and the feel of those incredible full lips crowded out all logic. She felt a familiar ache centered right below her stomach and wanted to inch forward and kiss that tempting corner of his mouth. But when his lips flared into a satisfied smile, she realized her mistake. One look at his eyes confirmed he'd caught her unguarded expression of desire. Her weakness gave him the advantage.

"I'll get your coat," she said, slamming the door in his face.

Keane cursed softly under his breath. He had just missed a permanent rearrangement of his nose by the plank-wood door. An instant later, the door opened again. This time a lovely, raven-haired woman with large blue eyes and shoulder-length curls stood before him.

"Ye must be the viscount."

Keane raised his eyebrows at the questionable introduction. The woman's grin grew wider, exhibiting a small gap in her near-perfect smile. Her beauteous face transformed into pure mischief.

"And you are?" Keane drawled, leaning against the doorjamb, his arms crossed.

The woman opened her mouth to answer, but before she emitted any sound, Esmeralda shoved between them and replied, "Edeltraud, her name is Edeltraud Dinkelspiel. If you'll excuse us for a moment." Again the door shut soundly in his face.

Inside, Esmeralda pinned Molly under a glare of green fire. "You touch that door and you can forget keeping Peter a secret from Jason Carter!"

Molly looked stunned. *"Musha!* Are ye threatenin' me?"

Esmeralda shook her head. "Don't you understand, Molly? That's Jason's *closest* friend. For all we know, Jason's told him all about you!"

"I havena lost me senses!" Molly protested. "I wasna goin' to give him me real name! But Esme—Edeltraud Dinkelspiel? A wee bit unlikely, I'm thinkin'."

"It was all I could think of!"

"Then ye best be leavin' the fast thinkin' to me, *mavourneen.*"

Ignoring the jab, Esmeralda paced frantically about the small kitchen. "What am I to do? I can't talk to him. Not since . . ." She trailed off, letting Molly fill in the silence with her own conclusions. She couldn't begin to explain what that snake outside was after: answers she couldn't give! She had to think . . . and fast. But instead of a clever explanation, all Esmeralda's head yielded was an ever-pounding pain.

Molly watched her friend make short work of her fingernails while trekking up and down the small confines of the room. A satisfied smile lit Molly's features. Esme was hooked, but good. And not a bad catch either—he had money, a title, and fine looks as well. She'd noticed his rich hair, more gold than brown, waving across his forehead. And he was taller than Esme by a head, with broad shoulders and nice eyes framed by thick dark lashes. The blighter would do nicely all right. Now the only question was, how to get the two hitched?

"Let me handle this, Esme. I'll get rid of him." She pushed Esmeralda behind the brick chimney stack. Its skinny niche would barely conceal her from the man at the door, but in a pinch it would do. "I'll give him his coat and send him on his way, don't ye worry."

Esmeralda let Molly take over, too upset by her confrontation with Keane to argue. Still she remained wary. "Molly, you won't mention marriage or anything silly like that?" Unconvinced by Molly's expression of hurt innocence, she continued, "We can plot and plan all you want *after* he leaves. But promise you'll give me a chance to explain things before you do anything about my . . . situation. Please, Molly? You know I would do the same for you—*have done* the same for you," Esmeralda corrected herself, watching Molly's expression sober from a look of mischief to one of unwanted responsibility.

"All right, Esme, have it yer way," she grumbled, granting Esmeralda the time she wanted.

Esmeralda hugged Molly and stepped behind the chimney.

Molly shook her head with grudging respect. That

Esme, she was a quick one to get her way. But she had a heart of gold. Why, if it weren't for Esme's unquestioning help, Molly would not have made it through her confinement. Aye, she owed Esme. Maybe it was time to exhibit some of Esme's kind of loyalty. In any event, waiting a bit would give her time to decide how to get Esme and the viscount married.

The viscount! She'd almost forgotten. Scurrying to the chair, she snatched up the coat and sash and carried them to the entrance. She flung open the door with a wide smile.

"Here is yer yacket, der lordship." Molly extended the garment to Keane.

Keane looked down at the petite woman with the doubtful accent. Something between German and . . . Irish? She really was quite dazzling, though, when she smiled like that. But his observation was clinical, not heartfelt. Esmeralda's smile had cut through him like a finely honed knife.

He took his coat and sash. "Please convey to the coward inside that it will be a cold day in hell before I leave here without some answers." Keane leaned forward casually. "I don't suppose you'd care to respond to a few questions?"

"Nicht speaken gutes English." The woman shrugged her shoulders.

"You were doing an amazingly good job when you first opened the door." Keane pointed out.

"Ick spricht nor ein bitchin," she replied, in what Keane considered a dismal attempt at German. She indicated a tiny amount by bringing together her thumb and forefinger until they almost touched. But he didn't believe she spoke little English—not for one minute.

"In that case, I'll just wait here for Esmeralda, shall I?" Keane stepped away from the door, his arms crossed, prepared to stand guard.

The raven-haired woman shook her head. *"Nein,* yer lordship. Feels *nicht gut,* Esme. *Nicht gut."*

"And she's going to feel a whole lot worse if I go in there after her!" Keane shouted, obviously addressing his remarks to Esmeralda inside the cottage.

Stepping out and shutting the door behind her, Edeltraud Dinkelspiel used her body to block the doorway. *"Nein!"*

"Oh, for God's sake!" Keane made short work of the woman's blockade and shoved the door open. As he entered the barren room, he was met by the shrill cry of an infant, but no sign of Esmeralda.

The German-Irish woman rushed in behind him, directly to a cradle at the hearth. She picked up the screaming child, patting the baby comfortingly on the back as she stared accusingly at Keane. *"Nicht, nicht gut!"*

Keane felt instantly ashamed at having awakened the babe. A quick glance around the room revealed he would not find Esmeralda inside: The window stood ajar—an easy avenue of escape.

"I'll show some uncharacteristic restraint this time and let Esmeralda play her little games. I know where to find her . . . she can't hide forever. But give her this message." He glared down at the small messenger. "I don't like unpleasant surprises when I wake in the morning— she promised me answers last night, and I plan on getting them . . . soon." He turned and strode to the carriage waiting in front of the cottage.

"Oh, and by the way." He paused before entering the coach. "I believe the phrase is *'Ich spreche nur ein bisschen.'* " He said the words in flawless German. Tipping his head in farewell at the stunned woman in doorway, he added, *"Auf wiedersehen."*

Molly stuck her tongue out at Keane's back. Unable to contain herself, she shouted as he mounted the carriage, "T'would be a cold day in hell before ye leave without yer answers, would it? Gettin' a wee bit nippy out, eh, yer

lordship?" Not waiting for a response, she shut the door
and went to lay the now-subdued Peter back in his cradle.
"Thinks he's so bloody clever!" She stepped toward the
window, hands on her hips, mimicking, *"Ich spreche nur
ein bitchin* . . . I mean *bisschen.* Just like Betsa always
says it! *Musha,* I thought I could manage it."

Leaning out the opened window, she brazenly waved at
the departing coach. When the conveyance turned down
the road, she shouted, "He's gone, *mavourneen.* Ye can
come back." Receiving no response, she yelled even
louder, "I said the blighter's flown. Get back in here! Bless
us and save us."

She watched Esmeralda emerge from the shed near a
copse of trees, glance furtively about, then hitch up her
skirts and run full speed back to the cabin.

"Well? Did ye hear what the blighter had to say?"
Molly asked once Esmeralda entered.

"Oh, I heard, all right. Did you have to pretend you
knew German?" Esmeralda followed Molly to the kitchen
where Molly donned an apron and began to make cornmeal mush for Peter's breakfast.

"And how's Edeltraud Dinkelspiel likely to be talkin' if
not in German, I ask ye?"

"Well, forget that for now. Help me think of a way to
get rid of him. He's going to ruin all our plans for Henry."

Wooden spoon in hand, Molly cornered Esmeralda into
a chair. "Let me tell ye somethin', Esme, Jason Carter is
no dummy. And that viscount of yers doesn't seem too
gullible, either. When they compare notes, they're not going to pay ye off, they're going to *run* ye off!" Molly gestured with the spoon as if it were a weapon. "When a plan
goes awry, ye got to learn to change yer horse midstream.
Our best bet now is the viscount!"

Esmeralda grabbed the spoon from Molly. "I don't see
why we should change our plans," she said adamantly. "If
anything, we're in a stronger position now."

Molly crossed her arms in front of her. "An' how ye figurin' that?"

Esmeralda licked her lips nervously, unable to answer immediately. Molly must be made to understand that now more than ever their plan to get money from the Carters made sense. In a way, the money *belonged* to Peter.

And to Molly as well, Esmeralda thought as she remembered all those months of watching Molly cry and lose her breakfast. Not to mention the leg cramps, the swollen ankles, the constant lethargy that prevented them from running their shop, and the incredible agony of Molly's twenty-two hours of labor. And those were only the physical symptoms. The emotional scars were there, too. She'd often heard Molly weeping on the pallet beside her, trying to muffle the sounds by burying her head in her pillow. At first, she tried to offer comfort, but she soon learned that only Peter's presence could give Molly solace. On those late nights Esmeralda would pretend to sleep in order to give Molly privacy, but it always tore her heart to hear Molly's tear-choked whispers, telling Peter how much he looked like his father while she held her child to her breast.

The money *should* come from Jason Carter. How dare he leave Molly in her hour of need, as if she weren't good enough for him. Molly was worth ten Jason Carters and more!

But Molly wouldn't accept so impractical a reason as revenge to carry out their plans. She had to come up with something else. Something Molly would believe. Something . . .

Esmeralda met Molly's impatient expression. "You don't really think Keane Marshall, Viscount Eldridge, would marry a lowly seamstress, do you, Molly? A woman with a muddied reputation? Weren't those the words you used?"

"No, Esme, ye got that wrong. Yer a lady."

"And how does Keane know that? Do I have some indelible mark that lets men know I'm quality?"

"Ye own a big estate," Molly argued stubbornly.

"Allen has Amberose! In Cincinnati, I'm just a poor seamstress trying to make enough money to live on."

Molly's anger dissipated. Her expression turned confused.

Esmeralda pushed her advantage, knowing it wasn't often she could put one over on the queen of manipulation. This was for Molly's own good. "Don't you see? That's why we need the money from the Carters. Once we move to England and I get control of Amberose, no one, not even Keane Marshall, will contest my title as a lady. Then, and only then, can I consider marriage."

Esmeralda walked toward the hearth and turned to observe Molly's reaction to her words. She had absolutely no intention of ever marrying Keane. Marriage would entrap her into the very kind of dependency that had permitted Allen to betray her. But she sensed that Molly would be more inclined to follow her plan if she thought her future with the viscount would be secured through it.

Now Esme was making sense, Molly thought. They needed the money to prove Esme was a lady! Then she could get hitched to the viscount proper-like. He wouldn't dare look down his nose at someone as beautiful and rich as Esme. But the Carters! It was too risky. What if Jason found out about Peter? "I agree with ye, Esme, but we'll be gettin' the money some other way. We've got to leave the Carters alone."

"But we're so close, Molly," Esmeralda exclaimed. "To give up now would be ridiculous."

"When Jason hears about last night from the viscount, the plan's as good as dead, Esme!"

"No, Molly. We can turn this to our advantage. Now I truly am a disreputable woman, like the actress and the singer. He'll want to pay me off as soon as possible." The idea dawned in her mind even as she spoke the words. "If Henry keeps seeing me, he'll look like a fool!"

Molly watched Esmeralda's expression with trepidation. She'd only seen that twisted expression on Esme's face once before, when Esme spoke about Allen. Why would she feel that strongly against Jason's brother? "Ah, Esme," she said softly. "I thought ye didna want the boy hurt?"

"Our plan can't ever really hurt him! He's fallen in and out of love with at least three other women in the past six months." Esmeralda returned to the sideboard, picking up the porridge bowl and stirring its contents with the wooden spoon. "And *they* were all paid off by Jason Carter. Henry's just a pampered little boy whose older brother pays for his entertainments, as if he were buying amusing pets!"

Esmeralda rhythmically slapped the spoon against the thickened mush. Getting well-deserved money from the Carters was not cruel! Cruel was leaving for a holiday with a woman who loved you and discarding her when she became pregnant. Only men had the power to be cruel. Should she and Molly give them that power in exchange for the short-lived ecstasy she'd experienced last night? No! *She* wasn't going to let any man have that kind of control over her again!

"Would you stop slapping that spoon!" Molly grabbed the utensil and porridge from Esmeralda's hands. *"Arrah,* yer going to break the bleedin' bowl!" She watched Esmeralda march back to the kitchen chair and flop down with her arms crossed. Molly sighed. "You may be right," she mumbled, staring down into the bowl. They were so close to getting the money. Two months' work would be destroyed if she backed down now. If Jason had not made the connection between her and Esmeralda by this point, he surely wouldn't now. And Esme needed the money to prove she was a lady! "But what do ye plan to be doin' about the viscount? He's not goin' to let ye gallivant around with Henry, not from what I saw here today."

The pounding in Esmeralda's head relaxed as a plan formed. "I'll tell him I'm going to break it off with Henry, but slowly, so as not to hurt Henry's feelings. I'll make that strutting peacock of a viscount think I'm leaving Henry because I'm enamored of him—but it must remain our secret! For Henry's sake."

"It might work . . ." Molly answered, despite her expression of doubt.

"Of course it will work! I'll ask—beg, if I must—for time to break the news to Henry as gently as possible."

The more Esmeralda thought about it, the more reasonable her words seemed. A smooth smile threaded across her face. While she tried to convince Keane it was he she loved, she would keep seeing Henry on the pretense that she needed to break things off slowly—all the while trying to get the money from Jason Carter.

Esmeralda shoved a much-bitten nail into her mouth. She would be playing a dangerous game. Even though she'd had too much to drink last night, she had no doubt that her physical attraction to Keane had not been alcohol-induced, not after her reaction to him in the cold light of morning. Could she do it? Could she pretend to be enamored without actually falling under his control? Dare she try?

Could she afford not to?

"I think it's worth a gamble, Molly. Just you wait and see. I'll be as sweet as molasses. The viscount won't know what hit him."

While the uneven road proved a challenge for the driver, the well-sprung carriage absorbed every jarring rut. Inside the coach, Keane was perturbed only by tumultuous thoughts about one disturbing redhead.

He was thinking about the strange events he'd encountered at the cottage. The house itself was in a deplorable state, and while the interior had been faultlessly clean, something in him twisted at the idea of Esmeralda living under such primitive conditions. There wasn't even a bed to sleep on, only a straw pallet he'd seen leaning against the hearth. The Irish girl and the baby apparently lived there as well. Was Esmeralda responsible for their welfare? That would certainly explain a need for money—the responsibility of caring for others besides herself provided a plausible motive for fleecing Henry. And yet it was still difficult to imagine her capable of such a scheme.

Keane pounded his fist against a leather squab. It was happening again. Despite all evidence to the contrary, he was talking himself out of believing the woman's perfidy. His gambler's instincts proved worthless where Esmeralda was concerned. He couldn't afford to let his guard down for a second with the woman—as he had done last night. To think that just when he'd convinced himself that all of Jason's ravings were unfounded, she'd nearly screamed out her confession. She'd actually said she wanted to ask Jason for money! And her outraged behavior, when she realized Jason was waiting for Keane in the salon, echoed too well that of a scheming woman thwarted from her goals.

Keane tamped down his anger. He'd been ready to get his answers last night, barely able to remain civil in his attempts to get rid of Jason. But when he returned to his room, the beautiful woman on his bed was asleep. Fuming with pent-up frustration, he watched the moonlight where it captured the loose tendrils of auburn hair and wondered how such angelic features could belong to a fortune huntress. Again, he doubted his assessment of the woman's character, just as he did now.

Well, he wasn't a complete fool. If she turned out to be a bitch like Alysha, always grabbing for the biggest purse no matter who was hurt in the process, he'd find out. And he knew well how to deal with that sort. But no matter what, it was time to exorcise her from Henry's life. She wasn't meant for Henry; last night had proved it. No, that luscious woman of passion was his own. He no longer searched for answers for anyone but himself. And he would have to be patient. The questions would wait until tomorrow.

Keane smiled. He looked forward to the interrogation.

Chapter Eleven

By ten o'clock Monday morning business was thriving in the Queen City. The stallkeepers on Pearl Street peddled sauerkraut and pickles from the many kiosks lining the open-air market, and shoppers milling about with baskets on their arms lingered undecidedly over the nearly fifty kinds of sausages sold there. Steamboats jammed the waterfront, each waiting for a chance at the wharf. Crowds on the landing grudgingly parted for draymen, who urged their horses forward, yelling profanities as they shuttled bales and barrels of goods through the crammed streets. Bookstores swamped lower Main Street, their shelves stuffed with the thrillers, "Yaller Kivers," and the many dailies, tri-weeklies, weeklies, ranging from the *Cincinnati Gazette* to the *Hochwächter*.

Amid this bustling activity, a small dress shop remained characteristically quiet. Inside its modest walls, Esmeralda MacClure pored over a recent issue of *Godey's Lady's Book*, resigned to the lack of business. She was therefore pleasantly surprised by the sound of a prospective customer opening the front door. Her delight ended when she stepped in from the back room and found Keane Marshall waiting at the entrance.

His buff-colored trousers and blue broadcloth coat accented his hard muscles, and she remembered well the feel of that strong body as it covered hers. He crossed his arms over his striped waistcoat, causing the cloth to bulge at the shoulders.

And she was supposed to humor this man? Trick him into docilely waiting for her to execute her plans against Jason Carter? Esmeralda felt her throat go dry.

"I believe we have some unfinished business, Miss MacClure." Keane pushed away from the door, stalking her like a predator.

"Hello, Keane." She smiled instead of giving in to her desire to turn tail and run. Holding her position, she met his advance like a good soldier. "I hope you didn't think me rude yesterday. My only excuse is a pounding headache. Please, sit down." She gestured to one of the ladderback chairs. She really should have been an actress, she thought; she couldn't believe how civil she sounded. But she would do whatever was necessary to make sure this man wouldn't ruin her plans for Jason. "How may I help you?" she asked, still smiling, though admittedly the line of her lips felt a bit tight.

Completely ignoring the offered chair, Keane grabbed her by the arms. "What game are you playing at now?"

"I don't know what you mean." Esmeralda pulled back, her smile slipping.

"Let's get right to the point, shall we?" Keane continued to hold her firmly. "Explain your departure in the small hours of the morning."

She saw the raging anger in his eyes, but her own ready temper did little to aid her attempts at docility. "Oh, I'm sorry," she replied sarcastically, continuing to tug against his hold. "I thought that was the way the thing was done. Or was I supposed to ask permission to leave first?"

Mindful of not hurting her, Keane let her step away, but he continued to stare her down. "You were supposed to provide answers to some very pressing questions!"

Esmeralda backed away from Keane's verbal onslaught, trying to feign ignorance. "What questions?" She threw the challenge out with as much bravado as she possessed.

"The questions we discussed before you became so conveniently ill!" Keane advanced, backing her up against the worktable. "Let me refresh your memory. You wanted money from Jason, remember? I want to know why. And I want to know now."

Esmeralda leaned back against the edge of the table. Reaching behind her for balance, she felt the bite of scattered buttons and braiding on the palm of her hands. Licking her lips, she gave her rehearsed answer. "I wanted to borrow some money . . . for a present . . . for Henry's birthday."

Keane didn't flinch. "You'll have to do better than that."

"It's true!" Esmeralda's voice rose in anger. Why didn't he believe her? It had seemed reasonable enough when she thought it up yesterday. "The shop's not doing well. I needed money to buy something for Henry. It was just a small loan." But for some reason she couldn't understand, her plausible explanation only fueled his anger.

"And were you going to explain our little encounter to Jason while you begged money for your beloved's present?"

Keane balked, surprised by her reaction to his question. *She's blushing, for God's sake!* he thought. *One minute she screams like a banshee, and the next she turns pink and rosy like a lady hearing something indiscreet.*

"I believe I was not completely in control that night," she said to his chest. Then, gathering some courage, she raised her chin and met Keane's amber eyes straight on. "And you took advantage of it!"

At that moment, Keane thought she looked extraordinary. He felt an awakening tug at his groin as he took in the tempting picture she created. In the sweet-smelling lavender dress she personified sensual innocence. Her red lips were wet, and her cheeks, flushed. Her startling emerald eyes glittered with anger—and perhaps something else? Yes, he felt it, too. The passion that always erupted when they were together, washing away all other considerations.

"Are you in control now?" he asked in a dangerously soft voice. Placing his hands on either side of her, he leaned on the table until their bodies touched intimately.

Esmeralda felt a hollow feeling at the base of her stomach. Her body tingled where it met Keane's. Although she experienced some trouble concentrating, she answered, nonetheless, "Of course."

Keane's head dipped down, and he began kissing the sensitive skin above her lace collar. At first she pulled away. But her resistance was feeble: a slight shift of her neck to avoid his lips. She remained enclosed within the space created by his two outstretched arms. And when he reached with one hand and gently explored the cloth below her breast, she leaned toward him for an instant before stiffening.

"So anything you do now is of your own free will? I'm not taking undue advantage?" he questioned between kisses.

Esmeralda wanted to pull away, really she did. But somehow her arms felt too heavy to lift. Rejecting the feel of Keane's mouth against her neck would require a Herculean effort, and his warm breath against her ear felt so good—too good to deny herself. Maybe she could just kiss him, then tell him to go away. When Keane's mouth covered hers, she instinctively parted her lips. Just one kiss.

For Keane, all thoughts of Henry vanished when Esmeralda opened her mouth under his. It was as if nothing had transpired since their night together. Apparently, no matter how angry they were, their mutual desire overwhelmed them both. Deepening his kiss, he reached up to stroke her breast and found the nipple had become a hardened point under the soft muslin. He heard her moan of pleasure as his thumb outlined the tip. Pushing his thigh between her legs, he felt a sweet ache build where she pressed close.

Esmeralda struggled for control. Not again! Heavens, how had things progressed so quickly from anger to passion? She had to keep her head—*she* was supposed to seduce *Keane*, romance him into doing her bidding. "Please." She pushed weakly against his chest. "Not here. Someone could see us."

Keane cursed softly under his breath. She had a point. The middle of a shop open for business was no place to make love. Seeing her face flushed with passion, he groaned. They needed more privacy for this little discussion. Grabbing her hand, he pulled her to the door, swinging it open with his free hand. He wouldn't play the gentleman again—not this time. But after he flipped the sign to read CLOSED and shut the door behind them, he nearly collided with the large, plump figure of Mrs. Greenfeld.

"My goodness!" the overblown matron exclaimed.

"My apologies, ladies." He included the wide-eyed Mrs. Percy in his greeting. "But we're late for an important appointment." Keane continued to drag Esmeralda to his waiting carriage.

"Miss MacClure, have you nothing to say for yourself?"

Esmeralda stared at the rotund woman and the stick-thin Mrs. Percy beside her, while Keane hauled her to the coach. Both virtually drooled at the scandalous behavior they were witnessing firsthand. Esmeralda fumed, thinking of the endless hours she'd spent tending these two, time that had not netted a single dime! Vicious biddies!

And now they'd found fodder enough for their gossiping tongues to last out the month. Seeing their expectant expressions, Esmeralda felt her anger get the best of her. Pausing at the door while Keane "helped" her step up into the carriage, she shouted, "Mind your own business, you old . . ."

Keane pushed her into the carriage and stepped in behind her. Leaning out the door, he smiled his apology to the two gaping women. "She really isn't herself today."

"Indeed!" Mrs. Greenfeld bristled.

"Good day, ladies." Not giving the women a second thought, he called to the driver, "I don't care where—just make sure it takes at least two hours to get there."

Keane closed the door and sat back against the squabs. He stared at the woman seated opposite him, their knees almost touching in the cramped quarters. Her arms were crossed before her, and her face set in a mutinous expression. Unable to stop himself, he burst into laughter.

"What's so funny?" she asked peevishly.

"You," he chuckled. Then, sobering a bit, "It was very unwise, what you said back there."

"Bosh! Those two have been searching for something to say against me for months. Now maybe they'll leave me alone." But despite her courageous words, she felt sick with disappointment. If only she'd held her stupid temper. She knew how the shop's highbrow customers would react to even a whisper of immoral behavior. She might as well close the doors forever now.

Keane watched Esmeralda's expression change from stubborn pride to despair. Clearly she regretted what she'd said to the women at the shop. He didn't much like to acknowledge his own participation in that little scene. While he'd been willing to expose her in front of Jason, it had never been his plan to ruin her reputation in the community. He watched as she stared desolately out the window. When a tear slipped down her cheek, he could no longer remain impassive.

Reaching across the small expanse, he pulled Esmeralda onto his lap. At first she protested, but then she nestled against his shoulder, her body trembling as she cried softly against him.

"Don't," he crooned while brushing the curls from her face. "Don't cry, sweetheart."

"Don't call me that," she sobbed.

Keane smiled. She still had some spirit left. "All right, sweets."

"Oh, Lord, why didn't I keep my mouth shut." She sat up, tears in her eyes. "But I was so *tired* of those two ninnies. And when I saw them there, their eyes bulging as if . . . as if I'd my skirt pulled over my head, I just couldn't stop myself." She tugged on the lapels of his coat, taking out her frustrations. "And that Mrs. Greenfeld," she said, warming up to her anger, "she's the worst. Why, do you know that woman has not purchased one item of clothing—not one—since we've opened our doors? Yet, in the past two months, she has practically *haunted* the shop. She and that Mrs. Percy. But do they bother to even pretend they're there for anything but malicious gossip?" She yanked harder on the lapels, her splendid eyes sparkling with unshed tears. At that moment, the liquid green of her eyes reminded Keane of a piece of malachite he'd seen once in France. "No . . . they . . . they've never even bought a . . . ribbon!" Esmeralda again leaned into his shoulder and sobbed.

"You don't need them, sweets," Keane murmured comfortingly.

"But you don't understand." Esmeralda met his sympathetic gaze. "They'll ruin my shop for anyone else. Once it's known . . ."

Keane took her face between his two hands, smoothing the skin under her cheeks with his thumbs. "Try not to worry. We'll think of something to explain what they saw."

Esmeralda brushed away her tears. Her eyes brightened with hope. "Do you think that's possible?"

Keane paused. If he were honest . . . no. "Of course. Just give me time. I'll think of something." He couldn't be so cruel as to extinguish her suddenly eager expression.

She sniffed. "Oh, if it were only possible." She turned on Keane's lap to face him better, her arms still around his neck. His body instantly responded to the move, and he drew her closer. "I really tried to make the shop work," she explained earnestly. "Mo—Edeltraud and I really worked hard so—"

"Shhh." Keane silenced her with his lips, gently pressing his mouth against hers. The gesture was so soft—more comforting than sexual—that Esmeralda returned his kiss without hesitation.

"It's not our fault there is so much competition here," she breathed against his mouth, her eyes closed.

"No, of course not." Keane continued to kiss her between words. "You couldn't have known."

"Mo—Edeltraud heard such marvelous things about Cincinnati." Keane dropped kisses across her lips. She accepted them eagerly. "We thought—"

"I know," he finished for her in a rough whisper. "The land of opportunity . . . money made by simply turning your hand over." He trailed his lips against her neck as he undid the buttons of her gown.

"Yes, that's what we thought." Esmeralda threw her head back. "Oh, yes."

In one swift move, Keane pulled Esmeralda onto the seat beneath him. He parted the gown off her shoulders and gazed at the tempting skin above her chemise. "The land of opportunity." He buried his lips in the exposed cleavage.

"Oh, yes."

Esmeralda burned from the inside out. Every spot Keane touched ignited feelings she'd never experienced. But as she trailed her hands over his firm muscles, she remembered her vow never to succumb to this taste of heaven again. Instead of folding her arms around Keane's neck and pulling his mouth to hers, she fought, struggling to move out from beneath him. Her efforts didn't even slow his sensuous assault. He continued to graze the skin of her neck with drugging kisses that sent shivers down to her toes. His thumb found and circled the tip of one breast. She grabbed his wrist and pulled his hand away— only to feel the warm fingers of his other hand caress her inner thigh as he inched her skirts up her legs.

With each new sensation she felt a need build. Inside her, something burned to be quenched, and she knew instinctively that Keane's tender touch would expertly sate this craving. And while the small voice of reason still chimed a warning for retreat, a more seductive message raged in her mind. Its sirenlike voice smoothly enveloped her, silencing any logic, until her hand released his wrist and reached for his silky hair. All she could think of was sensual: his soft breath against her ear, the tingling scent of lemon at his neck—and her desire to feel more.

Mindless of her precarious perch on the carriage seat, she pushed back the lapels she'd clutched before, helping him to remove his coat. Keane momentarily stopped his teasing kisses to take off his jacket and striped waistcoat, and then his shirt. The touch of his soft chest hair on her exposed skin and the feel of his rounded shoulders under her caressing fingers flooded her. Leaving the sinews of his back, she entwined her fingers in curls the color of warm caramel and pulled his mouth to her lips. His thighs felt hard and strong as they parted her legs, one knee on the carriage seat, the other balanced on the floor, pressing her leg against the edge of the seat. She could feel the rough wool of his trousers brush against the inside of her thighs.

"Esmeralda . . . Esmeralda, sweetheart."

The sound of her name was like a seductive breeze teasing her heated skin. And when Keane guided his tongue between her lips, she sucked eagerly, copying the gesture she'd learned from him in his suite. His groan of pleasure made her burn even hotter. She couldn't think. She didn't want to.

Keane lifted her skirt, dispensing with her last cloth barrier. He couldn't wait much longer. The feel of her skin as he caressed her thighs with his hands was achingly familiar. Their union was merely the culmination of what began a few nights past. Satisfied with his reasoning, he opened his eyes and examined the seductress beneath him. Her eyes were closed, her lips parted, wet, bruised, promising.

Esmeralda's eyes fluttered open. Through hooded lids, she took in the man hovering above her. His expression reflected his need—and something else? It was almost as if he were asking permission to continue. In answer, she threaded her fingers through his hair. "Kiss me." But despite her genuine desire and his expert kisses distracting from the gentle probing between her legs, she still experienced a moment of alarm when he started to enter her.

Keane felt her tense. He had promised himself he would stop at her slightest hesitation, no matter how difficult that proved to be. But his control did not serve him as well as he planned. She felt so good, so tight, he couldn't leave her now. Grasping her shoulders, he surged forward, planting himself deep within her.

A searing pain engulfed Esmeralda, overpowering her pleasure. She gasped and pushed at his chest, trying to escape what now felt like a suffocating embrace.

"I'm sorry, sweetheart. I didn't know—forgive me." Keane's insistent kisses soothed away the hurt. Soon the pain melted into a dull ache and then a fleeting sense of pleasure. When she stopped fighting, Keane deepened his kiss and began to move inside her. His body followed the rhythm of his tongue as he drew in and out of her.

Esmeralda felt a pressure build within, enticing her to strain toward him. She instinctively followed his lead until a wonderfully full feeling began to blossom deep inside her. Desperately wanting to attain the elusive state she sensed within her reach, she struggled until Keane admonished, "Relax, sweetheart." The words were featherlike caresses against her mouth. Without leaving her, he sat up on the seat and planted her firmly on his lap. Her knees straddled him, resting on the seat. The infrequent jarring of the carriage and its soft bouncing movement drove him deeper inside her.

"Just think of me inside you. You feel wonderful around me. Do I feel good? Do you like this?" Keane's lips left her mouth and kissed her neck as he worked her breast free of its cloth binding. His lips closed around her sensitive nipple and his hand reached between their bodies and intensified her enjoyment with gentle, rhythmic caresses at the apex of her pleasure.

"Yes," Esmeralda moaned, arching her back. "Oh, Keane."

With each stroke of his hand, a coil of passion tightened within her, threatening to explode. Esmeralda felt as if she were on the precipice of some unknown discovery. And then, when the feeling became almost unbearable, she felt Keane tense and groan. At that moment her tension burst and she floated into a warm, pulsing pleasure.

Keane stared at her expression of fulfillment, overwhelmed by a tenderness that he'd never felt for any other woman. Their lovemaking had been far more than mutual gratification of sexual desire. It had been something more intense—and frighteningly more permanent. As he watched, she gradually opened her eyes. He shifted her across his lap, feeling incredibly possessive as she rested her head against his shoulder.

"That was wonderful," she murmured.

"Yes, it was." Keane kissed the top of her head. "So why such a woeful tone?"

Esmeralda looked down, then released her hold on Keane. She smoothed the bunched cotton skirt over her lap, covering her knees. "I think that is rather obvious."

Keane pulled her hands away from her dress and wrapped her in his arms, hugging her tightly. She immediately hugged him back, trying to hide her shame by avoiding his eyes. But he would not allow her to regret what had happened. He kissed her forehead, her eyes, and then kissed her nose down to her lips until she was forced to lift her face to his in order to receive his kisses. Then he held her to him, as if by the pressure of his arms alone he could squeeze out all her doubts.

"You made me feel very special," he whispered.

She looked up, her eyes wide. "I did?"

"Yes." He smiled tenderly, then kissed the spray of freckles on her nose. "It makes a man feel special to know he's the first."

Esmeralda lowered her gaze. "I suppose it does."

"Sweetheart—"

She held her hand against his lips. "Please. Don't say anything more."

"But until we straighten—"

"Just for a moment?" She snuggled deeper into his embrace. "I want to pretend for a little bit longer."

Keane nodded. He'd do just about anything she asked at that moment. Thank God, she asked for little.

Chapter Twelve

Four days. Four unbearable, empty days. Keane tossed down the champagne that lay pooled at the bottom of his shallow glass with a carelessness that belied its excellent vintage. He stared at the image of a sunrise carved into the hearth's mantel of the Longworths' banqueting room, trying to lose himself in the clean lines of its federalist design. Four days without her warming presence. Four days of voluntary celibacy when he could think of nothing but the feel of her in his arms.

Uncomfortable with the direction of his thoughts, he shifted his gaze to see through the open doorway to the ballroom where many of Cincinnati's elite were enjoying the fine entertainment provided by their host. They celebrated the successful opening of the Hiram Powers exhibit. The artist himself was here; Keane had seen him in the hall admiring the scenic murals of the young Negro painter, Robert Scott Duncanson, who, like Powers, was one of Nicholas Longworth's protégés. But despite

Powers's talent, Keane had little interest in the lifelike statuary the sculptor created. His only reason for coming to the opening was dancing gaily in the next room, oblivious to the edict he'd given her at their last meeting.

Keane grabbed another glass of champagne from the banquet table, silently musing over its effervescence. While he'd guessed Esmeralda was planning to rook Jason, he suspected she had strong reasons for it. She wasn't the type to do it otherwise—he'd bet money on that. Still, despite any motives that might make her actions more palatable, he'd made it clear to her that she was to stop seeing Henry. Leaving her alone to maneuver young Carter from her life, however, had grated against him. She was his responsibility. In that carriage ride, he'd branded her as his own—Esmeralda was his. But she'd begged him for the time to break things off, and he'd agreed because he felt guilty about seducing her, a virgin. My God, who would have thought? Now, the past four days of endless waiting seemed an unnecessary torment. And he suspected she was no closer to ending her relationship with Henry.

Keane grimaced at his impatience. It was little enough to wait. Patience had always served him well in business and gambling—when had he lost his talent for it? Keane drained half his glass in one swallow, but the bubbling alcohol searing down his throat did little to erase the truth. The heart of the matter was that something about her drew him and made him forget what was right or sensible.

It was nice, that loss of control, so different from his past relationships, which had always been pleasant but restrained, without spontaneity. The raw feelings of a fledgling youth discovering his manhood had been smothered by Alysha's rejection. Ever since their disastrous breakup, he'd worked hard to suppress his emotions behind safe, unpenetrable walls, until he thought he'd lost the ability to be affected. Even now, when he was old enough to accept the hurt that sometimes followed, he held those emotions in check, unable to experience anything greater than strong affection. But with Esmeralda he'd felt intrigued, lustful, confused, delighted, possessive, excited; he'd been completely and irrevocably out of control. The walls were beginning to crumble. And the little minx dancing in another man's arms was the reason.

"There you are, Keane."

Hearing his name from across the room, he turned to find Jason winding his way through the couples in the banquet room. Keane immediately recognized the short, ugly man in a rumpled suit walking in Jason's wake. Though a queer duck, Nicholas Longworth was one of America's wealthiest citizens. An important property owner and vintner, he was also a leading patron of the arts. This room, and the many rooms of Belmont, the Longworth home on Pike Street, attested to his vast collection. While it was sparsely furnished with Duncan Phyfe furniture, the walls were a maze of paintings, all hanging from thick gold cords suspended from hooks in the molding.

Longworth's eccentric manner was well known. His plain and careless dress often made him look more like a beggar than a millionaire. Tonight he wore the requisite black frock coat, but its ill fit and need for pressing made him look frumpy rather than sophisticated. Keane glanced down Longworth's sleeve to his suit cuff where on many occasions he had seen scraps of paper pinned. Jason had told him these were notes reminding Longworth of important errands and appointments. Though a bit wrinkled, tonight his cuffs were bare.

"Nicholas just invited me to go trapshooting. I thought you might want to join us." Jason stepped aside to make room for Longworth beside him and Keane.

Keane smiled his welcome to both men. "Thank you for the invitation. But I must confess, I find shooting trapped pigeons trying to escape somewhat unappealing."

"Unappealing? A game imported from your own precious homeland?" With a sly wink, Jason added, "There's always straight shooting and heavy betting with the Cincinnati crowd."

Keane met Jason's jet stare, amused. "You do tempt me, Jason."

"Come," Longworth commanded. "I'll show you around my vineyard. I have some very promising plants that might interest you."

"I'd be delighted." Keane hid his triumphant smile behind his champagne glass. This invitation was exactly what he'd hoped for from Longworth. "I've been meaning to have a look at your new strain of Catawba," Keane added smoothly. He knew if he were going to invest in Cincinnati grapes, he'd need to cultivate his relationship with Longworth. It was Longworth's experiments with the native Catawba grape that had made wine making a success in Cincinnati. The man was a genius at horticulture. His work with strawberries had made the fruit, previously a European delicacy, popular and inexpensive for every individual, no matter how limited his means. That was the kind of experience Keane wanted to tap into. Even if he did pass on the vineyards here, Longworth's knowledge could easily translate into better grapes at the Eldridge vineyards in France and Germany.

"Good, good. I look forward to it." Without so much as a by-your-leave, Longworth turned and walked away, his attention now focused on the young sculptor who had just entered the room.

Keane raised his eyebrows to Jason in reaction at the man's abrupt ways. A dimple at each side of his mouth marked Jason's response to Longworth's departure.

"That's how I like the people I do business with." Jason's gaze followed Longworth across the room. "No shilly-shallying for Longworth, just plain-speaking." He returned his attention briefly to Keane before gazing back fondly at the short man in the rumpled suit, who was now speaking heatedly to Powers. "But don't let his rough manner fool you. Behind those shrewd eyes and coarse manner you'll find a strong mind and a generous heart."

"I'll take your word for it." Keane sipped the champagne, watching the two men beside the hall door. He nearly choked on his drink when he saw Esmeralda dressed in an organdy gown—a gown he would swear he'd seen displayed in her shop with a patron's name pinned to it—step out of the ballroom with Henry and head down the hall. Leaving Jason to fend for himself, Keane copied Longworth's abrupt departure and steered for the door to the adjoining parlor.

Esmeralda walked through the triple-hung window that opened onto the balcony. The enormous window, one of eight that spanned the outer wall of the ballroom, formed a doorway to the enticing breezes of the garden below. On warm, muggy evenings such as tonight, when the sweat of heated bodies pressed together caused ungenteel stains to appear on the colorful silk gowns and black frock coats, all windows remained open. But Esmeralda gave little thought to the heat, ignoring it and Henry beside her as she leaned against the iron rail. She was thinking about Keane.

He'd granted her time in which "to let Henry down gently," just as she'd plotted with Molly. But she'd been unable to meet with Jason Carter. She knew she had to work fast. After Mrs. Greenfeld and Mrs. Percy had seen her and Keane drive away together, there was no telling how long it would take Henry to hear about her indiscretion, if not through Keane, then certainly through the gossip mill. Yet four days hadn't been enough to advance her plan. She'd thought that after the Powers exhibit would be the best time. But now she dreaded approaching Jason Carter and repeating the words she'd been rehearsing.

She wondered if Jason suspected anything about her

relationship with Keane. After the carriage ride, Keane had promised to keep their involvement secret if she agreed to stop seeing Henry. Her cheeks grew warm with color as she thought about the intimacies she and Keane had shared. Again she'd underestimated his power over her. Revenge for Molly and Peter had cost her dearly. But then, for what did she need her virginity? And the things she'd experienced in his arms—it had almost been worth it.

Esmeralda sighed. Despite her outrageous behavior, she loved the way he made her feel. And their making love had accomplished one thing. Keane certainly believed she intended to leave Henry. She'd just have to make certain she was never alone with Keane; that way she would not lose control again. After she got Jason to pay her off, she could end things with Henry and leave for England with Molly and Peter. She needn't worry that Keane would be hurt by her departure; for him, she was just an entertaining pastime. The relationship she'd promised in order to buy time would be an inconsequential loss. Besides, she'd never demean Henry by publicly falling into Keane's arms after breaking things off between them. No, with Henry she planned to be as gentle as possible.

"You seem a million miles away." Henry's voice interrupted her thoughts.

"I'm sorry."

"That's all right, darling. I just hope this doesn't mean you're bored with me already." He laughed nervously, as if he sensed all was not well between them.

Esmeralda looked up into Henry's pouting expression. She knew many women found his little-boy face adorable, irresistible, even. But for her his childish vulnerability only made her stomach twist into tighter knots. Could she really do this to kind Henry? After she got her money, how would her sudden disinterest affect this gentle young man?

Stop it, she admonished herself. *Don't think about*

Henry. Think about Jason Carter and what he did to Molly!

But when Henry reached over and stroked her hand, she experienced a new wave of guilt. Heavens! She must get away and find Jason now, before she lost her nerve altogether.

"If you'll excuse me." She pulled her hand away too abruptly, as if his very touch were distasteful. Immediately she noticed her mistake and caught Henry's expression of hurt. Yet instead of offering reassurance, she turned to leave.

Henry grabbed for her wrist. "Where are you going?" His voice was edged with petulance.

"I just need to freshen up. I'll return shortly." She managed a smile before she stepped through the window to the ballroom.

Esmeralda skirted the dancing couples, catching her breath. She stepped through the doorway banked by two fireplaces and headed down the hall to the necessary. She had to find Jason.

Just as she passed the parlor across from the banquet room, an arm reached out and pulled her into the small chamber. Keane folded her into his warm embrace before the door even closed behind her. His kiss extinguished any protest against their indiscretion.

"Have you told him?" The warm, whispered words fell across her face between kisses.

"Keane, please. I need more time."

He pulled away, framing her heart-shaped face in his hands. With his thumb, he stroked the silky skin he'd just tasted. "Ask me for anything, sweets." His mouth lowered to hers. "Anything but that." He melded their lips in a bruising kiss, intending to wipe Esmeralda's mind clear of any thoughts besides the fit of his mouth against hers.

At that moment Keane and Esmeralda wouldn't have heard cannon fire, much less the slight noise of the door swinging open and someone walking in.

"So it's true."

The sound of Henry's voice catapulted them apart. Esmeralda's face turned brick red and even Keane appeared flushed with more than pent-up desire.

Henry stayed by the door, his expression sad and confused, much like a child who feels unjustly punished.

"Henry. I can explain—"

"Jason told me it wasn't true . . . just rumors."

"Henry—"

"No, please, don't say anything. Don't try to . . ." He looked down at his hands. "Don't lie."

Those words, spoken so softly, pounded against her heart with the force of a mallet.

"It's really my fault," he murmured. "I shouldn't have followed you. But I had to find out for certain . . . I had to know for sure if you were just like the others."

"The others?" Keane asked, surprised.

Henry smiled wanly. "Oh, yes, I knew Jason was paying them off. It was a game I played. Poor Jason wanted so much to protect me. But I felt sorry for them, even for Rosie, bless her greedy heart. I had so much, and they, so little." He chuckled softly, before taking a deep breath and meeting Esmeralda's confused stare. "I knew if I showed enough interest, he'd give them money to go away."

Esmeralda remained motionless, her heart beating against her chest as sharply as a fist. "You mean, you did it on purpose?" He'd seen them out of kindness? Actually trying to help them with his brother's money? "All those women . . . you knew your brother was paying them off?"

"I couldn't just give them the money outright. Jason would have had my hide!" His large brown eyes looked beseechingly at Esmeralda. "I thought it was rather clever to get Jason to pay them himself. But you were different. I lo—" He stopped himself from saying the words his face expressed so eloquently. Looking at Esmeralda as if they were alone in the room, his features settled into an unnatural expression of cynicism. "I hope you get a good price." He turned on his heels and left.

Esmeralda covered her mouth with her hand. She started after Henry, but Keane stopped her.

"Esmeralda, don't. Just leave him alone." His voice was gentle, but firm. He'd seen her face during Henry's speech. She'd been terribly upset by the scene.

Esmeralda struggled against him. "You don't understand! I thought . . . I've got to explain!"

"What did you think?" Keane asked, still keeping hold of her wrists.

Esmeralda twisted her hands out of Keane's grasp and screamed. "I thought he didn't care! I thought he was just . . . just a spoiled boy having fun!" She turned to the door, but again Keane stopped her.

"Please." Her eyes shone with tears. "I must explain to him."

"What can you explain?" Keane shook her, as if he could will her to understand the futility of her actions. "That you didn't mean to hurt him? That you feel *sorry* for him? Unless you can tell him that what he saw was a mistake and that you love him, don't go after him." And seeing her stunned expression, he explained softly, "Your pity will only hurt him more."

The sight of her tearful eyes and reddened features tore at something inside him. So he'd been right all along. She really wasn't malicious or callous, just too inexperienced to know better.

With agonizing clarity, Esmeralda realized what she'd done. Henry had never been anything but kind and considerate, but she'd willingly sacrificed him for the sake of revenge. She pictured him as he'd looked standing at the door, his expression pained but resigned. The love displayed on his face and his shattered expression of betrayal had struck her with agonizing familiarity. *Allen made me feel that way. Am I responsible for making someone hurt so much?* What kind of person had she become to do this to another human being? Had the pain festering within her the last nine years made her so unfeeling?

But she refused to accept sole responsibility for what happened. She narrowed her gaze at the handsome man still holding her in his arms. This never would have happened without Keane's involvement. *I was on track before he arrived.* Feigning an admiration she didn't feel was one thing, but betraying Henry with another man—allowing him to walk in and find her kissing Keane—only that kind of betrayal could cause the hurt she'd seen etched on his young face.

"This is your doing!" She started pounding on Keane's chest, her hands clenched into fists. "Why couldn't you leave me alone! If you hadn't come—"

"Stop this!" Keane forced her hands behind her back so her breasts pressed against his chest. But under the circumstances, he didn't feel desire. He knew she needed to vent her spleen on someone, knew that, in typical human fashion, she'd blame him for what happened rather than stand accountable for her own behavior. He saw the potential this scene had of destroying any relationship between them. That was one consequence he was not prepared to accept.

But Esmeralda had found her scapegoat. She clung to Keane's accountability like a lifeline. "You have no idea what you have done," she said, her tears dammed by anger. "I was going to talk to Henry. I would have told him what a friend I considered him to be and . . . and how much I cared for him. He didn't have to see this! He would have understood I didn't love him, and it wouldn't have . . . hurt," she ended in a high, choked voice.

Keane felt an ache inside him at her childlike look of pain. He released her hands and tenderly brushed the curls that tumbled down her back. "Oh, it would have hurt him, sweetheart." How could it not hurt to be rejected by this lovely woman? "You saw how much he cared. You couldn't shield him from that."

Esmeralda swiped at her tears with the back of her hand. "He would have understood! What he just saw . . . it's your fault." She pulled away from Keane as if his touch were poison. "Why couldn't you leave me alone?"

Keane began to reach out but dropped his arms instead, securing them in the pockets of his trousers. In a voice full of self-derision, he replied, "I wish I knew the answer to that question, sweets."

For a moment they stood unmoving, their eyes locked as if exchanging messages in some unspoken manner. But there was no communication, only misunderstanding.

Her chest heaving, her voice unsteady, Esmeralda turned away. "I'd like to be left alone now."

Keane stared at the graceful curve of her back. "I think not. We need to get some things cleared up."

Esmeralda laughed, incredulous. "We have absolutely nothing to say to each other." She spoke slowly, precisely, emphasizing each word.

"I disagree." Keane walked to the door and leaned against it. The soft sound it made as it clicked into place caused her to turn and face him. His arms crossed before him, he asked, "You did this for the money, of course."

The unexpectedness of his question struck her physically. Momentarily nonplussed, she stared in silence.

"I saw that cottage you live in." He looked at the borrowed dress, his eyebrows raised in question. "And business appears bad indeed."

Propelled into action by his disparaging tone, Esmeralda tried to push Keane away from the door. But shifting him was like trying to move a slab of granite.

"Do you need money, Esmeralda?" He grabbed her shoulders and forced her to stop her feeble display. "I can give you money."

So now he thought he could buy her off—just like any other arrogant man. Esmeralda experienced a depth of sadness she hadn't known existed within her. How she wished she could pay off her conscience in the same manner! How wonderful if she could offer Henry money to salve his wounds.

Keane realized his mistake too late. He saw Esmeralda's face reflect first hurt, then disdain. How could he make her understand? He wanted to provide for her. He'd asked about money not just to appease his conscience, but because he wanted ties between them, even if they were merely shallow monetary bonds.

"Lord Eldridge." Esmeralda jerked away from his grasp, her clipped English accent more pronounced. "Although at present my circumstances appear humble, I can assure you, it is only a momentary lapse." She straightened her back, and Keane almost smiled at the transformation from screaming termagant to prim lady. "My colleague and I will soon be traveling to *my* estate in England. There is only a small legal technicality to be cleared up, and I will again be Lady Esmeralda MacClure, Mistress of Amberose. I assure you, sir! Your financial assistance is not needed."

"Amberose?" This time he grinned. "You'll have to do better than that, sweets. Lord Kielder presides over that estate."

"Allen is not the Master of Amberose. Amberose is *mine!*" She stood before him, fists clenched. "Amberose is mine," she repeated, her voice softer but just as adamant.

Keane examined her earnest expression. He thought over what he knew of Lord Kielder, the man's unsavory reputation, the rumors that haunted his inheritance. He'd never met the man in person, despite their shared love of gambling—he'd done his best to avoid the fellow. Keane didn't play against cheats. What was the man's name? Allen? Yes, Allen . . . Allen MacClure. MacClure.

Keane stared intently at Esmeralda, a nagging memory pulling at the back of his brain. MacClure. MacClure. *It's uncanny, Eldridge,* a voice echoed from the past. *Has eyes that look right through you, almost as if he can read the cards from your hands. They're clear green, and hard as emeralds.*

Grabbing Esmeralda, he stared deep into her emerald green eyes.

Keane's look of disbelief only compounded the injury to her pride. "As I said, currently my colleague and I are experiencing—"

"Lord Kielder inherited Amberose some years ago." Keane examined her with an uncharacteristic look of awe. "He had a ward who disappeared under suspicious circumstances. It caused a lot of talk because he owed a substantial amount of money at the time. With his ward gone, the estate, the monies—everything became his." Keane tipped her face up toward his. "She was a girl no older than ten or eleven. Easily gotten rid of. Many claimed Lord Kielder did just that." Keane fingered her hair and smoothed the skin around her eyes. "Are you telling me *you* are that girl, Esmeralda?"

The question caused a pounding ache in her head. She pressed her fingers to her temples, trying to stop the pain, the memories.

"Are you that girl?"

She remembered the drunken conversation between the two men on the boat. *To the highest bidder she goes, then on to the slave markets. That's what Lord Kielder said. Get rid of the girl.*

"That's why you want the money, isn't it?"

Esmeralda's thoughts pounded against the black wall barring her memories. She could never remember what had actually happened before she'd awakened on that rowboat nine years ago. She could only recall the two sailors, their talk about Allen, then diving into the water and swimming for shore—Molly smuggling her aboard the ship to America. She had never remembered Allen's perfidy. Until now.

In her mind's eye, she saw Allen's glassy-eyed stare as

he pressed the handkerchief to her face. *I'm sorry, my darling. Truly I am.* The sodden handkerchief covered her mouth and nose. The acrid odor choked her. He had drugged her. Allen had followed her to the forest and drugged her! Then he'd given her over to those men. *To the highest bidder she goes, then on to the slave markets.*

"Are you Lord Kielder's ward?"

The soft, comforting tone of Keane's voice seeped through the nightmare images. Esmeralda tipped her head up. "Yes."

"Please, let me help you."

Drained, she melted into the support of Keane's arms. She wanted so much to have someone to trust, to believe in—to love her unquestioningly. As Allen had—Allen, who had drugged her and tried to sell her into slavery.

Keane felt her stiffen in his arms. But he never expected the resounding slap. Stunned, he massaged his cheek with his hand and stared at Esmeralda's fiery expression.

"Don't ever touch me again." Her eyes were cold and shuttered.

Keane's gaze narrowed. So that was the way of it. He could see the fear behind the facade of defiance. She might be a nineteen-year-old woman, but inside she was still the kidnapped child, running away, trusting no one. He recognized the wall she had so firmly placed between them in the frigid look of her eyes.

"I'm not giving up, you know. You'll have to deal with me sometime. You may even be carrying my child." He saw her eyes dilate with surprise, but she didn't say a word. Keane smiled tightly. "Good-bye for now, my lady." With a short bow he stepped out of the room.

Esmeralda watched the door close softly. Then slowly she walked to the corner of the room and slipped soundlessly into a chair.

Chapter Thirteen

When Keane arrived at his suite, he began drinking—slowly and steadily. At eleven o'clock Higgins retrieved the emptied brandy decanter, shaking his bald head at his master's uncharacteristic indulgence. While he replenished the liquor, the valet silently contemplated whether to use coltsfoot or quinine to alleviate the morrow's inevitable symptoms—then added a judicious amount of water to the cognac. But despite Higgins's efforts, half an hour later the Baccarat crystal hung perilously loose in Keane's hand.

Brooding over his snifter, Keane mulled over what he'd learned at the Longworths'. So he'd seduced not an experienced woman who made her living milking the rich of their money, but a naïve virgin—a lady not much older than Annabella. In his mind he pictured his sister, her sweet face set in a dreamy expression as she pored over the inevitable poetry book. How would he feel if for some reason Annabella should be alone, without help, at the mercy of a libertine . . . like himself? Keane tipped back his glass.

Now he knew what drove her to fleece Jason. It wasn't just the Irish woman or her child and the dismal conditions they lived in. She needed the money to accomplish some half-witted idea of getting back her estate from Lord Kielder. Keane barely tasted the smooth cognac. He drank mindlessly, concentrating on only his gloomy thoughts.

He had no doubt treachery was involved; the circumstances under which he'd first met Esmeralda and her current situation all pointed to it. Everything about her—her language, her manners—confirmed she was more than a common seamstress. That fact combined with what he remembered hearing of Kielder's intense green eyes, eyes that could be shared by a relative, now melded into a disturbing picture. She wouldn't be the first heiress put away by a greedy relative.

She'd mentioned a legal technicality she needed to clear up before again becoming mistress of Amberose. His hand tightened around the bell-shaped snifter. He didn't want her involved in anything dangerous—not without his help.

When the enamel Chippendale clock struck midnight, Higgins interrupted Keane's brooding by announcing Jason. As was his manner, Jason strode briskly into the salon, dropping his hat and cane on the barege chair at the door. His dark coat and matching trousers were immaculate, belying the late hour, and his dark curls were tamed into place by Madagascar oil. Keane fleetingly thought the hair tonic didn't suit Jason, then shook his head at the disjointed thought.

"I see you and Henry found a common solution to the charming Miss MacClure." Jason stopped before Keane and leaned against the rose marble of the mantel. "Didn't seem to give a damn about my opinion, so I left him crying on a friend's shoulder. Well in his cups, I might add. He was a little muddled about what happened, but I felt sure you'd pass along the story."

Keane examined Jason's demanding stance with cool brown eyes. "Go away, Jason." He was in no mood for an interrogation. Not now.

"The diplomatic Keane Marshall actually rude? Miss MacClure must be more talented than I thought if she's got you tied up in knots." Jason went to the sideboard and helped himself to a brandy. After taking a drink, he practically spit it out. "What the deuce is in this?"

"Water, I think." With a disappointed expression, Keane stared at the amber liquid that each turn of his wrist sent swirling inside his glass. The liquor had proved less than inspirational. "Higgins seems to be diluting the stuff."

Jason laughed. "Playing nursemaid again, is he?"

"Probably thinking up some vile concoction to feed me this very moment." Keane grimaced.

"Back teeth awash yet?"

Keane took a hard swallow. "Getting there."

"Then I want my answers now, before you muck up that keen mind of yours. Your health," Jason toasted.

Keane raised his glass in response. To be honest, he was actually glad for the distraction. But at the moment it wasn't a particularly easy story to recount. "Ah, yes. The sordid tale." Meeting Jason's intense glare, he lifted his brows mockingly. "The question is, where to start?"

"Enough, Keane. I want to know what happened."

Keane sighed. "Henry, Esmeralda, and I had an interesting encounter in the Longworths' parlor." Leaning against the tapestry headrest, he examined Jason from beneath drooping eyelids. "Unfortunately, Henry walked in during a particularly intimate moment." Seeing no change in Jason's coal dark eyes, he added, "We were kissing . . . passionately."

"I gathered that much from Henry's drunken mumblings," Jason answered dryly.

Keane raised his eyebrows. "What? No lecture?"

A measured smile crossed Jason's lips. "I can't think of a better way of showing Henry what the Scottish bitch was up to." He pushed away from the mantel and seated himself in the matching wing-back chair beside Keane. "As they say—seeing is believing."

Keane stared at the amber eddies in his glass. In his mind he pictured Henry's face during his emotional speech to Esmeralda. "I don't think you'd say that if you'd seen your brother as I did."

"I have seen him—downing my prize Kentucky bourbon as if it were sarsaparilla. He'll get over the hurt, and be much better for it."

"Perhaps." Keane thought about his own heartbreak at Henry's age. "The pain does lessen with time."

"But you're not telling me anything I don't know," Jason pressed.

Recalling Henry's confession about Jason and the women he'd paid off, Keane smiled. "No," he answered in a studied bland tone. "But then I haven't mentioned . . . I believe her name was Rose? Yes, Rose and her cohorts. It seems Henry's only interest in them was to relieve you of some funds." Keane bit the inside of his lip and waited.

"What?" Jason furrowed his brow, confused.

"The money, Jason. Henry knew about the money. He *wanted* you to pay those women off."

"The deuce you say!"

Keane laughed. Poor Jason thought he had everything under control. And all the while, he'd fallen victim to his younger brother's machinations.

Jason's disbelief remained for but a second before a thoughtful smile replaced it. "That sly . . ." He chuckled. "Who would have thought?" Then, taking a measured drink from his glass, he sobered a bit. "In any event, that's the end of Miss MacClure . . . and good riddance. There's really no reason for you to keep seeing her. Unless of course you and she have already come to some kind of understanding?"

Keane drained the brandy glass. "We have no agreement. But I'll do my damnedest to see that one is arranged."

"Well, that's your business, Keane."

"Correct."

"I don't have to remind you of the bitch's perfidy. You're not young and gullible—"

"Now who's gullible, Jason? How much did the greedy Miss Rose cost you?"

Jason's complexion colored. He shrugged his shoulders negligently. "I wasn't aware Henry had developed such a prankish streak. Still, I suggest you make *sure*—"

Keane laughed dryly, letting his empty glass drop to the Turkish carpet with a soft thud. He watched it roll away to the cold grate. "Nothing is 'sure' when it comes to that woman." Keane rose from his chair and stepped to the hearth, before turning to face Jason. "She needs my help."

For the second time that evening, Jason Carter was struck speechless. He didn't care for Keane's chivalrous expression, not one bit. He looked like some knight-errant ready to save his damsel in distress. "What kind of help does our poor Miss MacClure want?" He tried, quite unsuccessfully, to keep the sarcasm from his voice.

Keane raked his fingers through his hair. "I think she could be in some kind of trouble from a greedy relative." Keane returned to his chair and leaned over the armrest toward Jason. "You remember Lord Kielder, the gambler? The one the fellows at White's wanted to pit me against?"

"Yes, of course I remember," Jason said impatiently. "What does gambling have to do with that woman?"

"It's Kielder that's the connection. Kielder is an old Scottish title. It belongs to a lonely piece of rock in the northwest Highlands. The family moved to the Scottish-

English border years ago. The story goes that the old lord had a daughter late in life, to the chagrin of his nephew, who stood to inherit everything before her birth. When he died, the girl became her cousin's ward. And when she mysteriously disappeared—just in time for her cousin to inherit the hefty estate and pay off some rather substantial debts—there was talk. Lots of it." Keane paused, watching Jason's reaction. "Esmeralda is that girl."

"She told you that?" Jason asked suspiciously.

"Yes."

"And you believed her?"

At Jason's words, a shuttered expression closed over Keane's face.

Jason sighed. While most often blessed with an open mind, there were times Keane could be downright dogmatic. "Let's suppose she's that blasted girl—which I sincerely doubt—what do you plan to do about it?"

Keane did not answer immediately. What were his plans? How could he gain Esmeralda's confidence enough to help her? Unwillingly his liquor-fogged mind drifted back to the carriage ride. His skin burned with the remembered feel of her soft body against his. She had been so passionate in her responses. And a virgin! She'd never been with another man. And Keane knew with clear self-knowledge that he wanted to keep it that way. But only marriage would give him the right to dictate her actions—in and out of bed.

Marriage? Was that what he wanted? At thirty, he was certainly overdue for an heir.

Esmeralda for his wife. Honor certainly dictated that he marry the girl. His father had always taught him to live up to his duties. If her situation were different, if she'd had a relative to protect her interests, the fact that he'd bedded her would be reason enough for marriage. Should her being alone and powerless to force his hand—a mere quirk of fate—change the consequences of his actions? His father would say no. And yet Keane always imagined a different kind of woman to partner him through his duties as Viscount Eldridge. Someone not so fiery, not so independent.

Keane focused on Jason's questioning stare. What *did* he plan to do about Esmeralda? What indeed?

"I suppose I should marry her."

"You're not serious!" Jason exploded to his feet.

Keane shook his head. "I don't know, Jason. I just don't know." He leaned an elbow on the mantel, staring out the window to the dark streets.

Jason grabbed Keane's shoulders, turning him to face him. "Listen to me. I don't know what's going on inside that drunken head of yours, but I hope to God it's the brandy talking. I did not ask you to help me wrench Henry from that woman's grappling claws just to have you marry the chit." Keane pushed Jason away and turned to the sideboard intending to get another drink, but Jason dogged his steps. "Think of your family. What would your mother and sisters say if you returned to England with that woman as your viscountess?"

Keane smiled at the thought. "My mother would discreetly find out what all her favorite dishes are and instruct Cook to try to fatten her up. Charlotte would complain it was about time I married and invite her for endless cups of very proper tea. Annabella would read her poetry. And Nicky? Nicky would take her shooting and judge her by her marksmanship." Keane turned to Jason, and with what Jason considered a besotted smile, added, "She might have trouble winning Nicky over; I don't even know if she can shoot."

"Oh, she can shoot all right. Those pretty green eyes have left a sizable hole in your brain!"

Keane shook off his reverie. "Don't be overdramatic."

Jason felt control slipping away from him. "You can't be serious about this!"

"I don't know. I'm trying to do what's right."

"By marrying a—" Jason cut himself off with great effort. It was useless to try and badger Keane into careful thinking. He took a deep breath. "Just don't do anything rash. Think about the consequences."

"I promise not to go off for a license," Keane sarcastically replied.

"I'm not telling you anything I wouldn't tell Henry."

Keane turned and the two men's eyes met in a look of understanding. Keane offered his hand and Jason grasped it warmly. "Thank you, Jason. I've always considered you family as well."

Jason walked to the chair and gathered his hat and cane. Higgins stood at the door, patiently waiting to show him out. "We'll talk again soon. In the meantime, try to keep a level head." With a nod as a departing gesture, he stepped into the carpeted hallway of the Burnet.

It took him only until he'd reached his carriage to decide he needed to pay Miss MacClure a call. Keane really was like family; Jason would do no less for him than he would do for Henry. If he needed to pay off that Jezebel in order to save Keane from a monumental error in judgment, then he would do it.

It was best not to meet her at the shop, however. He wanted to make sure their meeting was not interrupted. He also wanted to catch her unprepared—a surprise visit to her home would probably be the best course. But he'd have to be quick. If she should get wind of Keane's proposal, he would never be able to persuade her to leave town and give up a fortune that rivaled even Carter Shipping's.

Chapter Fourteen

Esmeralda lay on her back, knees up and shoulder blades digging into the cool planked floor, as she held Peter above her on outstretched arms. Her simple brown skirt, with its many mends and slightly less than fashionable length, billowed out around her. The shirttails of her white cotton blouse bagged at the waist and wisps of hair surrounded her face where Peter had grabbed and pulled them loose from her tight bun. She cooed and giggled at him as she playfully bent her elbows and then straightened them, allowing their faces to touch momentarily before propelling Peter back to his perch above her. She imagined his delighted shrieks were loud enough to put a smile on Molly's face outside, where Esmeralda could hear her humming an Irish ditty as she hung the laundry.

While the morning was still relatively cool, the day promised to be just as hot and muggy as the preceding ones. As she played with Peter, Esmeralda contemplated staying and working at the cottage again, rather than taking the hot trip into town on the omnibus.

The shop had remained closed three cathartic days. Days in which she poured out her story, crying out her failures to Molly—who responded by reassuring and pampering her. Keane had tried to see her, but she steadfastly refused to speak with him.

The pig! All he wanted was to pay off his conscience. Well, she wouldn't make it easy for him. Let him stew. She didn't need money that badly! Not while she still had *any* alternative.

She sighed. Whom was she kidding, trying to act as if she didn't care about Keane? She cared . . . too much. Yesterday, when she'd gone to the shop intending to work, she was so jumpy with thoughts that the viscount might march in that she ended up spoiling the ruching on Louisa Holliston's gown. So she packed up her things in defeat and scurried back to the cottage, unable to face the possibility of confronting him.

Esmeralda laid Peter down on the floor beside her. She handed him his toy, a cornhusk doll she'd bought for him in town yesterday, and watched him immediately bite into it. At eleven months, Peter was exploring the world with his mouth. She pried the doll away from the death lock of his four front teeth. But when his face crumpled, threatening to erupt into cries of frustration, she handed the doll back.

Watching him happily gnaw on the doll's head, she smiled. Her trip into town had not been a total waste. It was on her way down Fifth to the omnibus station that she'd spotted the flyer announcing the *Eureka*'s voyage to California. In bold letters the handbill advertised the first American bark to set sail straight to the goldfields from Cleveland. The idea had struck her then that the goldfields were the answer to their financial woes. After her encounter with Henry, she had given up her thoughts of revenge against Jason Carter, sure she would never see a dime from him now. But the handbill had given her hope! She, Molly, and Peter could buy passage on the *Eureka* and sail to the land where men became millionaires overnight.

Esmeralda grabbed Peter, causing him to drop his doll, and lifted him over her head. "Don't you worry, darling boy. We'll make our own way—without anyone's help!" At Peter's gurgles of delight, she hugged him tightly. "Molly was right. I should have left the Carters alone. You're ours, Peter. Mine and Molly's. I wouldn't let those rich people take you away! And they'll never find us in California."

She rolled onto her stomach, carefully setting Peter on his back and tickling his stomach. She hadn't discussed the possibility of moving with Molly, but she would tell her soon. The ship was set to sail by the end of the summer, and they would need to make a thousand arrangements about the shop and the cottage.

Planning such a move was certainly a change for Esmeralda. In the past, Molly had always been the organizer of their dramatic adventures. But it was a *good* plan. Once they got to the goldfields, all the money they needed would be theirs, even if they didn't pan for it. Esmeralda had heard about the fortunes made by tradesmen selling their wares to the gold diggers at substantially inflated prices. But she wasn't out to cheat anyone. Not this time. She was willing to work hard for their gold, even if it meant sewing shirts for the men and doing their laundry.

The *Eureka* was also the safest way to California from Ohio. The ship would travel from the lakes through the Welland Canal and other waterways. Once it reached the Atlantic, the ship would sail past the Cape Verde Islands to Rio de Janeiro and around the Cape. They would then avoid the difficult trip overland across the isthmus. Although the voyage would take an estimated nine months, once they reached the goldfields their fortunes would be made.

Giving Peter an extra-large smile charged with the relief she felt, she realized she'd been waiting to tell Molly about California until she was sure she wasn't carrying Keane's child. That information had come this morning with her menses. She placed a gentle kiss on Peter's forehead. "You're the only babe I need, darling boy." Now she could forget about Keane and recapture her dreams of Amberose.

Stepping down from his carriage, Jason examined the whitewashed wooden house surrounded by walnut trees. Chickens pecked at the dry ground near a small vegetable garden, while a woman with her back to him was hanging laundry on a piece of twine stretched between the house and a large sycamore. He stared, surprised by the impoverished surroundings. With a twinge of conscience, he realized Miss MacClure's despicable acts could be motivated by more than simple greed. He quickly added five thousand dollars to the amount he'd determined to offer her, then stepped forward down the dirt path leading to the cottage entrance.

As he approached the sadly sagging porch, a small breeze carried the sounds of a hauntingly familiar melody. Jason stopped. Listening carefully, his body rigidly alert, he followed the soft humming to the side of the house where he'd seen the woman hanging the laundry. Looking at her more closely now as she bent to retrieve white rectangular cloths to hang over the twine, Jason felt a constricting pain in his heart. The ebony curls about her small stooped shoulders were achingly familiar, as was the gentle curve of her back, now swathed in a simple muslin dress trailing apron strings.

The color of the dress was blue. He'd always liked her best in blue. It matched her incredibly beautiful eyes.

"Molly."

When she heard the soft, resonant voice, Molly experienced a tightening thrill of recognition mixed with a curious sense of inevitability. She'd been waiting for this meeting, dreaming about it by night, fantasizing about it during the day.

So Jason had finally come.

She dropped the diaper she held and whirled around. A feeling of lightness blossomed within her. If she could have but one wish, it would be to stay with him, to be able to see him and feel his touch every day. But not as his mistress. *Not like Mother.*

He hadn't changed. His inky curls still refused to be tamed by hair tonic, and his clothes, a black jacket, buff pants, and striped waistcoat, displayed his conservative but fashionable bent. Despite the draping skirt of his coat, the jacket did little to disguise his powerful build, and his average height still towered over her five-foot-one-inch frame.

Molly stared up into his dark eyes, eyes that openly displayed love, and wondered with amazement how she'd ever found the strength to turn her back on that love almost two years ago. Wiping her hands on her apron, she stepped to him hesitantly. "Hello, Jason."

"My God, Molly." Jason enfolded her into his arms, hugging her to him. The feel of her body pressed against his was wonderful. He'd never quite given up on her. In his most secret dreams, they'd meet like this—as if nothing had changed, and time and separation were minor irritants that did not affect the great sense of belonging they'd always shared.

Jason continued to hold her wrapped in his arms, unwilling to release Molly and face the many difficulties her presence here posed. But being a man of logic, he finally pushed her away. "Why, Molly?"

"Oh, Jason, I canna explain."

"Under the circumstances, I believe an explanation is warranted."

Molly took in Jason's hardened features. So it had begun already. The touching moment of reunion was over and now the recriminations and bitterness would begin. This was precisely what she'd tried to avoid when she ran out into the night, leaving Jason and the magnificent sapphire necklace in the warm bed without her.

"I dinna think t'would do any good." She shrugged helplessly. " 'Tis best to leave things be. Just leave us—me alone." She turned to the cabin.

"Oh, no, you don't." Jason whipped her around to face him. "Running away is just too blasted easy. Answer me!"

She stared into his uncompromising eyes. Jason was so logical. An admirable trait for an attorney, surely. Yet the feelings she had about her mother could not be explained on the basis of logic. To someone who'd lived the pampered life of a Carter, Jason's offer of protection was more than generous.

As for love, she believed Jason loved her. But he had his prejudices; someone as socially important as Jason Carter could hardly marry an Irish street-urchin-turned-seamstress. Especially one who was the bastard daughter of an earl.

She furrowed her brow, thinking of how to answer his question most simply. Why had she left him and the security he'd offered? "Jason," she said softly. "What ye offered . . . it . . . it wasna enough." Seeing no reason to explain the more complicated aspects, she pivoted away, turning her back on his cold stare.

"I would have given you anything!" he called after her.

Molly stopped. "Oh, yes. Ye were generous with yer money."

Jason came up behind her. "No, Molly. I offered more than that." Placing his hands on her shoulders, he whispered, "I offered love."

Molly felt something die inside her. Would it ever register in that aristocratic brain of his—even that wasn't enough? What she'd wanted was marriage! But the thought of a Carter marrying so far beneath him could never occur to Jason.

"Didn't you realize how much I loved you, Molly?" he continued softly. "I told you often enough. At my hotel, on the picnics, in our bed at the cottage." He leaned over her shoulder, brushing his lips across the exposed skin of her neck, and she shivered in response. "You could have gotten anything, *anything* you wanted. Didn't you realize that? Somehow, you never struck me as naïve." He turned her to face him, and she saw his lips were curled, not with affection but with disdain. "Did you think I couldn't afford you? Well, you're wrong. There are very few things I can't afford."

"Ye can't buy *me!*" Molly pushed Jason away, her eyes shining with unshed tears.

The sounds of a baby's crying rent the air. She felt a cold explosion of dread in her stomach.

As if Molly's fears had summoned them, Esmeralda walked out the door carrying a red-faced Peter, screaming for his mother.

"I'm sorry Molly. Peter slipped and hit his head on the floor. . . ." Esmeralda's voice faded away when she saw Molly and Jason at the base of the steps.

The boy's increasing cries jarred Molly into action. Taking her distressed child into her arms, she cooed soft sounds while stroking his back and kissing the red mark on his forehead. Peter instantly quieted and began pulling on his hair, a gesture that signaled he was tired and ready for his morning nap.

"May I hold him?"

At Jason's question, Molly met the coal dark eyes she'd been avoiding. His face betrayed absolutely no expression as he lifted his son out of her arms. He held the boy gently, and Peter, surprisingly, did not resume his crying. Jason continued to stare down into the sleepy face, watching Peter suck on his fingers. Molly felt something stick uncomfortably in her throat at the sight of the two of them together.

"I presume he's approximately eleven months old?"

She could almost see the wheels turning: the attorney taking the facts and coming to the logical conclusion. A sudden fear clawed her heart and she wanted to snatch Peter from Jason's arms and run into the house—but she simply nodded.

As if sensing his mother's anxiety, Peter began to cry again. Jason attempted to comfort him by rocking the boy in his arms as he'd seen Molly doing.

"I'll take the bairn back." Molly held out her hands, but Jason continued to hold him. "Please, Jason, give him to me."

Jason expression was stubborn, like a man determined for a fight. "You can't keep him from me, you know."

When the child's cries turned louder, Esmeralda watched stunned as Molly just stood there, letting that man bully her. What was the matter with her? Didn't she know they could lose Peter? How could she let that man intimidate her?

Pushing her stunned friend aside, Esmeralda confronted Jason. They were almost of a height, but facing the man's brooding stare she could gather little assurance from that fact. She took a deep breath. "Mr. Carter, as you are not familiar with Peter's schedule, you would not know it is now time for his nap. If you please?" Esmeralda grabbed the wailing infant from Jason's arms and marched back into the house without another word. The door closed with a resounding slam.

Jason moved forward, intending to follow Esmeralda into the house, but the touch of Molly's hand at his elbow stopped him.

"Jason," she begged.

The pleading look marring her lovely blue eyes drained Jason's anger. Despite the startling sight of his child, he could not help his deep love for Molly. He couldn't smother the desire to comfort her and wipe away her fearful expression. So instead of going after his son, as he knew he should, he opened his arms to her. When she flew into his grasp and wept quietly on the sleeve of his coat, he felt something loosen its grip around his heart, and he swallowed his planned threats for paternity.

With his chin resting on top of her silky curls, he stroked Molly's back. "Why didn't you tell me?"

"Arrah, I tried," she cried into his coat. "I even came to Cincinnati to give'm to ye." Then, pulling away, she gazed up at him. "But after he was born, I wanted to keep the bairn. And I was afraid . . . afraid ye'd want him, too, and keep him from me."

Jason swept her back into the niche of his arms. So she'd been afraid he'd do exactly what he'd almost threatened: take Peter away from her. His son was a beautiful child—a big, strong boy, with the Carter brown eyes and black hair. He wanted him with an intensity he didn't know he could experience. But he also wanted the boy's mother.

"We have some serious discussing to do, Molly." He felt her tense in his arms and took pity on her. "But not today. I . . . I need to think." Holding her gently at the shoulders, he drew away from her. "I'll send a carriage for you. Soon."

Molly nodded, examining her apron to avoid meeting his eyes, but Jason tilted up her chin with his hand, forcing her to face him. For a moment, he stared at her with that same loving look he'd had before seeing Peter. Then he bent down and lightly brushed his lips against hers. Molly felt the gentle comfort of his touch as well as a flutter of excitement.

When he pulled away, Molly opened her eyes. Her gaze met his—he stared like a man starved for the sight of her. Stepping aside silently, he turned back to the carriage waiting on the dirt path, and Molly bit her lip to keep herself from calling him back. As if hearing her soundless cry, he stopped. Turning back to face her, he looked both tender and commanding, and she felt a deep longing to rush into his arms. But when he spoke, her longing froze to dread.

"When the carriage comes," he called back to her. "Be sure to bring Peter."

Chapter Fifteen

Esmeralda paced in front of the hearth, chewing on each nail with the concentration she used when pinking their most costly panne velvet. As she marched up and down the span of their small kitchen area, she agonized about what had happened. It was her fault Jason Carter had seen Peter. He'd probably come to the cottage to berate her about Henry. If only she hadn't gone outside with Peter in her arms!

At the first sound of the door opening, she rushed forward, only to step aside as Molly plowed through with a large basket of laundry perched in her arms. Tears bordered her eyes.

"Oh, Molly, I'm so sorry."

" 'Tis all right, Esme. I'm glad he came. In a way, I always knew he would. Now 'tis done and over with. I'll not be worrin' about it anymore." Placing the laundry basket on the kitchen table, she began folding the sun-dried sheets and diapers.

Esmeralda stared at Molly. She was folding sheets? Now? Well, perhaps her meeting with Jason had been so traumatic that she needed to do something by rote, something so effortless it took no concentration.

Picking up some clothes and folding them alongside Molly, Esmeralda slanted a glance at her friend. Despite the fact that her eyes were red and swollen, Molly seemed undisturbed—too quiet, almost docile . . . or was it resigned?

"What are you going to do about Jason?" Esmeralda asked softly.

Molly stopped folding and took a deep breath. "Nothing for now. He'll be sending a coach for us when he's ready."

"And you're going? Just like that?"

"Ochone, what choice have I?"

Molly gathered the folded laundry and set it on a chair beside the entrance. Esmeralda followed in her wake.

"Molly, you can't! For all you know, he could forcibly kidnap Peter and then you'd never see him again."

"Jason's not like that, Esme. He'd not steal his son."

"How can you be so sure?"

Molly turned to stare at Esmeralda as if she had grown a second head. "Bless us an' save us, would ye stop worrin'? Nothing's going to happen to the tyke."

Esmeralda stopped where she was, stunned. Why did Molly sound so annoyed with her? It was Jason Carter who was the problem. Quietly she watched Molly return to the table and continue folding clothes. She felt sick. She was supposed to be comforting Molly, the way Molly consoled her the past three days, not making Molly angry. Walking to the table, Esmeralda asked hesitantly, "You don't still love him, do you?"

Molly smoothed out a folded diaper and heaved a deep sigh. "Of course, I still love him. I'll always love Jason."

Her words sheared through Esmeralda's heart. She stared as Molly finished folding the clothes, making no attempt to help. If Molly still loved Jason Carter, didn't that make her vulnerable? Wouldn't he take advantage of her love and take Peter from them? She had to do something to save Molly from her own weakness! But what? Then she remembered the *Eureka*.

"Molly," she began excitedly, "I know a way to make sure that the Carters can't take Peter away from us." She grabbed the diaper Molly was folding and turned her away from the table. "Yesterday, when I was in town, I saw a poster for a ship going to California. It's leaving directly from Cleveland. Just think, Molly, the goldfields! Why, I understand you just go out and pick the gold off the ground, it's so easy. We could make millions! And Jason wouldn't follow you to California. Of course, the trip takes nine months, and the ship's not leaving until the end of the summer, but we could go to Cleveland and wait there. We could pack tonight—"

"Esme, I can't take Peter to the goldfields."

"But you can! The ship is going down the St. Lawrence to the Atlantic. It's perfectly safe. And all we need is money for the passage. Once we get there, our fortunes will be made!"

"I'll not be goin' to California," Molly insisted. Briskly she turned back to the laundry and piled the clothes into the basket. "I'll just have to take the chance that Jason will be fair about Peter."

"No, Molly. Don't do that! Please, listen to me."

Esmeralda grabbed Molly's hand, but Molly had finally lost her patience. She slapped Esmeralda's hand away. "I canna leave now! Not when I just found him!"

"But that's the problem, Molly. Don't you see? You love him. He'll use that against you!" And when Molly just stared at her, she continued, "It's because you love him that we have to escape. Otherwise he'll take advantage of you. He'll betray you."

Molly stared at Esmeralda. For the first time since they had known each other, Molly realized just how hurt Esme had been by her cousin. The poor bairn couldn't trust anyone. Silently she cursed the man to eternal damnation. As she took in Esmeralda's anxious expression, Molly's eyes softened. "Esme, me darling. Not everyone ye love betrays ye."

Esmeralda felt as if her throat were clogged with cotton wool. She couldn't make Molly understand. She was too blinded by her love for Jason to realize how he'd hurt her. "Have you forgotten what Jason Carter has done to you, Molly?" she sputtered. "How he only wanted you as his mistress? Now, he sees Peter, and how handsome he is, and Jason will do anything—say anything—to get him."

Molly shook her head sadly. "No, Esme. I don't believe that. Jason will be fair."

"He won't be," Esmeralda cried. "They never are. They pretend to love you, until you care so much you'll do anything for them. And when you're most vulnerable, when you look like you did outside, with your love glowing on your face, looking like you'd trust him with your life, that's when they strike. Molly, you can't take that chance!"

"Arrah, Esme, I can't afford not to." Gently taking Esmeralda's hand, she explained, "I ran away before, and what did it get me?" She smiled wistfully. "Oh sure, ye and I had dreams, lovely dreams that I wish I could make come true. But dreams dinna pay the rent—and the real world's not so nice. We barely have enough to eat! Look at ye." Molly shook the hand she held and wrapped her fingers around the slim wrist. "Skinny as a rail, ye be. And when we can't pay the rent, where are we then, me girl? Out on the street is what. I got to take me chances with Jason. If I don't gamble and trust him, then I've really lost. I can't be too scared to give him a chance. Do you understand? Maybe he'll never care enough to marry me. But he might care enough to love me and Peter, and help me make a better life for the bairn."

Esmeralda shook her head, trying to negate what Molly

was saying. She stared at her friend, an astonished look on her face. "You're not coming with me are you?"

"No, *mavourneen*. I canna."

"And if that scoundrel asks you to be his mistress, you're going to say yes, aren't you?"

"I don't know."

Esmeralda's heart skipped a beat. She'd thrown her question out as a challenge, to show Molly just how ridiculous her trust in Jason Carter was. But instead of realizing her error, Molly had admitted she might possibly leave to become Jason's mistress. Leave—just as Esmeralda's parents and Allen had left her. Molly was the only person she had trusted completely after Allen. And now Molly was going to betray her, too.

"It's a mistake, Molly. You'll see it's a mistake. I just pray it won't cost you Peter." Esmeralda swallowed a last plea to Molly. If this was how she wanted things, so be it. "I plan to be on that ship. It's not leaving until September. That should give us plenty of time to try and find someone to take over our lease at the shop. I only want enough money for the passage. The rest of it is yours and Peter's."

"Esme, don't do this. I don't want ye to leave. I'm sure Jason and I will work out some arrangement so that we can still be together. What will Peter and I do without ye?"

Esmeralda looked at Molly, trying to control her hurt and anger. "If you ever need me, you'll know where to find me . . . but I have to follow my own dreams. I have to get enough money to win back Amberose. I thought . . . I . . . thought we'd do that together." Esmeralda shook her head. "It doesn't matter. We won't lose touch, really we won't. And we have all summer to make plans."

"All right, Esme," Molly conceded. "If that's what ye want."

"I want . . . yes, that's what I want."

But when Molly tried to hug her friend for reassurance,

Esmeralda pulled away. "I brought some work home from the shop. I better get to it."

Esmeralda turned to the back of the room to retrieve her travel bag, ignoring the queasy, uneasy feeling in her stomach.

Jason slammed open the parlor door with the palm of his hand. Both of his parents stopped what they were doing, stunned. In the five years he'd served as head of Carter Shipping, Jason Carter had never come home in the middle of the day.

"I need to speak with both of you. As soon as possible. I'll be waiting in my study." Without a second look at either Derek or Samantha Carter, he turned and left the room.

The tatting shuttle slipped from Samantha's fingers and she looked to her husband.

Derek answered her silent question. "Whatever it is, it must be important."

Jason took the stairs two at a time. To think he'd gone to the cottage to solve Keane's problems! How the hell was he going to explain an illegitimate child? He'd always been so careful—he never thought . . . damn and blast! At the top of the stairs, he whipped around the newel-post and headed for his study. Once inside, he began to pace.

He'd spent the last two hours driving around in his carriage, thinking about what he should do. But the easiest solution had been the most abhorrent. He'd never kept a mistress, and he had no intention of demeaning Molly—and his son—by forcing that status on her. There must be some way to keep them near him, some way to have access to them without causing a scandal.

Marriage? Could he possibly marry Molly? In the lonely years since Charleston, he'd come to believe he'd made a mistake not offering marriage to her then. But now, he wasn't so sure. Her association with Miss Mac-Clure could mean any number of unsavory things. Maybe

Molly had intended to blackmail him or maybe this attempt to extract money from him through his brother was some sort of distorted revenge? Could he marry a woman capable of such double-dealing?

Jason stopped pacing long enough to pour himself a bourbon and swallow two mouthfuls. One thing kept him from believing her capable of such actions. The necklace. That necklace of sapphires was worth a small fortune, and she'd left it behind. No, Molly wasn't vicious or conniving. He believed her—she'd come to Cincinnati intending to tell him about Peter, but had shied away when she thought she might lose her son to his father. Wasn't that just like Molly? Trust no one, run away, and do for yourself. But that didn't explain Miss MacClure's interest in Henry.

When his parents walked in a few moments later, Jason was no more prepared to reveal Molly's and Peter's existence than he'd been two hours before. Yet he knew it was something he could not possibly keep from them.

"Please, sit down." He pointed to two Biedermeier chairs near the fireplace. After they seated themselves hesitantly, he turned to their expectant faces. But no words were forthcoming.

"Jason, darling, what's wrong?" Samantha's voice broke through the agonizing silence.

"I . . . I don't know how to tell you."

Watching the bewildered and tense expression that marred her son's handsome face, Samantha felt her pulse pound against her temples. "Darling, don't frighten me so. Please, just tell us what's wrong."

Jason sighed, then slumped against the chair of his desk. Taking a second to compose himself, he turned the chair to face his parents and sat down. Elbows resting on his knees, he leaned forward and played with the whiskey glass he held in his hands. Then he softly placed the glass on the table behind him and focused his attention on the concerned couple before him. "I have a child . . . a son.

His name is Peter. He lives with his mother just outside of town. In Walnut Hills."

Derek Carter bellowed, "A bastard—"

"—A grandson!" Samantha Carter gasped.

"My God, how could you—"

"When can we see him?" Samantha interrupted her husband. "And the mother, of course. We'll want to meet her as well. Do you think tomorrow would—"

"Samantha, will you shut up!" Samantha stopped her rambling. Derek's eyes remained riveted on his son. "How could you keep this from us?"

"I didn't know. I found out today."

A bit mollified, Derek sat back. "What are you going to do about this . . . this situation?"

"Don't you dare refer to our grandchild as a 'situation'!" Samantha could no longer hold her tongue.

"But, Sam, the child is illegitimate."

"We are not living in the *damn* Middle Ages." She paused, letting her scandalous use of her husband and son's favorite curse word sink in. Now she had their attention! "Illegitimate or not, that is my grandchild. Carter blood flows through his veins just as thick and red as it does in yours, Derek."

"I agree the boy is our responsibility. We'll have to make sure he and his mother are taken care of." The latter part of Derek's statement was directed to Jason.

"And made a *legitimate* part of this family," Samantha added.

Jason held up his hands, silencing the two before his father and mother could continue their argument. He hadn't asked them here for advice; he'd merely intended to apprise them of the facts. "I haven't decided what *I'm* going to do."

"If you ask my opinion," Derek said, "it's quite clear what you *should* do. I have friends in Virginia. I'm sure I could arrange something for the child and his mother there."

"Oh, no, Derek. How could you even think it, just to send them away like that?" Samantha asked, stunned at her husband's callousness. "And Virginia. Why, that's clear across the country."

"It's a simple matter of—"

"Father, Mother, please!" Jason's shout blocked Derek's defensive tirade. "I'm not going to send them away." His voice dropped to barely above a whisper. "I just found them."

The simple statement silenced both parents. The pain in Jason's eyes and his uncharacteristic expression of confusion made them reevaluate their positions.

Derek rose and walked over to his son. Patting Jason on the back, Derek tamped down his opinions with difficulty. "Of course, you'll do what you must, son. But please, think about what I've said. This could be the most crucial decision of your life. You're an important man here, Jason. People look up to you. Think about that and your family—then I know you'll do what's right."

Samantha joined her husband. She touched Jason's sleeve lightly. "How old is he? What's he look like?"

Jason smiled tightly; his throat choked up for a moment forcing him to pause. "Peter is almost a year old . . . and he"—Jason's eyes met his mother's in a look of bittersweet pride—"he looks like me."

Samantha nodded. "I knew he would."

Samantha peeked out past the bedroom door. The hall was empty. Only the soft hiss of the gaslight sconces broke the silence. Pulling the cowl of her cape over her head, she slipped out of the room and headed for the stairs. She was late. But Derek had taken an inordinate amount of time to fall asleep.

She smiled a secretive smile when she thought about her husband, happily snoring in their warm bed. They'd both shared the hurt and excitement they'd felt at the discovery of Jason's son. Their grandchild. And while

Derek was still stubbornly insisting it was best to send the boy away, she knew he'd come around to her way of thinking eventually. He always did. She just had to make him understand that the rhetoric he'd been spouting to Jason that afternoon was just moralistic poppycock. Bastard indeed. As if some quirk of fate could wipe out her grandchild's rights! Well, not while she lived and breathed would such a thing happen.

Hearing Jason's door open down the hall, she quickly ducked back inside the bedroom and waited. She held the door open a crack and watched as a servant walked past carrying an empty decanter. So Jason was still drinking. She frowned. Pulling off her cloak, she set it on a chair beside the door and slipped into the hall. The Coffins would have to wait. Jason needed her now.

She paused at the door to think. It was not as if this meeting were crucial, she thought in justification of her delay. There would be no black slaves newly arrived from across the river to freedom, in need of clothes, warm food, and comforting words tonight. She had no intention of missing even one of the abolitionist meetings she'd been attending faithfully for the past year; she would just be a bit late.

Samantha's heart pounded against her rib cage in the way it did when she made her midnight treks to Mr. Coffin's store at Sixth and Elm. While her activity as a supporter of the women's suffrage movement was tolerated by her family and friends, her involvement with abolitionists would never be. She was in a precarious position, a situation shared by many of Cincinnati's citizens. She lived on free soil, in a city separated by a thin strip of water from Kentucky, a slave state. And while Cincinnati was a city of idealism and humanitarianism, it derived its lifeblood from trade with the South. Carter Shipping was an integral part of that trade. Giving substantial amounts of money to those seeking to help black slaves to freedom was the only way Samantha had found to assuage her guilt for living off the fruits of slavery. But her activities were dangerous and she lived in constant fear of discovery.

Taking a deep breath to calm her racing heart, she slipped into the hallway and headed toward Jason's study. Her soft tap at his door elicited a gravelly response to enter. When she swung the door open, she smiled at the sight of her son seated by the fireplace. His red-rimmed eyes peered at her from beneath drooping eyelids—it was clear that he'd been drinking steadily. Still, he wore his coat and tie as fastidiously and correctly as ever.

Samantha shut the door softly behind her. "You're going to make yourself ill, drinking like that."

Jason held up his glass and examined the amber liquid as if he'd just now thought of that possibility. "God, I hope so." He gulped down another swallow of bourbon, thinking happily that no one in his house would dare water *his* liquor.

Samantha clucked her disappointment and gracefully slipped beside Jason. Removing his glass from his numbed fingers, she set it on his desk before taking a firm hold of his arm and helping him to his feet. "Time for bed now, darling."

"I might say the same for you, madame."

"A mother never rests while her children are in turmoil, Jason." She guided him to the door and out into the hall.

Now that he was moving, Jason realized his mother was right: He felt sick as a horse. He smiled. He'd rather concentrate on physical pain. He'd sought to stop the twists and turns of his mind as he imagined the agonizing scenarios of alternately losing and gaining Molly and his son. "I think you're right. It's time I get some rest." Pushing his mother's hands aside, he straightened. "Thank you, Mother. I think I know my way." But Jason's first step sent the hall reeling and he had to lean against the wall and wait for the topsy-turvy view to settle.

Samantha stifled a laugh. "I'm sure you do, darling. But it's been so long since I've been able to tuck you or your brother in." Again taking hold of his arm, they walked together to Jason's bedchamber. "Indulge me, please?"

Thankful for the steadying hand, but never willing to admit it, Jason grumbled, "Well, if you insist."

"Yes, darling. I insist."

Just outside his door, Jason stopped abruptly. He turned to face Samantha and almost fell in the process. Once he'd straightened, he asked, "Why are you still up, Mother? Not planning to hang any shoes on Mary Dicker's doorknob, are you?"

"Not tonight, dear." Samantha smiled.

"Good."

Once she'd guided him inside, Samantha helped Jason with his coat and tie. When she tried to take off his shirt, he stopped her. "Please, Mother," he said gravely. "I can do the rest myself."

Samantha sat on the bed next to her son. With a gentle hand she brushed aside Jason's black curls. Her normally impervious child looked more vulnerable than she'd ever seen him. Right now he reminded her of the quiet, serious boy she'd so proudly watched grow into manhood. Samantha sighed. "Does it hurt terribly, darling?"

Jason winced. "My head does feel like a mallet is pounding on it."

She smiled sadly. "That's not the hurt I'm talking about."

Jason met his mother's understanding gaze. "It hurts like hell."

"Do you love her so very much?"

Jason stared up at the ceiling for a moment, as if trying to compose himself. "Yes."

"You know, Jason," she continued to stroke his head, as if he were her boy of ten or twelve seeking comfort. "I've always felt that you've been waiting for someone special. And I was afraid you'd never find her. You're so very demanding." Taking his face in her hands, she said, "You've found her, haven't you?"

Jason looked down to his lap. After a moment, he nodded.

"Do I know her?"

"Possibly. She was designing dresses in Charleston when I met her. Now she lives with Miss MacClure. I imagine she's involved in the dressmaking business."

"Molly Egan?" Samantha gasped. And when Jason started at the name, she explained, "She's a very talented designer. I tried on several occasions to meet with her and order a gown, but she always refused. She claimed she was too busy. I found her attitude strange because the shop was so often empty."

Jason's lips formed a tight line. "I don't imagine she wanted to be too involved with our family—in case I might recognize her before Miss MacClure got her clutches on Henry."

"Oh, Jason, no. You don't think . . . ?"

"I don't know, Mother." Jason raked his fingers through his hair, shaking his head. "I don't know."

Samantha stared at her son. "But you still love her, don't you?"

With an agonized sigh, he answered, "Yes. I can't seem to help that."

Samantha patted his hand comfortingly, coming to a decision in her own mind. "Follow your instincts, Jason. They've always served you well in the past."

Jason shook his head sadly. "Not this time. I've always worked by logic. What I feel isn't logical."

Samantha stood briskly, anxious to get her plan started. "What you need is some rest, dear. Things will look clearer on the morrow. I'll send Albert to help you." Leaning forward, she kissed Jason's forehead. "Sleep now, darling. Things will turn out for the best. You'll see."

Jason appeared startled at her tone. "You're not to do anything, Mother! I don't want you involved in this."

She looked hurt for a moment, then said firmly, "You can trust me, Jason."

Jason looked a bit sheepish. "Thank you, Mother. I didn't mean to jump at you. It's just that I need to solve this for myself."

"I understand, dear. Now you lie back and I'll get Albert."

After returning from the third floor, where the servants slept, Samantha found her way back to Jason's study. Opening the top drawer to the large Biedermeier-style desk, she withdrew a creamy piece of stationery with Jason's name engraved on it. Lifting the sheet and slipping it into the large pocket of her skirt, she smiled.

Chapter Sixteen

Molly clutched the thick cream paper to her chest. Her hands were shaking. So soon? She'd hoped for more time to adjust—to think and plan. Taking a deep breath, she opened the missive.

Dark bold lines slashed across the single page. Following each word with her eyes, she sounded out the syllables the way Esmeralda had taught her, unconsciously mouthing the words. She stopped. Her heart doubled its beat. Could she be mistaken? She reread the confusing message, saying the words out loud to confirm her interpretation of the black ink lines.

"Esme!" she shouted. "Esme, come here!" Ignoring her own command, Molly rushed to the hearth, stumbling up to where her friend sat. Before Esmeralda could put down the two thin pieces of crepe she was sewing together, Molly shoved the stationery under her nose. "Am I readin' it right?"

"You know how to read just fine."

"Sure it can't be sayin' he wants me to meet his mother?"

Esmeralda set aside the piping she was sewing and took the paper from Molly's hand. Could it possibly be true? She read the bold script quickly and the burning coil in her stomach tightened with each word. Her eyes cool and distant, she met Molly's excited expression. "That's what it says."

"The blighter's cracked his wits." Molly grabbed the letter from Esmeralda and peered suspiciously at the message. When she'd reread the paper, she looked up with saucer-wide eyes. "He's been touched by the good people, he has."

Esmeralda could see by Molly's beaming smile that she was happy despite her words. Even though her own heart felt as heavy as lead when she thought of Molly with Jason Carter, Esmeralda forced a grin. "Why should you think him crazy? It's about time the man showed you some respect."

"Respect? To an Irish bastard who bore his child out of wedlock? I'll not be believing 'tis so."

Esmeralda rose from the rocker. "Believe it." Heading for the cedar chest in the corner of the room, she said reprovingly, "And you'd better stop wasting time ogling that note and start thinking about more practical things, like what to wear. The letter says he's sending the coach for you this afternoon. If you're going to meet the matriarch of the family, you should look your best." Esmeralda didn't want the Carters looking down their noses at Molly.

" 'Tis impossible," Molly whispered, still staring at the missive. " 'Tis beyond anything in me dreams. Jason, wantin' me and the bairn to meet his mother—" She clamped a hand over her mouth, stifling a gasp. "I canna go."

Esmeralda barely heard Molly from where she knelt, digging through the musty old clothes that filled the cedar chest. Finally she brought up a sapphire blue frock. "It's a bit worn, but it will look splendid with your complexion. See, Molly?" Esmeralda held up the gown. "It matches your eyes."

In a daze, Molly marched up and snatched the dress from her companion, flinging it back into the chest. "Did ye not hear me? I canna go!"

Esmeralda's heart thrilled at Molly's words. Had Molly changed her mind about Jason Carter? But then she saw her friend's look of total dejection. Molly wouldn't be happy without Jason, not now. "Nonsense," Esmeralda said with enthusiasm she didn't feel. "He wants you to meet his family. Do you know what that means? He cannot possibly intend to make you his mistress."

"Listen to me. I'll not be embarassin' Jason in front of his kin."

Esmeralda blinked her moss-colored eyes. "Surely he's explained?"

"Bless us an' save us! You're not *listenin'* to me." But when Esmeralda failed to react, she shouted, "I talk like the poor Irish street girl that I am! My brogue. I'll be soundin' more like their maid than the mother of Jason's son. Not this gown, nor all the finery in town could make me acceptable to the Carters."

Esmeralda shook her head slowly. Taking Molly's hand, she led her back to the rocker and sat her down in it. "Being Irish is not a crime."

"It might as well be in this town," Molly grumbled.

"How can you say so? There's many distinguished Irish citizens here. Why Mr. Sinton and—"

"I *can* read. I've seen the help-wanted ads for 'Protestants only' and 'Irish not wanted.' "

Esmeralda sighed. "Well, if you think it's so important, Molly, just speak without your brogue. You know how to," she gently reminded. "I spent years teaching you. You just choose not to."

Molly's lips remained pursed in a tight line. Crossing

her arms over her chest, she stared into glowing embers in the fireplace. " 'Tis been too long. I havena practiced since we left Charleston. I'll not be rememberin' how 'tis done."

"You can. It's just a matter of concentration," Esmeralda coaxed. "Try, Molly. You'll see. It will all come back to you."

Molly fastened her eyes on her friend. Taking courage from Esmeralda's assuring smile, she wet her lips. "How do you do, madame. I come visitin' . . . I *have* come visit*ing* upon Mr. Carter's request." She spoke the words as if she'd swallowed an egg. Whole.

Esmeralda erupted into laughter and Molly vaulted to her feet.

"I'm sorry, Molly," Esmeralda managed between gasped chuckles. She pushed the outraged woman back into the rocker. "It's just that you say it so seriously." Seeing the mulish set of Molly's mouth, she sobered her tone. "I really am sorry. It wasn't funny at all. You spoke beautifully."

"Not the *sidhe* themselves will get me in that carriage."

"Then you've changed your mind? You're coming with me to the goldfields?"

Esmeralda held her breath. She watched Molly closely, her eyes pleading for her friend to say they'd stay together. But after a moment, Molly shook her head slowly.

Esmeralda sighed. "Fairies or not, Molly, we both know you'll be in that coach," she said, stoically pronouncing the death knell to their friendship. "How else will Peter ever have the opportunities his father's family can provide?" She forced herself to sound convincing. "I still think you'd be better off with me in California. But if it's a choice between leaving you here to be the man's mistress or his wife, it's the latter role I wish for you."

Walking back to the chest, Esmeralda picked up the sapphire gown and shook out the silk foulard. Smoothing the wrinkled material against her so Molly could see it, she said, "Well, shall we get started? We've quite a bit of work if you're going to be presentable in time."

Biting her lip, her eyes shining suspiciously with tears, Molly simply nodded.

Molly swallowed a lump of anxiety as she looked out the carriage window to the magnificent granite structure outside. The row of giant Corinthian columns forming the front portico ticked past like an immense picket fence. Stretching horizontally from the main Greek-revival facade, two wings sprawled across the lawn, taking up a good chunk of the block. A brick wall surrounded the Carter residence like the barricade to a fortress. Molly tightened her hold on Peter.

So Jason lived in a bloody mansion. Had she expected anything different?

Jason's message that she was to meet his mother had made her as nervous as a cat in a dog kennel. That day at the cottage, when he'd said he'd be sending a carriage for her, she'd never anticipated this. Faith! What could she say to Jason's mother? "Hello. How do you do? Allow me to introduce myself, Mrs. Carter. I'm the mother of your son's illegitimate child." Would a large smile and a warm handshake make up for the circumstances of Peter's birth?

Taking Peter in her arms, Molly straightened his collar for the third time. At least she and Peter looked nice. The sapphire foulard had ironed out nicely and the seven narrow flounces and Mechlin lace Esme had added made it appear almost fashionable. With Esmeralda's help, she'd curled her hair with hot tongs so that the short black tresses peeked stylishly out from under her bonnet. Peter wore a simple white shirt, short dark pants, and a jacket Esmeralda had made for his birthday. But Molly had given up on the matching cap. He threw it off as quickly as she put it on him. Frowning, she looked at his slobbery smile. If only he didn't drool so much! No hope there.

With two teeth coming in, the poor tyke was a bleedin' fountain.

Molly felt the carriage shake to a halt and the driver jump down. With the help of a footman she stepped out, still holding Peter in her arms. A young man in a uniform appeared at the gate, as if he'd been waiting for their arrival.

"This way, Miss Egan." He gestured down the long paved walk beyond the wrought iron gate. "May I take your bag?"

Handing the man the large sack with Peter's things and balancing her son on her hip, Molly's gaze followed the daffodil-lined walkway that ended at the shallow stone steps of the portico. When her eyes met the sight of the intricately carved oak double doors, she caught her breath. Was she really going inside this palace? Molly shifted Peter off her hip and set him down on the limestone pavement before the gate. Taking his small hand in hers, she began leading him down the bouldered path. It was slow going, but she needed the time to compose herself.

If Jason wanted his mother to meet her and their son, it meant he was ready to make them a legitimate part of his life. Esmeralda was right—Jason would never ask Molly to be his mistress after she met his mother. Still, she could not believe it was so. She was a poor Irish girl, and Jason, he was one of Cincinnati's most important citizens. Dare she think, even dream . . . ?

Lord help her, but she'd regretted leaving him that night in Charleston. The past years had been unbearably difficult without him. But when she left Jason, she believed there was nothing worse than the fate of her mother —an aging mistress left behind after hardship had withered her beauty. And now, two years later, with their money situation so tight, she thought she would have to face that terrible choice: live as Jason's mistress and provide security for Peter, or keep her pride and face an uncertain future for her child. But no longer—her greatest hope was coming true. Molly took a deep breath, trying to control the joy threatening to burst her heart. Jason wanted her to meet his mother!

Before she could even raise the knocker at the door, a uniformed man she took to be the butler opened the wide doors and beckoned her in with a low bow. Stepping over the threshold, Molly felt her anxiety returning. She'd never seen such opulence! The floor of alternating gray and white marble slabs harmonized perfectly with the limestone walls. A basalt bust sat in the middle of the huge carved mantel over the fireplace. At the end of the entrance hall, to her left, stood a large staircase. A pair of tall Corinthian columns, reminiscent of the outside facade, bordered the base of the stairwell, topped by an arch depicting reclined figures. An intricately carved panel formed an oak screen from the archway to the ceiling.

The elaborate architecture allowed for only a minimum of furniture: two solid oak chairs with lion's heads roaring from the arms sat at each side of the fireplace, and in the middle of the room stood a highly polished table with a delicate china bowl centered on it. Above the table hung a bronze chandelier that echoed the carved designs of the oak paneling above the arched entrance to the staircase.

"The shipping business must be doing bloody well," she mumbled under her breath while continuing to gaze about the room with an awed expression.

"I'm sorry, miss. What did you say?"

Startled to find the butler at her elbow, Molly jumped. She clasped her hand to her pounding chest. "Nothing. I was just talkin' . . . talk*ing* to me—*my*self."

"This way, please." With a bored expression, the elderly man pointed to the arched door on the right of the fireplace. "Mrs. Carter is waiting for you in the White Salon."

Molly started at his words. Where was Jason? She'd

hoped he'd be there to greet her first. Just as she was about to turn and flee, the butler applied a slight pressure to her elbow and guided her through the door. Immediately, her heart started to thunder. She trod across the foyer locking Peter's hand in a death grip.

The door led to a spacious room with parquet floors. Velvet curtains of royal blue streamed down the pale blue walls from the ceiling to the floor. Molly waited silently as the uniformed man opened another door on the right and stood beside it patiently. Taking a deep breath, she marched through the opening.

The bright interior of the White Salon made a startling contrast to the darkened room outside. It took a moment to adjust to the sunny walls that reflected the light streaming through damask-draped windows. But once her eyes became accustomed to the light, she noticed a woman seated on one of two striped sofas. She was staring at Molly and Peter with intense interest.

Molly clutched Peter's hand tighter. *Molly Egan, you're about to pay for every sinful deed of your life.*

But the moment of imagined disapproval evaporated immediately when the woman rose gracefully from the sofa and extended her hands to Molly.

"Welcome, my dear." Tall, white-haired, and dressed in an elegant lime green tea gown, the distinguished woman glided across the plush carpet. "I'm Samantha Carter, Jason's mother. He has told us all about you. How terribly unfortunate he's waited so long to have you and Peter at our home."

Molly bobbed a curtsy, the way she'd always done when her father had deigned to visit. "How do you do, Mrs. Carter. I have come visiting—"

"Oh, please. Call me Samantha." The woman couldn't tear her eyes from Peter, who now struggled against Molly's grasp, eyeing the beautiful room like a pioneer ready to break new land.

Hanging on to Peter for dear life, Molly repeated her

rehearsed speech, "Thank you, Samantha. I have come visiting upon the—"

"And this must be Peter!" Samantha kneeled before the small boy. "I've waited a long time for you, young man. I'd say a good ten years too long!" She picked Peter up in her arms, her eyes moist with emotion. "He looks just like Jason did at his age."

Peter took one look at Samantha Carter and began to wail.

"Now hold on there, little sir. No crying for a Carter!" she admonished in a gentle tone. "Does my old face frighten you?" She offered Peter her thick gold chain with a lovely locket to distract him. Peter immediately stuffed the chain in his mouth.

"Peter!" Molly tried to extricate the costly jewelry from her son's grip, but Samantha Carter gently shooed her hands aside.

"Let the child be." Smiling at her grandchild, she continued, "How would you like a cookie? Grandmama had some made special for you. Can you say grandmama?"

Peter smiled and uttered some nonsensical sound, completely taken by all the attention he was receiving.

"Did you hear that?" Samantha looked at Molly with a besotted expression. "He said 'grandmama'!" Turning her attention back to Peter, she cooed, "You're such a very bright boy. Bensley, please," she said to the hovering butler. "A cookie for Master Peter." Taking Molly's hand with her free one, Samantha pulled her to one of the settees. She placed Peter on her lap as she sat down opposite Molly, letting him continue to play with the chain. "Now, do tell me all about yourself and the little one, dear." Samantha leaned forward, her attention now focused on Molly.

This was not how Molly had anticipated the afternoon. Horrified, she watched the butler bring forward a tray with tea and small iced cakes. Was she supposed to meet with Mrs. Carter by herself? "Where's—where *is* Jason?"

"Oh, he will be here in no time." Gathering Molly's discomfiture from her petrified expression, Samantha tried to put her at ease. "But let's talk about you, my dear." She placed a comforting hand on Molly's icy ones. "It must be terribly difficult to care for Peter by yourself."

A bit astonished by Samantha's genuine sympathy, Molly floundered. "It . . . it is difficult. Very difficult."

"And you've done a wonderful job; he's a fine boy. However did you manage?"

"Well, we had the shop . . . Esme and me—I mean, Miss MacClure and I run the dress shop on Pearl Street."

"But to be a mother and work at the same time. That shows a great deal of character."

"Thank you." *Can this woman possibly understand the hardship?* Molly wondered. Samantha Carter, who lived in this granite-and-marble castle—could she know what a struggle Molly's life had been? And yet, the look of empathy, of understanding, that shone from the woman's light brown eyes caused a raw ache in Molly's throat. She dipped her head down and focused on the butler's hand as he poured her tea.

Samantha picked up a cookie off the tray and handed it to Peter, but her eyes were still focused on Molly. "I believe if there were opportunities for women other than marriage, seamstressing, and . . . that other trade so many are forced into by hard times . . . society as a whole would be better served."

Molly looked up sharply. Hearing Samantha echo the very words she'd always said to Esme, Molly felt her jaw drop.

"So many wasted resources and talents." Samantha clucked. "To think that of the over four hundred medical students in Cincinnati not one is a woman. I refuse to believe those silly theories of Mr. Bly's or any other phrenologist who believes women are mentally inferior to men. Incapable of complex thought, indeed." She wagged her finger at Molly. "It's not a lack of intelligence that keeps young ladies out of such pursuits—it's a lack of opportunity. Don't you agree, my dear?"

"Why . . . why, yes!"

"Even the few who are educated are taught nothing of importance, the theory being that a woman of society should be idle . . . an ornament." She stopped, covering her mouth with her hand. "Oh, dear." Samantha chuckled. "I'm afraid I'm preaching again. Mustn't get me started."

"But I want to hear," Molly urged. "I agree with everything ye've said."

Samantha smiled warmly. "I thought you might."

For the next hour Molly sat listening to Samantha Carter with rapt fascination, enjoying herself thoroughly. Jason's mother was a marvelous person, full of wonderful ideas about women and their rights. As they discussed their similar philosophies about the women's suffrage movement, Samantha Carter interspersed questions about Peter and his first year of life. While Molly's nerves permitted only a few nibbles of one cake, and she let the tea sit in her cup without tasting it, within the first few minutes of their discussion she knew she liked Jason's mother tremendously—and that Samantha Carter in turn liked her.

Molly enchanted Samantha. Although Samantha seldom let herself think she could be wrong, this time she'd had her doubts. But not anymore. The petite woman seated on the settee opposite was not only beautiful, but intelligent—with solid ideas of her own, much in line with Samantha's own beliefs. And while she detected the lilting cadence of an Irish brogue, the woman's fine patrician features and delicate manners revealed she was not just a poor immigrant come to America seeking her fortune. She examined Molly's soft complexion, so pale it contrasted strikingly with her raven tresses and vibrant blue eyes. None could be more beautiful than the Black Irish, which Molly clearly was. And the delicate lines of her face were distinguished, almost aristocratic. Yes, Samantha could see why Jason had pursued Molly, and now loved her. She hugged her grandson to her; she'd done the right thing after all.

That was the last thought she had before Jason burst in the door.

"Mother, what's happened? What's the emergency?"

Jason stopped cold. Seated on the empire settee was his mother. Clutched protectively in her arms—his son.

"My God!"

"Jason, darling. You're home," Samantha said cheerfully. "Look who I've invited to visit."

Molly's heart sank at Samantha Carter's words. She stared at Jason and flinched when his menacing glare focused on her. "The note. It wasna from you." The words dropped like soft petals to the floor. "You didna ask me here?"

Seeing the effect Jason's presence had on the previously vivacious girl, Samantha Carter said soothingly, "I'm sure Jason would have . . . soon. I just tend to be a bit impatient. Isn't that right, Jason?"

"Impatient? That doesn't begin to explain . . . this is outrageous! You've really outdone yourself this time, Mother."

Jason stared at the beautiful sight Molly made. She looked gorgeous in the fine clothes. The vulnerable look on her face almost cooled the anger seething inside him—but not quite.

At Jason's steely voice, Molly gathered her reticule and extended her arms for Peter. The pleasant afternoon had turned bitter indeed. "Please, Mrs. Carter. If I may have Peter, I'll be takin' me leave now."

"Oh, no, my dear." Samantha held Peter protectively in her arms, out of Molly's reach. "You and Jason must talk."

"I'll not be staying where I'm not wanted."

"Sit down, Molly." Jason raked his hands through his jet hair. "This is between me and my mother."

Molly spun around to face Jason, the shame and disappointment she felt radiating from her. "Order me around, will ye, ye bloody blighter!" Her dark blue eyes shone, and her words choked in her throat. "I come here thinkin' . . . oh, what's the use." Swiping at her tears with the back of her hand, she stepped around the table to retrieve Peter. But Jason was beside her immediately, whipping her around to face him.

"What did you think? That I'd invited you here, after what you did?"

"Me?" Molly asked, straightening her shoulders. She'd be damned if she'd leave here looking the fool. "What did I do? It's what I did *not* do ye should consider, Jason, me love. 'Tis many a time I've thought of coming and dumpin' the tyke on yer door. It's a wonder I never made ye pay up, is what!" Molly screamed, while Samantha took a tentative step toward the door with Peter in her arms. "If he weren't such a fine bairn, I may have, too, and humiliated the lot of ye." Tears streamed down Molly's cheeks.

"But you didn't!" Jason bellowed. "Instead, you followed me to Cincinnati and skulked around Walnut Hills, waiting to pounce on me and my family." He paused, his features molded in a confused expression. "How could you keep Peter from me?"

During the wrenching scene, Molly and Jason remained oblivious to their son and his grandmother as Samantha handed Peter to the butler and shooed him out the door, stepping out behind him. It wasn't until he heard the key turning in the door that Jason noticed his mother had left the room.

Lunging at the portal, he turned the knob but found it locked. Jason pounded on the oak. "Open this blasted door!"

Samantha stood on the other side with a smile of victory. She tossed the key up in the air and caught it before shouting back, "Not until you guarantee I have a *legitimate* grandson."

"You can't do this!" Samantha heard the muffled shout through the thick door.

"I just have!" Pocketing the key triumphantly, Samantha Carter took her grandchild from the silent butler. "Come, Bensley. I believe Master Peter needs something more substantial than cookies."

Chapter Seventeen

Esmeralda leaned both elbows on the scarred and gouged surface of the worktable and carefully examined the hunting bonnet she'd just completed for Keane's sister. She turned the hat so that the life-size stuffed robin she'd spent twenty minutes carefully sewing to the hat's crown would face her. Thoughtfully tapping her chin with a forefinger, she wondered what was missing. The soft felt hat tapered to a point where she'd attached a row of multi-colored silk balls, all dangling at eye level. Three large orange bows cascaded down the back from the brim, contrasting nicely with the hat's pink band and chartreuse felt surface. Still, she wasn't quite satisfied with the effect. Something was definitely missing. Her eyes lit up when she saw a dark blue ribbon. Tying it into a rosette, she stitched the ribbon on top of the robin's head at what she thought a rakish angle. There—now the hat was ghastly enough!

Sighing, she leaned against the slats of the chair. She'd

come into town as a defense against the depressing hours
of waiting for Molly and Peter to return. But as usual,
business at the shop was less than diverting. To entertain
herself, she'd spent the afternoon plotting the makings of
a truly hideous hat. She'd planned each tasteless detail as
if Keane, and not his sister, were the intended recipient.
Now that it lay finished on the table before her, the satisfaction she'd felt in its planning fled.

Esmeralda pushed the hat aside in frustration. Keane
was like a deadly poison running through her veins and
seeping into her heart. Thoughts of him infiltrated her
dreams, her very soul. In her mind she raged at him,
screaming her insecurities, her fears about him and what
he made her feel. Their mock battles always ended with
passionate kisses, with his lips soothing the pain and lull-
ing her deeper into his power.

Love. She'd witnessed its effects on Molly. A strong
woman who had managed on her own for years by sheer
strength of will, Molly had crumbled like a dried biscuit
before the man she loved. It was an illness. And with
depressing certainty Esmeralda knew she could love
Keane. Why else would he have this control over her?
Why else did she reject his degrading offers of money
when she needed it so badly?

Looking into the lifeless glass eyes gazing at her from
atop the chapeau, she stuck her tongue out at the stuffed
bird. She felt terribly ill. Her head ached and her stomach
was none too settled. She should have stayed home. Pushing back her chair, she walked to the counter and retrieved the bottle of Brodie's Vegetable Specific. She'd
picked up the mixture at Brodie and Levy's Apothecary
Shop on Walnut and Third, hoping it would settle her
stomach. While it tasted vile, Mr. Brodie had said the
remedy never failed. "Always prompt and effective," he'd
stated proudly. "Had very favorable reports from the
cholera victims of '32 and the volunteers returning from
Mexico."

Esmeralda read the fine print on the bottle: "For diarrhea, dysentery, summer complaint, and cholera." Sighing, she pulled out the cork and swallowed another spoonful. So far, Brodie's Vegetable Specific hadn't helped either her uneasy stomach or the ache in her heart.

After returning the spoon and bottle to her bag, she glanced at the enamel clock on top of the shelves by the back room. If she hurried, she could still catch the omnibus back to Walnut Hills. Gathering her shawl and hat, she locked the door behind her and stepped into the muggy heat of the late afternoon. Out of force of habit, she turned to her right and headed toward Race Street. When she realized what she'd done, she did an about-face down Pearl to Main, avoiding her usual route by the Burnet House—that was no longer a place of interest to her. Turning on Main where Dodd's five-story building advertised in giant letters: UMBRELLAS, FANCY FURS, AND HATS, at the juncture of each story, she waved at the proprietor inside the store. Last week, she'd bought some of the materials for the hunting cap at William Dodd & Co. She smiled absently at the helpful Mr. Dodd as she passed the shop, thinking about what she'd read in the *Cincinnati Commercial* that morning.

The brig *Eureka* would sail on the fifteenth of September, having obtained the requisite permission from the British Government to pass through the St. Lawrence to the Atlantic. Although the advertisement suggested this was the safest and cheapest route to the gold diggings, and a rare chance to make a large fortune, Esmeralda lacked the two hundred dollars needed for cabin fare. The agent she'd seen at the public landing had suggested that credit was available with approved security, but she had no security. She owned nothing. More disturbing was the agent's announcement that passage was almost booked. She fleetingly wondered if Keane would pay two hundred dollars for a hunting bonnet.

Picking up her pace, she hurried toward Sycamore

Street, where she'd wait for the Walnut Hills omnibus, a yellow horse-drawn carriage affectionately named "The Rose." Esmeralda held her hand cradled against her stomach, no longer able to ignore the queasy feeling. By Fourth Street, her stomach began to cramp. Dropping her travel bag, she clutched her abdomen and waited for the pain to ease.

Keane gave the cab driver the address for the Pearl Street dress shop. Hoping that Esmeralda had come to her senses, he'd stopped by the shop once a day for the past three days—only to find the drapes drawn and the front door locked. He sighed in frustration as he stared out the carriage window and watched the grand buildings on Main Street drift by. Cincinnati was truly an elegant town. The seven hills overlooking it led to the eventual comparison to another grandiose city, Rome—although no one could seem to agree which of the many hills bordering Cincinnati actually made up the seven. It was indeed a great city, but he was ready to return to England. He'd decided not to buy the tract of land on Mount Auburn, despite Jason's recommendation about its potential for grapes. As soon as he settled things with Esmeralda, he planned to go back to the Eldridge estates. His solicitor was very anxious for him to return and had emphasized in his last letter that business dealings elsewhere needed attention. Keane had already spent more time in Cincinnati than he had on any of his previous visits.

As the carriage lumbered past Fourth, Keane's sharp gaze settled on a curious sight across the street. Immediately he recognized Esmeralda's huddled figure. Instructing the driver to stop and wait, he jumped down from the cab and raced across the crowded street, dodging several carriages and a few hogs as he ran to the opposite side.

* * *

"Are you all right?"

The sound of Keane's voice sent a second wave of pain through her anxious stomach. Keane! Of all the times for him to appear. No doubt her stomach problems were in part due to her anxiety over seeing this man. She'd known she'd have to face him sooner or later. But not today. It would be too humiliating.

Taking a deep, settling breath, she straightened. "Yes. I'm fine. I was just catching my breath. Now if you'll please excuse me, I'm trying to catch the omnibus." Esmeralda snatched up her travel bag and attempted to press forward past Keane.

"Wait." Grabbing her elbow, Keane guided her toward his cab. "I'll take you home. That is where you're going, isn't it? Back to the cottage?"

"Yes, but . . ." Esmeralda doubled over again, dropping her bag.

"My God, Esmeralda. What's wrong?" Keane hovered anxiously over her.

"Please . . . I'll be fine. Just leave me alone."

"I'm afraid I can't do that." Stepping forward, he started to pick her up.

"Oh, no." Esmeralda straightened, looking about the milling crowd with a horrified expression. "You mustn't. Not here." And when Keane looked unconvinced, "Haven't you done enough already! Must you humiliate me here, too?" Another sharp cramp silenced her.

"If you don't want me to carry you," Keane ground out through a false smile, his worry translating into anger, "I suggest you walk to the carriage . . . now." He motioned to the waiting cab.

Esmeralda nodded and stepped onto the paved street. While the cramping had eased, she was simply too tired to fight Keane. Let him take her home. How much longer could she have avoided him in any case?

Sensing her capitulation, Keane took her bag and helped her across the street to the hansom cab. Once settled inside the covered carriage, he trained his gaze on her face. She looked tired, as if her nights had been as sleepless as his. Her drawn expression worried him—her complexion was as sallow as the yellow muslin gown she wore. And young, she looked so very young and vulnerable as she stared out the carriage window. Keane tightened his grip on his walking stick. She needed him, even if she hadn't realized that simple fact yet, and it was his responsibility to help her.

"Esmeralda." He said the name quietly. "Let me help you."

"I don't need your help." Esmeralda bristled. She couldn't accept the pity she heard in his voice. For God's sake, would the man ever leave her alone? What more did she have to endure before she could leave Cincinnati behind her? As they headed uphill to the suburbs, Esmeralda stared at the passing streets, attempting to ignore him.

Keane frowned. Of course she wouldn't accept his help now. Not after the way he'd treated her. What did he expect? He'd taken her virginity, for God's sake. Well, he knew one way to make her listen. Leaning forward and taking her by the shoulders, Keane pulled her away from the window and turned her to face him.

"I've been trying for several days to speak with you, but you've avoided me up until now. I'm thankful that I finally have your attention; it's time you hear what I have to say. You said you were born a lady. I believe you." He took her hands into his. "And as a gentleman, I'm prepared to own up to my responsibilities."

Esmeralda furrowed her brow, not understanding what he meant.

"I will marry you, Esmeralda."

Keane saw her shocked look and leaned against the cushioned seat, satisfied. He *had* done the right thing. But the sound of soft laughter cut short his sense of relief. "May I ask what is so funny?"

His sober expression only increased her amusement. "It's just that . . . that you look so . . . so self-sacrificing!"

Keane's face revealed as much emotion as carved stone. "I hope my proposal doesn't offend you." Esmeralda waved away his mock protest with a gesture of her hand. Keane waited patiently, until she stopped her shallow laughter. "I gather your answer is no?"

She nodded and leaned back against her seat tiredly.

"May I ask why?"

"Of course." Her expression turned serious. "Because I don't choose to marry. Not now, not ever."

"So, it's not that you find me particularly offensive?"

Esmeralda shook her head, smiling at Keane's expression. He looked as if he'd just swallowed something quite distasteful. Her smile widened at the thought. Probably his pride! So now he wanted to marry her because he'd discovered, of all wonders, that she was a lady. What did he think she was before? Esmeralda stared across the carriage at the chiseled planes of his face. What an arrogant man, she thought. Before, his conscience had driven him to offer money. Now that he knew she was a *lady*, he was offering himself—for honor's sake, no doubt. Just another way to assuage his conscience. How honorable these men were; give them a pedigree—or a lovely son—and they snapped to, ready to smooth over their past wrongs . . . but for how long? No, she couldn't live her life depending on Keane and his conscience.

"What do you plan to do now?"

She slowly raised her head at Keane's question, feeling extremely tired. "I'm planning to go to the goldfields on the brig *Eureka.*"

"You're going to California? By yourself?"

"Yes."

"Are you mad!" Some of the frustration Keane felt at her laughing rejection projected into his voice. "You can't go to California, not by yourself."

"Why ever not?"

"You're a woman."

"You've discovered that, have you?"

Keane shook his head in dismay. "Do you have any idea how dangerous a trip like that would be for a woman alone?"

"Afraid some man might take advantage of me?"

"Listen to me!" Keane grabbed her shoulders and shook her. "What you're planning is a mistake!"

But as soon as he laid his hands on her, Keane knew it was he who was mistaken—from one moment to the next, her face changed from anger to pain. He released his hold, ready to apologize for his loss of temper.

"Stop the carriage."

"Esmeralda, I—"

She grabbed his walking stick and banged the door of the cab. Grabbing the door handle, she started to jump down. Keane tried to prevent her—the carriage had not come to a complete halt—but the hand she held clamped over her mouth and her sick pallor stopped him. Instead, he helped her down as best he could and tried to follow her as she ran toward the shelter of the woods.

"What's wrong?" he called after her.

Still holding her hand over her mouth, she doubled over with apparent pain. With a warning gesture, she halted his pursuit before she lurched forward, stumbling into the trees.

Keane stood staring at the clump of myrtles. He felt numb, paralyzed. Something was wrong—very wrong. In his mind he pictured Esmeralda as she'd looked on the street when he'd stopped to offer her a ride. She'd been doubled over, staring at the ground as if in pain.

"Shouldn't we go after her?" the driver called from his perch atop the carriage.

Keane thought about what she'd said when he'd found her on the street—*Must you humiliate me?* "No," Keane answered. "Not yet, anyway."

He paced by the carriage, then reached into his vest pocket and retrieved a cheroot. He lit the slim cigar, inhaled two puffs, and then stamped it out, kicking at the dirt as he did so. From the sounds drifting toward him, he gathered she was quite ill. He wanted to allow her the privacy she'd requested, but at the same time, he thought she might need his help. Pulling out his watch fob, he saw only minutes had passed since she'd fled to the trees. He settled for waiting, rationalizing that as long as he could still hear her out there, he knew she was all right. He lit another cheroot and waited. Then, suddenly, all noise from the woods ceased.

"Esmeralda." He tossed the cigar aside. "Are you all right?"

No answer.

"Esmeralda?" He dashed towards the copse of saplings.

"Please." The muffled cry drifted from deeper in the woods. "Go away."

Keane stopped, unable to decide whether he should stay where he was or charge after her. His indecision fled when he heard her anguished moan of pain. He sped to the woods.

Before he reached the trees he saw her stumbling toward him. Her shawl was half off and dragging in the brambles behind her. "My God, Esmeralda. What has happened?"

She bent over, clutching at her stomach.

"It's your stomach, isn't it? There's something wrong with your stomach."

Esmeralda nodded feebly. Then, weakly, she pushed against him as if trying to get away.

"Please, Keane." She looked pleadingly at him. "Go away."

"But you need help!"

Shaking her head, she continued to push him.

He looked at her drawn expression, speculatively. He hated to bring it up now, but the question had to be asked.

"Women sometimes feel ill like this when they're with child."

"No," she groaned weakly. "No child."

Keane felt his anxiety increase. He hadn't really thought it was something so obvious. He pressed his hand against her forehead. She felt warm.

"We'd better find a doctor." He started to help her toward the waiting carriage, but again Esmeralda grabbed her midriff. She tried to push Keane away and return to the woods. This time Keane was not so obliging.

"You need help. You can barely walk."

Esmeralda didn't respond but kept trying to pull away. Seeing that she was expending valuable energy, he let her go, intending to follow her this time, no matter what her objections might be. But after only a few steps, she turned and looked at Keane, a frantic expression on her face. Grabbing at the air, as if grasping for support, she crumpled helplessly to the ground.

Chapter Eighteen

"Open the door, damn it!" Jason pounded against the heavy oak. "Mother!" Rattling the doorknob in his left hand, he repeatedly slammed his right fist against the solid barrier. "Mother!" Hearing no response, he gave the wood a good kick. "Blast!"

Laughter filled the room, and Jason whisked around to face Molly. "You!" He pointed an accusing finger. "Don't you dare laugh!"

Chin up and arms crossed, Molly stood by the settee. Made crystalline by unshed tears, her eyes anchored on Jason with a haughty glare. "Then stop makin' an ass of yerself!"

"I will not be manipulated by my own mother!"

"Faith! Break the bleedin' door down, then!" she shouted, raising her voice to match Jason's.

"I wish to God I could!" He again fisted the door.

"Yer actin' like a bairn."

At Molly's reproving tone, something snapped inside

Jason. His inner turmoil froze into icy control, and he lowered his clenched hand. "You're right," he said, his voice deceptively soft. "I have absolutely no reason to want to leave this room. In fact, I should be thanking my mother." Slowly, Jason stepped away from the door and toward Molly, his lips turning up in a calculating smile. "I have you exactly where I've wanted you for a very long time."

Molly shivered. Sensing that his pent-up anger, only recently vented against the door, was now trained on her, she dropped her arms and backed away from him, strategically placing the empire settee between them.

Jason chuckled. "Go ahead. Run. You like to run, don't you, Molly? That's what you did in Charleston." Stalking her, he watched with satisfied amusement as she edged backward. Raising his eyebrows, he questioned, "But where to run now?"

"Ye . . . ye just leave me alone."

He shook his head, continuing to follow her with slow, purposeful steps. "Not this time. The circumstances are much too convenient to pass up. You and I, locked in this room together for who knows how long. Certainly long enough for a meaningful talk. Say, about . . ." Jason looked around as if searching for a topic of conversation. "My brother?" His face became deadly serious. "That should do admirably for starters." He purposely avoided the subject that mattered to him most.

"I didna know about yer brother." Molly felt a hard knot form in her stomach. He'd asked about the one thing she dreaded explaining, and she feared his cross-examination.

Jason leaned against the settee and crossed his arms. "A perfect combination of hurt innocence and confusion. I almost believe you. What a wonderful little actress you are."

"I didna know about Henry until it was too late," she yelled, desperate to make him understand. She hated taking the blame for anything, much less something for which she was truly innocent. "An' when I found out, I tried to call Esme off. I told her t'was no good, that Henry's family was too rich, too important. But she didna listen to me." Carefully keeping her distance, she continued, "I *told* ye before. We came to Cincinnati looking fer ye! I was wantin' to leave the bairn with ye. Only, when Peter came, I couldna give him up . . . not fer money nor security. Ye think I'd risk yer takin' the bairn from me if ye found us? I told Esme it was too risky, that she'd have to leave Henry be."

Jason's eyes narrowed, but he heard the conviction in her voice. Early in his law career, before he'd taken over running Carter Shipping, he'd trained himself to detect when a witness was lying, and nothing in Molly's story rang false. But it was too satisfying to see her squirm under his questions; he reveled in it with bittersweet satisfaction for the years he'd suffered after her abandonment. "If you didn't direct her to him, why did Miss MacClure get involved with Henry in the first place?"

"Sure as we were desperate. Bein' behind in paying the rent and all." Molly thought of how best to explain the scheme she'd hatched without sounding like a complete villainess. "Every dime we'd saved in Charleston went fer the shop. But we had not enough money—we were goin' to lose the lot, everything we'd slaved fer all those years in Charleston." Seeing a small dent of compassion in Jason's grim expression, she launched wholeheartedly into her story. "An' then Esme came up with this plan. She's a fine lookin' colleen, and I thought—I mean, *she* thought— Esme, that is—that maybe she could get the money from some respectable family if their boy was to ask her to marry. Our situation not bein' so good, I thought—I mean, *Esme* thought—the family would pay us to leave be." When Jason frowned, Molly quickly added, " 'Tis yer own fault she picked Henry. If ye'd not paid off them girls fer yer brother, Esme wouldna have chosen him. But

t'was easy to see that Henry was our—her best bet."
Molly lowered her head, trying to appear demure and
repentant. "Dinna be hard on Esme. She did it fer me an'
the tyke." She peeked up through her lashes to measure
the effect of her speech on Jason's hardhearted features.

"I don't give a damn about Esmeralda MacClure," he
said. "Only you. You and my son." Jason examined Molly
and her pose of innocence. "You actually expect me to
believe you're completely innocent in this scheme?" Jason
pushed away from the settee, targeting Molly as he
stepped toward her. He did indeed believe her version of
the story—to a certain extent. It made sense that she'd
want to keep Peter a secret once she decided to keep him
for herself. He could see she feared his family's power and
influence. But somehow he didn't think the elaborate plot
she'd just explained was Miss MacClure's invention. No,
this was definitely a scheme hatched in that pretty Irish
head. And while it did not much matter to him whose
idea it was—he could understand how desperation would
motivate someone to implement such a deed—he wanted
Molly to admit her part in it. The vengeful side of him
sought her admission as satisfaction for her desertion in
Charleston.

"Sweet, innocent Molly Egan." He prowled toward her
as she backed away, around the settee. He relished the
anxiety he saw chiseled on her face—while at the same
time her fearful expression scored him like a knife. He
sought her pain, realizing as he stalked her that his actions had little to do with his brother. Even now, after all
that had happened, he looked at her womanly curves with
longing and felt an awakening hardness in his groin. He
could still remember the joy of their lovemaking—and the
pain he had suffered when he lost her. He stepped closer.

"Get away from me, ye blighter."

"Such rough language." He shook his head with disapproval. Then he lowered his eyes to her lips, his expression turning intimate. "From such a sweet mouth."

"Och! Drochrath air!" Molly shouted, then fled around the settee, seeking to put as much distance between them as possible. But she miscalculated. Jason steered around to the other side, and she ran straight into his arms.

"Gaelic. Do you know when you last spoke Gaelic to me?" Jason's gaze pored over her possessively and his hands smoothed up her arms and around her shoulders to caress her back. The sweet feel of her body doubled his desire for her instantly. He sensed she too remembered the pleasure of their mating, for her breath became short pants as her heart raced against his chest. "You were naked . . . your soft little body pressed against me." He fitted his actions to his words, meshing her curves against his hips. The feel of her made him weak with memories. "But you said the words softly—not angrily. And when you said them"—he slowly lowered his mouth closer to hers— "you made me want you forever."

Molly opened her mouth against Jason's, her desire to fight paralyzed by the numbing sweetness of his words. As she'd often done in her dreams, she wrapped her arms around his muscular neck and pressed her peaked breasts against his solid chest. Her tongue flitted against his slightly crooked teeth, exploring the inside of his mouth, and she could feel the strength of his arms under the broadcloth suit as she ran her hands down from his shoulder. He smelled lightly of bay rum, a fragrance she'd come to associate with warmth and comfort. His strong blunt fingers outlined one ear and then brushed lightly against her throat before dipping into the gap between the silk neckline of her dress and her breasts.

Jason molded her body to his, reveling in his possession of her. The kiss was a mistake. The tactician in him sensed the error immediately. A long time ago, this woman had captured a small part of his soul. While dormant during their long separation, that part of him took over now. What he'd meant to be punishing, became tender and loving.

"Still so soft." He breathed the words against her lips, his fingers exploring the skin between her breasts, and he could feel her shiver as he again wet her lips with his tongue.

"Ye bloody rogue," Molly whispered, her hands creeping up his arms, gripping his shoulders as she returned his ardent caresses.

"You Irish witch," he chided back in a rough voice, nipping at her full lower lip.

Molly anxiously opened her mouth, seeking Jason's sweet taste. "I'll not be yer mistress," she asserted in a soft breathy voice.

"Whether you want to be or not, you'll always be the mistress of my heart."

Those words, so reminiscent of their last night together, propelled Molly from her fantasy. Henry and Esmeralda, even the loving touch of the man who held her, blurred as she remembered her reasons for being at the Carter mansion. It had all been a mistake. Jason had never meant to make her anything other than his whore. He hadn't sent the note. The fate of her mother loomed before Molly, effectively killing her ardor. With as much force as she could muster, she smashed her balled fist into Jason's stomach.

The unexpectedness of the blow had more effect than its strength. Grabbing his stomach, Jason expelled a low groan while Molly scurried to the opposite end of the room.

"Don't come near me, ye . . . ye . . . box-ankled hound!"

Jason dropped onto the settee, catching his breath. "What the deuce did you do that for?" he asked hoarsely.

"I'll not be yer mistress, Jason Carter! Not now, not ever!"

"Who the hell asked you to be?"

"You did!" she said accusingly.

"I did not—"

"Ye did! Just like before—at the hunting lodge in Charleston, when ye gave me them jewels. Even then ye were trying to buy me love when ye had it all for free."

Jason took a deep breath, as if testing to see if the pain had gone. Rubbing his stomach where she'd slammed her small fist, he rose from the settee. "I never asked you such a thing. And the necklace was a gift. It wasn't meant to buy anything."

"Ha! Ye canna fool me—I know the signs. First come the jewels, then ye sets me up in me own house. Only 'tis not mine—'tis yers, to do with what ye wants when ye no longer care fer me an' the tyke."

Jason stared at her, a niggling thought surfacing in his mind. He remembered Molly on that night before she'd left, when she had told him she loved him and they had made such sweet love. He'd called her the mistress of his heart then, and he'd always thought of her as such. That's why her abandonment had hurt so much. Could she possibly have believed he'd meant the endearment as some kind of cheap proposition? "My God, Molly. Is that what you thought? That I wanted you as my mistress? Is that why you left me?"

"Yer bloody right, that's why I left. I'll be no man's mistress."

"Molly—"

"Don't come near me!" she warned.

"Will you stop shouting and let me explain?"

She picked up the first object she could reach, a small porcelain statue of a girl in a shepherdess costume. "Dinna touch me. I'll not be fooled by yer lovin' kisses." She held the statue back over her head, aiming the projectile at Jason.

"Don't be absurd. Put that down before you break it." Jason stepped forward.

With astonishing accuracy, Molly hurled the shepherdess at Jason. He ducked. The porcelain missed his head by a fraction of an inch and smashed against the door. When Molly grabbed a second weapon, Jason lunged at her.

Outside in the hallway, Samantha Carter stopped in front of the door, carrying a small tray of sandwiches. It had not taken long for her curiosity to get the better of her. And while she was not adverse to listening at keyholes, she much preferred to have a legitimate reason for eavesdropping—thus, the silver salver of food. But when she came close enough to hear the muffled words streaming from inside the salon, she halted. Suddenly, the sound of shattering china rent the air.

"Oh, dear," she mumbled to herself. "I hope that wasn't the Meissen." With a slight shrug of her delicate shoulders, she broke off a piece of bread, popped it in her mouth and smiled. Her plan appeared to be working admirably. Reassured, she turned and headed down the hallway, back to the kitchen where she'd left Peter with a bevy of servants and his lunch.

Inside the salon, Jason tackled Molly to the carpeted floor. He grabbed her wrists before clawing fingers could reach their target, and pinned both her hands above her head. "It was a gift of love, Molly." With no little effort, he subdued Molly's attempts to throw him off. "You thought I wanted to make you my whore because I gave you that sapphire necklace, but you misunderstood. It wasn't meant to buy you."

"Then why'd ye ask me to be yer mistress?"

Jason transferred both her wrists to one hand. With his freed hand, he stroked her face. His heart pounded with the joy of discovery. She loved him! She'd never wanted to leave him in Charleston. Shaking his head sadly for almost two years of misunderstanding, he explained, "Mistress of my *heart*, Molly. The keeper of my love—not my kept woman, to be purchased and discarded. I couldn't do that to you . . . not then, not now." Gently he brushed her tears away with his lips.

"I don't believe ye," she cried.

"Why?" he whispered against her neck, nuzzling his nose against her ear affectionately.

"Because yer rich, and I'm just an Irish girl . . . and . . ." Tears choked off the words.

Jason stroked her black hair softly. "And?" he coaxed, wanting to soothe all her insecurities.

"Because," she stared up to Jason's warm brown eyes, scared to say the words. "I'm not a good person."

"You were always good to me."

"That's different. Ye were so easy to please."

Jason shook his head, smiling at the misconception. "Ask anyone. I'm a most demanding man."

"Oh, no," Molly corrected anxiously, forgetting to struggle against his loosened grip. "All ye wanted was to be loved . . . sure as that was the simplest thing in the world to do."

Jason felt a sharp pain radiate out from his chest at the raw love her words showed. Unable to continue looking at her tender expression, he hugged her, fitting his head in the crook of her neck. "Molly, how could I have been so wrong?"

Molly stroked the back of his coat. "I dinna blame ye for askin' me to be yer mistress, Jason. I understand. I just couldna do it . . . not even fer ye."

Jason pulled away. Leaning up on his elbows, he grabbed her shoulders and shook her lightly. "Stop this. I've already explained. You're being silly insisting that I'd only want you in such a sordid fashion."

Molly shook her head, denying his words.

"Yes, Molly, accept it. I love you." Seeing how the words affected her, he smiled tenderly. "I wanted you to be my wife even then. But I wasn't sure of my own judgment. We'd known each other for so little time. But that doesn't matter now. We have a child—and a future together, my Irish whirlwind."

"No. Ye dinna know."

"I know everything I need to know." He gently stroked

her temples. "It was all a mistake. You didn't leave me. You ran away thinking I wanted some cheap affair that could only hurt you because . . . because you loved me. You said it that night before you left. I understand now, Molly. And I'm sorry. Sorry for all the lost time and hurt." He leaned forward, kissing her roughly. "My God, Molly. Don't ever leave me again."

Molly felt as if she were suffocating. He didn't know. Jason didn't realize all the bad things she'd done. He thought she was a good person, someone he could love and marry. She had to explain. But her words were choked inside her by his loving expression. Finally a soft tapping on the door came to her aid.

Quickly, the two scrambled from the floor, for the first time aware of their compromising position. Straightening her clothes, Molly found her bonnet where it had fallen near the settee and quickly fitted it over her disheveled hair. Watching her struggle, Jason gently tucked in the loose tendrils, then gave her one last quick kiss for reassurance.

"Come in." Jason kept a firm grasp of her waist to prevent her from stepping away from him.

The door opened and Samantha peeked around the doorjamb. "I hate to interrupt, but a message just arrived for you, Molly." Stepping inside, she held out a square of paper. "The messenger said it was urgent." Handing the note to her, Samantha sent a concerned look to Jason. "Keane's man delivered it."

Molly took the folded sheet and opened it. The edgy feeling she'd had before was nothing compared to her reaction when she read the viscount's hastily written note:

Come to my suite at the Burnet. Esmeralda is asking for you. Hurry. Doctor says not much time left.

Chapter Nineteen

Keane sat beside the canopied bed, his knees touching the walnut frame. In his palms he held Esmeralda's thin fingers. His thumb gently stroked the knobby knuckles, following the tapered fingers to their tips where they ended in short, bitten nails. He smiled, remembering how she would jam a finger in her mouth, then yank it out, as if recalling some prior scolding. Sometimes she would keep biting, too involved in her thoughts to be conscious of her bad habit. He touched the pads at the ends of her fingers, examining their blunt-tipped softness, then trailed his thumb back to feel the webbing where her second and third fingers met. Her skin felt rough and papery dry, like a discarded peel from a potato.

Looking at the figure on the bed, Keane hardly recognized Esmeralda as the woman he'd held passionately at the Longworths' party a few nights before. A blue tinge colored her lips and her face looked pinched and tired. Only the auburn curls identified her. He took a long tendril of soft hair and wrapped its silken length around his index finger. The lock formed a feathery tip that jutted out from his hand and served as a soft brush. He used it to paint away lightly the pain he saw etched on her tired face. But despite the softness of his brush strokes, the pinched lines remained.

Keane sighed, letting the copper curl slip from his finger. She slept fitfully under the influence of laudanum mixed with camphor—a remedy given by the second physician who had seen her. Keane had driven out the first doctor. The fool's recommendation that they submerge her in a bath filled with frigid water and then administer a purge had been ludicrous. The second physician, although at first more promising, had also been a disappointment. One look at the patient and he'd shaken his head sadly, stating he'd been called too late. Too late? She'd been fine until this afternoon. But that was the nature of the disease, the doctor had explained. Men who woke in the morning in good health would fall to the ground by midday and be buried that night. With the spring thaw, the Angel of Death had traveled up the Mississippi to the docks of Cincinnati.

Esmeralda was dying of cholera.

It wasn't a pretty disease. Keane felt sure that if she were in any condition to protest, Esmeralda would be mortified at his washing and dressing her. But while he'd cleansed the filth her body expelled so violently and wrapped her in his nightshirt, he'd been glad for something useful to do.

With Higgins's help, he changed the soiled linens regularly, trying to keep her clean and comfortable. Afterward they'd burned the sheets in the fireplace. He didn't want anyone at the hotel alerted to her condition. The fear of cholera had caused more than one riot as locals attempted to route the scourge from their homes. The hotel management would not appreciate a cholera victim under its roof, and he'd had to pay dearly to buy the silence of the two physicians who had tended her already.

Suddenly Esmeralda cried out in her sleep, flailing her hand wildly out of Keane's grasp. He grabbed both hands and began massaging them as he had been doing on and off for the past hours. They felt so cold—icy as death. He tried warming them with friction. The rubbing calmed her; it seemed to relieve the painful cramps she'd complained of earlier.

When she opened her eyes, Keane took the opportunity to lean her forward and tip a glass of water to her dehydrated lips. He had to force her to sip the water slowly; she drank with a raging thirst. When she finished, she dropped back against the pillows, unconscious. At every opportunity, he tried to fill her with liquid—but it was useless. One way or another, the water would drain from her almost immediately. It was as if life itself were slowly leaking from her, leaving behind only a dried shell.

Keane rubbed his hand over his face. He felt so utterly helpless! He'd sent a note to Miss Egan at the Carter home after learning from Esmeralda during a lucid moment that her friend was there. He'd also sent Higgins out to find another physician, hoping that this time the prognosis would be better than the last. So far, neither Esmeralda's friend nor Higgins had appeared, and Keane was forced to wait in his suite—alone with his fears.

Although he was not an overly religious man, it was times like these that made him look to a higher source for guidance. His Anglican upbringing certainly provided a base for his short prayers, in which he outlined all his past sins and promised improvement. The last time he'd gone through a similar litany had been at the deaths of his father and his older brother, Phillip. Back then he'd accused God of indifference. Now older and wiser, he knew even God could not take back death. Yet he just couldn't accept so final a verdict for Esmeralda.

Too late, the doctor had said. It just couldn't be too late!

Keane stroked her hot forehead. *Dear God, just let her live and I swear I'll take care of her. Bring her back to me, and she'll never want for anything. I'll be responsible for her. But don't let her die! Please, don't let her die!*

A loud knock brought Keane out of his reverie, and he reluctantly left Esmeralda to answer the door. At the entrance stood Jason and the woman who had called herself Edeltraud Dinkelspiel. Molly Egan—Jason's Molly? Keane glanced down. His friend was holding the woman's hand possessively in his. So he'd found her at last.

"Miss Egan?"

"Where's Esme? What's happened to her?"

Keane pointed to the door leading to his bedchamber and stood aside as the petite Irish woman raced by without a backward glance.

"You look terrible," Jason announced with characteristic bluntness. "What's the matter with Miss MacClure?"

Keane turned to face Jason, raking his fingers through his hair. "It's cholera."

The curt words visibly stunned Jason. His own brother had almost died of cholera and he knew the devastating effects of the disease. Few survived once they'd contracted it. Having a sense of Molly's close relationship with the sick woman inside, Jason turned with concern toward the bedroom. "I'd better go in."

Keane followed him into the bedroom, where they found Molly tending her friend. She swabbed Esmeralda's face with the wet handkerchief he'd left in a basin at the side of the bed.

"Sure as there's something terribly wrong. Have ye sent fer a healer?" Molly's voice sounded low and frightened.

"Yes. Two. My valet's looking for a third."

"And?"

"Molly, come away." Jason attempted to pull the handkerchief from her grasp.

Molly pushed Jason's hands away, nearly overturning the porcelain bowl on the bedside table. "Tell me what's wrong?" She directed her shrill question to Keane.

"The doctors say cholera," Keane answered, quietly.

"Oh, no!"

"Molly, we have to leave now." Jason again tried to coax her from the sick bed.

"Nay. Nay, I canna. She's me friend, Jason."

"For a moment, then. Please, we need to talk."

After a bleak look at the face peeking out from under the white linen sheet, Molly nodded absently, allowing Jason to steer her out to the salon. When he shut the bedroom door behind them, Molly fell into his arms, seeking comfort.

"Oh, Jason. She looks so sick."

"She is very sick." Jason thought ominously of the bluish skin and pinched face. "Henry almost died of cholera when he was just a child. I'm afraid your friend looks a lot worse than my brother ever did."

"Nay!"

"Listen." Jason continued to hold her to him, even as she tried to pull away after his morbid prediction. "We have some important decisions to make, and they must be made very quickly. If cholera is back in Cincinnati, we have to leave before the epidemic takes hold."

"I will not leave Esme!"

"Think of our son," he admonished. "He's only a babe. He'll surely die if he contracts cholera. Would you want that?" Molly shook her head. "Then we *must* leave. Your friend . . ." Jason hesitated to say what he really thought her chances of survival were. "She's with Keane. He'll take care of her." He'd seen the concern on Keane's face when he'd opened the door. Clearly, his commitment to the woman was deeper than Jason had ever believed possible. Keane would take care of her. And although under normal circumstances Jason would have tried to persuade him to leave as well, as much as Jason hated to admit it, at the moment it suited his purposes to have Keane stay.

Molly shook her head, tears in her eyes. "Ye dinna understand. If it weren't for Esme, we wouldna have a son. Sure as she saved me life and Peter's. After two long days of labor, I didna have the strength or courage to go on any longer. Only Esme wouldna let me give up. She badgered me, screaming that I had to work fer the life of me bairn. She gave me the will to try. I'll not give up on her now!"

Jason's face clouded at Molly's recounting of Peter's birth. The woman dying in the next room was responsible for helping Molly bring their child into the world. For that he would forgive her anything, even her treatment of his brother. Yet what good could anyone do for Miss MacClure now? Surely, when one weighed the risks against the benefits, it was not worth exposing Molly to cholera.

"Look at me." Jason smoothed Molly's black curls away, cupping her face in his hands. "If I thought our staying here would help—"

"I'll not be leavin'. Not fer ye—not even fer our bairn. I'll not be leavin' Esme to die!"

"Molly—"

She grabbed Jason's lapels. Her voice edged with hysteria, she begged, "Ye can take him—ye an' yer mum. Take Peter away to a safe place."

Jason examined her wide-spaced eyes. He read in them a determination as hard as iron, a loyalty he'd always known existed—and had been frightened he'd lost when she disappeared in Charleston. "I'll stay here with you."

Molly's face brightened. Then, gently, she stroked the side of his face with her hand. "I love ye, Jason. Truly I do. I dinna want ye to get sick as well. Please, take our son, and care for him. I'll be stayin' here with Esme as long as she needs me."

Jason merely shook his head and leaned forward to kiss

her lightly on her lips. "We'll stay together this time, shall we?"

Molly smiled tentatively, still frightened by the total acceptance she saw in his eyes. "All right, me love. Together."

"We'll have to go back and make arrangements with Mother. She'll want to take Peter and the rest of the family out of the city." At Molly's nod, he took her hand in his, trying to give some encouragement.

Hands clasped together, they returned to the sickroom.

Keane barely noticed their entrance, his attention was so focused on the unconscious woman on his bed. God, she looked so ill! He searched his mind for some remedy, anything that he could do to help her. But he could think of nothing. Soaking the handkerchief in the porcelain washbowl, he wrung out the cloth and applied its moist comfort to her forehead. As he did so, he felt Molly's cool, sure hands take the linen from him. Giving her an appreciative look, he stood to let her take his place. He felt Jason's reassuring hand on his shoulder as he watched Molly tend Esmeralda.

"Sir! I found a doctor."

The sound of his valet's voice immediately lightened the gloomy atmosphere inside the sickroom. Giving Jason and Molly an anxious glance, Keane spun around and left to greet the new arrival.

His hopes dropped at the sight of the physician's youthful appearance. Standing next to Higgins was a man much younger than the doctors who had preceded him—he couldn't possibly be older than his late twenties. His youth reeked of inexperience. But Keane tried to take courage from his valet's proud expression.

"This is Dr. Paul Anderson, sir. I've explained the *viscountess*'s condition," Higgins said meaningfully.

"You did well," Keane silently approved his valet's quick thinking. While the subject had not come up with the other physicians directly, Keane knew they'd all assumed Esmeralda was his wife.

Transferring his black satchel to his left hand, the doctor stepped forward, extending his hand in polite greeting. "Viscount Eldridge. I wish we could have met under better circumstances."

Keane took in the man's pleasant expression and blond good looks. Both characteristics seemed incongruous for one who dealt with death on a daily basis. Yet when he shook Keane's hand, some of the doctor's youthful enthusiasm transmitted itself, and for the first time that afternoon, Keane felt hope. "Please, call me Keane. This way." He indicated the bedchamber. "My wife's resting in here."

Keane led the doctor to the room where Esmeralda lay, still unconscious. One look at his patient and Dr. Anderson quickly shooed Molly away, not waiting for an introduction to the couple by the bedside. He sat down and felt Esmeralda's wrist for a pulse. After a moment, he touched and pulled the skin of her arm and shook his head.

"Your wife is very ill."

"I understand that," Keane said impatiently. From the corner of his eye, he caught Molly's start at the use of the word wife. "That's why I sent for you."

Dr. Anderson examined Esmeralda's eyes with a worried frown. "What have you been giving her?"

"Laudanum with camphor. Five drops mixed with brandy every two hours."

"Well, it's much too late for that, I'm afraid." The doctor looked to Molly and Jason. "If you'll excuse us, I would like to speak with the patient's husband alone."

Molly appeared about to protest, but Keane interceded. "The lady is a close friend of my wife's."

"Be that as it may, the fewer the people in this room, the better it is for the patient. The atmosphere should be preserved as pure as is possible. That means any unnecessary occupants should be removed."

"Of course, Doctor." Jason looked over his shoulder at Keane as he hooked his arm through Molly's and led her out before she could argue. "We'll be waiting outside if you need us."

Keane nodded. When the door closed behind the couple, he turned anxiously to Dr. Anderson. "Will she be all right?"

"No, she will not be all right." The doctor's calm brown eyes met Keane's sympathetically. "Your wife is a very sick woman. I'm afraid from all the symptoms she exhibits, she can only be suffering from cholera."

Keane felt fear coil around his heart once again at the doctor's bleak expression. This time he refused to listen to any predictions of doom and death. "Well, thank you for your time, Dr. Anderson. If you'll leave a bill with my valet—"

"Keane," the doctor said softly. "She's in the collapse stage. She'll be dead before morning."

Keane felt his stomach plummet. "I cannot believe that," he said angrily. "There must be something that can be done. I just can't stand by and watch her die!"

"I won't soften the blow. She is far beyond the premonitory and congestive stages. If I'd been called earlier, her chances for survival would have been greatly increased. The effects of medicines at this stage are measurably lost. Absorption is so completely arrested that remedies remain in the alimentary—"

"But you weren't called earlier," Keane ground out, frustrated by the doctor's cool delivery of medical jargon. "I want to know what you can do now!"

"For victims this far gone, I recommend a *venous injection.*"

"Which is?"

"We inject liquid right into the veins. It's considered radical, and not widely accepted, but I have used it on cholera victims with some success."

"What exactly is *some* success?"

"Because it's only used on those considered beyond hope, any life saved is considered an achievement," the doctor said bluntly.

Keane silently digested the bitter odds.

"At this point, I would say it's your wife's only chance outside of divine intervention." Seeing Keane's indecision, the doctor took up Esmeralda's limp hand and pinched her skin. "You see how blue and cold your wife's hands are, and how her skin distends when I pinch it, but fails to return to its normal shape when released?" Keane felt his stomach roil at the sight of her tented skin. "Her blood is in a black and thickened condition, impeding secretion. The newer theories focus on bringing salts into contact with the black blood of cholera. The most successful have injected aqueous and saline fluids into the veins directly, in order to throw the fluid immediately into the circulation. In one out of five cases, the patient's condition improves almost instantly."

Keane stared at Esmeralda's pinched and blue face, as well as the drawn and puckered skin of her hands. Whenever she awakened, she drank with a great thirst. He sensed that what she needed desperately *was* water. He didn't know anything about medicine, but this remedy made sense to him.

"There are dangers," Dr. Anderson warned. "I don't want to be overly optimistic. I heat my instruments as I personally believe this inhibits infection. I also strain the liquid twice through leather in order to prevent any particles from entering the system."

"Without this therapy, will she die?"

"Most certainly."

Keane walked over to the side of the bed. He caressed Esmeralda's feverish face with slow, loving strokes. "You don't give me much choice."

Dr. Anderson's cool gaze remained on Keane. "You can always call another physician. But at this point, I must warn that time is of the essence."

Keane thought of the two other doctors who had attended Esmeralda. A fourth opinion would do no good. While Paul Anderson was young, he seemed competent, and Keane appreciated his blunt assessment, despite its cruelty. Most importantly, Anderson was the only doctor who had given Keane *any* hope. Facing the biggest gamble of his life, he looked down at Esmeralda's haggard face for the reassurance she could not give him. He stroked her hair, the only part of her still filled with life.

She was deteriorating with alarming speed. The situation called for a quick decision—now was not the time to start doubting his own intuition.

"We'll do as you say."

Chapter Twenty

"She looks worse."

Keane ignored Molly's pessimistic assessment and continued to wash Esmeralda's arm with a cloth soaked in a nitrate of lead solution. Dr. Anderson had left the disinfecting agent behind with instructions that Keane use it to cleanse both the room and its patient.

"I still dinna think it proper fer ye to be here."

"That's a rather interesting belief since this is in fact my room, and you are merely an invited guest."

"Hmph! She shouldna be here at all. Sure as she'd be better off at the cottage, with me takin' care of her." From her side of the bed, Molly washed Esmeralda's neck with quick, efficient swipes.

"She collapsed—getting her to a doctor as quickly as possible was my sole concern, not a side trip to Walnut Hills."

"Maybe. But as soon as she's well, I'll be takin' Esme

home. She's not really yer wife, an' ye can stop pretendin' 'tis so."

Keane merely grunted at the oft repeated remark. For the past two hours, the woman working across the bed from him had been nothing but a nuisance. It seemed Molly resented any help he could give Esmeralda and wanted the care of her friend to be her sole responsibility. When the doctor had told them how to disinfect Esmeralda by bathing her with a dram of nitrate dissolved in water, Molly had argued vehemently against Keane's doing so, stating that his care of her sick friend was highly improper. But Keane bitingly replied that she could rest assured—he did not find an unconscious woman sexually arousing. Turning beet red, Molly sputtered something about being capable of bathing Esmeralda without his help, and Keane reluctantly agreed to let her deal with Esmeralda's "private parts," as Molly referred to them.

He thought the whole thing rather ridiculous. He was more familiar with those intimate parts of Esmeralda's anatomy than Molly would ever be. But he gave in just to get the Irish harridan to leave him alone. He joined in later, helping to wash Esmeralda's arms and legs, and none of Molly's arguments could sway him to leave. He found it intolerable merely to stand by, waiting in the salon with Jason, when there was something physical he could do to help Esmeralda.

"When is the doctor coming back?" Molly asked for the third time.

"I don't know. Soon." They were all anxious for Dr. Anderson's return. He'd left over two hours before, saying he needed to find his assistant and get some equipment. Keane himself wondered what was taking so long.

After putting the cloth back in the washbowl filled with the disinfectant, Keane gently placed Esmeralda's hand at her side. The room smelled strongly of nitrate mixed with the pungent odor of coffee. Following the doctor's instructions, Higgins had sprinkled the nitrate solution on the floor and furniture. Then, mumbling something about doctors not knowing half as much as they pretended, his valet had set ground coffee beans on a heated plate near the fire, announcing that his method was the proper way to purify the atmosphere. Despite the strong smell of both mixtures, the room reeked of impending death.

Incredibly warm from the blazing fire heating the room, Keane swabbed his perspiring neck with his handkerchief. Warmth was another precaution the doctor had insisted on. He'd explained that cold moisture was to be avoided at all costs. In addition to pure air and a dry environment, he'd instructed that Esmeralda be clothed in flannel. Apparently anything that would keep the skin's surface warm and clean was considered beneficial.

"Here you are, sir." Higgins entered carrying a ceramic cup on a silver tray. Keane took the drink gratefully and turned to the bed. The tonic was made of brandy and water, with ten drops of chloroform mixed in. It was supposed to stop the vomiting. But when he neared the bed, he saw that Esmeralda was still unconscious. He'd have to wait before he could administer the remedy.

Placing the cup on the nightstand, Keane arched his back, stretching his tired muscles. He'd been hovering over Esmeralda for five hours now. The cloying smell of illness permeated the room. Though disguised by the smoking coffee grounds and the nitrate solution, the odor sickened him. He looked out at the balcony with longing.

"Go ahead," Molly said gruffly. "I'll keep a watch on 'er till ye get back."

He smiled his thanks before stepping out on the open-air balcony. Hoping a smoke would calm him, he lit a cheroot. He'd long ago discarded his jacket, and although the evening was cool, he remained outside to savor the fresh air. The night sky shone with brilliant lights from the heavens, looking so peaceful, belying the anxious activity within his suite. What would he give to repeat the past weeks, he thought, to relive the moments when he'd held Esmeralda in his arms and she'd breathed strongly against his chest, returning his warm kisses with as much passion as he offered? He pictured her as she looked the night they almost made love in this very room, her burnished hair streaming to her waist and her emerald eyes flashing. She'd been like a sorceress, seducing him with her innocent magic. If he'd known then how little time they'd have together, would he have acted differently?

Keane shook off his morbid thoughts. It was getting more difficult to ignore the signs of death. Yet he wouldn't give up hope. He couldn't. He had this strange feeling that as long as he believed she'd live, the possibility remained, hanging from the fragile thread of his faith.

Inhaling one last puff, he dropped the cheroot to the stone floor of the balcony and ground it out with the heel of his boot. Gazing at the stars again, he saw a flash of light streak across the black sky. Some said falling stars represented souls returning to heaven. He shivered. Not Esmeralda . . . please . . . not her.

The sound of the French doors opening breached his gloomy thoughts. Keane turned. Lodged between the open doors stood Jason, gesturing to him.

"Dr. Anderson has returned," he said softly. But when Keane turned to go inside, Jason stopped him. "He's brought another doctor with him and . . . a lot of equipment. I don't believe Molly should be here during the treatment. It looks . . . frightening." He glanced away for a moment, then met Keane's eyes steadily. "I'd hate for Molly's last memories of Miss MacClure to be of death. But if you feel we might be of some help?"

"No. No, please take Molly away. What the doctor described doesn't sound pretty. I wouldn't want to subject anyone to it, much less someone who cares for Esmeralda as much as Molly does." He'd actually be glad to have her out of his hair, but he didn't think it necessary to reveal that detail to Jason. For some reason, the Irish termagant lost her shrewishness with Jason as easily as she found it around Keane.

"Thank you." Jason laid his hand on Keane's shoulder. The two friends exchanged a silent message of encouragement before returning to the sickroom.

Inside, Dr. Anderson was setting up several glass beakers, a burner, and some rubber tubing. A large syringe lay across a towel on the Chippendale bureau. Molly's eyes were glued to the bizarre instrument, the body of which was about the size of a large jar. Jason immediately went to her side and whispered something to her. Keane watched Molly shake her head sharply, her face set in a stubborn expression. Her eyes remained riveted on the syringe. Jason again whispered to Molly. Keane's lips pressed in a tight line. It looked as though Miss Egan was going to require some persuading.

He turned, seeking Dr. Anderson's help. When he saw the doctor busily measuring some crystal powders, he waited, dreading any disruption of what appeared to be a delicate procedure. He stood by until the doctor stopped and looked up, giving Keane his attention. "Doctor," he said. "I don't want the young woman present during the procedure."

"I quite agree. Even though we've taken the precaution of purifying the room, it really is best to have as few people present as possible. I must ask everyone to leave before we begin the therapy. You, of course, may stay." His no-nonsense gaze lighted on Keane. "But I warn you, it won't be pleasant."

Keane nodded. "If you could please ask them to leave now. I believe the suggestion would be better received from you."

"Of course." Dr. Anderson quietly approached Jason and Molly. But they were so caught up in their argument, issued in low whispering voices, that they remained both unaware of the doctor's and Keane's presence.

Dr. Anderson cleared his throat loudly. "I'll be starting

the injection process soon. I'll need everyone to leave the room—except the viscount, of course."

"Why is he staying?" Molly asked, her arms wrapped tightly across her chest.

Dr. Anderson raised his eyes, surprised. "Because he's her husband."

"He's not . . ." She stopped, riveted by Keane's unwavering gaze.

"I'll take care of her for you. I won't let anything happen," Keane assured her.

Unconvinced, Molly pulled Keane aside, beyond the hearing of the doctor and Jason. "Listen ye blighter, she's special!" Tears glistened in her eyes. "She's . . ." Molly's voice choked, preventing her from finishing.

Keane gripped Molly's hand, trying to make her understand how much he cared for Esmeralda. "I know, Molly. I'll watch over her. Trust me. I won't let her slip away from us."

Sapphire eyes anchored on his as Molly measured Keane's sincerity. For a moment he felt an odd sensation, as if Molly's gaze were reaching deep into his soul, touching some dark, private part of his thoughts. Then her turbulent blue eyes calmed and she slowly lowered them from his. "Aye. I'll trust her care to ye."

Walking past Jason to the bedside, she leaned forward and lightly kissed Esmeralda's forehead. After one last stroke of her hand, she turned and left. Jason silently followed.

When the door closed softly behind the couple, Keane turned to Dr. Anderson. "All right. Let's get started."

Feeling as if he were in the midst of a nightmare, Keane helplessly watched as the doctor's assistant transformed the elegant bedchamber into a medical laboratory. Large glass jars filled with clear liquid were everywhere. Rubber tubing, which he'd seen the assistant clean earlier with lime, lay strung across the furniture. One full jar was being warmed over a burner. White papers once filled with crystalline powders littered the floor.

Rivulets of sweat dripped down Keane's forehead. Wiping his face with a handkerchief, he watched Dr. Anderson check the temperature of the warming liquid with a thermometer. Apparently satisfied, the doctor then took the large syringe in hand, submerged its tip, and pulled back on the plunger. When it was completely full, he attached the tip to the end of the tubing, filling it.

"All right, I'm ready." Doctor Anderson looked at his assistant. "Let's insert the tube."

Keane cringed at the doctor's words. He knew what they were going to do; Anderson had explained the procedure in great detail. Still, Keane felt a terrifying dread when the assistant inserted the steel needle into Esmeralda's arm. As he watched, her arm jerked once. Even in her unconscious state, she seemed to feel the needle's insertion. He pressed his lips together and waited.

The assistant wrapped a cloth around her arm and kept a firm grip on the tubing to prevent it from moving. Dr. Anderson had warned that if air or a particle should get into her blood, she might suffer from an embolism and die.

"Is there anything I can do?" Keane asked anxiously.

The doctor shook his head, concentrating on continuing the flow of liquid by slowly pressing on the plunger of the syringe.

Keane stared at the immobile figure on the bed. The covers had been tucked underneath her arms, and the sleeve of his nightshirt pulled back off her forearm where a cloth now held the tube with a ball valve in her vein. For once, he was thankful she was unconscious. He almost desired the same antidote for the pain gripping his insides. The tension within him tightened as he watched her. Though frozen in a strained and pinched expression, her face still held a bit of the magic beauty that had first drawn him to her.

For half an hour, the doctor continued to pour liquid into her system. The concentration stamped on the faces of the two medical men, each with his own exacting duties, was phenomenal. Keane simply sat on the tapestry chair at the foot of the bed, watching. And praying.

All at once, Esmeralda's body began to shake and jerk. Dr. Anderson swore under his breath. Keane's heart shot into his throat.

"What's happened? What's the matter?" Keane sprang from his chair, alarmed by the assistant's futile attempts to keep Esmeralda's arm still.

"Rigors," Doctor Anderson responded in a tight voice. "Usually this doesn't occur until after the therapy is complete."

"What can I do? For God's sake, tell me what to do!"

"Keane, if you want to help, you'll stay calm and try to keep your wife from tearing that tube from her arm!"

Without hesitation, Keane stepped to the side of the bed opposite the assistant and placed both hands on Esmeralda's shoulders. At his touch, her body arched and fought him. Her spasms grew stronger and more frequent. Sweat dripped down Keane's face and back.

"Sir! Keep her still!"

Seeing the assistant's anxious gaze on her arm, Keane climbed on top of the bed and straddled Esmeralda's convulsing body. He covered her completely, pressing her flat against the bed.

"Hold on, sweetheart, just hold on," he whispered, his mouth next to her ear. "Don't fight us! We're doing this for you. God, help me, Esmeralda. Don't leave me. Please, help me." Her body jerked against him. He felt as if he and Esmeralda were locked in a struggle for life, fighting this terrible disease together. More frightened than he'd ever been in his thirty years, he continued to spill out his fears in a hushed voice, telling her how much he needed to have her with him. He explained how wonderful life would be after she got over her illness and the care his family would show her. And over and over again, like a prayer, he told her how much he needed her to live.

The spasms ended as abruptly as they'd begun. Both doctor and assistant expelled a collective sigh of relief, but Keane's breath remained clogged in his throat.

"I believe the rigors have subsided—at least for now. We may need your assistance again, Keane."

"Yes," he answered, his voice shaking. Kissing her cold cheek, he slipped off the bed and looked down at her face. Her hair had spilled wildly around her. He gently smoothed the curls from her closed eyes.

Pulling his chair next to her, he sat down to the endless waiting. He thought about those anxious moments when her body had spasmed beneath him in a parody of love, and the words he'd whispered so desperately. It was true —he needed her. To lose such beauty, such spirit for life— no, he just wouldn't accept it.

Keane looked at her hand beside her still body; the contrast of the stark white sheet against her skin heightened its bluish tinge. He trailed his thumb along the curve of her fingers to their blunt tips. Seeing her lax hand cradled in his infused him with memories of a similar scene. That day so many years ago, the day he'd learned of his father's and brother's deaths, the room had also been stiflingly hot. Then, it had been his mother's hand he'd held —and her grip had not been slack.

His mother squeezed his fingers to numbness, in the throes of another contraction. "Keane, they're dead. My Nicholas . . . Phillip, gone!"

"Mother, calm yourself." Keane glanced at his mother's stomach where it protruded under the sheets. He met Charlotte's steely gaze. His sister had said the shock of the accident had brought on labor—something they must try and stop at all costs. The baby's premature birth meant certain death for the posthumous child of Nicholas Marshall, and possible death for his mourning widow.

"They said it was a sudden squall, that they could not

possibly prepare." She moaned. The room was overly warm from the boiled water they kept ready. Keane stroked his mother's heated brow with his free hand, trying to soothe her. "Marcus won't even let me *see* them. I want to see them one last time!"

"Uncle Marc is right," Charlotte said from behind him, her voice imbued with the strength she'd inherited from her father and not from her mother, who was edging on hysteria. "Seeing Father and Phillip"—she glanced at Keane—"it would be too much for you."

"You have to think of the child." Keane knew the reasons for his uncle's edict and Charlotte's wariness. He'd not spared himself the sight of the bloated bodies, distorted by the salt water they had swallowed in death.

His brother dead. The heir to the Eldridge title and lands. He'd had so much to live for. Phillip had been trained from birth for his role as the future viscount, while Keane, at nineteen, only played at Oxford while gaming the night away at his favorite clubs, more often than not relying on his innate intelligence rather than his study habits to succeed. Hearing his mother's sobs, he could think only one thing: *God, why hadn't it been me? Why didn't I die instead? I was the better choice.*

When he'd received the missive to return home, he'd done so immediately. Even stoic Charlotte's voice had shaken as she explained the details of the sailing accident. He knew then, with a killing certainty, that he could have saved them. If only he'd gone with them, as his father had asked . . . Keane was the better sailor; he could have brought them through the storm. The guilt of remaining alive after two such wonderful and necessary individuals had been swept away by careless fate clawed at him.

"Mummy, I'm scared," Annabella's soft voice called from the bedroom door. Managing a gentle smile, Keane beckoned his seven-year-old sister to his side. After quickly crawling up on the bed, she leaned into the niche of his arm and began sucking her thumb as she twirled a lock of white-blond hair in her fingers. Keane felt an ache in his chest watching his sister revert to habits she'd abandoned with babyhood.

"My children! Who will take care of them with Nicholas gone? I can't do it alone! They need a father."

"I'll be their father," Keane assured his mother.

"You're a boy still." A wan smile flitted across her lips as she reached up to caress his cheek. "My wild boy."

"Mother." He took her hand from his cheek, gently kissed it, then pressed it to her protruding stomach. "This child is more than a brother or sister to me. I will raise it as my own. I'll love and cherish, scold and punish." His voice dropped. "Just like Father."

His mother began to weep softly, and Keane cradled Annabella to him as Charlotte came to his side, placing her hand on his shoulder. Keane hugged both his sisters. In turn, they leaned forward to surround their mother with their arms, becoming a blanket of comfort, smothering her grief.

Keane again squeezed his mother's hand, welcoming the reassuring grip, then felt her grasp relax until it became Esmeralda's whitened hand nestled in his. He inhaled deeply as the past crisis faded into the present one. He'd always believed he should have been the one who died—not Phillip. He recalled how he'd tried to hide from that guilty knowledge with drink and gambling. But ironically, from that moment on, he could not lose. His incredible luck drove him to greater folly. Daringly he'd bet thousands on the turn of a card. But almost as if the fates were mocking him and his greater loss, he would win. He looked down at Esmeralda's pale face and continued to caress her cold knuckles. Would he always win at the trivial, just to lose what really mattered?

Reaching out, he lifted a strand of copper hair and rubbed it between his fingers. Remnants of her haunting beauty still lingered on the death mask her face had become. This woman, lying unconscious in his bed, needed him. For his family, he had been only a substitute, and though he'd provided for them to the best of his ability, he was still a replacement for the lost originals. But here was a woman, a girl really, foolishly trying to take on the world. She needed him. And he needed her. In her, he had found a reason why he—not his brother—had survived: a special woman, meant for him and no one else. And to lose her?

God in heaven, how could he lose her, too?

Not again. Please, not again.

Taking her cold fingers, he rested his forehead against their clasped hands. "Esmeralda, stay with me," he whispered against her icy skin. "Don't leave me behind."

Chapter Twenty-one

Molly could not fit the key into the lock, but Jason's warm, sturdy grip around her shaking fingers guided the key to its mark. With a firm twist of his wrist, the cottage lock clicked, and Jason pushed the door open with one hand. The other he slipped around Molly's waist to guide her inside.

Once he'd shut the door behind them, Jason hugged Molly to him. In the darkened room, he heard what sounded suspiciously like a sniffle. Reaching up, he traced his finger underneath her eye, wiping away the moisture he found there.

"Your friend is receiving the best of care, Molly. There's nothing more you or anyone can do. The rest is out of our hands." He felt Molly's silent nod against his shoulder.

"Wirra, it's just that . . . she looked so bad. Not at all like me Esme. Oh, Jason."

He tightened his hold. "I know, darling. I know." He

could think of no words to reassure her. Despite Keane's efforts, Jason thought Miss MacClure's chances of surviving poor.

"If ye'd known her. If ye'd seen her like I have," Molly cried. "Esme's a good colleen. She don't deserve to be hurtin' so. The times she helped me an' the tyke, put herself out to make us happy." Jason felt her shift her head up to look at him, but the dim moonlight outside did not penetrate the room's darkness. "I even think she gave up her food fer me an' Peter, there not bein' enough fer all of us to eat our fill." He heard Molly choke back her tears. "I told her not to. I told her she'd get sickly."

"Her falling ill was not of your doing, Molly. I won't let you blame yourself."

"I canna help it. I keep thinkin' maybe if I'd forced her to eat more, not been so generous with me portions to Peter . . ."

"Molly." Jason set her away from him, shaking her slightly. "Cholera can strike anyone: young, old, rich, poor. . . . When my brother fell ill, he wasn't lacking for anything, much less such basics as food." Jason rubbed his hands up and down her arms, comforting her. "We don't know what causes cholera. No doubt your friend would have fallen ill under any circumstances. You can't take the blame for this."

Molly sniffled, drying her eyes with the back of her hand. "I suppose yer right."

Jason kissed the top of her head and gave her a quick hug. "Of course, I'm right. I'm always right—remember that."

Molly smiled for the first time that evening, thinking how often she'd said the same words to Esmeralda. "Oh Jason, me love, if ye truly believe that's so, I've a lot to teach ye."

Jason frowned at her teasing words. "Go light a lamp. I can't tell your mood in the dark."

Molly scurried across the plank-wood floor to the

hearth; Jason followed behind her at a slower pace. When the soft, yellow glow of the oil-and-rag lamp revealed the room, the shabbiness of their surroundings struck Jason like a blow to his chest. "My God, Molly." He glanced about, taking in the lone table, the aging sideboard, and the ragged horsehair settee held steady by a rock placed strategically where a leg was missing. The only bit of life was a brightly painted pine cradle by the hearth. Jason thought of the elegantly furnished rooms set aside for his future offspring and the abundance of luxury he'd been raised to expect. "Why didn't you come to me for help?"

Molly softly blew out the spill she'd used to light the fire. "Ye know the answer to that."

Jason turned and gathered Molly into his arms. He pressed her face against his chest, fitting his chin on top of her head. "I can't stand the thought of you and Peter living like this."

Molly pulled away, and Jason realized he'd made her uncomfortable. "I've seen worse," she mumbled under her breath while stepping around him. "I'll be gettin' the bairn's things ready."

Jason watched Molly kneel before a cedar chest and rummage through the clothes inside. He could barely contain his desire to grab her and shake her. Why hadn't she come to him, for God's sake? Peter was his son! He should have the very best, not this . . . this . . . squalor. Jason jammed his hands in his pants pockets, tamping down his useless anger. If he and Molly were to have a successful marriage, he'd have to forget the past, learn to accept it. "You might as well pack up everything. We can leave Miss MacClure's clothes at the Burnet. After we speak to Mother, I'll take you to the Gibson."

Molly stopped her riffling and leaned back against the chest. "An' what would I be doin' at the Gibson?"

Jason raised his eyebrows at her hostile tone. "You can't very well stay here."

Molly stood. Planting her legs wide on the floor, she crossed her arms. "An' why is that?"

Nonplussed by her aggressive stance, Jason eyed her warily. "Just look at this place. It's . . . it's primitive. Not to mention completely secluded. I will not leave you here alone. Not for a single night."

"Happens to be where I've been livin' for almost two years."

Jason flushed, condemned by her words. "Yes. But that was before. I'm here to help you now, Molly." Then, unable to contain himself, "As I would have done if you'd come to me from the beginning, rather than hatch that crazy scheme of yours!"

"I'll not be goin' to the Gibson!"

Jason grabbed her by the shoulders and shook her. "I'm through catering to your willful pride. You're going to be my wife, Molly. You'll do as I say."

The collective glow of lamp and fire reflected in her heated gaze. "An' I suppose you'll be settin' me up at the Gibson until the weddin'?"

"Yes."

"An' after we get hitched, I'll move into that grand house of yers, and we'll live happily ever after with Peter?"

Jason hesitated for a moment, suspicious of her amiable questions. "That's right."

"An' when people come to visit, they'll see me bairn and say how cute he is—and how he looks just like his father."

Jason smiled. "Yes."

"An' call him a bastard!" Molly swung away from Jason. Staring into the fire with deadly earnest, she wrapped her arms tightly around herself. "They leave me and the bairn alone in this town—we're not important. I've always pretended I'm a widow lady to any who asked, an' no one cared enough to question it. If we marry, that will change. It won't take long to make the connection, not with Peter the spittin' image of ye. I'll not have me bairn named bastard."

Molly's reasoning stung Jason to his core. But he refused to let any obstacles stand in the way of their being together. "What do we care what others say? They're just words, Molly."

She spun around to face Jason, her fists balled at her sides. "Words hurt, Jason," she choked out. "They . . . hurt."

Her twisted expression gripped his heart. "Molly." He stepped forward, intending to wrap her in his arms, but the lift of her chin and her rigid stance held him back like a wall. Instead, he stood before her and asked softly, "What words hurt you so badly?"

She remained silent, as if judging the wisdom of revealing too much. Then, tentatively, "Bastard." Her blue gaze weighed the effect of the name. "Misbegotten," she continued more forcefully. "Whore's daughter . . . by-blow." She hurled the words at him, shouting them.

"Stop!" Jason grabbed her, pulling her head against his shoulder, trying to smother the painful names against him. "Stop this!"

"Love child . . . child of shame—" Lifting her face to meet his, her eyes brimming with tears, she confessed, "I'm a bastard, too."

"Oh, Molly." He folded her head against his shoulder.

"That's why I canna be yer mistress, Jason, me love. No matter what I feel fer ye. I canna go the way of me mother."

"I'm not asking you to, Molly. I want you to be my wife."

"But I canna! Sure as ye must realize that now."

Jason cupped her face in his hands and tilted her head up toward his. "Why? Because your father never married your mother? Does that cruel fact make you bad or evil?" And when she didn't answer, he asked, "Does it make Peter evil?"

"Nay, not Peter! He's not to blame fer me sins!"

"Then why must you suffer for your mother's?"

That question, asked so softly, plummeted Molly into confusion, the comparison between Peter and herself too parallel to dismiss. "But it's not the same," she battled, unable to condemn her child to the pain she'd lived with, and equally unable to shed the guilt she'd carried for the circumstances of her birth.

"And how is it different?"

"Peter's just a babe. I've done things." She lowered her gaze before whispering, "terrible things."

"What"—he lifted her chin with the crook of his finger—"things?"

Molly wet her lips nervously. "I . . . I've lied."

"In my business, we call that a negotiating tactic."

Molly searched his eyes, looking for disdain, but reading only amused acceptance. "I've stolen," she blurted out.

Jason looked about the sparsely furnished room. "Not very successfully, I'm afraid. I've done better against my competitors. Next?"

"It was *me* plan, Jason. Not Esme's." She spoke haltingly, her words clogged within her by fear. "I thought of the plan to marry her off to some rich blighter."

"That, I'd already guessed," he said dryly. "But why? Why search out my brother? Why not come to *me* instead?"

"Oh, no, Jason." Molly's eyes widened. "Truly, I didna know t'was yer brother Esme culled."

Jason frowned. "She just *happened* to choose Henry?"

"Sure as he was the only choice, yer paying off anything in a skirt that looked his way twice. Poor Esme, I never told her ye was Peter's father. She thought she'd done good findin' Henry."

Instantly, Jason's features softened, any lingering doubts finally quelled. He smiled. "Your plan rebounded, didn't it? It came right back home to roost."

Molly nodded solemnly. "The whole time I wanted money to leave without ye knowin' about the tyke. But instead, we hook up with yer bleedin' brother."

Jason smoothed the curls away from her face. "Is that it? Confession finished?"

"You expect more?" She pulled away, angry that he'd not taken her seriously. *"Arrah,* that's enough to have me arrested!"

Jason drew her back into his arms. "It's not enough, Molly," he softly murmured against her mouth. "Not nearly enough to make me stop loving you."

Molly tried to shake herself free. "Ye dinna understand."

Jason subdued her weak struggles without effort. "What don't I understand?" he asked between gentle kisses.

"Ye canna love me, Jason."

Jason smiled, staring down at her earnest expression. "Oh? And why is that?"

"Because"—the words became muted—"I'm not lovable."

Jason cradled her against him, stroking his hands up and down her back. "Oh, Molly, me dear," he said, mimicking her Irish lilt. "If it takes the rest of me life, I'll make you see you're wrong."

He burrowed his face against her soft neck, inhaling her light scent of roses. Gently he nuzzled his lips against the warm flesh where her neck met her shoulder. She rewarded him with a responding shiver. Reaching behind her, he unhooked the top fastener of her gown.

It had been a long time since he had undressed a woman. After Molly's flight, he'd dedicated his energies to his work, propelling Carter Shipping into the top tier of commercial enterprises in the city. His work had been his passion, and his isolated instances of sexual gratification had been perfunctory, without emotion. Now, looking down at her lips parted with passion, he wondered how he'd ever believed he could live without her. He tightened his hold around her waist, and Molly threw her head back, arching against him. Her uninhibited response opened a floodgate of unsatisfied physical and emotional needs. His long period of abstinence made caution impossible.

He couldn't seem to remove her clothing fast enough. Sensing his impatience, Molly helped with the many fasteners and hooks that barred the feel of his flesh against hers. How she'd dreamed of this moment . . . to be in Jason's arms again, experiencing the heat and longing only he could create. "I love ye, Jason." Molly blinked back tears of relief.

"Good," he said gruffly. "We're in agreement, then."

She smiled at his matter-of-fact tone. Even in his lovemaking, Jason had always been practical. "What about Peter?" she sighed, enjoying the soft kisses he trailed from the base of her neck to her ear.

"I'll think of something," he murmured softly, working to untie the lacing of her corset. "And if I don't, we'll set my mother's ingenious brain to it. Not a wagging tongue in Cincinnati will be safe."

"What could your mother do to stop the gossip?"

He thought a moment. "She'll go out in the middle of the night and tie shoes to their doorknobs." He continued to loosen her corset.

"What?"

"Never mind. I'll explain later."

As Molly tore off his neck scarf and unbuttoned the top fasteners of his shirt, he kissed her neck and bare shoulders. When she reached the third button on the white linen, she lowered her head to the middle of his chest and began kissing the skin exposed as she unhooked the mother-of-pearl buttons. Unable to resist, she stroked the silky hairs on his chest with her tongue, eliciting a low moan from Jason. She continued to the next button, as he pulled her down with him to the floor in front of the hearth.

Lying on top of him, Molly parted his shirt, spreading it open, off his shoulders. Her corset lay on the floor beside her gown, and she lifted her hands over her head to help Jason pull off her cotton chemise. Very slowly, with her eyes locked on Jason's passion-darkened gaze, she lowered her breasts to his chest and rubbed against him. The satisfying friction created by the curly hair covering his muscles caused the tips of her breasts to harden and peak.

"I love ye, Jason. With all me heart."

"Molly."

Alternately biting and tenderly kissing his musk-scented skin, Molly progressed down his neck to his muscular chest. The flat nipples surrounded by soft, black hair tempted her, and she licked and sucked at each before continuing her magic down the black vee that ended at the top of his trousers. Once she reached the cloth band of his pants, her hands furiously unfastened the opening and reached inside for the thick shaft she knew lay within. His eyes closed, Jason groaned and stroked her hair, urging her to continue. In answer, Molly encompassed him in her hand and squeezed while stroking up and down his length in what she knew was a satisfying rhythm. Everything she knew about lovemaking she'd learned with Jason. She longed to weave every moment they'd experienced together and relive them all now.

Before long, Jason grabbed her hand to stop her erotic motion. Opening his eyes to meet hers, he pulled her body to cover him and reached down to remove her drawers. He rolled her on her back and quickly discarded the rest of their clothing before covering her with his body. He reached down between her legs and the feel of her moist and ready passion excited him even further. Burying his face between her breasts, he parted her legs with his hands and stroked the insides of her soft, inviting thighs as he gently pressed against her. When he glided inside her, feeling her warm and tight entrance pulsing around him, he experienced a sense of completion so profound it frightened him.

"My God, Molly," he moaned.

"Dinna stop, Jason. Please, not now." Sensing his hesitation, Molly wrapped her legs and arms around him, tying him to her.

Her sensual plea divorced him of all thought. Jason plunged forward and deepened their connection. At that moment, the muscles surrounding his erection contracted and Molly's moan of satisfaction propelled him into sexual oblivion.

A short while later with his body collapsed on hers, Jason kissed her with such tenderness that she felt her throat tighten and tears well in her eyes.

"Oh, Molly," he sighed. Then he wrapped her in his comforting embrace and hugged her to him, vowing they'd never part.

Chapter Twenty-two

Keane watched from his balcony as the orange-pink glow
of dawn crested the indigo hills, suffusing the morning sky
with light. He lifted his cheroot to his lips, taking another
deep drag from the cigar. His fears for Esmeralda seemed
a little less chilling in the light of the new day, but the
night had been a trial. They'd repeated the injection of
fluid at midnight. As the clock over the mantle chimed its
twelve strokes, Keane had watched Esmeralda carefully
for signs of distress as the doctor and his assistant pumped
more liquid into her veins. Thankfully, this time she'd not
experienced rigors, but the procedure had left Keane exhausted both physically and mentally. His collar open, his
shirt sleeves rolled up his arms, he'd waited outside for
the past two hours, watching the dawn fold back the blue-
black sky of the night. He needed a shave and a bath. But
more than anything, he needed to know Esmeralda would
be all right.

As if his thoughts had summoned him, Dr. Anderson

slipped past the French doors and onto the balcony. Keane looked up apprehensively.

"My wife?"

"Is doing fine." He placed his hand on Keane's shoulder. "She's going to make it."

"Thank God." Keane's chin fell to his chest. He wanted to cry . . . to laugh . . . he didn't know which, anything to release the anxiety he'd kept bottled up during his vigil.

"Come in and see her," the doctor said with a smile. "I think you'll be pleased."

Keane threw the cheroot to the floor and pushed past the French doors to the bedchamber. He went immediately to Esmeralda's side, sitting on the edge of the bed next to her. Examining her beloved features carefully, he saw the remarkable changes she'd undergone in just the past hour. There was a hint of pink to her skin, replacing the gray-blue color of illness. Her face looked fuller, the sharp planes taking on more of its natural heart shape. Despite the dark circles beneath her eyes, to Keane, she looked more beautiful than ever.

"I've left some medicine with your valet."

Keane stood, turning his attention to Dr. Anderson as he instructed Keane on Esmeralda's care. Both the doctor and his assistant had packed their equipment and looked ready to leave.

"Take care of her, Keane."

Keane shook the doctor's hand. "How can I ever repay you for saving my wife?"

Dr. Anderson smiled, that same youthful grin that had given Keane such hope when they'd first met for its optimism. "I also left a sizable bill."

"She's worth every penny and more."

"It's a miracle that she lived, you know." Keane nodded at the doctor's words. "You should thank a higher source than myself for intervening. God has given you a great gift, Keane." Dr. Anderson tipped his hat in parting. "Take care of it."

"I will."

After the doctor left, Keane sat down beside Esmeralda. Bringing her hand to his lips, he kissed her skin lightly. She slept peacefully now, for all the world resting as if nothing had happened. But for Keane, the night had wreaked incredible changes.

He thought of Alysha—how dead she'd left him inside and the cynicism he'd cultivated over the years after her rejection. He'd believed he'd never again be able to admit to the emotion that held him so powerfully as he watched Esmeralda sleep. But now he felt free to speak it at last.

With a smile, Keane leaned over and brushed his lips against hers. He whispered against her mouth, "I love you, Esmeralda," then curled up on the bed beside her.

Keane folded the newspaper and shoved it under his arm. He tossed a coin to the newsboy and adjusted his hold on the two dozen blood-red roses he'd just purchased. Taking the steps two at a time, he climbed up the stairs to the columned entrance of the Burnet, tipping his hat to a group of ladies as he did so.

Two weeks had passed since Esmeralda had fallen ill and there was still no news of cholera in the papers. But it would come. He'd seen the pigs and dogs roaming the streets like good soldiers on patrol. Sanitation, the only known precautionary measure against the spread of cholera, was pathetically insufficient in the city. Keane well remembered the epidemic of '32. Soon business would be overwhelmingly good for the undertakers and gravediggers.

Life after cholera was against the odds.

Climbing up one of the grand staircases to his suite, he thought about the small miracle he'd left this morning in his canopied bed and a smile spread across his lips. She'd been playing cards on her lap, clothed in a pink dressing gown that emphasized her glow of health, as if survival had never been a doubtful wager.

He'd beaten the odds; he'd beaten death. He had Esmeralda back.

Whistling under his breath, his step light, Keane swung open the door to his suite. Immediately, Higgins was there to greet him.

"How is our patient doing this morning, Higgins?" Keane handed his fragrant bundle to his valet.

"Feisty as ever, your lordship."

Keane whipped off his jacket, and exchanged the coat for the flowers. "Tried to foist your witch medicine on her again, did you?"

Higgins beamed. "Threw the cup right back at me."

"Good." Keane slapped his valet's back, sharing in Higgins's rising spirits. "She'll be up and about any day now."

"My thoughts exactly, my lord."

With subdued impatience, Keane turned toward the bedchamber. But before taking a step, he again faced his valet with a thoughtful expression. "Threw the cup at you?"

"Yes, your lordship."

Keane grinned. "I'll try to remember that tactic in the future."

Keane arrived at the door to the bedchamber he'd vacated two weeks before. Tapping softly, he waited for the melodic response. When it came, a smile spread wide across his lips.

Esmeralda tried to ignore the butterflies Keane's presence always created. Today he was dressed in fashionable black twilled cotton trousers and a striped waistcoat. His handsome countenance had its usual devastating effect on her peace of mind. All smiles, he pulled up a chair and placed his gift of roses across her outstretched arms. The crooked curve of his wide lips made her heart contract, as did the warm expression in his amber eyes. She buried her nose in the flowers and inhaled their rose fragrance as if it were a tonic against her weakness.

"Do you like them, sweets?"

"They're beautiful. But where do you suggest we put them?" Her eyes narrowed as she looked about the flower-festooned room. "The only place left is on top of my head!"

Keane threw his head back and laughed. "You'd look lovely, even with flowers sprouting from your head. But I'll have Higgins put some of these in the salon."

Esmeralda frowned. How easy it would be to succumb to his seductive charm. "I remember reading somewhere that plants take up the air in a room. Is that your plan, your lordship? You wish to do away with me by smothering me with flowers?"

Keane's smile turned warm and intimate. Taking one of her hands, he placed a soft kiss at the pulse point on the inside of her wrist. "I fought too hard for the privilege of keeping you to do away with you now." Before she could complain about his intimate touch, he squeezed her hand gently and placed it back on top of the velvety petals.

Esmeralda felt herself flush. Keane's actions during her recovery confused and tantalized her. At every opportunity, he would touch her. Not in any manner that was offensive, but it was unsettling nonetheless. And often she would catch him looking at her with an almost possessive gleam in his eyes. According to Molly, Keane had been responsible for bringing her back from the dead. And during the past two weeks, he'd been completely dedicated to her quick and comfortable recovery. Every time she'd suggested she should move back to the cottage, he argued that she was not well enough. And whenever Dr. Anderson came to check on her progress, Keane interrogated the poor man mercilessly about her health.

On a daily basis, Keane presented her with lavish gifts: flowers, little ceramic figurines, chocolates—lots of chocolates, which she loved. He called her "sweets" constantly now, a teasing reminder of her love for the tasty confections he brought home. During what could have been depressingly lonely evenings, he dined with her, eating his simple meals from a tray by her bedside, and regaling her with funny stories of his childhood until she felt she'd recognize his sisters immediately on sight. On those evenings together, she'd seen another Keane—a man devoted to his family, who missed the support and friendship of his father and brother, both of whom he'd told her had died in a drowning accident. And a man who seemed to care for her a great deal.

He frightened her—his almost loving attentions threatened her resolve to leave for California as soon as she was able. But she must get to the goldfields! She needed the money to win back Amberose. Amberose was her dream —not this charming man whose smile alone could make her breathless. Each day she planned her trip to California with a determination born of desperation.

She must remember what care and companionship had yielded her in the past: betrayal—her cousin's, and now Molly's, who seemed to grow more committed to Jason each day. Like a catechist, Esmeralda repeated to herself that Keane acted out of guilt for her lost innocence. His care during the last weeks was his payment for seducing her in his carriage. His sense of honor was such that he was even willing to marry her because he'd taken her virginity. He didn't love her—he pitied her. She wasn't special.

And yet looking at Keane now, his features fixed in a boyish expression of excitement over his gift of roses, she couldn't help *feeling* special. She remembered that Molly had once likened Keane to a snake. Esmeralda considered what she'd read about the cobra's dance, how it mesmerized its victims until the snake struck them dead. After all she'd suffered from those who "loved" her, would she succumb again to the emotion's deceiving allure? No, she must depend on no one but herself.

"How do you feel today?" Keane's mellow voice from her bedside broke through her depressing thoughts.

"Fine." Angry at her breathy voice, she cleared her throat, striving for a commanding tone. "But if I don't get out of this bed soon, you're going to find me howling at the moon one of these nights."

"We can't rush your recovery."

"Rush? I've been confined to this bed for an entire fortnight! Higgins spends his days thinking of bizarre concoctions—each more vile than its predecessor—to drown me in. You feed me chocolates and pastries as if they had some medicinal properties. If I don't get some sort of exercise soon, I'll . . . I'll get fat!"

Trying quite unsuccessfully not to smile, Keane said, "I understand you've put a stop to Higgins's helpful efforts."

Esmeralda folded her hands over the roses before mumbling, "I warned him yesterday I'd not drink another drop of that poison. He should have believed me." She looked up, contrite. "I didn't mean to hit him. I merely wished to let him know I was quite serious when I said the 'remedies' *must* stop. I aimed for the wall behind him. I can't help it if he ducked right into the cup's path."

"I'm sure he's learned his lesson. You'll not have to worry about his potions again. As for going to fat"— Keane reveled in the glow of health emanating from her pinkened cheeks and sparkling eyes—"I was only trying to satisfy what I saw was a decided sweet tooth. You didn't have to eat the chocolates, you know."

"It's practically torture to stare at those heavenly confections and *not* eat them," she replied peevishly.

Keane smiled. "In the future, I'll see that no such temptations appear on your plate."

Esmeralda thought for a moment. Then, unable to help herself, "Well, maybe one."

"One?"

"Yes." Esmeralda focused with undue concentration on

the cover as she smoothed her hands over her lap. "One of those cream-filled things with the almond icing."

"The iced puffs?"

She nodded, biting her lip. At that moment she reminded Keane of his ten-year-old sister Nicky when she was caught pulling one of her many pranks. "I'll let Higgins know."

A smile of delight threaded across her lips. "I really will get fat, you know."

For a moment, Keane remembered a pale and shriveled Esmeralda. He forced himself to focus on her rosy complexion and full pink lips, until the garish apparition faded, freeing him of his cold fears. With a sigh of relief, he lowered his gaze to the tempting swell beneath her bodice, outlined by the folded covers pressed against her. All thoughts of his patient's weakened condition fled, and a swift, almost painful, desire gripped him.

A slow, determined smile pulled at his lips. "We'll think of some form of exercise for you, sweets." Esmeralda raised her eyebrows at the odd remark, and Keane quickly added, "In any event, we'll have to wait until Dr. Anderson says you're well enough. I won't let you push yourself."

Esmeralda waved away the speech she knew was coming. "I know, I know. I was deathly ill and must take special care of myself until I get my strength back."

"It sounds as if I've been repeating myself."

Esmeralda nodded, trying to sound grave, but having trouble not laughing. *"Constantly."*

Keane reached over and brushed a curl off her face. She really looked like her old self—better, actually. When he first met Esmeralda, she was thin, too thin, her lovely face made unnecessarily angular by what he knew now had been hunger. She had a fuller, healthier look about her. He furrowed his brow. She'd soon be well enough to leave.

Keane stood and stepped away from the bed. "We

should talk about what happens after you're fully recovered," he said softly. "You understand, of course, that your trip to California is now completely out of the question."

Esmeralda felt herself bristle, the lovely feel of his hands brushing against her face forgotten. California was her escape; it was the means to achieving her dreams. What did he mean, she couldn't go? Trying to keep her tone civil, she stated, "I hadn't heard anything that required a change of plans. Tell me, your lordship, is there a travel ban of some sort? Or has the *Eureka* sunk?"

"Neither." The muscles at Keane's jaw tightened. "You know I can't let you go."

"I wasn't aware I needed your permission."

"What would have happened to you if you'd caught cholera on board ship or in California? Who would have helped you then? Surely, you can see how foolish your scheme to go to the goldfields alone is!"

"But I did not catch cholera on the *Eureka* or in California. I am now in perfect health, and while I greatly appreciate your past assistance, I believe I am sufficiently recovered to take care of myself."

"It so happens, I made inquiries on your behalf, and the *Eureka* is fully booked." Keane quickly calculated how much it would cost him to buy out the passage. He'd buy the entire ship if he had to!

Esmeralda felt her heart pound in her chest. Booked? But she had to get to the goldfields. "The *Eureka* can't be the only passenger ship going to California."

He revised his calculations to include other ships, then decided it would be much cheaper to bribe all the shipping agents on Front Street. About to shout she could just go ahead and *try* to find passage, Keane checked his anger at the sight of the mutinous twist of her lips. He would get nowhere trying to bully her. And yet, after two weeks of watching over her and caring for her, he felt as if he'd earned a say in her future. Together, they had beaten death! Fate had deemed that they be together. Taking a deep breath, Keane counted to ten mentally. Around the count of five, an incredible, outrageous plan began to form in his head.

"You have the money to purchase the fare, of course?"

"No. Not yet." Esmeralda's hands tightened into fists. "But I'm sure I'll get it."

"In that case, I have a few options you may want to consider first."

"For example?" she asked guardedly.

Keane strolled toward her and sat on the chair by her bedside. "My offer of marriage still stands."

Unlike in the carriage, this time Keane delivered his proposal without any signs of self-sacrifice. Gazing into his brandy-colored eyes, Esmeralda saw nothing but warmth and tenderness. His admiring regard and the softness of his expression brought to mind her own confusing reactions to him. She shivered. Marry Keane? The man who could cause her to completely forget herself just by the touch of his hand?

"As I said before, your lordship, I have no intention of marrying."

Keane smiled, undaunted. "Somehow I expected that would be your answer. Perhaps my second suggestion is more to your liking." Keane stood and walked toward the fireplace directly at the foot of the bed. Leaning one shoulder against the mantel, he crossed his arms. "I have a business proposition for you." Seeing he had her attention, he continued, "You plan to get your estate back, correct?"

Esmeralda nodded.

"I am willing to finance your attempts to get legal title. I'll pay for your passage back to England and for your living expenses and the legal fees pending the resolution of your claims."

"And what do you get out of this?"

"Fifteen percent of the estate's earnings for twenty-five years."

Esmeralda watched him suspiciously. It sounded *too* good. There had to be a trick. "What if the estate doesn't clear its costs?"

"Fifteen percent of the *net* earnings," he explained. And after a moment, "And an equal vote on all major financial decisions."

"And if we disagree on a venture?"

"The deadlock would be broken by an unbiased third party, acceptable to both."

Esmeralda bit a nail. "Do we put this in writing?"

"Just say the word, and I'll have Jason draw up the papers."

Money! At last enough money to fight Allen! And she wouldn't have to feel guilty about how she got the funds, or depend on some nebulous chance of striking gold! She was negotiating with what was truly hers: Amberose.

Keane pushed away from the mantel and advanced toward her. His eyes almost incandescent, he stood at the foot of the bed. "There is one small condition."

Esmeralda's stomach fell with disappointment. "I should have known."

"I'll need to oversee the entire process of regaining your estate."

She narrowed her eyes. "Why?"

"Because I want to make sure it's done right. I'm willing to invest a great deal of money in the venture, but I refuse to do so on blind trust. You understand, of course." The right corner of his mouth curved upward in a challenging smile. "This is just business."

"And what would your supervision entail?"

Keane stepped toward the side of the bed. "I want my own solicitors to handle all the legal transactions. I want to be involved in all negotiations for the estate."

"But that would require that we work together a great deal."

"It would."

Esmeralda considered Keane's stipulation. Now more than ever she felt a desire to flee from his handsome face and gentle touch. It was all too disturbing, fighting the suffocating feelings she had for Keane. Yet to have the means to get back to her home at her disposal and turn her back on it seemed unthinkable.

"Is that the extent of your conditions?"

"Yes."

"How much time do I have to consider your proposal."

Keane's smile reeked victory. "All the time you need, sweets."

Esmeralda bit on her nail nervously. All the money she needed. Hers. Now. No more struggling. No trip to California . . . but she'd constantly have to fight her attraction to Keane—not give into her feelings and risk betrayal.

Smiling like the cat that swallowed the canary, Keane held up his hand as if he'd just recalled a last item of discussion. "One more thing I should make clear. I will, of course, have to accompany you to England. That I consider would be part of my supervision of the project."

"You don't trust me very much, do you?"

"As I said, this is business. And," he continued, strolling back down the length of the bed, "as I have a reputation to maintain, I don't think it would be wise for us to travel together without some kind of civilized arrangement."

"What kind of *arrangement?*"

"Well"—Keane sat on the edge of the bed, beside her— "marriage comes to mind as very civilized."

"Lord Eldridge, you seem to have a problem understanding the word 'no.' "

"If you're so set against marrying me, becoming a viscountess, and being rich beyond your wildest dreams," he stated in a dry tone, "I would agree to *posing* as married."

Esmeralda discarded the idea outright. "Couldn't we have a chaperone—like Molly, for instance?"

"Unless it has escaped your notice, Miss Egan is previously engaged."

Esmeralda wrinkled her nose. It was true. Molly's visits the past weeks always included Jason Carter. From the smoldering looks those two gave each other, Molly would probably turn her down flat, just as she'd refused Esmeralda's suggestion to go to California. Molly's abandonment of Esmeralda hardened her resolve. "Well then, someone else could serve as a chaperone. I'm sure we could find someone eager to be hired—"

He shook his head. "I prefer to keep things simple—just the two of us. Come now, Miss MacClure. Why haggle over details? You've proved yourself an accomplished actress in the past. Posing as my wife should give you no trouble." He lifted his brows. "Should it?"

"You mean, the whole agreement hinges on whether or not I agree to travel with you as your wife? That's part of your condition?"

"I'm afraid so."

"You should have said so at the beginning!"

"Would you believe, I'd hoped you'd agree without my insisting?" Keane leaned forward, closer to her. "That perhaps you'd marry me for my money, if not my good looks?"

Esmeralda ignored his mocking words. "How long would we have to pose as a married couple?"

"Until we reach England should be sufficient."

"After that, we're on our own?"

"The very second we touch ground, you're a free woman."

Esmeralda looked away from Keane's penetrating gaze. For goodness' sake, how could she even hesitate at such an offer? All the money and legal support she needed to get back Amberose. Yet even as she scoffed at her wavering, she wanted to scream "no" and run from Keane and the warming comforts he'd provided. And she suddenly knew why. She loved him. Even though she wanted desperately to deny it, there seemed no escaping the feelings she had for this man. Just as Jason had captured Molly's heart, Keane had hooked hers well and good.

She felt trapped by her own desires. Yet could she afford to refuse him? Could she turn her back on her dreams just because of her fears of love?

She really had no choice.

She was about to sound her agreement when she met Keane's amber gaze. The immediate effects his gentle look and charming smile had on her pulse kept her quiet. Heavens, he was so handsome, so charming. The cloying tendrils around her heart that she'd come to identify as love squeezed tighter.

She swallowed. All the money she needed—a sure thing —and all she had to do was face this man on a daily basis for the short voyage to England.

"All right," Esmeralda croaked. Then, clearing her voice, she answered more forcefully, "Yes, I agree to your terms. As long as we're in public, we'll act as a married couple would."

Arms crossed and leaning against the bedpost of the canopied bed, Keane's smile looked triumphant. "You won't regret this, sweets. You've made a wise decision."

"Not like I had a great deal of choice," she mumbled.

Ignoring her sulky tone, Keane stood beside her. "I believe now that we are in agreement, all that's left is for us to seal our bargain."

Esmeralda looked up warily. "Is that a regular procedure? I mean, don't we wait for the legal documents?"

"Certainly, but gentlemen always shake hands as a show of good faith after concluding an agreement."

Keane's sultry expression from directly beside the bed caused Esmeralda to catch her breath. "But I am not a gentleman."

"Then we'll just have to improvise," Keane murmured,

as he dipped his head down and captured her lips in a gentle kiss.

Esmeralda felt her desire for Keane flare instantly, like a smoldering flame igniting under a breath of air. His soft moist lips moved across hers tentatively at first, cautiously, but when she reached up and wrapped her arms around his neck, unable to help herself, Keane licked at her lips with his tongue until she opened her mouth to him. Hesitantly, she brushed her tongue against his. Keane immediately deepened the kiss and brought a hand up to brush against her satin-clad shoulder. But when his touch dropped to her breast, Esmeralda started and pulled away, remembering her faltering promise to resist Keane and the temptation he presented.

Keane reluctantly pulled away from Esmeralda. This was precisely what he'd dreamed about during the two weeks he'd watched her recover. Seeing her here, in his bed—dressed in the delightful creations he had purchased for her—had made him want her more than ever. And yet today was the first day he'd acted on his desires, afraid that she was too weak to respond to him before now. Their verbal sparring had assured him that she was fully recovered, and the smoldering kiss they'd just shared removed any doubts he had about her health. He had her back. Thank God, he had her back.

Slowly, he stepped away from Esmeralda. She looked so confused, it made him smile. The trip to England stretched out before him, giving him more than ample time to make sure she could never leave him. He planned to make the most of this opportunity. He'd tried the honorable way. Hadn't he offered marriage sincerely, without trickery? Of course, he'd known she would refuse. She was obsessed with her desire to recapture her estate, and for some reason she seemed to believe an emotional involvement with him would stand in her way. But he'd learned long ago how to use people's desires for his own gain. By couching his proposal as a business proposition, in which it appeared he had something to gain financially, he'd known he would persuade her to let him help her. She'd walked right into his plans. Judging from her response to his kiss, Esmeralda would be his long before they ever reached the shores of home.

"I'll let you rest now, sweetheart." Keane said gently. Tucking the sheets around her, he bent over her and placed a chaste kiss on her forehead. He couldn't help smiling at her wary expression. Time. All he needed was a little time and the minx would come to accept their life together.

Esmeralda watched Keane silently close the door behind him as he walked out of the bedchamber. She slowly let out the breath she'd been holding. Heavens! What had she just agreed to!

Chapter Twenty-three

Esmeralda looked down on the jewel-like colors covering the counterpane. A dress of Tibetan merino was spread majestically across one corner of the bed, while the elegant folds of emerald-colored gros de Brazil swept over an Alpaca poplin gown. She was familiar with each material, having worked with them when making dresses for her clients—other people's dresses. Picking up the silk cord of the poplin, she pulled its smooth length across her fingers. But these gowns were hers—an entire wardrobe, fashionable and expensive, selected for her trip back to England. Keane had purchased the clothes some time ago, but she'd only recently been well enough to make use of them. Now, almost three weeks after her recovery, she sifted through their luscious colors each morning, making the difficult decision of which to wear.

Lovingly she smoothed her palms over the rust foulard she'd chosen for this morning. Turning toward the full-length mirror, she stared at her reflection. The close-fitting gown made her look almost regal. The skirt, trimmed with two deep flounces, fell in graceful folds around her, and the high bodice outlined her generous curves. A faint memory—a time when she'd expected to wear fine clothes —gently nudged her as she fingered the silk.

The click of the opening door drew her attention away from her image in the mirror. Molly marched in, a gown of teal blue swirling about her small form as she slammed the door behind her.

"Why did ye not tell me?"

Esmeralda stared, stunned by her friend's vehemence. "Tell you what?"

Her arms crossed uncompromisingly before her, Molly backed Esmeralda against the tester bed. "Don't ye pretend with me. I heard all about it! Imagine, me findin' out ye've married from Jason!"

"Married?"

Molly's eyes flew open. "Yer not goin' to deny it now, are ye? Bless us an' save us! Do ye not trust me? Oh, maybe I was a bit harsh with the viscount afore he married ye. But it was an act, see? I had to let the snake know he was to do the proper thing." Molly enfolded Esmeralda into an enthusiastic hug. "I'm so happy, *mavourneen.* Now nobody can hurt ye."

From over her friend's shoulder, Esmeralda watched the door open and Keane sweep in. Her eyes narrowed. "Well, if it isn't my *husband.*" Her voice dripped acid sweetness as she extricated herself from Molly's python hold.

Keane stopped dead. Exactly what he'd hoped to intercept when he'd heard Molly mumbling something about marriage as she barreled toward the bedchamber had already happened. So Jason had done a little improvising after drawing up the contract for Keane and Esmeralda. Well, there was nothing for it now but to play the scene out as best he could.

Flashing a winning smile, he hooked an arm around

Esmeralda's waist and tugged her to his side. "I saw no reason not to let Molly and Jason know."

"I can think of *one* very good reason."

"She thought you might not approve." Keane smiled his explanation to Molly. "She wanted to break the news to you herself, but I must have let something slip to Jason." Of course, Jason knew all the details of Keane's agreement with Esmeralda. Apparently his friend had seen fit to ease Molly's worries by telling her that Keane and Esmeralda had actually married.

"But 'tis wonderful news!" Molly again hugged Esmeralda, then pumped Keane's hand up and down enthusiastically. "I knew ye'd do yer duty. No hard feelings?"

Keane looked down on the little virago who had made his life nothing but hell for the last weeks. Each day she'd appeared at his door, demanding better care of her convalescing friend. Each day had given birth to a new complaint: He wasn't feeding her right; Esmeralda didn't get enough sun. But the most prevalent complaint had been the one thing he'd refused to change—Esmeralda's presence in his suite. At times Molly's visits had broken down into shouting matches, with Higgins pulling him to one corner and Jason taking control of Molly. Keane forced a congenial smile. "Of course not. You were only trying to protect Esmeralda from my lascivious attacks."

"Exactly," Molly chimed in wholeheartedly, then turned to Esmeralda. "But why did ye not let me know sooner ye were gettin' hitched? I'd of stood up fer ye." Molly's eyes clouded up. "To think I missed yer weddin'—"

"It couldn't be helped," Keane explained. "As soon as the doctor thought her up to it, we rushed right across the river to Kentucky. After all, if anyone should get wind of her staying here without the benefit of matrimony . . ."

Molly nodded. "Yer right. I dinna want her reputation to suffer. T'was best to do it with as little fuss as possible.

Still"—Molly took Esmeralda's hands in hers— "I'd have given anything to be there, *mavourneen.*"

"You didn't miss a thing, Molly." Esmeralda looked up at Keane, her smile a mere gnashing of teeth. "Why, everything happened so quickly, I almost feel as if . . . as if it didn't happen at all."

Keane gave her waist a squeeze. "Perhaps we should repeat the ceremony—it might be more memorable the second time around."

Esmeralda pressed her lips together, biting back a heated reply. "That won't be necessary." Uncoiling his arm from around her waist, she sashayed around Keane. "If you'll excuse us, *darling.* I want Molly to go over my new wardrobe and see if I need anything else for the trip." She glanced pointedly at the door.

For a split second he almost refused, thinking of the havoc the Irish termagant could raise if she even smelled a whiff of deception. But he didn't think Esmeralda would tell her friend the truth; she would have done so already if that had been her intention. He nodded once. "Of course. I'll be working at my desk if you need anything." At the door, he paused. "Remember, sweets, our ship leaves in two days. We wouldn't want *anything* to delay our plans, would we? Be sure to purchase whatever you need today." He shut the door behind him silently.

"*Wirra,* if that ain't the strangest . . ." Molly turned accusingly to Esmeralda. "Ye married to the blighter or not?"

"Oh, Molly, stop worrying so much. Everything is working out just fine." She led Molly to the bed. Shifting aside some of the gowns, Esmeralda plopped down on the edge, seating Molly next to her. She turned to face her friend, examining her with surprise. "You look . . . marvelous . . . glowing."

Molly flushed. Her sapphire eyes grew dreamy. " 'Tis Jason. I've never been so happy. I love him so much. Bein' with him and Peter . . . 'tis the happiest I've ever been."

Esmeralda felt her throat tighten. Jason Carter was the reason for her friend's joyful expression. Despite Esmeralda's many warnings, Molly had thrown her lot in with him. She'd truly lost Molly. Esmeralda hoped her friend's happiness would last.

"But I still worry—Jason bein' so important here in Cincinnati," Molly continued, a slight frown marring her brow. "I'm afraid someone will figure out he's Peter's father."

"I thought you said his mother would come up with some marvelous plan?"

Molly smiled. "An' that she did, bless her heart. I'm supposed to be some long-lost relative. Married to some cousin of theirs. That explains why Peter looks so much like a Carter. I fell into hard times after my husband's death and was ashamed to come to them right off for help. They took me in as soon as they discovered who I was." Molly frowned. "Not that I'd believe such a story meself, but Samantha says when she's through with this town they'll be beggin' to invite me to their social whirls. Plans to drop a few hints about me father bein' an earl and that some of me designs are worn by royalty. She says that will have them sniffin' around me in no time. There's only one catch."

"What?"

"I'm not to speak a word to anyone until she completely breaks me of me brogue." Molly stuck her tongue out in distaste. "She says if I want people to forget I was just one of the town's seamstresses, I'll have to learn to speak like a lady. Has me locked up in that country house of theirs, practicing every day with her an' some book on manners. 'Do come in and have some tea. The opera was wonderful tonight.'" Esmeralda started laughing at Molly's sour expression as she repeated the polite phrases. *"Arrah,* 'tis a bloody waste of time, I'm thinkin'."

"Well, I'm glad to see Jason's mother is having more success than *I* ever had."

Molly turned to face Esmeralda, her expression sad for the first time. Gripping her hand tightly, she said, "I'm goin' to miss ye something fierce, me girl."

"Me, too, Molly."

"Ye'll be happy with the viscount, won't ye, Esme? I did the right thing, makin' him marry ye?"

Seeing her friend's eyes darken with concern, Esmeralda pulled Molly into her embrace. "You did the right thing. We both did."

When the door flew open an hour later, Keane was ready. He watched Esmeralda march in, her fisted hands swinging with each step, and he smiled. He'd been looking forward to this meeting—he knew it was as inevitable as the sun's rising. When she stopped before his desk, planting both hands on her hips, he pushed back on his chair and rested casually against it. "Do come in," he drawled.

She ignored his sarcasm. "Our bargain was not to start until we boarded the ship."

Keane thought about explaining he'd had nothing to do with Molly's misinformation, but seeing the fire burning in her eyes and the way her tempting breasts, beautifully presented by the snug fit of her bodice, rose and fell as she breathed, he decided against it.

That would end the fun much too quickly.

"Oh, I see." He crossed his hands behind his head, preparing to enjoy himself. "We were supposed to board the ship *unattached*. Somehow I thought being secretly married *before* boarding, rather than appearing miraculously as man and wife sometime in between here and England, made more sense. How thickheaded of me."

"And arrogant! Not to mention high-handed, obnoxious . . . and . . . and . . . bumptious!"

"Bumptious?" Keane lifted a brow, feigning shock. "Certainly not bumptious?" He grinned. "You wound me deeply."

"We need to establish some rules," Esmeralda pressed.

"I will *not* be controlled! I *will* have equal say in this . . . endeavor."

Keane remained silent for a moment, studying Esmeralda. Arms crossed before her, she looked as determined as the goddess Diana before a hunt, and just as beautiful. "Rules, I understand." Keane unwrapped his arms and leaned forward on his desk. "What are the rules to this game, sweets?"

"The papers I signed gave you a say in *financial decisions,* not how to run my life. I am still my own person! I cannot believe you would go about telling people—my friend in particular—we are married before we've discussed the how and when of it."

Keane picked up a quill from his desk and played with its feathered tip thoughtfully. "As it happens, I didn't." Dropping the pen, he stood and walked around the writing desk. Esmeralda followed him with her eyes, turning a slow pirouette until her back was to the desk and Keane stopped in front of her. "Jason came up with the idea of telling Molly we were married all by himself. I had nothing to do with it. In fact, today was the first I've heard of it."

Esmeralda had the grace to blush. "You could have told me that."

"I just did." Keane looked down at her full, tempting lips and his mood sobered. It had been a long time since he'd kissed her—not since they'd sealed their bargain the week before, when she'd still been confined to bed. He brushed the back of his knuckles against her heated cheek. Her skin felt so smooth and warm.

Esmeralda jerked her head away from his touch, but held her ground. "I mean before now—why didn't you say so when I first came in?" The right corner of Keane's mouth barely curled upward and Esmeralda felt a familiar weakness in her legs.

"It was an experiment." Keane stepped closer, backing her up against the desk. When she tried to step around him, he simply placed his hands on the desk behind her, surrounding her with his arms. As she watched him warily, he reached with one hand and dug his fingers into the burnished curls at her temples, threading through the soft tendrils to her scalp. He could feel her breath become short and difficult. When she tried to pull away, he grabbed her face with both hands and held her head tightly so she couldn't move. "I wanted to see your eyes when you're angry. The color changes. Did you know that?"

When she didn't respond, he stepped closer. Her hips met his. Her breast lightly grazed his chest. He tilted her head up so he could see her eyes and still hold her close. "The color gets deeper, darker when you're angry. I wanted to compare—wanted to see if I could make them darker still."

"I don't think I like your experiment." There was just a hint of fear in her voice.

Lowering his mouth to hers, Keane replied, "I think you do."

Esmeralda tried to push Keane away, battling him and her reaction to his kiss. When that had no effect, she attempted to shift her mouth from under his, but he kept her face imprisoned between his hands. The softness of his lips, the very taste of him, soon wrought its magic. Logic, fear, and a gamut of other emotions that warned her against succumbing, were washed away by the tide of sensual adrenaline coursing through her veins. Slowly she wrapped her arms around his neck, lacing her fingers into the soft curls that barely reached his collar. When he slanted his mouth across hers, she parted her lips in welcome.

He smelled clean and fresh, a lemony scent mixed with a trace of tobacco. He tasted as sweet and delicious as any confection she'd craved. With her hands she traced the shape of his shoulders—wide, taut against the broadcloth of his suit. She could feel one muscular thigh nudge her legs apart, and it felt good, so good to press against it.

"My God, Esmeralda." The words were a plea against her lips. "If we don't stop now, I don't know if I'll be able to."

Slowly, painfully, she became aware of her position. She was leaning against him; his knee was between her legs so that her skirt fanned over each side of his thigh and she was practically riding it. Her aching breasts were crushed to him and her hands clutched his shoulders.

She felt her face heat up with the realization of what she'd been doing. Twisting away, she pushed Keane back and stepped away from him, a bit stunned by what had just happened.

Keane looked at the spot where a moment before he'd held a passionate, very participating Esmeralda. Now there was only air. He sighed and let his arms drop. Next time he'd keep his mouth shut.

"That's not exactly what I meant when I said we should stop."

"How do you do it?" Her voice sounded a bit awed.

"Do what?"

"Make me forget everything. Where I am. Who I am. What I should be doing."

Keane smiled sadly and shrugged. "You make me forget, too."

"No. You're always in control—you're doing what you want!"

"If you're honest, you'll admit you are as well," he said softly.

Esmeralda shook her head. "What I want has nothing to do with this. I need only your money. I don't want anything else!"

"Not even love?"

Esmeralda looked alarmed. "Especially not that."

Keane watched Esmeralda thoughtfully. The very idea of his loving her sent her into a panic. Until he discovered the reasons behind her fears, he'd never be able to help her overcome them. And the only way he was going to do that was to stay close. "All right. Money it is, then." He grinned. "Are you sure you wouldn't want"—he glanced down his body before raising his eyes to meet hers—"anything else in the bargain?"

The reproving look she shot him told him she wasn't in a joking mood.

Esmeralda squared her shoulders. "I want to talk about the rules."

"Ah, yes." Keane folded his arms and leaned against his desk. "Every game needs rules. We were about to establish the ones for this particular sport. Have you something specific in mind?"

"Yes," she answered immediately. "No touching."

Keane became deadly serious. "Out of the question."

"It's not negotiable. No touching, no kissing . . . no physical contact."

"And how on earth are we supposed to play the happily married couple?" he argued.

"In private," Esmeralda amended. "No touching in private."

Keane thought for a moment. "What do you mean, 'It's not negotiable'?"

Esmeralda took a deep breath. "I'll walk out of here without a second thought. We can forget the whole agreement."

"That's not very sporting of you, sweets," he stated dryly.

"Sporting is for gentlemen. I'm no gentleman." *Just a survivor,* she added to herself.

Keane examined her with the concentration he would use against any opponent he intended to beat. Was she bluffing? Would she really walk away from his offer? He sighed, relaxing against the desk. He'd stay his hand for now, wait until he had her aboard the ship. Then he would be in a better position to negotiate. "Your way it is, then. No touching."

Esmeralda let out the breath she'd been holding. She was safe. As long as he didn't touch her, she would be fine —no distractions, only Amberose as her goal. "It's settled, then." Glancing at the pile of missives waiting for him on his desk, she added, "I'll leave you now. I've kept you long enough as it is." She stepped to the door, then turned back and explained, "I really think this is for the best." After his curt nod, she left.

Keane stared after her, his face expressionless until the door shut softly. Only then did he permit himself to smile. No touching indeed. Nothing would keep him from Esmeralda. Her love was a prize he'd wanted too much, for too long, to give up now.

"We'll play it your way, sweets," he murmured to himself. "At least until we get aboard ship."

Chapter Twenty-four

Esmeralda took Keane's proferred hand for balance as she stepped down from the hansom cab onto the dirt road. She looked up and squinted against the high noon sun. Smelling the pungent scent of coffee from the New Orleans Coffeehouse, she felt suddenly nostalgic and glanced about the bustling activity of the public landing, drinking in the scenes she'd taken for granted over the past year. Heavily laden drays rumbled down Front Street. Across the willow-fringed river, nestled at the base of the Kentucky hills, were the cozy manufacturing towns of Covington and Newport, both easily accessible by ferry. Steamboats of fairy architecture lined the quay opposite the row of massive warehouses and rich stores that made up the public landing. As her eyes surveyed the parade of brick and frame buildings, she silently mouthed, KANAWHA SALT, BISHOP WELL & CO., and PROTECTION INSURANCE COMPANY, reading the board signs one last time.

"There's Jason and Molly." Keane pointed down the wharf to the couple waving at them. "You go ahead. I'll direct the furniture car to the *Embassy* and make certain our trunks get on board."

Esmeralda held back the shiver of anticipation generated by Keane's words. Today was her first real step toward regaining Amberose. She was on her way to England—on her way home.

"Go on." Esmeralda felt Keane's gentle nudge. "I'll join you in a minute."

Walking around the many barrels and bales piled before the docked steamboats, yet careful not to step too far into the busy traffic, Esmeralda made her way down Front Street. When she met Molly halfway down the road, she returned her friend's embrace, feeling eerily removed from the warm gesture. She could not imagine what it really would be like to be separated from Molly, who had been friend, confidante, and mother for so many years. Even the touch of Molly's cheek, wet with tears, against hers did not make the parting seem real.

"I know 'tis selfish of me, but I dinna want ye to go."

"I wish you were coming with me." She glanced up at Jason. "Just like we always planned."

Molly pulled away, shaking her head. " 'Tis where me and Peter belong now, *mavourneen.*" Molly smiled at Jason with a look so loving, Esmeralda felt it like a blow.

"I've already asked Molly to be my wife," Jason said, grasping Molly's hand in his.

Esmeralda didn't miss the possessive gesture. "So Molly said. And when is this blessed event to take place?"

Molly blushed. "Jason's mother thought we should wait till next spring. Get the town used to me bein' related and all before Jason starts courtin' me."

"A wise decision."

"To which I have not agreed," Jason added.

Esmeralda met Jason's cool expression and silently hoped he'd not betray her friend.

"More wedding plans?" Esmeralda heard Keane's deep voice call from directly behind her. She half-turned to meet him before he stepped to her side and wrapped an arm around her shoulders. She flashed him a warning look, which he ignored as he leaned down and pressed a quick kiss to her cheek. "In public," he whispered, "the happily married couple, remember?" With a wide smile, he added out loud, "An institution I recommend highly, marriage. Isn't that right, sweets?"

Molly's joyful smile stopped Esmeralda's denial. "Highly," she echoed archly. She couldn't admit the truth now. Molly thought all of Esmeralda's worries had ceased with her marriage to Keane.

Molly took a handkerchief from her reticule and dabbed the linen daintily to her eyes before blowing her nose lustily. "I just knew it'd all work out between ye."

Keane smiled warmly at Molly, feeling quite expansive now that he was about to put an ocean between himself and the Irish termagant. But when he saw Jason suddenly stiffen and stare at something behind him, Keane turned, following the direction of Jason's gaze.

There, leaning against the pillar before the City Insurance Building, was Henry.

Jason stepped forward, but Keane held up his hand, stopping him. "I'll handle this. It's business I need to take care of before I leave, Jason. I should have dealt with him before now." With a quick nod to the ladies, he turned and left to confront Henry.

Keane strode forward. He was a bit surprised by Henry's appearance. He'd learned from Jason that over the past weeks Henry had avoided all social functions, choosing instead to come home early and get drunk in his room alone. Watching Henry now, Keane saw the boy step away from the front facade of the building and plant both feet firmly apart, his clenched fists at his sides. Keane grimaced. He should have anticipated this reunion, should have gone to see Henry before this.

Keane stopped directly in front of the brooding young man. Then, casually, he placed a booted foot on the top step leading up to the front portico of the insurance company and leaned forward, resting his forearm on his knee. "How are you, Henry?"

"As well as could be expected." His mouth a belligerent line across his face, Henry crossed his arms in front of his chest. After a moment, he nodded toward Esmeralda. "How is . . . she?"

Keane smiled at Henry's avoidance of her name: His statement revealed both anger and concern. "As you can see, she's fully recovered. You should have come to see her. I'm sure she would have liked to talk to you. Explain things."

"Where? At your suite? That was where she was staying, wasn't it?" At Keane's nod, Henry snorted. "No, thank you. I think I've been sufficiently humiliated already, don't you?"

Keane pressed his lips together. He thought of telling Henry that he and Esmeralda had married, but discarded the idea immediately. He owed Henry the truth.

"I've offered to marry her, Henry."

Henry's only reaction was a slight tightening of his lips and for the first time since Keane had met him, his expression reminded Keane of Jason.

"How very noble of you," Henry drawled.

Keane sighed. This was more difficult than he'd anticipated. "I suppose I was being noble when I first asked her. My second proposal was . . . different. A matter of the heart, you might say." He smiled with self-derision. "She refused me." And at Henry's slightly raised brow, Keane explained, "Apparently, marriage was never in her plans."

Henry's hardened expression wavered slightly. "And now?"

"I'm escorting her back to England."

"She refused marriage to become your mistress?"

"Hardly," Keane snapped, not liking Henry's tone.

"We're returning to England to complete a business venture together. It really isn't my place to tell you why. You really should have let the lady explain." Keane pushed away from the steps. "I'd appreciate your not discussing this with anyone, particularly Molly. Your brother has seen fit to tell her we've actually married. A story to ease her mind." Keane held out his hand, a final attempt to reconcile. Henry ignored the gesture, staring at Keane with a sullen expression, until Keane dropped his hand to his side.

"Even if she was at my suite," Keane challenged. "It amazes me that for all your professed love, Henry, you never bothered to come see her—even when we thought she'd die."

Keane's barb achieved the desired results, and Henry's expression became immediately contrite. "I don't mean to sound callous. It . . . it affected me greatly when Jason told me of Esmeralda's condition. And I was truly relieved to hear of her recovery." Henry shrugged his shoulders helplessly. "But you must see how difficult this all is for me to accept? You understand, Keane—I cannot truly forgive either one of you."

Keane nodded. He stared at Henry for a moment, assessing the effect of his next words. "I'm not sorry about the end result of this mess. Esmeralda could never have made you happy in the long run." Keane stopped Henry's angry rejoinder with his upraised hand. "I know that is difficult for you to accept. I am, however, very sorry about how the whole business came about. I'm not trying to make excuses, but originally I thought I was helping you when I tried to draw her attention." Seeing Henry's scowl, Keane closed off that particular avenue to discussion. "In any event, I'll not bother you further. Maybe the next time we meet, you'll understand why I did what I did. Perhaps someday we can again be friends."

Henry pursed his lips together, trying unsuccessfully to

hide his pain. "I sincerely doubt that, Keane." He choked on the words.

"Well, there's nothing left for me to say, is there? Goodbye, Henry." Keane turned back to the wharf.

"How very simple this all turned out for you, Keane." Keane whipped around. "You're wrong—"

"First, you set out to pursue the woman *I love,*" Henry continued, his face becoming a deep red, "which you very well knew I did before you even met her. Then, after watching me make an absolute *ass* of myself trying to keep her interest, you bed her." Henry stepped toward Keane, his chin held high but his voice shaking.

Seeing that Henry's raised voice was drawing attention, Keane grabbed Henry's sleeve and steered him to the alley behind the insurance building. Only after he made sure no one was around did Keane release Henry's arm. "I've tried to explain the situation to you," Keane murmured, trying to soothe Henry's ego.

Not the least bit mollified, Henry shouted, "Explain? You come here, not even *pretending* to be the least bit repentant, and toss an apology at me, like a bone to some poor hound you feel sorry for. It's clear you've washed your hands of the whole affair, ridding yourself of any guilt because you've asked me to shake hands and be friends." Standing in front of Keane, Henry's gangly height almost brought the two men nose to nose. "Well, I'm sorry, *old friend,* but I won't make things as easy as all that!"

Before Keane could stop him, Henry slammed his open hand across Keane's cheek and Keane's head snapped back from the unexpected blow.

"I won't fight you, Henry." Keane ignored the burning pain in his cheek.

"The hell you won't!"

Henry stepped back to take a better swing, but this time Keane was prepared. Ducking to the left, he managed to avoid Henry's fist. But the miss didn't even give Henry pause. Like an angry bull, he lowered his head and charged.

Keane grabbed Henry's head as it collided with his stomach, expelling an audible "whoosh" with the hit. Losing his balance, Keane fell over backward still holding Henry by the neck and head. Both men hit the dirt, one on top of the other.

"This is insane!" Keane managed to croak when he'd caught sufficient breath to speak.

"I'll make you think twice before taking what's mine!"

Henry continued to score punches, before Keane managed to get his foot between the two of them and catapulted the maddened boy off him. The sound of splitting seams rent the air, and Keane swore soundly under his breath. He managed to get off the ground before Henry again rushed him. Not bothering to pull his punches, Keane slammed his powerful fist against Henry's chin.

With a look of utter astonishment, Henry staggered back from the force of the blow, stopping only when his back hit the wall. His head struck the brick with a soft thud, and Henry crumpled on the ground, leaning against the wall in a daze.

Standing in front of the stunned man, Keane tried to catch his breath. "I'm sorry I did that, Henry," he panted. "And I'm sorry I've caused you so much pain. But understand this: What I did, I did because I love Esmeralda, whether I knew it at the time or not. I have pledged my life to seeing her happy, and I've sworn to take care of all her future needs. I was willing to cheat even death for a chance to make her love me, and I sincerely doubt you can claim such an emotion since you did not *once* stop by to inquire if she were dead or alive because of your damnable pride. And now that she's well, nothing will stop me from having her by my side."

Henry looked up at Keane with a dazed expression and wiped his mouth with the back of his hand. Amused, he saw that his hand was now stained red with blood that trickled from the side of his lips where Keane's fist had made contact. "My God, Keane," he said, his voice raspy. "I really do believe you've fallen for her." Then, for some unexplained reason, Henry began to laugh.

Keane looked on, breathing heavily. "What," he asked, "is so funny?"

Still chuckling, Henry rested his head against the wall and looked up at the astonished man hovering over him. "Don't you see?" Henry chortled. "This is the best revenge of all! You actually *love* her!" Then in a serious tone, "And she'll leave you. Just as surely as she betrayed me, she'll do the same to you. I don't have to hurt you, Keane." Henry smiled. "Your punishment is as well as delivered."

Keane stared down at Henry's satisfied expression, first with amazement, and then with distaste. Bending down into a crouched position that brought his eyes almost level with Henry's, Keane grinned a not-so-nice smile and said, "Would you care for odds on that?"

Chapter Twenty-five

Esmeralda dabbed at the perspiration on her forehead with a handkerchief. Glaring at the pounding heat of the afternoon sun, she silently cursed the wealth of material on her person. In the muggy heat of early summer, her new cotton corset, layers of petticoats, and lined travel suit weighed her down like iron chains. There was something to be said in favor of poverty after all—poor people didn't wear so many clothes.

Wadding up the sweat-soaked square of linen, she stuffed it back into her reticule and shifted her weight from her right leg to her left, preparing to continue her vigil by the gangplank. A few feet away, Keane stood before their piled trunks, mouthing instructions to one of the porters, an attentive Higgins erect behind him. As Keane leaned closer to the packet worker, Esmeralda noticed a gleam of white where the dark broadcloth sleeve of his jacket should have met the material at the back. A rip in the sleeve of his coat? Picturing the torn knuckles of his right hand, she had a vague idea of how the rip got there.

She, Molly, and Jason had all anxiously watched Keane's conversation with Henry, rooted to their places by the river's edge while Keane and Henry removed themselves to the alley behind the City Insurance Building. When Keane returned minutes later—his jacket dusty despite noticeable attempts to brush it clean, his hair a bit more tousled than usual—with no Henry in sight, Jason loped forward, demanding an explanation. Keane's glance over his shoulder to the alley sent Jason running with Molly trotting behind him. That was when Esmeralda had first noticed the raw knuckles of Keane's hand. She tried to get him to explain what had happened, but he just smiled tightly and looked at her strangely—as if he were examining her for some mysterious flaw he'd not noticed before.

Esmeralda shifted her vision from Keane to the line of steamboats trailing down the dock behind him. While the ships were a familiar sight on the public landing, she thought them an odd-looking lot. Each was a side-wheeler with three decks sprawling above the water line, making them seem top-heavy. At first glance, they appeared ugly and boxlike, but as she examined the packets, she found something almost gracefully fairylike about the elaborate filigree woodwork and the two crowned chimneys at the fore of each ship.

Esmeralda heaved a sigh of relief when Keane left Higgins to deal with the porter and joined her at the gangplank. Her pulse picked up as Keane offered the crook of his arm, almost challenging her to turn down his escort. Chin up, she looped her arm through his and together they turned to face the four officers in uniforms with gold braid and dress boots who lined the walkway up to the ship.

Arms linked, she and Keane followed a gloved steward up the plank and boarded the *Embassy*. On the main deck, they strolled forward past the engines, pantry, and kitchen, while the steward pointed out the different sections of interest. Esmeralda half-listened as she stared over the railing at the roustabouts and stevedores loading the packet. She caught sight of a family and watched them, intrigued as the father gave his two small boys a pat on the head and his wife a quick hug before nudging them to board the ship without him. Joining the roustabouts, the man piled a bundle of wood onto his shoulders.

She stopped and leaned over the railing. "Do passengers help with the loading?"

The steward looked to where she pointed. "Some can't afford the three-dollar deck passage downriver, so they help wood-up when we need fuel. But you don't have to worry about the deck passengers, ma'am. They sleep and take their meals here. They won't be bothering the cabin passengers."

Esmeralda felt her stomach tighten. If not for Keane's help, she too might be forced to buy passage with the people below and camp out on deck, exposed to the elements. Another reason to feel obligated.

At the front of the ship, two staircases of polished woodwork swept gracefully up to the promenade deck. Esmeralda and Keane climbed the curving stairway on the right to the ship's main cabin. A wide corridor the length of the boat, the main cabin looked like a long tunnel separated by two rows of staterooms on either side. From its elaborately carved, bracket-supported ceiling hung glittering cut-glass chandeliers, and varicolored carpets covered the floor. Furnished with polished inlaid wood, deep sofas, and fine oil paintings that hung on the door of each stateroom, it reminded Esmeralda of a hotel lobby. There was even a piano at the curtained entrance to the ladies' cabin at the back. As he led them past the gentlemen's bar to their stateroom, the steward explained that the main cabin did double duty as the social hall and dining room.

Just as the steward stopped before the entrance to their room, Esmeralda caught sight of a beautiful blond woman across the cabin. She was dressed in a stunning ruby gown, and an elderly gentleman hovering beside her fitted the key into the door of what was obviously their stateroom. Her beauty alone drew attention, but Esmeralda found herself staring at the woman because she was in fact staring at them. Or more precisely—at Keane. Esmeralda peeked up at Keane, who was also watching the blond beauty. Quickly, she glanced back in time to catch the woman smile and nod at him. A blinding, unexplainable rage tore through Esmeralda, so intense she felt it like a physical pain. She looked back to catch Keane's reaction to the flirtatious nod, but he just turned away, intent on the steward's recitation of the dining schedule.

Esmeralda swallowed her ire and stepped into the room as the steward swung the door open. There she met another challenge to her composure. The room was small—very small—and was dominated by a curtained bed that seemed enormous in the room's tiny confines.

Keane took in Esmeralda's anxious expression with amused tolerance. He could guess the source of her unease. While steamboats were considered the most elegant form of travel, easily outdoing the cramped quarters of a stagecoach, the fifteen-foot-square stateroom provided little privacy. He smiled. Just the perfect site to play his first hand.

After the steward shut the door behind him, Keane turned and asked with studied nonchalance, "You look a bit pale. Is there a problem?"

"Where are you going to sleep?" she blurted out.

Keane stepped around Esmeralda and casually leaned against the bedpost. He glanced over his shoulder at the bed. "There seems to be ample room for both of us."

"We can't . . . you don't think . . ."

"Nothing to worry about, sweets. I don't steal the covers and I rarely snore."

Esmeralda clasped her arms across her chest. "I'm not sleeping in that bed with you."

Keane raised his brows. "Oh? And where do you plan to sleep?" He looked about the room as if searching for an imaginary second bed.

"It's *you* who are sleeping elsewhere."

Keane glanced from the armchair to the washbasin. "Where would you suggest? The floor looks rather firm. Or perhaps I should bunk in with Higgins?"

"The chair appears very comfortable," she countered.

"You're joking?"

Esmeralda shook her head, arms still crossed before her.

"Esmeralda . . ." Keane stepped forward, ready to take her in his arms, but she ducked around him.

"You promised. No touching in private. That most certainly includes while we sleep!"

Keane started to insist, but looking at her stubborn expression said nothing. Better to bide his time and gain her confidence. Only then could they truly become intimate, the way he dreamed. "The chair it is then," he said softly. "But I warn you," he added with his most charming smile. "I'm not my best without a good night's sleep."

Esmeralda held back a sigh of relief. "I'll take my chances."

"Would you care to join me for a walk on the promenade? It will be some time before the luggage gets here. I'm told leaving port provides a magnificent view of the city." He motioned toward the door, holding out his hand for hers. "Shall we?"

She almost reached out to clasp his hand before she remembered: *no touching*. Taking a deep breath, she stepped to the door, careful to walk around his outstretched hand.

Esmeralda stared down at the violet gown of Turkish satin spread across the bed. It was one of the most beautiful gowns in her new wardrobe. Satin knots caught at intervals the rows of pleats decorating the skirt, and a deep, rich lace, set nearly plane so that its pattern showed distinctly, trimmed the off-the-shoulder sleeves and neck. She'd planned on saving it for a special event. But something—to be honest, someone—made her want to look her best tonight.

While she and Keane had strolled up and down the guards on the promenade, they'd met Cecilia Burton and her aging husband. The blonde, more stunning up close than she'd appeared from across the main cabin, fairly cooed when the captain introduced Keane as Viscount Eldridge, and Keane had been his most obnoxiously charming self. Esmeralda could understand the smile and the soothing compliments, but the kiss on Mrs. Burton's gloved hand—that, in her estimation, had far exceeded the necessities of etiquette.

So now, feeling like a good soldier plotting strategy, she'd laid out her best weapon: an off-the-shoulder gown that showed both her coloring and her figure to advantage. She'd stopped analyzing her desire to keep Keane's attentions from the cloying Mrs. Burton, deciding it was just unseemly that she, supposedly newly married, should not be able to maintain her husband's attention. It had nothing to do with a weakening of resolve. No, she was just as intent as ever to regain Amberose and leave Keane.

That small doubt taken care of, she'd prepared to don her weapon—and discovered that, like any good general, she needed assistance. She couldn't button the gown by herself.

A quick review of her trunks revealed that all her dinner frocks were of similar design. So for the past fifteen minutes she'd stood before the bed, expecting Keane— who had already dressed and retired to the gentlemen's bar to give her privacy—to enter at any minute and find her in her undergarments.

*　*　*

Keane tossed his cheroot over the railing into the Ohio. Just about now Esmeralda would be standing clad only in her undergarments, staring at some beautiful gown, trying —but not succeeding—to fasten the thing without assistance. Sauntering down the cabin to their stateroom, he grinned. Not hiring a lady's maid had been a despicable tactic, something akin to an ace up the sleeve. But his time *was* limited. He needed to break her resistance down before they reached England, where she'd be free to go about her business without him. Whatever it took, he planned to make Esmeralda his wife, and Henry's predictions be damned.

Smiling at his vehemence, Keane stopped before the door to their stateroom. She could always do that to him, make him lose control of his emotions, act like a young pup sniffing at his first bitch. And for a man who had spent the last ten years with a tight rein on his emotions— growing ever more urbane, feeling at times almost soulless —Keane acknowledged that losing control had not lost its thrill.

Keane tapped softly on the door before fitting the key into the lock. He hoped supper would not drag on interminably. While he was eager to offer his assistance in fastening Esmeralda's gown, he so looked forward to helping her remove it.

The chair, after all, did not look so comfortable.

Esmeralda perched nervously on the edge of the bed, holding the bodice of her gown against her with both hands. When she heard the soft tap against the door followed by the key turning, the beat of her heart jumped into double time. She took a deep, steadying breath as she watched Keane sweep into the room and close the door behind him with a soft click. He appeared almost wolfish in his black frock coat and pants—dangerous and devilishly handsome. Esmeralda pressed the satin more tightly against her. When he smiled at her like that, she always felt a bit breathless.

"It occurred to me you might need some assistance dressing." Keane could almost taste triumph. While Esmeralda had actually donned the gown, it hung lax against her shoulders, held up only by her clutched hands. "Unfortunately, I was unable to find a lady's maid willing to travel with us to England."

"You tried to find a maid?" Esmeralda's eyes grew wide, before she dropped her gaze to her lap. "I hadn't thought of it."

Her voice was so soft, almost apologetic, that Keane felt his sense of victory teeter miserably. No, she wouldn't have thought of a maid. She was too accustomed to serving others to think of servants for herself. "Stand up and turn around, sweets. It will be my pleasure to play the part of lady's helper."

Esmeralda almost giggled at the image of Keane as maid. His good humor made him seem a little less intimidating than he'd first appeared when he'd entered the room dressed in his black finery. Esmeralda stood and turned her back to Keane, lifting her waist-length curls over her shoulder with one hand while the other held the front of her bodice in place.

Keane stared at the smooth, pale skin of her back. She'd managed to fasten the buttons up to her waist, but the sight of exposed flesh above that made Keane grapple for control. For a moment he remembered what her soft skin felt like against his mouth and he ached to wrap his arms around her and bury his lips in her smooth neck. Keane swallowed hard, wiping his mind of the seductive image. He had to get hold of his desire. Stepping forward, he started reciting Latin proverbs to himself while he hooked each tiny button in place.

Esmeralda could feel Keane's warm breath against her neck. She closed her eyes and shivered. It had been a long time since he'd kissed her. Two days. An eternity.

Keane felt Esmeralda lean back against him. He fastened the last button, then, softly, placed his hands on her shoulders and slid them down her bare arms to her hands. He laced his fingers through hers and wrapped their arms across her stomach, pulling her flush against him. "Esmeralda," he whispered against her neck, brushing his lips across her lilac-scented skin.

The knock at the door thundered across the small room, jolting Esmeralda from her seductive haze. Keane cursed softly under his breath, and she bit her lip in frustration. It had happened again. Despite her resolve, despite all her promises and vows, the minute Keane had touched her, she'd melted against him, ready to beg for his kisses. She slumped against the bedpost, fixing her gaze on the door as Keane opened it to admit the first officer. She silently thanked the young gentleman for his timely intervention.

Keane stared down at the blond, blue-eyed Mr. Dalton. Nothing short of an emergency evacuation could justify this particular interruption. "How may I help you, Mr. Dalton?"

"The captain requests the honor of your presence at his table, and that of your wife, of course"—he beamed a smile at Esmeralda—"as his guests this evening for supper."

Mr. Dalton's beatific smile assumed his news was pleasing and of great importance. Little could he guess that right now Keane was valiantly suppressing his desire to shut the door in Dalton's bright, eager face. "It will be our pleasure," Keane drawled. "Please convey our acceptance to Captain Halderman."

"That I will, sir. Madame." Dalton stepped back with a smart click of his heels. But before he could finish his most proper bow to Esmeralda, Keane slammed the door shut.

Chapter Twenty-six

A pleasant smile plastered on her lips, Esmeralda quietly endured Cecilia Burton's unctuous recital while eviscerating her bread roll with her fingers. After the first officer's premature departure, Esmeralda had managed to evade Keane's next assault by insisting on a walk on the guards before supper. But the incident in the stateroom was just the beginning of a trying evening. Seated between Keane and the first officer, and directly across from Esmeralda, Mrs. Burton kept the eyes of all six men at the captain's table riveted on her bulging cleavage and batting eyes.

To think Esmeralda had thought her violet gown daring! The trollop—for no other word adequately described tonight's performance—opposite her had her audience ogling her breasts, attentive as to when they would actually pop out of her low décolletage and plop onto the pristine linen tablecloth in front of her. Esmeralda watched helplessly as Cecilia once again turned her lovely indigo eyes on Keane and "accidently" brushed her breasts against his sleeve—for the third time since the fowl had been served.

"What exactly *does* a viscount do?" Cecilia cooed. "It must be ever so exciting."

Esmeralda swallowed a piece of bread and felt it stick in her throat as Keane bestowed his most dazzling smile on the blonde.

"I'm no different from any other businessman."

"I know one thing he does damn well," interrupted Cecilia's husband from beside Esmeralda. "Gambles. Lost more than I'd like to admit playing faro against him this afternoon."

"A lucky day for me, Mr. Burton," Keane demurred. "I'm certain you'll win it all back at our next game."

"Oh, no. Learned my lesson, I did. I don't play against professionals."

"Perhaps I may interest you in a game, sir?" the slim gentleman with a pencil-thin mustache asked from the far end of the table.

"How exciting!" Cecilia clapped her hands and bounced in her seat, causing James Dalton's eyes to bulge open as he stared at her breasts. "Mr. Devol is a professional riverboat gambler."

"You can count on me as well," chimed in the man seated on Esmeralda's right, a short, dark-complexioned gentleman with a thinning hairline and a Yorkshire accent. "Though I may not be able to keep up with the two of you."

"Of course, Mr. Winton." Keane nodded his acceptance.

"May I watch?" Cecilia pouted prettily as she squeezed Keane's arm for a little extra persuasion. "It would be simply dreadful of you to play in that stuffy gentlemen's bar where I'd miss all the excitement."

"Now, Cecilia . . ." Mr. Burton began, sounding more like an indulgent father than a husband.

"Oh, please, Tommy. I would so *love* to see a game."

Esmeralda pushed her untouched chicken and vegetables from one side of her dinner plate to the other, thinking unkind thoughts about the reasons behind Cecilia's marriage to a man twice her age.

Mr. Burton hesitated. "Well, it's up to the gentlemen playing."

"You will say yes?" Cecilia stretched a perfect smile on her lips for each of the three players, and again brushed her breasts against Keane's arm.

Esmeralda's fork dropped with a loud *clank* onto the Limoges china plate.

"Excuse me," she muttered under her breath.

Keane just barely contained his laughter. While he'd hardly noticed Cecilia Burton—being quite familiar with and completely uninterested in the invitation she'd been directing his way since they met—he'd certainly begun paying attention when he saw how much Mrs. Burton annoyed Esmeralda. He practically crowed with delight when he first realized that the beautiful redhead across from him was suffering from a fit of jealousy.

"If Mr. Winton and Mr. Devol agree, I would consent to playing a game on Texas deck. I wouldn't want to deprive Mrs. Burton of the night's entertainments." Keane imbued the final phrase with special meaning and watched Esmeralda's reaction from the corner of his eye. She looked as if she were contemplating using her fork for some purpose other than spearing her chicken. Keane's smile widened. "Would you care to join us, Esmeralda?"

"Oh, no, thank you."

Keane admired her casual tone and responding smile. She looked almost cheerful—if one didn't notice her eyes, which had turned the iridescent green of swamp fire.

"In fact," she continued, "I'm afraid you must excuse me. I have a dreadful headache. I think I shall retire early."

"Why, of course, Lady Eldridge." The captain stood

solicitously. "I shall send the ship's surgeon to see you. He will prescribe a powder."

"That's very kind, Captain Halderman, but I'll be quite all right with rest."

Keane was already at her side, pulling her chair out for her. "Shall I escort you back to the room?"

"I would hate to keep you from your *game,*" she said with exaggerated sweetness, her smile tight.

"Do come back," Cecilia coaxed. "It will be a dreadfully dull evening otherwise. That is"—Cecilia's gaze barely flitted across Esmeralda before her indigo eyes returned to their original target—"if your wife's health permits."

Esmeralda watched Keane closely, waiting for him to choose between her and Cecilia's charms.

"If my wife feels better, I shall meet you gentleman— and Mrs. Burton, of course—on the Texas deck later." Keane bowed cordially to all. "Thank you for your hospitality, Captain Halderman." His hand at the small of her back, Keane guided Esmeralda toward their stateroom across the main cabin.

Winding her way around the tables to the forecastle, Esmeralda silently seethed. How very diplomatic of Keane. *If* she felt better, he'd go slithering right *back* for further ogling. Well, Cecilia Burton could jolly well have him—this night and any other night. What did she care with whom Keane spent his time? It just irked her that he'd shown such poor taste, that was all. The woman's pathetic fawning had been embarrassing.

Keane swung open the door and stepped in after Esmeralda. He watched her walk to the bed, then turn abruptly and stare back at him. Shoulders squared, chin high, her emerald gaze slashed across the room to challenge him.

"Do not let me keep you," she snapped.

"It will be hours before the others make their way to the Texas deck for the game," he answered casually, stepping toward her. "My concern now is you and your head-ache. How are you feeling?"

"Well enough not to need your help, thank goodness. Please, hurry along to Mrs. Burton's side. I'm not sure she'll manage long without your entertaining company."

Keane grinned. "She does seem to be a bit taken with me."

"Practically salivating would be a more appropriate description, I believe."

"Poor Cecilia. You do her an injustice. The woman is bored, and I just happen to be the entertaining sort."

"Injustice?" Esmeralda warmed to her subject. "I'll tell you what's unjust! The way you cater to her simpering. 'Would you care for more wine, Mrs. Burton? A bit more aspic, perhaps?' You encouraged her disgusting display."

"I was simply being a suitable dining partner. And I would hardly term the woman disgusting," he added dryly.

"She was eating you up with her eyes, as if you and not chicken had been served up for supper!"

The small laugh lines at Keane's eyes deepened. "Surely you exaggerate."

"And if she thrust her pendulous breasts at you one more time, I thought I would become positively *illl!*" Esmeralda pulled her shoulders back, causing her breasts to press perilously against her own décolletage. Batting her eyes in an exaggerated manner, she chirped, " 'Being a viscount must be ever so exciting!' "

Keane leaned against the washstand, tapping his fore-finger against his chin thoughtfully. "You have the voice right, but the thing with the shoulders . . . I think that's not quite right. Perhaps you should try it again?"

Esmeralda's eyes narrowed dangerously. "Get out!"

"What?"

"GET OUT!" She pointed to the door.

"The woman is a hopeless tease. She means nothing to me."

"Well, that's a shame, because it's with her drooling over your shoulder while you play cards that you'll be spending the evening!"

"That's not what you truly want, sweets."

"I want you out of this room, now! I don't care what you and that . . . that strumpet do."

"Don't you?" Keane stepped to her, his expression serious, his eyes riveted on hers. "Don't you really care?" His voice was hypnotizingly soft as he backed Esmeralda against the bed. "That's strange." He stopped, towering over her. "For a moment there, I thought you cared very much."

Esmeralda stumbled up against the bed, almost falling onto it. "You're wrong. I shan't care if you never return."

"Oh, I'll come back, sweets." He lowered his lips to hers.

"Don't touch me."

"What are you afraid of?" he asked softly. "Are you afraid of this?" Keane pressed his lips against her warm dry ones, marveling at their softness. He felt her breath quicken. She tried to twist her face away, but he captured it between both hands.

Esmeralda felt herself falling into a dark abyss of sensual pleasure. Keane's mouth covered hers, warm and moist against her skin. She could feel his tongue's sweet touch coaxing her lips to part for him. Unable to help herself, she opened her mouth and wrapped her arms around his neck, melting against him. His taste intoxicated more powerfully than the Madeira wine that was served at supper. She leaned forward, pressing against the strong muscles of his chest. She felt him reach behind her. The gown's tight hold loosened and he unfastened her dress to her waist, still kissing her breathless.

When her knees held the strength of warm taffy, Keane pulled away slowly. "You see? There's nothing to be afraid of, sweets." He examined her darkened eyes from beneath hooded lids as he took her arms from around his neck and set them gently at her sides. "It's just a kiss, after all."

Esmeralda stared at Keane in stunned surprise as he turned and walked to the door. "Wish me luck." He grinned. "I plan to win a lot of money."

Screaming with frustration, Esmeralda grabbed a pillow from the bed and threw it. It hit the door just as it closed behind him.

Keane clamped his teeth down on his cigar and fanned open his cards. A pair of twos, hardly promising. He looked up to Devol, who was seated across from him.

"Three cards."

Keane watched as the dealer tossed the requested number with an expert twist of his wrist. Each card slid across the table with a soft whisper and landed facedown before Keane.

It was just the two of them now. Winton, Dalton, and even the charming Mrs. Burton, had all retired long ago. It had been a diverting evening. Devol was a talented gambler, and Cecilia Burton's antics to get Keane's attention had been almost as entertaining as Dalton's reactions to them. But Keane's mind was no longer on the game, and for the last hour the pile of coins before Devol had steadily increased.

Keane finished the last swallow of whiskey in his glass and waited for the betting to begin. It didn't take long before he folded his cards and tossed them onto the table toward Devol. "That's it for me."

Devol smiled thinly. "Just when my luck turned."

Keane flipped open his pocket watch, suddenly impatient to return to the stateroom. It was just past two in the morning.

"Another time, perhaps."

"Certainly," Devol replied with a nod. "I look forward to it."

Straightening his jacket as he stood, Keane dropped his

cigar to the deck, careful to stamp it out. Explosions from the boiler engines and fire were the greatest causes of death on the steamboats traveling up and down the Ohio. With a curt nod at Devol, Keane turned to go down the stairs.

So far, his strategy had taken its toll on his patience. After the first officer's interruption of a very promising encounter, Keane had determined it was not good enough just to get Esmeralda into bed. That part was easy. Keeping her there was the problem.

In the past, bedding her had accomplished nothing—she would just regret it, then stiffen her resolve to keep her distance. He must get Esmeralda to come to *him,* without first kissing her into numbness. Her jealousy of the charming Mrs. Burton was an unexpected bonus—of which he planned to take full advantage. He estimated that the combination of Cecilia and the undeniable attraction Esmeralda felt for him should work to his benefit. He planned to touch her, kiss her, caress her, at every opportunity, until she sought him out and admitted they were partners in love, not just in business.

Kissing her this evening after supper, then leaving to play cards on deck with Devol, had almost broken his resolve. Not even a fast game of cards could stop Keane's mind from wandering downstairs. Enticing pictures of Esmeralda asleep in their bed had flashed through his head all evening, effectively destroying his concentration.

When Keane opened the door, a low moan from the bed drew his attention. She'd shut the curtains over the bed, but he knew exactly how she would look. She would be lying still, her rose-pink lips slightly parted, one hand curled softly against her cheek. . . . Keane shook his head clear of the seductive image. He was going to have to do better than that if he planned to get any sleep tonight.

He smiled thinly when he noticed the blanket and pillow set out on the armchair. Imagining his six-foot height cramped into the chair, he sighed heavily. He should have had another drink before coming downstairs to face these sleeping arrangements. Keane heard another moan come from beyond the bed-curtains. Make that a full bottle of Kentucky's best.

With a grunt, Keane stripped off his jacket and sat down to pull off his boots. He had just unbuttoned his shirt when the screaming began.

Chapter Twenty-seven

Esmeralda was drowning.

The salt water burned her throat, choking her. Clawing at the murky darkness, she inched forward, then slid back, deeper into suffocation. Her legs tangled in the water plants, and clinging tendrils sucked her down. The vines wrapped around her arms, strapping them to her sides. She couldn't move, couldn't fight. The lighted surface of the water dimmed. She wasn't going to make it; her lungs were bursting. She opened her mouth to scream. Water rushed in to smother her.

"Esmeralda? Esmeralda, wake up!"

The words seeped through the darkness, reaching her. She clung to them, rode them to the surface of her consciousness, until she felt her weighted eyelids flutter.

"Open your eyes, sweets. It's just a dream. It can't hurt you!"

Esmeralda wrenched her eyes open and gasped for

breath. Her legs and arms were tangled in the sheets. Keane hovered over her, shaking her awake.

"Keane!" She pried herself free of the blankets and flung her arms around his shoulders, hugging him as if he were an anchor to the real world.

"Sweetheart, are you all right?" Keane rocked her in his arms. "You were screaming. Look at you." He brushed the damp tendrils from her face. "You're soaked. Was your dream so frightening?"

Esmeralda clung to him. Breathing heavily, she nodded. "I've never remembered before; I've always forgotten the dream once I wake up. But I remember this time." Esmeralda began to sob softly. "I remember."

Keane held her against his bare chest where his shirt hung open. He could feel her fragile shoulders shaking under the thin cotton of her nightgown, and his heart knotted. Her chilling screams still echoed in his mind. "Would it help to talk about it?"

"I don't know . . . I wanted to remember . . . I always thought . . ."

"Shhh. Wait a minute. Catch your breath. We've got all night, sweets."

Esmeralda nodded against his chest. "I want to talk about it. I need to tell you." The hysteria in her voice settled. She knuckled her eyes clear of tears, and sat up on the bed, nuzzling against the haven of Keane's arms. "I was dreaming about what happened nine years ago."

As she spoke, her voice sounded frightened. Moonlight streamed through the small porthole past the parted bed-curtains and lighted her pinched features. "My cousin, Allen MacClure. Lord"—she stumbled on the words—"Lord Kielder. He hired . . . men to take me away. Only I woke up and escaped to the forest. Allen came to look for me. He found me . . . and I think he drugged me. I couldn't understand . . . I still . . ." She looked down at the sheets, fighting back tears.

Keane tightened his hold, trying to give her the strength she needed to continue.

"He said something about the estate." She shook her head as if trying to remember. "Something like, Father shouldn't have left it to me. But it *was* mine—not Allen's." Keane smiled, seeing some of the old spark in her eyes as she looked up at him. But then the light in her eyes dimmed. "And I would have shared everything with him. I tried to explain that . . . but he wouldn't listen. He looked mean. Frightening. As if he hated me." One tear slipped down her cheek, and Keane brushed it away before pulling her head to his shoulder. He smoothed his hand over her tangled curls, trying to soothe her pain.

"I never remembered Allen's part until that night at the Longworth's, when Henry found us together." Her voice sounded weak even though she spoke close to his ear. "I only knew of his involvement because I overheard my captors talking about it. But I always had these horrible nightmares." She shuddered. "The water . . ."

"Go on," he urged, knowing she must dispel her ghosts. "Tell me about your dream."

"I wake up on a small boat with these men, the men Allen hired. They were talking about selling me to the highest bidder." Keane's breath caught in his throat. Instinctively he tightened his grip around her. "I get scared and I dive into the water before they know I'm awake. I know how to swim, and I make for shore. I almost drown. That's what I was dreaming about. Drowning."

Keane grew cold. *Drowning.*

"Like my father and brother."

"Oh, Keane." She blinked back her tears, suddenly focused only on his pain. "Of course. How could I forget! I'm so sorry."

He half-smiled and kissed her forehead lightly. "That was over ten years ago. I've had plenty of time to heal those wounds. But sometimes"—he said the words softly, like a child telling a secret—"sometimes I dream of drowning as well—and I know it can be awful."

She shivered. "It was. But I could hear you calling to me, and I hung on to the sound." She burrowed deeper into his embrace. "It was as if I was following the words to the surface of the water. Then I heard you tell me to wake up."

To Keane, her voice seemed to reach deep inside and burn into his heart. Again he thanked God for giving him this beautiful woman-child to love and cherish.

Scooping her up off the bed and into his arms, he pulled back the covers before settling her under them. Then he slipped in beside her, still clothed in his trousers and shirt.

"Keane, I don't think—"

"Not a word." He settled in, spooning her against him. "I plan to just hold you."

Esmeralda sighed. "That would be nice."

Keane felt her relax, then nuzzle into his side, seeking his warmth and assurance. Together they fell asleep, dispelling their own particular demons with the strength each received from knowing the other was there.

It was about one o'clock when the *Embassy* started through the canal. From atop the Texas deck, Esmeralda waited, perched on one of the benches that lined the walls of the pilothouse, and stared out over the calm waters.

The canal appeared as if cut out of solid rock, leaving just room enough for a ship to pass without colliding with its high banks. The *Embassy* traveled backward through the man-made waterway to the Mississippi—a maneuver that Esmeralda imagined made the trip safer. Captain Halderman had already shown himself to be a cautious man; he'd ordered the ship's cargo unloaded and hauled overland when Esmeralda could see that other ships traveled through the canal loaded to the guards. Still, it felt strange to watch the stern cutting its path through the placid waters captured by the canal gates.

At the moment, however, the awesome sight of the *Embassy* leaving the Ohio River held only half of Esmeralda's attention. Another phenomena captured her interest. Out of the corner of her eye, Esmeralda studied Cecilia Burton as the woman plied her charms on Keane with impressive persistence. To Esmeralda's satisfaction, Mrs. Burton's vast arsenal—batting lashes, simpering compliments, and outthrust breasts—appeared to be wasted on Keane. While listening attentively enough, he acted cool and detached—polite but uninterested.

Esmeralda smiled. Ever since Keane had waked her from her nightmare two days before, he'd been—she hesitated even to form the idea in her mind, but yes—he'd been kinder, more considerate. He no longer acted the urbane gentleman humoring her, mocking her and her naïvete at every turn. He'd even returned to sleeping on the chair without complaint. And while he spent a great deal of time in the men's lounge gambling, Esmeralda had the distinct impression he did so only to avoid Cecilia Burton, who after the first game on the Texas deck haunted that deck with suspicious regularity.

As if sensing her thoughts, Keane glanced over at Esmeralda. Their eyes met and she caught her breath. Slowly the right corner of Keane's mouth lifted with a smile that reached his eyes and caused her to lean against the wall for support.

He was such a handsome man, she thought, with handsome manners—when he chose to make use of them. She started to stand and go to him, then caught herself. Best to stay where she was, safely seated across the room. She sighed and turned to look out over the ship's decks at the approaching bridge. It had never occurred to her that she'd have to fight *liking* Keane as well as their physical attraction to each other, but in the past weeks since he'd helped her recover from cholera, she'd been doing exactly that.

Keane's smile froze in place when Esmeralda looked

away. Try as he might, he couldn't seem to get beyond her fears. It made him angry to see that haunted expression whenever she realized she'd let her guard down. Sometimes he wanted to take her and shake her—or better yet, kiss her until the frightened look melted from her face and she clung to him. But he understood her fears now. He knew why she fought against love: Love had betrayed her.

Keane felt a burning pain in his stomach when he recalled her cousin and the blackhearted means he'd used to disinherit Esmeralda. When they arrived in England, Keane planned to make certain Lord Kielder could never have the power to hurt her again. He realized part of what drove him was revenge for Esmeralda. But not just because Lord Kielder's actions conflicted with Keane's idea of fair play. In a small sense, what Keane had planned for Esmeralda echoed Lord Kielder's despicable methods.

After hearing her nightmare, Keane had reevaluated his tactics to achieve marriage—and decided to discard tactics all together. Esmeralda was a hurt young woman who needed to learn how to trust. Try as he might, Keane knew he couldn't manipulate or trick her into trusting him. Trust would either come or it would not.

It frightened him to think that the valuable time he had left with Esmeralda would be spent without plan or strategy. That he would actually have to let her go if she chose to leave him when they reached England. But after holding her, and watching her cry as she recounted her cousin's betrayal, he knew he could never lie to her or trick her as Lord Kielder had done.

She would either grow to trust him—or she would not. It was as simple as that.

"I don't believe I have your full attention, Lord Eldridge. That is very disconcerting to a woman's vanity."

Keane reluctantly turned his gaze away from Esmeralda. "I'm sorry, Mrs. Burton. My mind wandered. You were saying?"

"I was remarking on how long it's taking to get through the canal."

"It's the ship ahead of us, ma'am," explained the pilot from behind the wheel. "They're removing the chimney stacks to get under the canal bridge. It shouldn't be much longer, though."

"I should hope not. This trip is getting frightfully boring." Cecilia unpursed her lips and smiled slyly at Keane. "Perhaps you—and your wife—would like to join Tommy and me later for supper. We could think of some ways to liven things up?" Cecilia's indigo eyes swept up and down Keane's length making him almost laugh at her transparency.

"I'll speak with Esmeralda."

From across the pilothouse, Esmeralda watched Mrs. Burton's self-satisfied smile and seethed. How dare that woman sit there and ogle someone's husband like that? It mattered not that Keane answered with polite but unenthusiastic replies. In fact, his obvious disinterest only served to emphasize the woman's perfidy. Would she ever leave Keane alone?

"Excuse me, Lady Eldridge. Might I join you?"

Esmeralda looked up at David Winton. Smothering her choler, she smiled and gestured toward the bench next to her. Mr. Winton, whose stubby, round proportions reached no higher than Esmeralda's chin, hunkered down next to her.

"It's a lovely view of the canal from here."

"Yes, it is," Esmeralda answered politely. "We're so close to the banks, I feel as if I could step right onto them from the deck."

Mr. Winton laughed. "It certainly does seem so, though I wouldn't advise it. The ship stops for no one. Why, I've even heard of families split apart because one member doesn't make it back on board before the ship leaves the harbor after wooding up."

"That's dreadful!"

"Oh, it's not nearly so bad as it sounds—there being so many ships passing through. Who's ever left behind just hops aboard the next packet a little smarter for the experience."

Esmeralda examined the man with the thick Yorkshire accent with interest. "For an Englishman, Mr. Winton, you certainly seem to know a lot about river travel on the Ohio."

Winton flashed a gap-toothed smile that instantly brought Molly to mind. The reminder made her nostalgic for her friend. She did so miss Molly. Esmeralda warmed to the man next to her, trying to ease the pain of losing Molly through Mr. Winton's company.

"I know a bit about the home turf as well," Winton added with a wide grin. "Enough to wonder what Viscount Eldridge is doing in Cincinnati with a wife he didn't have when he left England."

His words so contradicted his pleasant expression that, at first, Esmeralda actually questioned her hearing. Her smile faltered. "We met and married in Cincinnati," she answered coldly, no longer amused by Mr. Winton's conversation.

"Now, don't get all frosty on me." Again he smiled winningly. "I have a real soft spot for romance, and as soon as I saw you and the viscount, I said to myself, 'Now Davey, there's a story worth hearing.' "

Still a bit unnerved by the man's questions, but weakening to his outspoken style and friendly demeanor, Esmeralda answered hesitantly, "We haven't been married long, actually."

"I knew it! I could tell by—I hope you don't mind my saying this"—the gap-toothed smile widened—"by the way you look at each other. Lord, I do love a good romance." Mr. Winton pulled off his hat and brushed a few wisps of hair back over his balding pate before replacing it with a frown. "But one thing puzzles me, Lady Eldridge. You're English?"

"Scottish and English."

Winton nodded, then leaned forward conspiratorially. "I'm sure there's another good story in how you ended up in Cincinnati married to the viscount."

Esmeralda laughed at his theatrical whisper. "Nothing as interesting as all that. For the past year and a half, I've lived there—temporarily. Until I could settle things with my estate."

"Your estate?" Winton's brows lifted.

"Amberose," she said automatically. Mr. Winton's easy manner put her at ease, making her speak without thinking.

"That's up by the Scottish border?" At Esmeralda's nod, he continued in a puzzled voice. "Doesn't that estate belong to . . . Lord Kielder?"

"Allen may have possession of my home now, but Amberose is mine. Now and always!" A bit ashamed by her vigor, she continued in a more subdued voice, "You'll have to excuse me, Mr. Winton. My cousin is truly a sore subject with me."

"Oh, it's quite all right," he assured her. "As I said before, an interesting story."

Keane listened to Esmeralda's exchange with Mr. Winton, losing every other sentence to Cecilia Burton's recital of the various sights in New Orleans. But when he heard his name and that of Esmeralda's cousin, he excused himself to Cecilia and stepped in to intervene. There was something about the seemingly innocuous Mr. Winton that Keane didn't quite trust.

"Hello," Keane interrupted the two, who were continuing their discussion in lowered voices. Smiling at Esmeralda, he extended his hand to her. "If you'll excuse us, Mr. Winton, I'd like to take my wife out onto the guards. The pilot suggested we'd have a better view from there while the ship sails under the bridge."

"Of course, Lord Eldridge. I, too, must be returning downstairs." Winton's smile to Esmeralda was much more familiar than Keane would have liked. "Thank you for sharing your story with me, Lady Eldridge."

Esmeralda stood beside Keane, ready to leave. "My pleasure, Mr. Winton. I'm sure we'll speak again later."

Winton bowed his head. "I look forward to it."

Keane frowned, escorting Esmeralda toward the door. "What were you speaking about with Mr. Winton?"

"We were just talking about home and river travel. I'm sure nothing as riveting as your discussion with Mrs. Burton," she added acidly.

Keane winced. Cecilia Burton was still a sore subject with Esmeralda, even though he tried his damndest to stay away from the woman. He should spend more time with Esmeralda, even if it did make her nervous. Maybe that would discourage Cecilia and prove to Esmeralda that his interests were firmly entrenched in her and not in the married American woman.

As they left the pilothouse, Keane looked back over his shoulder to make sure Cecilia would not follow them to the guards. But what he saw instantly centered his attentions on the gentleman from York.

Mr. Winton appeared to be scribbling notes on a piece of paper.

Chapter Twenty-eight

Esmeralda watched Cecilia Burton sip her champagne like a satisfied cat lapping cream, then gaze up at Keane and titter. Fuming, Esmeralda gulped down a mouthful of champagne from her glass. Try as she might, she could not see the allure of so forward a woman. Yet every eligible gentleman seemed to hover close by, waiting for some hidden signal from Cecilia that his turn had arrived. And arrive it would, for Mrs. Burton was nothing but egalitarian in her flirtations. What truly amazed Esmeralda was that Cecilia managed to target her special attentions on Keane without losing her audience of admirers.

Since her unfortunate meeting with Cecilia in the ladies' lounge earlier that day, Esmeralda was feeling even less charitable than usual toward the woman. When she'd walked into the lounge and had seen Cecilia wave a greeting to her, Esmeralda managed a half-hearted smile in her general vicinity before finding an empty chair as far away from the American woman as possible. But Esmeralda's efforts to avoid Mrs. Burton were wasted. Soon Cecilia slithered up to Esmeralda, her sewing in hand. She plied Esmeralda with question after question about what it was like to be married to a viscount, while mercilessly stabbing away at her bit of cloth. Which members of the royal family did Esmeralda know? How did the nobility spend the season? The questions had been endless and, surprisingly enough, had all been delivered in a friendly manner. Just when Esmeralda dropped her guard, beginning to wonder if she'd misjudged the woman, Cecilia began her ugly insinuations, implying that only an extremely bored husband could prefer another woman's company and gambling to spending time with his wife. Esmeralda was so furious she left immediately—but not before commenting that Cecilia's sewing showed as much talent as that of a trained dog.

Keane did not prefer Cecilia Burton! Granted, it had been three days since he last kissed Esmeralda, but he was just following the rules of their bargain. Rules she had come up with—necessary rules that would make parting easier once they reached England.

So why did the very thought of leaving him cause Esmeralda's stomach to churn?

Esmeralda sighed and sipped her champagne, instantly depressed. She'd made certain Keane never touched her. And when that hadn't helped, she'd seen to it that they spent as little time together as possible, meeting him only for their meals. But try as she might, she couldn't squelch her growing feelings of love.

Whenever she walked into a room, she found herself searching for him. If he was there, her heart would soar and she'd immediately step toward him, drawn to him despite herself. And if she didn't see him, her heart would drop in disappointment. Whenever she woke, she would glance out from behind the curtained bed and watch him scrunched down, sleeping on the chair. His hair tousled in sleep, his squared lips slightly parted, he looked so peaceful. So lovable.

Esmeralda sighed. Maybe it was too late. Maybe once you loved someone, you could never stop loving him.

Now she understood why Molly hadn't been able to leave Jason. She'd been overly harsh in condemning Molly. Molly hadn't betrayed her—she'd just followed her heart.

A particularly loud titter from Cecilia drew Esmeralda's attention. Looking across the room, she saw Cecilia press up against Keane and whisper something in his ear before laughing behind her hand and flashing him a naughty look. Esmeralda's anger smoldered. She'd had enough of the cloying Mrs. Burton and her fawning over Keane. If she didn't take some action, Esmeralda felt sure she would burst. Without a second thought, she signaled one of the uniformed men serving champagne.

"More champagne ma'am?" the man asked while taking Esmeralda's empty glass.

Esmeralda shook her head. "Bordeaux. I would prefer a glass, a large glass, if it's not too much trouble."

"No trouble at all, ma'am."

When the man returned with the glass of red wine, Esmeralda didn't even bother to take a sip before wending her way across the room to where Cecilia Burton held court.

Keane watched Esmeralda wind her way around the dancing couples toward them and held back his sigh of relief. He intended to ask her for a dance, and her "no touching" dictum be damned. He'd done more than was humanly possible to make her feel comfortable around him, to trust him. But every time he thought he was making some headway, he'd hit a new layer of defense. Well, she could at least dance with him. He was thoroughly sick of Cecilia Burton's simperings and sexual innuendos.

Just the thought of holding Esmeralda in his arms

again, even if it were for no longer than one waltz, made Keane grow excited. Damn, but this trip was getting more uncomfortable by the day.

He'd created his own hell, of course. Every evening he was faced with that luscious pale back as he fastened Esmeralda's dresses. And at night, when they retired, helping her remove her clothes was worse than any torture he could have imagined. So often he'd reach over, almost grasping her shoulders to smooth the material off her skin and take her in his arms. Then he'd remember: no touching. Turning his back on temptation, he would huddle into the cramped quarters of the armchair.

The idea of bunking with Higgins was rapidly gaining allure.

With a smile, Keane stepped aside to allow Esmeralda to join their circle beside him and Thomas Burton. But surprisingly she ignored the created space and nudged Cecilia Burton aside, settling in between her and Keane. He almost laughed, but the beaming smile on Esmeralda's face, aimed at the unlikely object of Mrs. Burton, caught his interest. He saw the glass of Bordeaux, and frowned. He'd always thought Esmeralda preferred the sweeter white wines from Germany that the ship's large stores offered.

"You looked like you were enjoying yourselves so much," Esmeralda said with an enthusiasm she'd never displayed around Cecilia. "I thought I'd join in on the fun. My husband can be so very entertaining."

"Most assuredly so." Cecilia smiled wickedly up at Keane, as if sharing some secret with him. "But I'm disappointed." She pouted. "Despite all my hints, Viscount Eldridge hasn't asked me to dance, yet."

"How very remiss of you, Keane," Esmeralda scolded. "You simply must do your duty with Mrs. Burton. Why I see they're starting—" Esmeralda turned sharply toward Cecilia, as if looking to the band, and dumped the entire glass of wine down the front of her dress. A huge scarlet stain ran from the neckline to the waist of Cecilia's white satin-and-lace gown.

"How dreadfully clumsy of me," Esmeralda said in a voice devoid of any remorse.

"You did that on purpose!"

"Now, darling . . ." began Mr. Burton.

"It was on purpose, I tell you." Cecilia glanced around their company, seeking confirmation from the witnesses, her face distorted into ugly lines of anger. "You bitch!" She turned to look accusingly at Esmeralda, whose features were settled in bored amusement. "You little—" She lunged forward.

Keane stepped in front of Cecilia's path, intercepting her. As unobtrusively as possible, he turned her from her target and escorted her to her husband's side. "I believe your wife needs a change of clothes." Keane flashed Mr. Burton a stern look. "As well as better manners."

"*My* manners!" screeched Cecilia. "Look to that bitch you've married if you want to improve someone's manners. . . ." The angry tirade trailed off as Thomas Burton herded his wife toward their stateroom.

Cecilia Burton dispensed with, Keane turned to face Esmeralda.

With an expression of complete innocence, Esmeralda shrugged her shoulders in Gallic nonchalance. "I must have slipped."

"Gentlemen, if you'll excuse us?" Keane grabbed Esmeralda's hand and hauled her through the milling crowd that had gathered at the first sounds of discord. Esmeralda barely kept pace behind Keane without tripping as he pulled her along. When they arrived at their stateroom, Keane yanked open the door and dumped Esmeralda inside before slamming it behind them. Leaning against the door, he crossed his arms and stared across the room at her.

Esmeralda stared back, her face set in a mutinous expression.

"What on *earth* did you think you were doing back there!" he shouted.

"I was getting rid of a problem."

"A problem? That woman held so little interest for me that I would not even place her in the category of acquaintance, much less problem!"

"I thought differently."

"So you just . . ." Keane groped for the words. ". . . Just . . ." Unable to stop himself, he began to see the humor in the situation and his anger lapsed. Soon the room filled with the sound of his deep throaty laughter. "Dumped . . . a glass . . . of wine on her dress?"

Esmeralda could feel her lips twitch. "I would have dumped it on her head if I thought I could get away with it."

"My God, but that's rich!" Keane continued to laugh and soon Esmeralda joined in. "The look she gave you. Medusa couldn't have done better." Keane's laughter turned to soft chuckles. "I thought she was going to scratch your eyes out."

"She probably would have if you hadn't stepped between us."

"I really can't believe you did it." Smiling with admiration, he stepped forward and swept up Esmeralda's hand before executing a gallant bow and kissing it softly. "Thank you for saving me from Mrs. Burton's ruthless clutches."

Esmeralda beamed. "My pleasure."

Still holding her hand, Keane moved closer. "My virtue *was* at stake, you know."

"What virtue?" she asked dryly.

Keane pulled her closer still, shifting her into his arms. "The things that woman said to me . . ."

Instantly recalling Cecilia's lascivious looks to Keane, Esmeralda demanded, "Such as?"

Keane thought for a moment, then shook his head. "No. I cannot possibly sully your ears with it." Then lowering his voice to conspiratorial softness, "But, I do believe the woman proposed sexual favors."

"I should have thrown the wine in her face."

Keane laughed merrily. "God, I love you." He said the words naturally, as if he said them to her every day, then he leaned down to kiss her.

Immediately, Esmeralda pulled out of his embrace. She backed away, her features wiped clean of any humor. The same haunted expression he'd come to despise radiated from her.

"You shouldn't touch me." She said the words like a lament.

"For God's sake, Esmeralda. Is that all you have to say to me? I just told you I love you and you stand there looking at me like a cornered animal!"

"We agreed, no touching . . . it was part of the rules."

"The rules be damned!" Keane marched forward, then stopped midstride. A slow, ruthless smile formed across his lips.

"Those rules are very important to you, aren't they, sweets?" He watched her closely, stalking her until she backed up against the bed. He lunged forward. Startled, she fell on top of the bed to avoid making contact. "We don't have to break the rules," he said, climbing up the bed behind her as Esmeralda inched up the covers. He continued until he straddled her, forcing her up against the pillows. "I won't touch you—not unless you want me to."

"What are you doing? Let me up!"

Keane's voice was soft and mesmerizing as he lowered his face to Esmeralda's. "Go ahead, push me off."

Just as Esmeralda tried to get up, Keane eased his lips down to hers. She gasped and fell back against the pillows. With a merciless smile, Keane continued to lower his lips until they hovered just above her mouth. His breath caressed her lips. "You don't want to break the rules?"

"Keane." The word was a hopeless whisper.

"I'm listening." Keane blew softly against her ear and Esmeralda shivered. "I'm not touching you." Keane stroked her face with his soft breath, almost nuzzling her neck. "Hmm. You smell so delicious."

"Keane . . ."

"Like flowers. I love how you smell, Esmeralda." His lips almost brushed hers. "I love how you taste: sweet, like the chocolates you like so much."

"Keane . . . please."

"Please, what?"

"Please . . ." Her breathing became rough, as if she were fighting. And she was—fighting herself. Even though he hadn't touched her, his nearness, the scent of champagne on his lips, the mere memory of his kisses seduced her. His mouth was so close, and his chest hovered above hers, almost brushing her breasts, making her ache for the touch. Closing her eyes, she whispered, "Please . . ."

"Break the rules?"

"Yes."

"I don't know if we should." He blew the words softly in her ear, sending another shiver through her.

Esmeralda arched up to kiss him, but Keane pulled away. She stretched up toward him, and he leaned further away, teasing her. Beyond thinking, Esmeralda wrapped her arms around his neck and pulled him down to her.

It was all the encouragement Keane needed. His mouth slashed across hers, meshing their lips together. He threaded his fingers through her loose curls and let his weight settle on her soft frame.

"When are you going to admit you love me, need me as much as I need you?"

Esmeralda answered by deepening their kiss. She could feel his hands caress her face and neck. Pulling his lips away, Keane touched his tongue to her ear and Esmeralda gasped with pleasure. Slowly he tasted every crevice, feeling her shudder beneath him. "I love you, Esmeralda." He whispered the words before softly biting her earlobe.

Esmeralda was on fire, burning from the inside out. Wanting only to feel his warm skin against hers, she pulled at the lapels of Keane's dinner jacket. He quickly began unfastening her dress and they disrobed each other between heated kisses and whispered endearments.

When Esmeralda lay back against the counterpane, na- ked, Keane held his breath. She was so beautiful. The moonlight shone on her pale skin, making it seem almost iridescent. Her hair fanned across the pillows behind her like shimmering copper. He knelt above her, straddling her thighs, and reached out to cup one warm breast with his hand. He brushed the tip with his thumb until it formed a hard nub.

Esmeralda sat up against him and wrapped her arms around his stomach, burying her face against the hard muscles there. She could feel his erection thrust up be- tween them and the memories of how it felt to have him inside her swept through her, causing a warm explosion below her stomach. Keane stroked her back gently, then leaned forward until he pushed her down on the bed. Slowly he slid down her length, gently nipping and kissing her salty skin. Stopping at her breasts to suckle each softly, he took one in each hand, then continued his path down. The curls at the apex of her thighs were a brighter color than the muted copper tones of her auburn tresses. They drew him like a mesmerizing firelight. Spreading her legs gently with his hands, he kissed the soft insides of her ivory thighs and then lost himself in the flame-colored curls.

She protested at first, struggling to move him, but he continued to taste and kiss her until she moaned and bur- ied her hands in his hair with acceptance. The savor of her moist flesh drove him to the edge of his endurance. But still he held back. He wanted their union to be her most fulfilling experience yet. Replacing his mouth with his thumb, he moved up to her stomach and kissed the small mole next to her navel. Then he returned his lips to her tantalizing breasts, while his thumb continued to stroke the small bud hidden within her moist folds of skin.

Esmeralda pressed against him, and he knew what she sought. Burying his tongue deep in her mouth, he parted her legs with his knees and thrust into her moist heat. The minute he entered her, her muscles contracted around him as she found her pleasure. A short while later, he spilled his seed deep within her.

When Keane slipped down alongside her, Esmeralda spooned her body against his and sighed. Languid and satisfied, she nuzzled against his neck, inhaling the lemony scent he wore.

"I love you." Keane placed a gentle kiss on her temple.

Esmeralda tensed. Seconds dragged like minutes before she whispered softly into the darkness, "And I love you."

Keane felt an overwhelming joy spread through him. He cuddled her closer. "I've been waiting a hell of a long time to hear you say that."

"I didn't want to admit it." Esmeralda turned and stared into Keane's eyes. "To you or myself."

"Why?"

"Because . . . because I've been desperately trying not to"—she looked away—"love you."

Keane took her chin in his hand and raised her face up to his. "Because of your cousin?"

She nodded silently, her eyes pleading for reassurance.

Keane leaned forward and cupped her face in his hands. "People who love you, truly love you, don't betray you." He stroked the side of her face, touching his thumb to her full, bruised lips. "They don't seek to hurt you for their own gain. They cherish and protect—and put *your* needs before their own wants and desires." He smiled boyishly. "Or try their damndest to. But never hurt," he said, his voice suddenly very serious. "They don't cause pain; they seek to cure it. Your cousin didn't love you, Esmeralda. Not the way I do." He touched his lips to hers. "If you don't believe that yet, give me time. I'll prove it to you. I swear it."

Keane sat up, removing his signet ring from his pinkie. Taking Esmeralda's hand, he slipped it on her index finger, the only finger it would fit. "You wouldn't wear a wedding band for our mock marriage. Wear this ring as a token of my love. It was my father's and means a great deal to me."

"Oh, Keane, I couldn't—"

He pressed his finger across her lips. "Wear it. Whenever you begin to doubt my love for you, I want you to look at this ring and remember. Remember how much we struggled together when you were so sick. And remember how I make you feel when we're one. And always, *always* remember that I love you."

Keane slipped down beside Esmeralda, fitting her body against his in a firm hug. Esmeralda felt a sizable lump lodge in her throat. She wanted to believe Keane—desperately. But somehow, she sensed he didn't understand. Allen had loved her. She knew that, just as surely as she knew how much she loved Keane.

Love could betray.

Chapter Twenty-nine

Allen MacClure, Lord Kielder, narrowed his eyes at the disturbing headline. When he saw the paper at his club, he immediately returned to his lavishly furnished London town house. In the study, he spread the newspaper on the desk, the article concerning him front and center. Leaning back against the brocade armchair, he tapped his fingers rhythmically on the desk, trying to determine how best to waylay the trouble this bit of news could cost him.

All his careful plans, the work of a lifetime, undone by some greedy imposter? It was something he could hardly permit.

Allen picked up the paper. With long, tapered fingers, he tore out the article claiming that Lord Eldridge had married abroad and was bringing home his heiress bride. The woman called herself Esmeralda MacClure. She claimed to be the true heir to Amberose, the Northumberland estate that had for the past nine years financed Allen's rich life-style and gambling. Once he had the newspaper story in hand, Allen threw the rest of *The Times* down on the Aubusson rug and kicked it aside. The article he placed on the desk.

For a moment he explored the possibility that Esmeralda had survived after all these years. He stood and walked to the gilded mirror on the wall of his study. Sharp green eyes, the color of bottle glass, stared back at him from the mirror. The stylish superfine coat showed his figure to advantage; his reddish curls looped down over his ears, granting him a youthful appearance that belied his two and thirty years. He touched his hand to his full lips and tried to imagine the same mouth on a woman. Through some trick of his mind, for a split second he actually saw a woman with his features reflected in the glass. The blood rushed to his groin.

Ridding himself of Esmeralda was the one thing he truly regretted. He'd loved that child. She'd been so utterly beautiful—a perfect reflection of himself. Even at ten, she'd showed such promise. . . . But the old man's will had been explicit. The same document that had given him the right to her guardianship had sealed the girl's fate. Dear God, how he *missed* her! He'd had such plans for their future before the will.

Allen tore his eyes away from his reflection, suddenly angry that it would *not be* Esmeralda returning to him. How dare some woman try and pass herself off as his long-lost cousin? He grabbed the article off the desk, shredding it to pieces between his long, fine fingers. Already people stared when he walked into the club. His solicitors predicted dire consequences to his finances unless the rumors were squelched. But it wasn't the article's scandalous implications about his past that made him toss the torn pieces of paper in the fire, then grab the inkwell and throw it against the mirror, shattering the glass that mocked him with its vision of a mate in his image. As he watched the India ink drip slowly to the rug, he admitted to himself that it was this deep longing—the desire, ignited after so many years, to hold her in his arms—that incited his rabid anger.

Allen dropped to the floor and leaned his head against the desk. *Esmeralda. Dear Esmeralda,* he thought. *If only I could have had you and the money both.*

Esmeralda leaned back against the seat cushion, exhausted by the long coach ride. Ever since they'd arrived in England, they'd been cooped up in this carriage, stopping only to eat and rest briefly at an occasional roadside inn. Did the man never get tired? Another lurch of the carriage made her stomach roil, and she flashed Keane an accusing stare. He answered with an encouraging smile that seemed to say: *Buck up old girl; we're almost there.* Attacked by another wave of queasiness, she nonetheless squelched her childish urge to stick her tongue out at the picture of health seated opposite her. Somehow she didn't think he'd understand that his continued energy during their harrowing journey from Southampton made her feel frail and inadequate.

Blast that man and his stamina! She hadn't wanted to mention the illness she'd experienced the last three mornings of their crossing—she hadn't wanted to think about it herself. It seemed perilously similar to the illness Molly had experienced the first months of her pregnancy. So Esmeralda had convinced herself that it was only seasickness and agreed to their present exhausting pace to Eldridge Manor.

She sighed, recalling their past month together. A week of it had been spent in New Orleans, where they rested, discovering the city—and each other. But the crossing to England had taken its toll. A wave of nausea made her swallow her gorge. She was just tired, she reasoned. This queasiness and the lateness of her menses were unrelated. They had to be.

Esmeralda had yet to come to terms with her feelings for Keane. She loved him, and she knew he cared deeply for her as well. In his arms she found a completeness that she knew instinctively she'd feel with no one else. But try as she might, she still couldn't trust Keane.

He sensed her mistrust. It made him short-tempered. Simple discussions often erupted into loud arguments— arguments they resolved in bed. Still she couldn't seem to stop her wariness. No matter how beautifully Keane made love, no matter how tender and loving his gaze, a niggling fear shattered her belief in him.

After all, she'd believed in Allen's love.

So when Keane asked her to marry him, the morning after they'd first made love on the *Embassy,* she begged off, claiming she needed time to think about his proposal. During their crossing, she'd still been unable to commit herself to a real marriage. Marriage meant the kind of dependence that had given Allen the power to hurt her. But she couldn't accept the alternative—leaving Keane. As a compromise, she agreed to go to his estate near Salisbury, where she would stay with his mother at Eldridge Manor while Keane arranged a meeting with his solicitors and Allen.

Esmeralda shuddered. Allen. Amberose. The end of her long struggle was nearing.

"Not much longer now, sweets."

Esmeralda grimaced. "You said that hours ago."

Keane smiled at her impatience. "We'll be there before dark. I sent a messenger ahead of us at the last stop so my mother will be expecting us. Everything will be ready for your comfort. I promise, you'll get some needed rest soon."

Resigned to the wait, Esmeralda leaned back against the squabs and sighed.

"Wake up sleepyhead, we're here."

Esmeralda felt a gentle nudge wake her. She must have dozed off. Feeling tired and queasy, she stifled a shudder.

Tired. Nauseated. Just like Molly when she'd been expecting Peter.

Squelching her frightening thoughts, she stepped down from the carriage. If it hadn't been for Keane's steadying hand, she would have tripped and fallen right on her backside. There, lined up in front of a huge Tudor mansion, was a row of servants, all dressed in pristine uniforms and all beaming with friendly smiles. At the head of the line was a short, matronly woman with pink cheeks and snow-white hair. Beside her, a tall, feminine replica of Keane hovered over a petite, angelic blonde. Next came a breathtakingly beautiful girl, with jet black hair and a murderous look in her gold-colored eyes that were trained right on Esmeralda.

Keane's mother and sisters. Esmeralda would know them anywhere.

She felt as if she were facing a firing squad.

Keane pulled Esmeralda forward, flashing her an encouraging smile. He gently embraced the white-haired woman as she placed a motherly kiss on his cheek.

"Mother, I hadn't quite expected this . . . reception."

Her eyes moist with emotion, Keane's mother smiled up to her son, who towered over her. "It's not every day you bring home your viscountess."

Esmeralda felt faint. She looked at Keane, but he appeared to be just as confused as she.

"Well, aren't you going to introduce us?" asked a sharp, efficient voice from behind her. Esmeralda turned her gaze to the replica of Keane. *Charlotte, the eldest.*

"Of course." Keane stepped aside and motioned Esmeralda to stand beside him. "Esmeralda," he said, careful to avoid using her last name, "let me introduce my family. My mother, Katherine, the Viscountess Eldridge."

Katherine stepped forward and gave Esmeralda a heartfelt embrace, before kissing her on both cheeks. There were tears in her eyes. "We've waited so long to meet you." Glancing back at Keane, but still holding Esmeralda's shoulders, Katherine said softly, "She's lovely, Keane. I couldn't have chosen better myself."

The queasy feeling in Esmeralda's stomach increased tenfold.

"Stop fawning over her, Mother," Charlotte exclaimed. "Give us all a chance." Taking her mother's place, Keane's eldest sister, a few inches taller than even Esmeralda, took up her hand and grasped it warmly. "You'll get used to Mother and her sentimentality. I'm Charlotte Cheshire. Unlike Mother, I knew he would get around to doing his duty soon. It's just like him to do the thing abroad and avoid a fuss. Though I must say, he could have warned us." Charlotte stepped aside with military crispness and motioned to the two girls behind her. "Come, Annabella, Nicky. Help me welcome Keane's bride to her new home."

"Bride?" Esmeralda gulped.

"I knew it!" The dark-haired girl, her exultant face wiped clear of the murderous expression, ran to Keane's side. In her hand, she carried a torn piece of newspaper. Keane picked her up with practiced ease, and she clung to him like a monkey. "It's a lie. I knew it wasn't true!"

"Katherine Nicole! Behave yourself!" Charlotte barked, ready to pry her from Keane's arms until he waved her away.

"It's a lie!" Nicky screamed back at Charlotte, still clinging to Keane. "Just look at their faces! They're as surprised as we were!" Then, turning her anxious gaze to Keane, "The newspapers lie all the time, don't they?" She waved the scrap of paper in her hand. "It says you're married to some awful Scottish heiress—but you wouldn't do that!" She stabbed Esmeralda with an accusatory look, then buried her face in Keane's shoulder, hugging him even more tightly. "She's awful. I hate her. Make her go away—"

"That's enough, scamp." Keane unwrapped Nicky's

arms from around his neck and put her on the ground next to him, taking the paper from her hand.

"But it's not true—"

"I said, that's enough!" Keane commanded, cutting her off with quiet authority. A look of betrayal dawned on her beautiful face, and the young girl turned and fled back into the manor house.

"Nicky!" Charlotte shouted, only to be ignored.

"Oh, dear," Keane's mother whispered under her breath.

Keane grinned a tight smile that didn't reach his eyes. "Perhaps we can dispense with the formal introductions today, Mother?" He glanced at the row of waiting servants, and at her nod, excused the lot. "Shall we continue this inside?" Wrapping a possessive arm around Esmeralda, he waited patiently as his sisters and mother marched stoically up the entrance steps. He and Esmeralda followed quietly in their wake.

Once inside, the Viscountess turned her concerned gaze back to Esmeralda. "You must think us awful, my dear. Nicky can be so headstrong, and she's so . . . so . . . possessive."

"I believe I can explain things to Esmeralda, Mother. If you'll excuse us? I'd like to speak to her in private. We'll meet in the library for a *proper* introduction in ten minutes. Charlotte, you'll make sure Nicky is there?"

Charlotte nodded curtly, her gaze hardening into the expression of a general planning his next assault.

Esmeralda followed Keane through the long entrance corridor. Once they reached the walnut double doors of the library, Keane guided her inside and motioned her to a chair. Smoothing out the scrap of newspaper he still held, he walked to the hearth and read it. After a moment, he started to chuckle. He handed the newspaper to Esmeralda and waited.

"I don't know what to say." She glanced up, confused. "How could they know about our meeting in Cincinnati?

And this part about my returning to England to fight Allen for Amberose, how could they know all that?"

"David Winton," Keane stated dryly. "If I don't miss my guess. He spent the entire trip plying you for information. I even remember seeing him take notes once. I thought it strange at the time. Our dear Mr. Winton must work for *The Times of London,* and he managed to dig up enough information about you to publish a story about our 'secret wedding.' " Keane laughed again, this time without humor. "It has all the makings of a dreadful romance. 'Dethroned heiress marries viscount in the colonies. Vows to regain her home.' "

"What do we do now?" she asked helplessly.

Keane walked across the room. Taking her hands, he pulled her up from the chair. His face set in a serious expression, he whispered urgently, "Marry me. In secret. No one need ever know we weren't married in Kentucky." Folding her in his arms, Keane continued, "It's what I've always wanted, Esmeralda. And if you're honest, you'll admit it's what you want as well."

Esmeralda met Keane's earnest expression of love and felt it carve its mark on her heart.

"Marry me," he whispered again.

Her heart beat speeded up. Marry Keane. Marry. Forever.

"Let me love you for the rest of your life, Esmeralda."

She closed her eyes. The queasy feeling inside her stomach reminded her of other possibilities. What if she were at this moment expecting Keane's child? She opened her eyes and met his loving gaze. Instantly, all thoughts of a possible child fled when she stared at his anxious amber eyes.

It's what you want! shouted the voice within her.

A sense of freedom swept through her, so intense she stumbled against Keane. *It's what I want.*

"Yes," she whispered back.

Keane grabbed her around her waist and twirled her

around in the air. Her giggles of happiness joined his mellow laughter. He kissed her with an intensity that transported his joy right to her heart and exploded in a feeling of loving warmth.

At the soft knock on the door, Keane pulled his lips away from hers. A beaming smile lighting his features, he gazed into Esmeralda's eyes. "Come in!"

Slowly his family marched inside, a reluctant Nicky dragging in behind Charlotte. Keane turned Esmeralda to face them.

His voice strong with pride and love, he made his announcement.

"Ladies, this is Esmeralda MacClure Marshall, the new Viscountess Eldridge."

Esmeralda looked across the long dining table at Keane while she took a tentative sip of the turtle soup. No responding queasiness occurred. Smiling to herself, she settled back to enjoy her meal, suddenly feeling quite ravenous.

She would have preferred having a tray sent up to her room, but when Keane's mother gave her the choice of eating alone or joining the family, Esmeralda could see it was the latter choice that would make Lady Eldridge smile. So she'd changed her traveling suit for a pale pink satin dress with silver brocade trim and joined the others in the dining room. Since Keane's return to Eldridge Manor with his bride marked a special occasion, ten-year-old Nicky, who Esmeralda was told usually ate in the kitchen, sat on her left with Annabella beside her. Directly across from them were Keane's mother and Charlotte. Charlotte and her two sons were staying at the manor while Charlotte's husband was away on business, but the boys had already been put to bed.

Obviously trying to humor Nicky out of her sour mood, Keane asked, "Did you miss me, scamp?"

Nicky grumbled a noncommittal answer into her soup.

"Mind your manners, Nicole," Charlotte commanded sharply.

Nicky looked up from her soup, and for a moment, her unique topaz eyes softened as she looked at Keane, her face aglow with hopeless worship. "I said I missed you very much. I hate it when you go away."

"Maybe now Keane will be staying closer to home?" Katherine gave Esmeralda an affectionate glance.

Nicole looked as if she'd rather have Keane stay away than have a new wife keep him at home.

"Please," Annabella said softly. "Don't mind Nicky. She's just terribly jealous. It's not enough that she has Uncle Marc fawning over her constantly. She wants *everyone's* attention."

With a quick look to check if Charlotte was watching, Nicky stuck her tongue out at Annabella, causing Esmeralda to choke on her soup. Nicky flashed a look of triumph.

Esmeralda returned her attention back to the angelic Annabella. Unlike Nicole, whose dark tresses stood out among the fair-haired Marshalls there, Annabella's hair was almost white. Her large, clear blue eyes and round face reminded Esmeralda of Keane's mother. Esmeralda predicted Annabella's soft prettiness would make her upcoming debut a success. Charlotte's handsome features, on the other hand, reflected Keane's caramel-hued hair and amber eyes. Tall and slender, she towered over the shorter, more rounded Annabella and Katherine. Only Nicky stood unaccounted for, her ebony curls and eyes the color of the finest yellow sapphire looking like no one else's. Esmeralda wondered whom Nicky favored with her pixy-sharp, exotic features, and thought perhaps it was her father. Esmeralda sensed that of the women seated around the table, Nicky would grow into the true beauty and clearly outdistance her sisters.

"Nicky can be a real discipline problem," Charlotte said, louder than necessary. "That's because Uncle Marc and Keane spoil her. I've told Mother she should let Nicky stay with me and Charles. I wouldn't indulge her antics the way the men do."

"Keane doesn't spoil her," Annabella defended. "Why, remember the time she put a frog in his bed? She never did that again!"

Curious, Esmeralda asked, "Why is that?"

Annabella's eyes grew saucer-wide and her full pink lips curled in disgust. "He made her eat it."

"It was a very small frog," explained Charlotte, as if the punishment were nothing. "And he had it cooked. Why, if it weren't for those beady eyes staring up at you, you'd think she'd been served a dish fit for a prince. Besides," she added, with a meaningful look to Nicky across from her. "He only made her take a bite. I would have made her eat the whole thing—raw!"

"I wouldn't have been stupid enough to put it in your bed!" Nicky said, not bothering to disguise her tone of superiority. Then, with a sudden light shining in her eyes, she turned her gaze to Esmeralda, whom she'd pointedly ignored all evening. "Do you like frogs?"

"Not to eat," Esmeralda replied warily.

An impish smile threaded across Nicky's red lips. "I didn't think so."

"I hope you're not planning something foolish, scamp?" Keane asked with deceptive softness.

"I was just being friendly." Nicole returned to her meal, a curious smile on her face.

Esmeralda sat before the vanity, combing her hair. She loved them, all of them, even—or maybe especially—the pixy, Nicole. It had been so long since she'd felt the warmth of family surrounding her. She'd been only Nicky's age when her parents died. Yet tonight, she felt wrapped in a blanket of familial love.

It was clear how much the women in his family respected and loved Keane. Over dinner, his mother had chatted about the *ton* gossip, obviously enjoying having her son's ready ear. Charlotte discussed her husband's business, asking Keane's advice on this investment and that. Everyone seemed to defer to him. Annabella also asked his help—what color looked best on her for her debut, and would Keane practice some new dance steps with her? Nicky, happy to have Keane's attention, languidly related every hunting feat she'd accomplished with the aid of her uncle, and Keane patiently listened until Charlotte finally cut her sister off, scolding her for being a chatterbox.

Later, when Esmeralda presented them with the gifts she and Keane had bought in New Orleans, they "oohed" and "ahhed" their appreciation. Even Nicky's face lit up when she saw her hunting cap, which was a far cry from the hideous hat Esmeralda had designed in Cincinnati. Afterward, when Nicky left for bed, they all gathered about Esmeralda, including her in their discussions as if she'd always been a part of their family. Just thinking about it now made Esmeralda's throat feel thick and her eyes dangerously moist.

To be part of a family like Keane's, after all those lonely years with only Molly, and then eventually Peter—it was just too wonderful.

With a sigh, Esmeralda put away her brush and walked over to the bed, ready to throw back the counterpane and get some needed rest. But just as she reached for the quilt, a small jerking movement under the sheets by the foot of the bed made her hold back. She stared hard at the bedcover, and the movement was repeated. With dawning suspicion, Esmeralda threw back the covers.

There, at the foot of her bed, was a very small, very green frog.

"Ribit!" it chirped.

Esmeralda clapped her hand over her mouth to keep from laughing aloud. With a wary glance to the door connecting her room to Keane's, she picked up the frog.

"You're one frog that won't be anyone's dinner," she said, stroking the amphibian's head lightly.

"Ribit," he answered. Quite thankfully, Esmeralda imagined.

Hearing the doorknob turn, she looked about the room desperately. Finding no better option, she threw the frog into the tall vase by her bedside just as Keane entered the room.

He was wearing a satin dressing gown that molded his wide shoulders and showed his muscular legs as he walked. Esmeralda caught her breath. His eyes burned with the same intensity as the smoldering flames in the hearth.

"Now that we really do plan to marry, you're not going to insist we wait for the wedding to be together, are you?" Strolling forward, Keane asked the question jokingly, but Esmeralda could see he was anxious for her answer.

"Ribit!"

"What was that?" He stopped, looking around for the source of the sound.

Immediately, Esmeralda ran across the room, launching herself into his arms. She rained distracting kisses across his lips. "I don't want to wait. Ever." Throwing her inhibitions aside, she kissed Keane with all the love she felt for him.

Keane instantly responded. He began to remove her nightgown, but Esmeralda pushed him toward the door. "No, not here. I want to sleep with you in your room."

Keane swept her up in his arms, and Esmeralda locked her arms around his neck, burying her lips there. "Just as long as we're in the same bed, I don't care where we sleep," he said in a rough voice.

He stepped through the doorway to his room and, cradling Esmeralda in his arms, kicked the door shut behind him. He carried her to an enormous bed of dark wood. Its intricately carved headboard loomed a good four feet high, almost covering the wall. Throwing back the covers, Keane tossed Esmeralda on the the bed and dived after her. Laughing, they wrestled each other, their weapons kisses and loving strokes. The mock battle ended with groping hands while each tried to disrobe the other and still keep their mouths locked in a feverish kiss. When they lay naked, Keane got up off the bed and pulled back the drapes. Moonlight filled the room.

With a wicked smile, he blew out the lamp. "This is how I like you best."

"Bathed in moonlight?" Esmeralda giggled.

Keane shook his head. "Naked."

He lunged for her on the bed and Esmeralda's laughter erupted into high-pitched squeals as she fended him off with a pillow. Keane tossed the barrier aside easily and pulled her beneath him, holding her wrists pinned to the bed as he hovered over her.

"Now I have you under my power, wench."

Breathless, she stared up at him with her heart shining in her eyes. "You've always had that, my lord."

Keane sobered instantly. Releasing her wrists, he cupped her face in his hands and lowered his lips to hers. "God, I love you."

Esmeralda's hands caressed the warm skin of his back, sliding down to his muscular buttocks as she opened her legs to him. Keane glided inside her in a perfect fit and began moving his hips in small circles. Throwing back her head, she followed his erotic rhythm as he pulled her hair over her breasts, watching her nipples part the waterfall of curls. Keane brushed the tips lightly with kisses, then traced the aureolas with his tongue, sucking each nipple into his mouth until he heard a satisfied moan from Esmeralda.

She raised her legs and locked them around his hips. Her fingernails dug into his shoulders as she felt herself inching toward the edge of sensual oblivion. His hands worked their magic on her breasts, his fingers gently rubbing the tips as his mouth tortured her earlobe and neck with soft kisses and endearments. He felt so good, so wonderful inside her, she never wanted the pleasure to stop. But then the familiar explosion seized her and she gasped as she reached the haven of fulfillment only he could give her.

They lay on the bed, nestled against each other, relaxing, but each reluctant to let the other slip away into sleep. With their hands and mouths they acknowledged the evening was still young and this was a mere respite in their journey of discoveries. Esmeralda watched the stars through the window, listening to the night sounds as Keane played with her hair.

Esmeralda propped herself on her elbow and ran a finger down his chest to his stomach. "I love the color of your skin. It looks like coffee in the morning with lots and lots of cream." She leaned over him and licked the nipples surrounded by his chest hair, then looked up and smiled. "Rich and smooth. All over."

Keane stopped stroking her hair as she picked up his hand, examining his wrist for a change in skin color. But there was none. She glanced down at his hips.

"Why, that's the natural color—"

Keane flipped on top of her, meshing his hips against hers. "You're not the only one with exotic ancestry." Taking her hand, he planted soft, moist kisses from her wrist to the inside of her elbow.

"Well?" She shuddered as delicious sensations ran from her stomach to her toes. "Do I have to guess?"

"Would it matter?"

She could see from the look in his amber eyes that the answer worried him. That surprised her. Didn't he know how much she loved him? "Of course not. How could you even think—"

He took her face in his hands and kissed her with such

love that she felt as if she were the most precious thing on earth. When he finished the kiss, leaving Esmeralda quite breathless, he grinned. "Then I refuse to reveal all my secrets before the wedding." He continued his path of kisses from her elbow to her shoulder, his hand stroking the soft skin of her inner thigh. Slowly, teasingly, his hand inched upward.

Somewhat distracted, Esmeralda plunged into the game nonetheless. She thought of Nicky and her exotic dark looks. "Gypsy blood! That's why you're so good at bamboozling me."

Keane shook his head. "Something much more royal, sweets. I sincerely doubt you'll guess."

"The King of the Gypsies," she said breathlessly, losing her concentration to the pulsing desire building with Keane's stroking fingers.

"Something like that." He pulled her beneath him, and Esmeralda felt him seeking entry before he drove inside her.

"Oh, dear," she gasped with pleasure. "Already?"

"Always."

Hours later, Esmeralda eased out from under Keane's arm and off the bed. She didn't let out the breath she'd been holding until she'd stood and watched him for several minutes, sure she hadn't awakened him. She stared at her beloved, his golden skin shimmering with moonlight as his chest rose and fell in a steady rhythm. She looked at the warm spot on the bed beside him longingly, then forced herself to turn on silent feet and pad back to her room. She was a woman with a mission, after all.

Once in the hallway, the frog wrapped safely in a handkerchief, she made her way to Nicky's room. She knew the way from a tour earlier that evening. But when she carefully turned the knob, she found Nicky's door locked.

She bit her lip. She had to show Nicky she wouldn't be tricked. Somehow she sensed she had to earn the girl's respect, but once she had it, nothing would shake it.

Esmeralda thought. How could she possibly get into the room without . . . A slow smile formed on her lips. Could she do it? It had been so long since . . .

There was only one way to find out.

Chapter Thirty

Lord Kielder stared down at Lady Elizabeth Remick's distorted features. Allen had always thought it quite comical the way a person's face screwed up during the act of love, as if it were torture rather than pleasure. As he plunged deeper into Lady Remick's delectable body, shifting a little to the left, then pressing himself still further inside, he rubbed against her point of passion and watched with great interest as Elizabeth's mouth drooped open and a thin stream of spittle oozed free of her lips. She emitted a low moan.

Elizabeth always moaned.

Some women screamed. A moan was only slightly more dignified.

Just as Lady Remick's shudders subsided, Allen pulled himself free of her tangle of arms and legs and swung his feet over the edge of the bed. His phallus was still erect and rock hard.

A few minutes later, Elizabeth reached for him with her soft, expert hands, but Allen gently set them aside.

"I want to give you pleasure. . . ." Elizabeth whined.

Allen examined the angelic features, the pleading soft blue eyes and flowing blond hair. "You already have, darling. It pleases me to pleasure you."

He smiled and thought, *She really is a whore.*

"But . . . you're so . . . so uninvolved." Elizabeth lowered her voice. "It's degrading, really."

Allen felt himself grow flaccid just looking at her pouting mouth. "Get some sleep, Elizabeth," he said in a sharper tone than he'd intended. He displayed his warmest smile to take the sting from his words.

Elizabeth's pleading afterward was the most insufferable part of this ritual. He really must look for a new mistress. But he owed Lord Remick a great deal of money, and so far Elizabeth had been able to keep the old goat from calling in the vowels Allen had signed.

Like the others, Elizabeth served her purpose. They were all so easy to manipulate.

Allen padded across the room, completely at ease with his nakedness. He knew that Elizabeth and her contemporaries found him irresistibly attractive. Like a Greek god, she'd said just this afternoon. He sensed that she watched him as he strutted across the room. *Starting to pant for me all over again,* he thought with no little disgust. He stopped at the window, reaching for a cheroot he kept on the table next to it.

Watching the busy London traffic below, Allen thought again about stopping by his solicitors' office. He wanted the cloud over his title cleared as soon as possible. Last week's announcement that his long-lost cousin had returned to reclaim Amberose had cut into his gambling funds severely. No one was as willing to front credit for the measly piece of Scottish rock that went with the Kielder title. No, it was the illusion of the Northumberland estate and its past wealth that gave him money and power. And no imposter would take that away from him.

But they'd made him wait—the Eldridge solicitors. Stalling until the viscount made his appearance. Allen smiled. He'd always wanted to take on Eldridge. Now was his chance.

He inhaled deeply on his cigar, his thoughts returning to Esmeralda. If only such a woman could exist for him. The vision he'd seen in the mirror, himself in female form, emerged in his mind. He closed his eyes, shaking off the torturing apparition that could never be. He'd made certain Esmeralda would never return to claim his inheritance. It was too late for regrets now.

Allen sighed, blowing the bluish smoke through slightly parted lips.

"Allen? Please, come back to bed."

So the slut is hot again. Allen tossed his cheroot down on the plank floor of the seedy room. He'd find no pleasure in Elizabeth's arms today. His pleasure would come later, and as always, he'd find it alone.

The childish screams woke Esmeralda just after dawn. Still groggy, she heard Keane mutter a curse under his breath as he flung the covers aside and grabbed his robe from the foot of the bed. By the time she was fully awake, Keane was already out the bedroom door. Esmeralda swallowed back the nausea she felt upon waking and quickly followed.

When she arrived at Nicky's door, she almost burst into peals of laughter. Nicky stood beside her mother, her head pressed against Katherine's comforting bosom and her eyes wide as she watched Keane gingerly remove the sheets with a broomstick obviously provided by one of the servants who hovered by the doorway.

There, at the foot of the bed—where Esmeralda had placed him while Nicky slept the drugged sleep of the young—was Nicky's frog. The comical expression of disbelief on the young girl's face was almost Esmeralda's undoing. She bit the inside of her lip to keep from laughing and giving herself away.

"See Nicky. It's only a frog." Keane sent a wry look at Esmeralda over his sister's head.

Nicky marched over to the bed, her jaw still open. "How did *he* get *there?*"

"Looks like someone was playing a little trick on you, scamp. Maybe your days of practical jokes have caught up with you?"

Nicky whipped around. Her gold eyes grew impossibly wider as she met Esmeralda's smug smile. "But my door was locked. I made sure . . ." Nicky followed Esmeralda's gaze to a spot behind her. The curtains fluttered open with the soft morning breeze.

"He could have gotten in through your window," Esmeralda suggested innocently. She watched the girl scurry across the room and peer over the sill at the trellis Esmeralda had nearly broken her neck climbing. It had been quite a feat to climb and still keep her teeth clamped on the handkerchief holding Nicky's frog. Esmeralda felt quite proud of herself this morning. "You really should take better care of your pets, Nicky. You never know where they could end up if you don't keep track of them."

Slowly, Nicky turned toward Esmeralda, a look of pure admiration on her face.

"Why do I get the feeling I'm missing something?" Keane asked, his eyes narrow as he looked from Esmeralda to his sister.

Katherine shooed Nicole back under the covers. "Into bed with you, young lady."

With a knowing smile, Esmeralda walked with Keane to the door, but the sound of Nicky calling her name stopped them. When Esmeralda turned to see what the child wanted, Nicky smiled a beautiful, accepting smile and asked, "Can you shoot a gun?"

Esmeralda shook her head. "Not very well, I'm afraid."

Nicole watched Esmeralda for a moment, as if coming to some weighty decision. "I'd better teach you, then. Meet me at the stables at ten." That taken care of, Nicky gave her mother a quick kiss on the cheek and turned on her side, away from the door.

Escorting her down the hall, Keane gave Esmeralda an admiring glance. "I think you just made a friend."

Esmeralda grinned. "I hope so."

Much later, when the creeping light of dawn turned into brilliant morning, Esmeralda propped her chin on Keane's hard chest and gently stroked the short wiry hair there. She sighed, completely sated. They always made such beautiful love together.

The sheets lay bunched at the foot of the bed and Keane reached out to stroke the red tresses winding down Esmeralda's bare shoulders.

"I love your hair," he told her.

Esmeralda flipped onto her back, still propped against Keane. "Shall I cut it and give it to you as a present?" She glanced about the room. "You could hang it over there by the mantel as a prize."

Keane smiled and reached down to kiss her. "It would be worthless without your lovely head attached."

"Ah, so it's my head you're after."

"Your head, your shoulders, your hands"—Keane kissed each portion of anatomy as he named it—"your beautiful breasts. Hmm, the mole next to your navel—"

"All right, then." She laughed, taking his head in her hands and guiding his face back to hers. "I shall remain in one piece for you." She kissed him tenderly on the lips.

"I love you, Esmeralda. Marry me soon," he breathed the words against her mouth, kissing her with growing passion.

"How soon can it be arranged?" she whispered, returning his kisses with equal ardor.

"Tomorrow?"

Esmeralda pulled away and shook her head. "Your

family would find it strange if we left just when we've arrived."

"At the week's end then."

Esmeralda smiled sadly at Keane's fervor. "I'm sure this will be much more complicated than you believe to arrange."

"A marriage?"

Esmeralda touched her finger to his lips, trying to stem the growing frustration she heard in his voice. "A secret one that supposedly occurred over a month ago."

Keane sighed and leaned back against the pillows. Esmeralda settled into the crook of his arm. "It shall be done as quickly as possible," he said adamantly. After a moment, he asked in a deceptively quiet voice, "I'm still wondering how you managed to get up that trellis without killing yourself."

Esmeralda stiffened, then smiled impishly. "How did you know?"

"I found leaves and twigs on your side of the bed."

"You did not!"

"No, I didn't." He kissed the tip of her nose. "How else could you get that damn frog in her bed?"

"You're not angry?"

"As if that would matter," Keane scoffed. Esmeralda took a playful swat, but Keane captured her hand and kissed her wrist. "Nicky was going to be hard to win over. I think you just did it."

"I think I did, too." Esmeralda propped up on her elbows to get a better view of Keane. His tousled hair and hooded eyes made him look more desirable than ever. Trying to turn her thoughts to a less seductive subject, she asked, "Why do you call her Nicky? In the library, you introduced her as Katherine."

"Katherine *Nicole.* Katherine for my mother, Nicole for my father, Nicholas. We prefer Nicky as a tribute to my father. She was born after the drowning accident. Besides," he added in a lighter tone, "two Katherines could be confusing."

"You brought Nicky up, didn't you? That's why she's so attached to you."

"I suppose I've always treated her more like a daughter than a sister. My mother wanted me to be a father as well as a brother to Nicky. Though I've tried hard to fit both roles, I'm afraid I'm away too often on business to do the thing properly. Thank goodness she also has my Uncle Marc, my father's brother." Keane smiled as if recalling some fond memory. "Mother asked me to name her when she was born. I thought it fitting that she carry both my father's and mother's names—she was the last thing their love for each other ever created."

Esmeralda looked at Keane. Her heart felt as if it had just outgrown its slot in her chest. "That's terribly romantic."

Keane smiled and hugged her roughly. "Sentimental," he corrected. "I'm not the least bit romantic. I leave that to Byron and those sorts."

Esmeralda pressed against his warm chest. Sentimental, romantic, a good father—and husband. She was beginning to believe in Keane and his love.

She was beginning to trust.

Chapter Thirty-one

Keane watched Esmeralda pace back and forth in front of the library fireplace, gnawing unconsciously on her nails. She wore a gown of striped Peking silk and she'd tied her long curls back off her face with an olive green ribbon that matched her gown. Despite her frown and the tight lines around her lips, Keane thought she looked more lovely than ever, glowing even—but her pacing was starting to get annoying. She'd wear a trail through the Turkish rug soon if she didn't stop.

"Esmeralda, sit down. You're making *me* nervous," Keane complained.

Esmeralda abandoned the hearth and settled into a large empire-style chair with an audible *swoosh*. She clamped her hands tightly on her lap and stared up at Keane. "When will they *be* here?"

"Soon."

"But your solicitors haven't even arrived yet!"

"They will."

Esmeralda looked unconvinced.

"If you're going to be this nervous, sweets, I suggest you go for a visit to Charlotte's apartments and let me take care of this meeting."

"It's *my* estate we're discussing."

"When Lord Kielder comes, you can trust me to take care of your interests."

Esmeralda shook her head firmly. "I've been waiting nine years for this moment, and I'll not let anyone, not even you, take care of it for me." Her features softened. "Don't you understand, Keane? I *need* to be here. I have to see Allen."

Keane understood, all right. That was precisely why he'd not tried to talk her out of attending in the first place. If he had his way, she'd never see Allen MacClure again. That man was trouble; Keane sensed it. No one with a shred of humanity could have done what he did, not for all the money in the world.

Keane sighed. It was all happening so fast. Too fast. He'd thought he and Esmeralda would have a few quiet weeks together here at Eldridge Manor. That they'd get married, and then he and his family could show Esmeralda the love and care she needed to heal the wounds of her childhood—before she had to face the past. But the day after they arrived, he'd met with his secretary and gone over the months of correspondence. There had been two urgent messages from his solicitors. Apparently, Lord Kielder was chomping at the bit.

Now, barely a week after their return, Esmeralda was about to meet Allen. And Keane had a bad feeling about the reunion.

Allen stared up at the palatial dwelling and felt a slight twinge of envy. Once Amberose had been as magnificent, but he'd let the house run down. He preferred living in London. Stepping down from his carriage, he waited for Messrs. Gellman and Pernich to disembark. He straightened his blue wool coat and fastened the brass buttons. When his two solicitors stood beside him, he made a show of looking over the Tudor mansion.

"It's quite pleasant. Very . . . rustic."

The two gentlemen beside him glanced nervously at each other before nodding their agreement.

"Shall we, gentlemen?" Allen mounted the stairs to the front entrance. "Our imposter awaits."

Allen and his entourage followed the butler through the maze of halls. Silently Allen assessed the value of each rug, chair, and tapestry, being quite familiar with their quality. He'd sold many similar objects and furnishings from the Northumberland estate to finance his gambling.

When the butler announced them, Allen let his solicitors lead the way into the room. He feigned disinterest until his eyes locked with those of a tall, distinguished man of approximately his age standing in front of two elderly gentlemen. A cool, calculating smile spread across his lips. "Eldridge." Allen stepped forward, his hand extended.

Immediately he sensed something was wrong. His smile wavered as the man, who could be none other than the viscount, ignored Allen's greeting and visibly paled.

"My God," Allen heard Eldridge whisper.

"Allen," a voice called from behind him. The familiar sound echoed inside his head, becoming soft and childlike. *Allen. Help me.*

Slowly Allen turned around to meet his mirror image. He smiled with pure joy when he saw her.

"Esmeralda." He said the name almost worshipfully.

Keane couldn't believe his eyes. They looked so much alike, like twins, only Lord Kielder stood a few inches taller and his features were slightly less feminine. They were like beautiful matching china figures. Many claimed he and Charlotte looked alike—but nothing like this. He watched Kielder walk slowly toward Esmeralda until he stood right in front of her. Seeing them standing there, facing each other, Keane had an eerie sense that nothing he was witnessing was real.

Esmeralda stared up at Allen. He looked exactly as she remembered, as if he hadn't aged in the past nine years. He still stood tall, with broad shoulders. His auburn hair waved back over his brow, and his emerald gaze still held warmth and love. She closed her eyes and shook her head. No, not love—she was mistaken. Allen hated her; he wanted to hurt her, to take away her home. But when she opened her eyes, the look of caring was unmistakably there. She wanted to cry when she smelled the warm, comforting scent of tobacco and pine trees that was distinctly Allen.

"Esmeralda," he repeated softly.

Allen stretched his hand out to her. Unable to stop herself, she looked down and placed her hand in his. He pulled her into his embrace.

"My darling girl. I've waited all these years. I thought you were dead." Allen held her tighter. "It's a miracle. I can't believe you've come back to me."

"A very touching performance, Kielder," Keane cut in. "I'm sure you're very surprised to see your cousin after you masterminded her abduction."

"See here now, Eldridge," warned one of the solicitors. "One should not go about making such accusations."

Despite the solicitor's intervention, Keane's words had their intended effect. Esmeralda again felt the cold waters of the Thames drawing her under—Allen's hand pressing the soaked linen to her nose and mouth. As if these powerful images had some physical effect, she found it difficult to breathe. *Get rid of the girl. That's what Lord Kielder said.* The words echoed louder and louder in her head.

"It's true," Esmeralda shouted, pushing out of Allen's embrace. "He paid men to kidnap me. He wanted Amberose for himself!"

"My God, Esmeralda. Is that what your captors told you?" The sincerity of his voice was frightening. And confusing. "I searched everywhere for you. I offered rewards. I thought there would at least be a request for money—I prayed for it!" He took up her hand once more. "Esmeralda, I told you not to play in those woods. But you wouldn't—"

"Stop it!" Esmeralda covered her ears with her hands.

"Darling . . ."

"Stop! You're lying!" Esmeralda cried. "I remember, Allen. It took me nine years, but I finally remembered what you did!"

Allen looked over to the group of men gathered behind them with a sad expression. He shook his head, slowly. "She was ten years old . . . I'm afraid the experience has . . . affected her."

Esmeralda gasped. He sounded so concerned, so sincere. So believable. She saw the doubt dawning on the men's faces; one of the Eldridge solicitors even cast her a sympathetic look. She turned to Keane, feeling helpless.

"Come home with me, darling." Allen gently took her hand, pulling her toward him. Esmeralda leaned away, shaking her head desperately. "All the things you love are home. Nanny, Cook—all the people who care for you."

"Take your hands off my wife." Keane stepped between Esmeralda and her cousin and pushed Kielder away. Esmeralda dived into Keane's arms.

Allen looked physically struck. "My God. After all my efforts to find you—the pain I felt at losing you . . . you believe . . ." Pressing his lips together, he looked away, as if gathering strength to continue. When he looked back at Esmeralda, one lone tear slipped down his cheek. "I don't know what your captors told you, or what you've imagined from that dreadful experience, but it's not true, darling. Think about the years I cared for you. You were like a sister to me. I loved you. I could never hurt . . ." Allen's words choked off. After a moment he locked his emerald gaze on Esmeralda, his eyes shining with unshed tears. "I hope with time, darling, you'll come to realize how wrong you are. You know where to reach me."

Allen turned and walked out. His solicitors followed.

At that moment, Esmeralda's doubts began.

Keane played distractedly with the end of his quill. He was—as he'd been doing all day long—worrying about Esmeralda.

She'd been so confused after Allen had left, and Keane could tell that the bastard's performance had gotten to her. And it had been good. More than good—brilliant. How he could shed that tear at precisely the right moment . . . even the Eldridge solicitors had been taken in, advising Keane not to press charges on behalf of his wife. After all, they argued, Esmeralda would get Amberose; Lord Kielder hadn't denied her identity.

Keane twisted the top of his quill viciously until it snapped. As if the bastard could deny so clear a family resemblance.

No, Kielder had played it like a master. It galled Keane to no end that the bastard could actually get away without paying for his heinous crimes against Esmeralda.

Hearing a soft knock on the study door, he looked up at the mantel clock, happy for the interruption. Supper would be served soon. It was a good time to quit for the evening. Shouting, "Enter," Keane put down his quill and waited as Esmeralda opened the door and stepped in.

She held a folded piece of paper out to him. "It's from Allen. He sent this to me yesterday, after he left. He wants me to meet him at Amberose." She handed the missive to Keane. "He says he wants to explain things to me."

Keane cursed under his breath as he read the carefully worded missive. "That bastard." Keane crumpled the paper between his hands with the relish he'd use to wring Kielder's neck. "He'll pay for this. I swear it to you, sweets. He won't get away with what he's done."

Esmeralda shook her head. "I felt the same at first;

that's why I didn't mention the note before now. But I've been thinking . . . about my dreams." She looked up and the confusion Keane saw in her eyes made him wince. "What if Allen is right?"

"Don't do this, sweets. Don't start doubting now."

"It was so long ago. So much of what happened I only started to remember recently. Maybe I just imagined the part about Allen drugging me. I couldn't remember what happened for so long; I blocked it out . . . I *was* young, Keane. It all seems so blurred now, like a dream." She shook her head in confusion. "I have to know, Keane," she pleaded. "If he can explain . . . I have to give him that chance."

Keane was up and around his desk instantly. He took Esmeralda's shoulders and shook her. "Listen to me. That man is dangerous . . . more than you know!"

For a moment Esmeralda's eyes cleared, but then the doubting cloud filmed over them once again. "I have to go, Keane. For us. I have to understand—"

"No, absolutely not! I forbid it. I won't let you walk into the monster's den."

"It's my home, Keane."

"Your home is here!" he shouted. Trying to maintain his rapidly failing control, he lowered his voice, but his tone was just as commanding. "You're not leaving, and that's final."

Esmeralda looked up, puzzled. "You can't keep me here. We're not even truly married."

Keane grabbed her by her hand and pulled her to him. "Understand this, Esmeralda. You're my wife in every sense of the word. I fought heaven and hell for you. I even beat death to keep us together! And your charlatan cousin is not going to beat me on this."

"You're talking as if I'm something you won in a poker match. Is that how you see me? A possession that you have a right to watch over and control?"

Keane closed his eyes tight, silently praying for

strength. "You're not going. I'll do anything it takes to stop you. I'll lock you in the closet if I have to! Do you understand me?"

A spark of defiance showed in her eyes.

"Do I have to lock you in the closet, Esmeralda? Answer me, damn you!"

In a bitter voice, Esmeralda replied, "No, Keane. You don't have to lock me up. I'll be a good little wife for you. I'll do as you say."

With a look of complete disdain, she turned and left.

Esmeralda ran down the hallway to her bedchamber. Once there, she slammed the door and leaned back against it, tears streaming from her eyes. She glared across the room at the door that led to Keane's chamber, then viciously pulled off his signet ring she always wore and threw it on the floor. Taking a deep breath, she waited for her heart to stop pounding. When the beating slowed to a dull pain, she took a small satchel from the bottom of her armoire and began packing. From her dresser drawer she removed a small bag of gold coins Keane had given her to buy gifts with in New Orleans, thankful now that she'd been thrifty with her spending.

A few minutes later, Esmeralda sneaked out the servants entrance to the stables. It didn't take much to bribe the stableboy for a mount into town. Once there, she'd look for a conveyance to Northumberland.

As she pulled the horse's reins and kicked it into a canter, a small figure ducked out from behind the shadows and ran into the stables.

Keane glanced up at the mantel clock, then back to the half-empty decanter of brandy he'd been nursing since Esmeralda stormed out of his study. The creeping light of dawn was just seeping through the crack in the heavy curtains. Keane pushed back his chair and stood. Morning already. He should go check on Esmeralda.

He regretted their argument. He'd been too strong, too

possessive. But the idea that Esmeralda—who had suffered so much at her cousin's hands—could be so easily deceived, had galled him. Still, he should not have threatened to lock her up. He'd go to her now and apologize. If it was so important to her, they'd go to Amberose together. But under no conditions would he let her go off, half-cocked, by herself.

Thinking of the wonderful way he planned to apologize, Keane made his way to their rooms. But when he tapped on the connecting door to her chamber, he received no answer. He swung the door open.

The room was empty.

It was obvious that Esmeralda hadn't slept there. He searched frantically for some clue to her whereabouts. Then he saw it.

Walking to the middle of the room, he bent down and picked up his signet ring.

"She left last night."

Keane turned sharply to the door. Nicky stood in the shadows in her night rail, her eyes red and swollen.

"She left because of me, didn't she?" she hiccuped. "Because I said I didn't want her here that first day. But I thought she knew . . . that I'd changed my mind." She lowered her head to her hands. "Uncle Marc and I were teaching her to shoot. I thought . . ."

Keane shook his head. "No, scamp." He got up and gathered his sister into his arms. "We had a fight. I said some . . . mean things. She left because she was mad at me."

Nicky's eyes cleared, as if a great weight had been lifted from her shoulders. "Well, then—you must go after her. You have to bring her back!"

Keane looked into his young sister's earnest eyes. Through a trick of the light, or maybe because he was so tired, her light topaz eyes shifted in shape, reminding him of Henry Carter's doe-soft gaze. Somewhere in the back of his mind Keane remembered Henry's warning: *She'll leave you. Just as surely as she betrayed me, she'll do the same to you.*

"I followed her into town." Nicky's childish voice grew high with excitement, interrupting Keane's thoughts. "I overheard her hiring a coach to Northumberland—"

"Northumberland?" So she'd gone to Amberose. To Allen.

Nicky nodded. "You have to go after her."

Again, Henry's taunting prediction blared through his head. *She'll leave you. She'll leave you!*

Keane shook his head clear of the disturbing voice. To hell with Henry's predictions. He had a coach to catch.

Chapter Thirty-two

Esmeralda jolted awake. The vintage springs of the carriage exaggerated every rut in the road, making sleep nearly impossible. Restlessly she shifted her weight from her left side to her right, cursing the plank-hard seat. She'd hoped to find better transportation at Leeds, but this had been the only conveyance willing to take her further north. Adjusting the skirt of her muslin gown, one of two she'd managed to pack when she left Eldridge Manor, she sighed. Tired, she was so very tired.

The grueling voyage and her worries had taken their toll. She'd had to keep an iron grip on her feelings during the entire trip, she missed Keane so terribly. Just thinking of him brought an onset of depression. She'd tried to make him understand! She needed to know the truth about her cousin, not just for herself, but for them—for her *and* Keane. Until she knew for certain what had happened to her those many years ago, she could never truly trust anyone completely. And without trust, what kind of marriage could they have? But before she could even explain, he'd dictated to her what she could and could not do, as if she were a possession to be owned and controlled!

Esmeralda swayed to the left as the coach turned off the road. A wave of excitement engulfed her, overpowering her inner turmoil. With a shaking hand she pulled aside the carriage curtain and stared out into the gloaming. The eerie twilight revealed little, but she could feel the coach slowing, coming to a halt. Her heart raced. She grabbed the door and swung it open, letting herself down before the driver could offer assistance.

In the gloom, she could barely make out the entrance to Amberose. An icy knot formed in her stomach and she pulled her shawl tightly around herself. What the creeping fog hid, her memories provided. In her mind's eye she could see the limestone structure and its slate roof with aching familiarity. The darkened interior puzzled her; she'd sent a note from her last stop. She should be expected. Yet only a faint glow from a window in the second story revealed that anyone was home. Frowning, she made her way up the steps to the entrance, instructing the driver where he could find the stables.

Something was wrong, terribly wrong. Missing a step, she fell to her knees to avoid tumbling backward. Crumbling mortar under her palms cut into her skin. Peering closely, she saw a stone step had given way under her weight. She stood and walked more carefully as she climbed to the front doors. She rapped on them loudly. No one answered. Turning the knob, she pushed the door open. The hollow creak of old hinges echoed inside the mansion, making her shiver.

The front entrance hall was dimly lit by two torches jutting from the wall sconces. The gloomy light bounced her shadow off the walls of the large and empty chamber. Gone were the priceless tapestries handed down through generations of MacClures. Gone were the beautiful furnishings she remembered playing among as a child. Dusty cobwebs hung from every corner and crevice.

A soft cry fell from her lips and she scrambled from room to room. Everywhere it was the same: empty, covered with dust, uninhabited. She rushed up the stairs to the second story, again almost falling when a rotting step collapsed under her feet. The floorboards on the second floor creaked ominously as she raced to the library where she'd seen a light shining from outside. Swinging the door open, she stopped at the threshold and stared inside.

Allen leaned against the mantel, holding a glass in his hand. The fire within the hearth lit his face with an unnatural glow.

A slow, warm smile settled across his face. He gestured to the near-empty room around him with his glass. "Welcome home, darling."

The impact of his words made her step back. She watched, stunned, as Allen calmly placed his glass on the mantel and walked toward her, extending his hands in greeting.

"I've been waiting for you. I knew you'd come, but when I got your note you'd be here tonight, I was delighted." He grasped her cold hands in his. By contrast, his warm clasp seemed to burn her fingers. He pulled her gently into the room. "Come in, come in. Sit down and rest." He looked about the room for some kind of chair and, finding none, smiled apologetically. "Or perhaps you'd rather stand?" He chuckled softly then pulled her closer to him. "I'm so very glad you came." He reached up and gave one of her curls a playful tug.

"What has happened?" she whispered, finally finding her voice. "All the furnishings, the servants . . . ?"

Allen smiled sadly. "Gone."

"That's all you have to say?" Esmeralda glanced about the room. A rat scurried across the hearth. "Dear God, Allen. What have you done to our home?"

Allen sighed wearily. "I had to sell some things." He

shrugged his shoulders. "I ran up a few . . . debts."
Then, taking her shoulders in his hands, he added, "But
that's not important now." He examined her, as if memo-
rizing every feature, and smiled softly. "I have you back.
You don't know, darling . . . how much I regret." He
hugged her fiercely to him. "God, to have you back. So
beautiful, so . . . grown-up."

Esmeralda felt an ugly thought form inside her head.
She stared at the fire over Allen's shoulder and saw her
image staring back from the dim mirror over the mantel.
She looked ghostly white and her eyes were wide emerald
splotches on her face. With a odd sense of detachment,
she asked, "What do you regret?"

He held her at arm's length, his features settled in a
confused frown. "Why, sending you away. It was a dreadful mistake. But I was so afraid . . . afraid you would
marry and your husband would take it all away. I didn't
know how things could *be* between us."

Allen smiled. He took his finger and traced her mouth,
looking down at her almost with longing. Esmeralda
shuddered, revolted but drawn to him at the same time.
She saw love in Allen's eyes, love that confused her because she wanted so desperately to respond to it. They'd
been so close when she was young; he was like a brother.
She'd always depended on him for everything. It was Allen who held her and comforted her after her parents'
deaths. Allen, who taught her to ride, who dried her tears
when she cried after a fall.

She shook her head, confused by the intimate glow in
his eyes. "I don't understand."

Allen sighed. He spoke as if he were explaining the
obvious. "He bequeathed everything to you, all the
money, the estate, I acted out of anger. It should have
been mine—"

"I was my father's only child. Amberose and everything in it belongs to me."

"No!" A chilling light appeared in Allen's eyes, and his

grip tightened painfully on her shoulders. "I, my darling, am *our* father's first and only *son*. He should have left everything to me! Do you understand?" He shook her. And when Esmeralda tried to pull away, he continued, "Must I explain the whole tiresome story? I'm your half brother, Esmeralda. Born of a moment of indiscretion, true, but his son nonetheless! When it appeared that your mother would never have any children, our father brought me here to Amberose. I was resurrected as a long-lost nephew." Allen laughed. "He even forged papers to the effect, not wanting the Kielder title and fortune to escheat to the Crown. But then you were born." He stroked her hair away from her face ever so gently. "I tried to hate you, truly. But I couldn't. You see"—he tipped her head up with the crook of his finger—"you always loved me so. You'd follow me around with so much admiration in your childish eyes." Allen sighed. "How could I help but love you back? When the bastard left it all to you, I could have killed you then, I was so angry. But when I tried, you just looked at me with those trusting eyes, eyes that were an exact replica of my own. I could no more kill you than kill myself." His voice dropped an octave. "You always looked so very much like me, even then."

Esmeralda fought his mesmerizing voice. "You sold me into slavery!"

"How was I to know you would grow up like this? Oh, I imagined. I dreamed of it. But the reality . . . you are so very stunning, Esmeralda." He took her to the mirror and stood behind her. "We were meant to be together. We are mirror images of each other," he whispered. "You have grown to be a beautiful woman. . . ." Allen turned her around to face him. "The female image of myself."

Allen lowered his face to hers until Esmeralda felt his soft lips press against hers. Instantly, his lurid spell was broken. She tore her mouth away from Allen's, struggling.

"Don't fight me, darling," he panted. "It was meant to

be. I made a terrible mistake sending you away. Forgive me, darling. I'll make it up to you." Allen whispered the words furtively against her cheek, still grasping her to him. They twirled about the room in a parody of a waltz, Esmeralda desperately trying to dislodge Allen's hands. With her nails she made to claw at his face, but Allen pulled her hands behind her and slammed her up against the wall. His hand hit an old sconce and it fell to the floor. The tattered and aging curtain beside them burst into flames.

Esmeralda struggled to get away from Allen's grip. The heat of the burning curtain sent waves of panic through her. It felt as if she were reliving her nightmare—when he'd held her down, smothering her with a handkerchief —but this time it was smoke that burned through her lungs, gagging her.

Allen's mouth covered hers, stifling her cries. They battled as spots of flame drifted across the room, igniting everything. The ancient floorboards became kindling for the burning draperies. But Allen seemed unaware of the fire around him. He buried his tongue deep in her mouth, releasing her only when she bit down hard.

Esmeralda stumbled back. Coughing from lack of air, she looked up and saw Allen's terrible face as he wiped the blood from his mouth with his hand. The fire around him made him look demonic. He stepped to her, his arms outstretched and menacing. Esmeralda inched back, then turned and ran for the door.

Just as she crossed the threshold, Allen grabbed her hair and pulled her back into the room. He struck her with the back of his hand, and she fell against the door from the strength of the blow and saw stars. Fighting to stay conscious, she crawled backward, attempting to escape, but Allen simply grabbed the hem of her skirt and dragged her to the center of the room before falling on top of her.

"You shouldn't have done that, Esmeralda." He looked

at her with the same glazed expression he wore in her dreams. "You know how much I care about you, darling. I love you, really I do."

"Please, Allen," she cried, fear and smoke choking her. "Stop this!"

"Do you love me, darling?" he crooned between kisses, squeezing her breast painfully. "Do you? Say it. I want to hear you say it."

"No, Allen!" She threw her head left and right, trying to avoid his mouth. "Please, don't do this!"

Esmeralda coughed, unable to breathe from the smoke and Allen's stifling kisses. With her last bit of strength, she rolled over on her side, sliding out from beneath Allen and crawling toward the door. When she felt him tugging at her skirt, she turned on her back and kicked out. He stepped aside easily, laughing at her feeble attempts to escape. Fire raged uncontrolled around them. Panting for breath, she watched as Allen calmly walked toward her, a smile of triumph on his lips. At the last possible moment, Esmeralda came up on her knees and pushed him.

Allen stumbled back until his foot hit a weakened floorboard. With a sharp snapping sound, the floorboard cracked beneath him, and Allen propelled himself backward to avoid falling through the hole in the floor. He landed on the hearth, his head hitting the brick with a sickening thud.

Stunned, he looked up at Esmeralda, barely able to lift his head. She watched horrified as he reached out toward her with one hand. "I love you, darling. Please . . . I love . . ." His head fell back to the floor.

Esmeralda stumbled to his side. The room was thick with smoke. "Allen," she called. And when he didn't respond, she reached out to shake him conscious. Blood oozed out from beneath his head, staining the brick hearth. Not knowing what else to do, Esmeralda grabbed Allen's arm and began to drag him toward the door. His head left a trail of red on the floor boards, further sickening her. The room began to spin and dim. Coughing she scrambled for the door, dragging Allen with her. But it, too, burst into flames.

Esmeralda stepped back from the searing heat. Unable to gather a breath, she wheezed. The room darkened. She felt herself fall to her knees beside Allen.

Her last thought before she blacked out was that she had fallen into hell.

Keane watched the eerie glow on the hillside with a chilling premonition. The past three days he'd ridden like a man possessed, trying desperately to make up for Esmeralda's half-day lead. A week ago he thought he would catch her easily. If his horse hadn't thrown a shoe, he would have intercepted her—but fate had placed an added barrier before him, and try as he might, he would not reach Amberose before her. Now he raced with his heart in his throat, sensing that Esmeralda was at this very moment in grave danger. He whispered added encouragement to his mount and stared at the ominous light that wavered and shifted like the flame of a candle in the night.

When Keane circled off the road and up the manor drive, he felt like screaming in rage. Flames licked hungrily at the sides of the building and flicked out from the windows of the second story. He pulled his mount up next to a waiting carriage before the front portico and jumped down.

"Where is she?" he shouted to the driver, whose blackened face and scorched clothing attested to thwarted rescue attempts.

"Second floor, I think. But ye can't get up the stairs. I tried. It's like bloody hell in there."

"Where's the trough?"

"Up around back by the stables."

"Do you have a blanket in the carriage?"

"Aye."

Keane flung open the carriage door and grabbed the

folded blanket from the seat. Mounting his horse, he sped to the trough and dunked the blanket in the murky water within. Returning to the house, he untied his scarf and wrapped it around his nose and mouth. The soaked blanket around him like protective armor, he climbed the steps.

"Ye'll never make it!" warned the driver.

Without hesitation, Keane dived through the front doors.

He found the stairs quickly and ducked his face behind the wet folds of the blanket before climbing the steps two at a time. He lost valuable time searching several rooms before he found the center of the inferno. With a silent prayer that Esmeralda be anywhere but trapped by the raging fires within, he jumped through the doorway and became engulfed in flames.

Keane rolled to the floor, smothering any fire that might have caught on the blanket. The smoke-filled room was empty except for two bodies lying unmoving on the floor. Keane instantly recognized the man and woman who resembled each other as much in death as they had in life. With a shouted curse, he immediately discarded the possibility that Esmeralda could be dead and bent down beside her. He gathered her up in his arms and wrapped her and himself in the blanket. The floorboards creaked ominously.

With one last prayer that they leave this hell alive, he plunged through the burning doorway.

Chapter Thirty-three

Esmeralda's eyes fluttered open, then shut quickly against the blinding light. Her throat felt raw and scratchy and her lungs hurt when she inhaled. She peeked through her lashes but didn't recognize her surroundings.

"Sleeping Beauty awakes at last."

The familiar voice sent a shock wave of longing through her. Slowly she turned her head and looked over at the man seated next to her bed. A full day's stubble on his chin, his amber eyes bloodshot, Keane sat with his arms crossed, staring at her.

"Where am I?" she asked groggily.

"Where you belong—in my bed. Although this bed happens to be in the inn nearest Amberose."

She nodded her head, slowly remembering Keane carrying her here the night before. There had been a doctor, and someone else . . . it was all very hazy.

Keane leaned forward, and whispered next to her ear, his voice urgent, "Never, *never*, run away from me, Esmeralda. No matter what I say, no matter what our differ-ences—and there will be many—don't leave me. God, I almost lost you." He picked up her hand, and kissed her knuckles. "How often can I fight death for you and win? Sweets, we can't go on beating the odds."

Esmeralda smiled wanly. With her fingertips she touched his lips softly. "I'm sorry. I was so angry. I didn't think you understood."

"That you loved your cousin and wanted to believe he'd not betrayed you? Oh, I understood. Too well. That's what made me so furious. To see your eyes so full of hope and longing, and know that you'd only be disappointed—or worse yet, trust him and be destroyed. He nearly took you from me forever."

Esmeralda heard the fear in his voice—and the love—and her smile deepened.

Then she remembered.

"Allen?" She tried to sit up, but Keane pressed her gently back against the pillows. She searched his eyes for her answer, then fell back in despair. He was dead. Esmer-alda squeezed her eyes shut, reliving the fiery inferno from which she'd tried to save Allen. He might have been evil, but she'd never wanted him dead.

"I couldn't save him, sweets. I barely got there in time to get you out. The house burned to the ground."

"Amberose." She said the word softly, bidding her dreams good-bye.

Keane stroked her fingers with his. "It's only a house."

She shook her head, staring out the window at the countryside. "It was my dream. My reason for living."

"You have another reason now." Keane placed her hand on her abdomen, covered it with his, and pressed it there. With a look so tender she felt her heart swell, he met her eyes. "The doctor examined you when I brought you here. Our child, Esmeralda. Is it reason enough?"

Unable to speak, she was so filled with emotion she simply nodded.

"We can build Amberose again, as a legacy to our children," Keane murmured and she felt tears well in her eyes as he intertwined his fingers with hers. "But love and trust," he continued, "those will be harder to achieve."

"I love you, Keane."

He shook his head sadly. "That's not enough. Without trust, we have nothing. Will you run from me every time I get angry?"

"Will you threaten to lock me up when you do?" she countered.

He smiled and traced her lips with the pad of one finger. "I can't help words said in anger. It's my actions you should judge me by."

She nodded, understanding.

"Can you trust me, Esmeralda?"

She turned her gaze to his expectant face. Softly she touched his cheek. "My cou—Allen . . . hurt me. Very badly. I always feared love, because I thought it would betray me, as he did. When I thought, even for a moment, I could be wrong—that Allen had not been the culprit I'd been led to believe—I sought the truth, hoping it would cure me of my fears against love—our love. But now I see that there are different kinds of love. Allen was sick, terribly sick. I should not judge what love can be by his actions." A tear slipped down her cheek. "You have always, *always* made me feel dear, and loved. Love me, Keane. Love me as you always have, and trust will come."

Keane kissed her hand softly, then wiped her tear away with his finger. "I give you fair warning—a clergyman has been sent for. You'll not leave this bed, much less this room, until we're wed, good and proper." He reached inside his coat pocket and retrieved his gold signet ring. Placing it over her finger, he pushed it into place with the words, "I love you, Esmeralda. Now and forever. I promise to put your needs before mine, to cherish you and love you always. Have we a bargain?"

She smiled. "A bargain well made."

"Excellent." The right corner of Keane's mouth lifted into a melting smile. "Now I'll fetch the doctor to see you. He's been waiting downstairs."

"Wait!" Esmeralda's urgent voice stopped Keane where he stood. She looked up at him and frowned. "I may be no gentleman, your lordship, but I know when a businessman has been remiss."

Keane raised his brows in question. "And what have I forgotten?"

Taking his hand, Esmeralda tugged him down until he leaned close to her. "You forgot to seal the bargain."

"Ah!" Keane smiled, then whispered against her mouth, *"Very* remiss indeed," before he closed his lips over hers in a kiss fit to seal the bargain of a lifetime.

Epilogue

Eldridge Manor, 1854

Esmeralda sat in her bed, propped up by a mound of pillows. She felt tired and her muscles ached, but she was very proud of herself. In her arms she cradled Phillip Nicholas Marshall, her son of five hours. At her side was her daughter Marina, whom nature's palette had colored with the hues of her mother, but whose crooked smile and fine eyes reflected her handsome father.

Esmeralda smiled; Phillip would look like her.

Shouting voices made her start, until she realized who was arguing. She pressed her lips together and turned to her daughter.

"Auntie Molly and Daddy?" Marina asked.

Esmeralda nodded. "I'm afraid so, darling."

Marina screwed her face up in concentration, reminding Esmeralda of Keane in one of his more pensive moods. "Why is Auntie Molly always mad around Daddy but smiles so much around Uncle Jason?"

"I don't know, darling. You might ask her sometime."

Just then the door burst open and Molly strode inside. *"Arrah!* I tell you, *mavourneen,* the man's got the brains of a—" Molly caught Esmeralda's warning look and smiled at Marina. "Good morning to you, my darling colleen. Come to see your brother, have you? What do you think of the tyke?"

Marina wrinkled up her nose. "He looks very . . . pink."

Molly plopped down on the bed next to Marina and stroked Phillip's downy blond hair. "Well, that's the way bairns look when they're born."

"Samantha's a baby and she doesn't look half so bad," Marina remarked with earnest concern.

Molly smothered a laugh. Winking at Esmeralda, she explained, "Yes, but they all start out kind of ugly-looking. You have to let 'em ripen up—like fruit." And at Marina's skeptical look, Molly added, "Why, even Peter looked a little half-baked when he was born."

At the mention of her favorite playmate, Marina's face lit up. "Well, Peter looks all right now!"

"You see! Just give the tyke time. He'll not let you down." Molly turned her attention to Esmeralda. "About that . . . charming husband of yours."

"Yes, Molly?"

"He's got this craz—inaccurate idea that you should rest forever and a day. Now I explained to him, quite sensibly, mind you, that you should be out and about as soon as possible, taking in some fresh air and the like."

"Keane does tend to be a bit overprotective."

"Keeping you cooped up here is not good. You should—"

"She should be resting," Keane interrupted from the doorway.

"Daddy!"

Marina ran to her father and jumped into his arms, hugging him tightly.

"My dearest Molly," Keane said with a sarcasm that was not lost on the adults in the room. "I believe Samantha has awakened from her nap and is calling fiercely for her mother. Jason is quite at loose ends. It seems you're needed urgently in the nursery."

Molly *humphed* loudly, then gathered up her skirts and swept past Keane to the door. "I'm not finished with you yet, viscount."

"I'm sure I'll have the pleasure of your erudite discussions again soon, madame."

When Molly shut the door behind her, Keane carried Marina to the bed. "What do you think of your new brother, pumpkin?"

Marina looked over his shoulder at the sleeping Phillip, then gently patted her father's back, as if comforting him. "It's all right, Daddy. He's going to ripen soon. Then he'll be as handsome as you!"

Keane looked puzzled and Esmeralda laughed.

"I'm sure you're right, pumpkin." Keane's eyes met Esmeralda's as he mouthed "I love you," before smiling proudly at his son.

Esmeralda felt her heart fill with almost painful satisfaction. Watching Keane holding their daughter in his arms and looking proudly at their son, she thought, as she often had over the past five years, about all her old doubts and fears. It seemed quite ironic that of all the things she thought were important—Amberose, revenge, money—the one thing she shunned, a total commitment to this special man, had brought her the most happiness.

When she'd fallen in love, she thought her heart had betrayed her, but now she knew it had guided her true. She finally understood: At the heart of what matters is love.

Author's Note
and
Acknowledgments

The historical personalities and places mentioned in this book all existed. I did, however, stretch a few facts. For example, the Burnet House opened in 1850, a year after I have it operating, and Hiram Powers, the great American sculptor, was living in Italy at the time I have him celebrating his art opening in Cincinnati. But both the Burnet and Mr. Powers are such important parts of Cincinnati's history during this era that I couldn't resist making them a part of my story.

I would like to thank the organizations that helped keep historic Cincinnati alive for me: the Cincinnati Historical Society, the Taft Museum, the Krohn Conservatory, the John Hauck House, and the Sharon Woods Historic Village. Reading about a place is fine, but walking through Esmeralda and Molly's cabin at the Sharon Woods Village, listening to the docent describe how the triple-hung windows work in Nicholas Longworth's home, looking at street maps and lithographs from 1849, make a book come to life.

This book would not have been possible without the help and encouragement of some very special people: Mary Bicos, Leila Posakony, Consuelo Carreras, and my mother, Olga Gonzalez. My wholehearted thanks for the endless proofreading, the encouragement, pep talks, and the baby-sitting.

Watch for

White Tiger

USA TODAY BESTSELLING AUTHOR

OLGA BICOS

Visit